THE THIRD WOE

THE THIRD WOE

Book Two of The Third Peril Trilogy by
L. P. Hoffman

www.hopespringsmedia.com

The Third Woe
Book Two of The Third Peril Trilogy
By L. P. Hoffman

www.TheThirdWoe.com
www.TheThirdPerilTrilogy.com
www.LPHoffman.com

Scripture taken from the New Living Translation. Copyright © 1996, 2004, 2007. Used by permission of Tyndale House Publishers. All rights reserved.

Published by Hope Springs Media.
www.HopeSpringsMedia.com
P.O. Box 11, Prospect, Virginia 23960-0011
Office: (434) 574-2031 Fax: (434) 574-2130

International Standard Book Number (ISBN):
978-1-935375-06-7

This book is a work of fiction. Names, characters, businesses, places, events, and incidents are either the product of the author's creativity, inspiration, or used in a fictitious manner, or part of the public domain. Any resemblance to actual people, living or deceased, or actual events is purely coincidental and unintentional.

Printed in the United States of America.

Cover and book design by Hope Springs Media and Exodus Design. Original cover artwork by L. P. Hoffman.

Dedication

This book is dedicated to God whose Word inspires and compels me. With deepest gratitude, I want to thank those whom Christ has woven into the fabric of my life: my husband, Paul, for his love, patience, and steadfast contributions to this project; my daughter, Desiree, who can brighten the darkest day with her smile; my son, Fritz, who awaits a Heavenly reunion with those he left behind. Special thanks to my editor, Adele Brinkley, as well as Phil & Annette Hertzler and Michael Prevost for their keen eyes, insight, and encouragement.

Prologue

Tassels of corn waved in the sultry summer breeze, but Joel's eyes were keen for anything out of the ordinary. He cocked his head to listen, a feckless pursuit, for the damp ground would muffle the sound of any movement. Still, instinct warned him that something was not right.

Joel slipped through walls of corn and peered up and down each long row. He saw nothing in either direction but a vanishing point.

Something rustled, and the young man's breath caught in his throat. A trickle of sweat snaked down Joel's temple, and he stood as still as a statue.

Minutes passed. The fear Joel felt was palpable. *I'm imagining things,* he told himself and forced a smile. *I'll laugh about it later.*

A shadow fell across his path. Joel gasped and raised his arms defensively as a flight of ravens circled overhead. *Man up,* he chided himself.

Joel tried to re-trace his footsteps through the cornfield, but the country road where he had parked his car proved challenging to find. He crossed row after row in the direction from which he'd come, but the view never opened up as expected. Confused, he thought, *Did I get turned around?*

At the base of the corn stocks, Joel stooped to examine his footprints. The markings from his boots were obvious, but they seemed to end between rows. *There's got to be a logical explanation*, he reasoned.

Joel heard the sound again, the same chilling din that had drawn him into the field in the first place. A prickly sense of foreboding crawled across the young man's flesh. *What is it?*

The noise grew louder. *Like a buzzing*, he thought, shaking his head. *No, it is something else.* Joel looked up toward the wispy clouds and watched the blue sky darken.

The air thickened and a deafening sound, like the hissing of a thousand steam kettles, pierced his ears.

Gray shimmering fingers of movement seemed to reach downward. In an instant, the cornfield was swallowed by a veil as black as sackcloth, and Joel was pummeled by living, crawling matter!

Slapping insects from his face, he cried out. In a panic, Joel willed his feet to run. Locusts were landing, jumping, and fluttering before his eyes in a swarm so dense they seemed to choke oxygen from the atmosphere.

Blood coursed through Joel's veins furiously and his heart raced as he beat a panicked path through the cornfield. Beyond the swarm, the sun had been reduced to shimmering specks of light. He groped blindly ahead, pulling insects from his hair and beating them off his arms. Something caught Joel's foot, and he tripped and fell headlong. Like living, writhing quicksand, the ground swallowed him alive.

Part 1
After The War

My hope is built on nothing less
Than Jesus' blood and righteousness;
I dare not trust the sweetest frame,
But, wholly lean on Jesus' name.
On Christ, the solid Rock, I stand;
All other ground is sinking sand.

Edward Mote—1834

Chapter 1

California

Friday, April 5th

    Joel opened his eyes and felt a rush of relief. *It was just a nightmare.* Still, the vivid impressions lingered.

    Overhead, from the upstairs bedroom, floorboards creaked with heavy footsteps. *Haus is moving around,* he figured. Sometimes Joel imagined his oversized roommate crashing through the ceiling of the old federal-style college house. It wouldn't be a pleasant sight!

    Joel stretched beneath a tangle of damp sheets, rolled over, and gasped! On his pillow, a locust was perched like a sentinel, its shiny emerald eyes just inches from Joel's face. His reflexes kicked in, and he batted the tiny creature into the air. The locust fluttered to the window, its wings buzzing against the glass. *Stupid bug!*

    Joel threw off his covers, reached for his cell phone on the bedside table, and stared at the time.

    "Oh, crap!" he yelped and then launched to his feet like a rocket. He found a wrinkled pair of jeans, shimmied his medium frame into the pants, scooped a t-shirt from the floor, and jammed it over his head. After shoving his feet into a pair of flip-flops, he burst into the living room that he shared with three other roommates. "Hey! Has anybody seen my car keys?" Joel searched frantically among the leftover beer bottles and junk food wrappers that littered an old crate coffee table.

Finn appeared in the kitchen doorway and said, "Bro, I'm not your nanny." He leaned against the threshold and eyeballed his housemate. "What's got you so twisted around the axle?"

"I'm late for a lecture." Joel flipped the couch cushion where he'd sat the night before. "There's stuff growing down here!"

"Which Professor?"

"Neville Squire—Poli Sci."

"You're toast, Bro. Might as well neuter yourself before you go and save him the pleasure." Finn walked into the living room and lifted the lid on a pizza box. He called out, "Dibs on the last piece," and shoved a curled piece of pizza into his mouth.

"You're not helping!" Joel knocked the empty box aside and spotted his key chain. "Score!" He snatched them from the coffee table and then dashed out the door.

Joel maneuvered his Jeep Wrangler among the Beaux-Arts Classical architecture of the UC Berkley buildings. He was going fast enough to warrant a speeding ticket from the campus police, but it was a risk he was willing to take. His roommate Finn had not been exaggerating about Professor Neville Squire. The man had a God complex.

Looking for a place to park, Joel circled Wheeler Hall. He had to settle for a space nearly a full block away. He grabbed his backpack and sprinted.

Inside the building, Joel paused to catch his breath and nodded at a kid that he recognized from their political science class. Kyle Lobosco was loitering anxiously just outside the open door of the auditorium. "Squire hasn't started the actual lecture yet," Kyle whispered and then rolled his eyes. "He's giving a dissertation on his favorite subject—himself."

They stood listening to the political science professor who always managed to weave his academic pedigree into the lectures. "Well-respected Rhodes Scholar…," *Blah, blah, blah.* "Master's Degree—Doctor of Political Science…," *Blah, blah, blah.*

"Maybe we can slip in unnoticed," Joel said.

"You go first."

Joel crept up to the door of Wheeler Auditorium and hung close to the jam trying to summon nerve. The opportunity arose when the sleeve of Squire's wrinkled tweed jacket brushed across his podium and one of his papers fluttered to the stage.

With agile stealth, Joel slipped into the auditorium and hunkered into a seat in the back of the room.

The professor scooped up the paper and didn't miss a beat, "As you all know, I am the author of three books: Squire's International Studies, The New Global Paradigm, and Game Theory & Social Revolution. Trail blazers, rave reviews…," *Blah, blah, blah.*

Neville Squire swept his gaze over the expanse of young faces. The corners of his mouth pinched smugly. "As an expert of note, my publisher has recently asked me to analyze the war that took America by surprise six-and-one-half years ago."

Suddenly, the Professor stopped. He peered intently over

the little round glasses that were perched on the tip his nose. Then, like a gun from a holster, Squire's left hand slid from the pocket of his khaki slacks, and he pointed a finger toward the double doors. "You there!"

All heads turned to see the kid who, moments before, had been standing beside Joel.

"Come forward!"

For an awkward second, the student visibly seemed to shrink, and then, as though resigned to his fate, he squared his shoulders. Lobosco moved toward the platform like he was walking to a military tribunal.

Professor Neville Squire stood against a backdrop of golden curtains staring down at his student. "How nice of you to grace us with your presence."

The student stared at his feet. His response was low and inaudible to his peers.

A look of contempt spread across the professor's face. "Ladies and gentlemen, it appears that Mr. Kyle Lobosco has been rather flippant about your time and mine! Now, he assures me that it won't happen again!" Cynical laughter puffed through Squire's cheeks.

Kyle squirmed under the bead of the professor's protracted stare.

Seconds passed before Squire spoke again. "You are correct, Mr. Lobosco. It will not happen again! This interruption will, however, be reflected in your grade. Now leave this hall." The professor flicked his fingers dismissively. "Maybe, by my next lecture, your sense of decorum will have evolved."

Joel felt a rush of empathy as his classmate walked past.

Before exiting the lecture hall, Kyle Lobosco turned, locked rage-filled eyes on Dr. Neville Squire, and then slammed the auditorium door behind him.

The professor clasped his hands upon his podium. "Well, then, where were we?" He cleared his throat and began. "Ah, yes, the war that took America by surprise.

"Nearly seven years ago, the United States of America experienced what has come to be known as 'The Third Peril.' I shall recap the events that preceded this coordinated attack. It began a few weeks earlier with a mass divesture of stock by foreign investors. This was dubbed an 'act of economic terrorism' by the former president, Thomas Atwood." The professor paused and sniffed. "One of the many diplomatic blunders by the previous administration."

Here he goes again. Joel braced himself to endure another bashing of the former president. To his surprise, the professor shuffled some papers on the podium and moved on.

"Political and military analysts of the highest caliber have come to view the mass divesture as one of two brilliant diversions, the other being the strategic ruse that lured our Pacific Fleet to the Formosa Straights. Let me summarize the Third Peril."

Squire cleared his throat, took a sip from a water glass, and began, "On that fateful October night, a large part of the power grid failed, affecting the Great Plains and upper Midwest regions. Under a blanket of darkness, operatives slipped across the Canadian Border and swiftly implemented their pre-determined tasks with single-minded purpose. Feedlots were poisoned, and farmlands, granaries, and silos were torched as far south as Nebraska."

He paused for effect. "Squadrons of fighter jets soon followed, swooping across the border and into North Dakota with eagle-eyed precision. Infrastructure was targeted: military installations, refineries, bridges, and large commercial farms. That strike claimed the lives of 735 citizens, yet the collateral damage that was inflicted by this attack is still felt by consumers at grocery stores and gas stations… But I digress.

"On that historical night in question, along the US-Mexico Border, a different strategic outcome was planned. Foreign operatives were assigned the task of sabotaging various water impoundment structures. This mission failed, however, after the enemy was intercepted by a citizen militia."

A spattering of hoots and cheers issued from the student body, but these quickly faded when the professor cast a disapproving glare over his tiny, round-rimmed glasses.

Squire waited until the room was silent and then forged on. "Halfway around the world, an unsuspecting US Navy Pacific battle group had steamed right into the middle of a carefully organized ambush. Upwards of 10,000 sailors perished." The professor lowered his head for a few seconds of silence.

When Squire spoke again, his words carried a breathless excitement. "Finally, my Dear Ones, I come to the coup-de-gras! In the early morning hours, a disabled nuclear submarine—planted by one of our presumed allies—detonated at the Norfolk Naval Station. An orange fireball lit the sky and vaporized anyone within a mile radius of ground zero. Those outside the blast zone were literally blown from their beds, but for many civilians, the worst was yet to come. Imagine, if you will, the wide mouth of the James River empty, nothing but a gaping hole where a Russian nuclear submarine had once been docked. The water blown out to sea now rolled back with a fury. A massive wave formed and hurled itself eastward, striking Norfolk, Hampton, Portsmouth, and Newport News."

Squire stepped from behind the podium and began to pace on the platform. "Nearly a half a million Americans perished that fateful morning. The aftermath was also devastating. Many of our citizens succumbed to hypothermia due to rampant power outages. Transportation gridlocks cut off vital food and medical supplies. The economy, infrastructure, and military were badly damaged. In short, Dear Ones, our nation had been demoralized!" Something in the professor's tone conveyed approval.

"As information began to trickle in, President Thomas Atwood could only respond with impotent outrage, for this attack had been orchestrated by a well-organized global coalition. Leaders from around the world, acting in unprecedented unity, had engineered a brilliant military coup-d'etat with swiftness and discretion. With a few quick mortal blows, the international playing field had been leveled."

The professor held up a finger to punctuate the next point. "But, all was not lost. In the face of national humiliation, one man rose up with the courage to lead us into our diplomatic future. President Ira Corban has championed three actions that have had enormous implications for the international community. Can anyone here name them?"

Neville Squire's gaze darted around the hall as hands raised. He selected a young man with a pony tail seated on the front row.

The student stood, coughed nervously, and began, "The

World Reserve Bank Charter (WRB), the North American Coalition Treaty (NAC), and the Global Unity and Economic Recovery Treaty (GUERT)."

"Correct!" Squire puffed as the boy settled back into his seat. "As many of you know, our global economy was facing an unprecedented crisis. Fiscally irresponsible countries were draining nations that had sound monetary policies. It became obvious that something must be done. Alistair Dormin, Chairman of the WRB, proposed a solution that would even the international playing field. This plan called for extraordinary action. In order to address core issues, all nations agreed to cede economic sovereignty temporarily to the WRB Chairman for a seven-year period. Now, in just over three years since the implementation of GUERT, we have seen remarkable results."

The professor laced his fingers together and leaned over his podium. "Alistair Dormin's fiscal genius has already turned chaos into order. Never in the history of mankind have we seen our global economy work in such unison."

"Is there anything we cannot achieve when we join hands?" Neville Squire blinked back tears. "Now, in his second term, President Ira Corbin is realizing the birth of another dream—to see a united North American continent. Very soon, the NAC Treaty shall be signed. This international agreement is much more than an economic partnership with Canada and Mexico. The NAC Treaty leads us one step closer to a world without borders." He stopped in front of a white board and wrote these words: Revolution and the Evolution of Civilization.

"Sometimes it takes the heat of a forest fire to regenerate

the forest. Change is often birthed painfully, Dear Ones. It is through this lens that we can learn to embrace our enemies as instruments of social evolution. Let us not forget that in a gesture of reconciliation these same countries have stepped in to help us rebuild after the Third Peril."

Squire returned to his podium. "The time has come to cast off the limiting restraints of nationalism and to embrace our global future!"

Joel crossed his arms and struggled to appreciate what he was hearing. The professor spoke of those who attacked the US as though they were heroes. *What about patriotism and the soldiers who gave their lives to protect America's interests?* he thought.

"The great visionary and songwriter, John Lennon, implored us to imagine society as a utopia free from the ravages of war and religion," Squire continued. "Today, these dreams of a dreamer are becoming reality. The cleansing tide of revolution is scouring away the stain left by small-minded nationalists. Globalism, once vilified as a monetary beast, must now be embraced as a tool, a powerful economic connector useful toward building a unified world society!"

What an ego, Joel thought, as he watched the professor run fingers through a wild mop of sandy hair.
"The shell of our nation's super power has cracked. Today, 'we the people' are emerging into a changing new world." Squire threw open his arms. "Signs of new life are all around! Narrow-minded ideologies, such as deeply-rooted theology, are being replaced with blessed tolerance. Today, hate crimes are prosecuted, even those once cloaked behind the mask of religious freedom. Cross-cultural respect is now nurtured, a

fact evidenced every time our school children recite the Pledge of Allegiance to the World!"

Squire basked in the applause that punctuated his speech and then consulted his notes. "State-sponsored mental health clinics and federally-subsidized anti-depressants have helped millions of citizens to cope with the scars left by the war. American welfare and health care programs have engineered fraud-proof systems, thanks to the use of radio-frequency identification—RFID—chips." Professor Squire flashed a rare smile. "These are just a few of the social-justice initiatives that have blossomed since the war. Think of the possibilities."

In the row in front of Joel, a guy leaned toward a girl to his left and said, "Squire really believes all this bull."

The young woman snarled, "What? And you don't?"

As far as Joel was concerned, the kid was right. Squire was painting some kind of utopian image of post-war America. The truth was the country was still struggling, both socially and economically.

"And now, Dear Ones," the professor droned, "I have time for a few questions."

As hands shot up in Wheeler Auditorium, Squire pointed. "The young lady with short blond hair and glasses."

She rose, tall and gangly. "Yes, I was wondering what we can do to help society embrace our new social paradigm?"

Neville puffed. "That's an excellent question!"

Joel couldn't see the girl's face, but something told him that her nose was three shades of brown.

"You have already taken the first step by enrolling in my class," the professor said. "Simply put, you must carry this message of regeneration. Raise it like a banner in the face of narrow-minded resistance."

"I have a question!" someone said.

The voice was familiar. Joel searched the large auditorium for the speaker and froze upon the hoary head of an old man who stood in the front row. He was wearing a loose-fitting Hawaiian shirt. *It can't be*, Joel thought.

"I was just wondering where God fits into all this humanism stuff? I mean, just take a gander back through history. It's pretty clear that when folks are left to their own devices, they usually make a mess of things."

Squire's face pinched in distain. "I'm sure I wouldn't know."

"Oh? I'm sorry, Professor," the old man said without a hint of guile. "I didn't mean to embarrass you in front of all your students." Laughter rippled through the cavernous room.

"It's 'Doctor Squire.'" The professor glared. "Sir, are you a student?"

The old man twirled the tip of his long, white beard. "I guess you could say I'm working on my Master's in the University of Life. So, I figure as long as I got a pulse, I'm a student."

"I don't appreciate being trifled with!" Squire bellowed. "If you are not registered with this class, then you are trespassing!" The professor turned his red face back to the podium, began to shove papers into his briefcase, and said, "That's all for today."

Joel shot from his seat as young people spilled into the aisles. He craned his neck above the crowd, waved his arm, and called out, "Zeke!" It was futile to push through the crowd, so Joel waited beside the main doors searching the throngs for his friend. The auditorium emptied, but the old man was gone.

As Joel walked back to his Jeep, he punched "Mom" on his cell phone.

She answered on the third ring.

"Hey, Nora."

"Hi, Son. I've been missing you!" Nora seemed to understand why Joel still could not bring himself to call her, "Mom," even though she was his birth mother. "How is everything going?" she asked.

"Fine," he said. It was always an awkward exchange. There was so much about college life a mother shouldn't know. "Hey, you'll never guess who I just saw," Joel said. "Zeke!"

"You're kidding! How is he?"

"Don't know—that's just it—I saw him in the crowd, but then he just disappeared."

Nora laughed. "Well, that's Zeke for you! Still, I can't believe he didn't stick around to see you. Maybe he doesn't know you're a student at UC Berkeley."

"Zeke knows," Joel said with certainty. "He always knows."

On the other end of the receiver there was silence. Even across the miles, Joel could tell when his mother was anxious. "What's wrong?"

"You don't think he'd mention who you really are. I mean, it would be bad if word got out. You'll be graduating this spring, and so far, everything has gone so smoothly."

"Nora, it's okay. Don't worry." As he walked back to his Jeep, Joel listened to his mother's stories about the characters that frequented Nora's Bargain Bin. Once a grand hotel, the second-hand store had become a local hub and outreach center.

"It's getting so busy here," she told him. "I think I'd keel over from all the work if it wasn't for Gertie and J. J."

"Give them all my love," Joel said before ending the call.

He unlocked his Jeep Wrangler, climbed behind the wheel, and then drove aimlessly around campus looking for the old man who had changed his life.

Chapter 2

California

Friday, April 5ᵗʰ

Club music was bumping from the backyard when Joel arrived back at the "Ozone," the nickname given to the party house that he shared with three roommates.

Finn was standing near the rear of his tricked-out Ford pickup talking to some girls from his study group that met over at the Moffitt Library. "Just in time, Bro." he dropped the tailgate. "You can help me tote the brew."

Three cases of budget beer were in the truck bed, along with a plastic kiddie pool and a large platter of hot wings. "What's up?" Joel asked.

"Crack open a cold one. It's pool-party time!"

"A bit early in the season, don't you think?" Joel rubbed his arms. "It's not that warm yet."

Finn grinned and nodded. "Yeah, but don't tell that to the ladies." He lifted the kiddie pool over his head like a giant lampshade and headed for the backyard.

Joel followed with his arms loaded.

It was a little before 5:00 on a Friday afternoon, but a sizeable crowd had already gathered to ease into the weekend. A couple of blonds wearing minimalist beachwear smiled at Joel as he unloaded the bottles into some ice-filled coolers.

"Hey, Toadie. Crank up the valve, Bro!" Finn yelled, after he set the pool in place and lifted the garden hose that was snaked through an open window. The hose spit, sputtered, and then spilled warm water into the pool. "I'll be back in a nanosecond," Finn said as he dashed off.

Big Haus lumbered through the backdoor, wearing a frilly apron over a speedo. In one hand, he held a platter full of burger patties and in the other a bag of buns. "The grill-meister has arrived!" he announced.

"I think it's against the health code to cook in an outfit like that," Joel joked. "Come to think of it, isn't there a law against a guy your size wearing a speedo?"

Big Haus pointed the spatula at Joel like it was a scepter. "Silence, Peasant. When you taste my heavenly culinary cuisine, you will grovel at my feet."

Finn returned from his truck with a party platter of wings and set it down on a lop-sided picnic table. Then he hoisted a red plastic cup. "Listen up, Preppies. I propose a toast."

Joel grabbed a beer and twisted off the cap.

"Here's to chillin'!" Finn yelled.

Everyone whooped and whistled in response, and some of the younger Berkeley students downed their drinks. Joel pretended to take a sip and then set his bottle down. His first two hazy years at Berkeley had taught him that the only surefire way to avoid trouble was to avoid alcohol. When tempted, Joel thought back to the night his college career nearly ended after an all-night party. Luckily, the cop had decided to give a warning instead of hauling him to jail for public intoxication.

Joel, although of legal drinking age now, had a deeper reason for abstaining. From the day he was accepted into UC Berkeley, the rules had been clear. If Joel's true identity was ever discovered by anyone, he would be asked to leave the university. Drinking was just too risky.

Haus flipped the burgers on the grill and then launched into a rave dance, his ample girth swaying like gelatin.

Finn blasted him with a squirt gun, and some water droplets sizzled on the grill. The fight was on! The one thing Haus never joked about was food. He locked Finn's head under his arm and wouldn't let up until his roommate begged for mercy.

Finn grimaced. "Bro, remind me to get you a stick of Old Spice."

Joel leaned back against the house and kept an eye on some bikini-clad girls swirling their toes in the water.

Toadie stuck his head through the open window and followed the line of Joel's gaze to the kiddie pool. "Dude, I thought you and that little dark-haired waitress who works over at the Seabird Grille were tight?"

"I'm just doing a little harmless bird watching."

"Those Loth girls are a bit breezy for me." Toadie croaked out a belch. "But, that chick from the Seabird Grille you've been hangin' with... now, she's some primo arm candy." A wistful grin spread across Toadie's face. "I wouldn't mind takin' that babe on a stroll through the Glade."

"Her name is Coco, and she's off limits!" Joel growled at his roommate.

"Okay, chill. Man, you've got it bad." Toadie punctuated his concession with another belch and then pointed to an interesting character with a long, white beard and Hawaiian shirt. "Who invited the homeless dude?"

"I don't believe it." Joel watched his old friend stroll over to the picnic table with a plastic barrel of cheese balls and a six pack of blue sports drink. "Zeke," he yelled, "it's good to see you!"

"Good to be seen!" The old man grinned.

Finn wandered over and took a loud slurp from his Solo cup. "Who's your little ZZ Top friend?"

Joel made the introductions.

"Anybody who brings cheese balls to a party is okay by me. Hell, yeah!"

"I make it a policy to just say 'No' to hell. Besides, Young Fella," Zeke said, with a twinkle in his eye, "those cheese balls would be burnt to a crisp there."

Finn chuckled. "You're a hoot, Ol' Bro. Help yourself to a cold one!"

"Nah, that stuff makes you stupid." Zeke grabbed a bottle of sports drink and twisted the cap. "Blue Berry Blast. Now, this stuff will knock a big hole in your thirst. Has a nasty tendency to turn my lips blue, but I don't mind."

The plastic cup slipped from Finn's hand. He dove to catch it, stubbed his toe on the picnic table, and then let out a string of profanities.

Joel and Zeke watched him hopping on one foot. Finn's heel came down onto the edge of the kiddie pool, spilling a stream of water over his bare feet. He fell on his butt, and the partygoers roared with laughter.

"Yup, like I said, that stuff will make you stupid," Zeke said to Finn, then he looked earnestly at Joel. "You've grown up nice, but I'm not surprised."

"Can you stay?"

"Wish I could, Kid, but there's someplace I need to be." Zeke's pale, crystal eyes locked on Joel. "I've got a message for you—kind of like an early graduation card from God."

Joel pushed his hands into his jean pockets. "I'm listening."

The Apostle Paul said, "When I was a child, I spoke and thought and reasoned as a child. But when I grew up, I put away childish things."

"I don't understand." Joel followed the old man to the front yard of the party house. "Is God telling me to grow up?"

"That's a question you should be asking Him. I expect God will make it all clear in time." Zeke swung open the dented and rust pocked door of his old Rambler station wagon.

"I can't believe this old relic is still running after all these years," Joel marveled.

"You referring to me or the car?" Zeke climbed behind the wheel and cranked the window down. "A little dab of Gorilla glue and some fresh duct tape here an' there. Would you believe she still gets great gas mileage?"

The old man fired up the engine and reached out for a handshake. "I'll be seein' you around." As the Rambler rolled away, Zeke looked back and hollered, "Ponder that word, Kid. Things could get a little rough from here on out."

⸺∞⸺

After the sun went down, it didn't take long for the evening cool to chase the revelers from the pool party at Joel's place.

Drawn by the lure of big screens, ESPN, and cheap pitchers of beer, Haus and his clique of sports addicts had set out on their usual Friday night pilgrimage to the Bear's Lair.

The rest of the party crowd had moved inside the Ozone. The kitchen was jammed with warm bodies and loud chatter. As usual, Toadie was playing disc jockey—anything from rap to country—and jacking up the volume with each drink. A green-faced girl stumbled into Joel, covered her mouth, and raced for the toilet.

In the living room, Finn was defending his X-Box FIFA championship. Joel watched the raucous competition for a few minutes and then elbowed his way toward his bedroom, where he fiddled with the padlock. Things in a college town had a way of disappearing, a lesson Joel had learned the hard way. He slipped into his room, changed his shirt, and slapped on some cologne. In a few hours, the Seabird Grille would be closing, and Coco would be getting off work. He punched out a text message, punctuated it with an emoji, grabbed his jacket, and headed out the door.

Downtown Berkeley was busy as usual on a Friday night, but nothing could have prepared Joel for what he saw when he turned onto San Pablo Avenue. It was crawling with cop cars and response units. The road had been cordoned off. Joel pulled alongside a uniformed officer. "What's going on?"

"Move along."

Joel found a parking space a block away and then hurried toward the local hangout where his girlfriend worked. The

Seabird Grille, normally filled with patrons conversing quietly in booths or hunched over lamp-lit tables playing board games, was now the epicenter of police activity. Several times, Joel tried to pass through the barricade, but without success. He waited and watched with a worried eye. In front of the restaurant, a couple was giving a statement to a lawman.

When the man and woman turned and made their way up the sidewalk, Joel asked, "Hey, what's going on?"

"Some psycho with a machete tried to kill us all!" the woman cried.

Joel's mouth went dry. "Was anybody hurt?"

The man put his arm around his date. "The bartender was bleeding when the paramedics got there, but it only looked like a flesh wound."

"Anybody else?" Joel pressed.

"I'm not sure—maybe that waitress. Look, it all happened so fast."

The couple rounded the corner, and Joel tried again to slip past the police line. "My girlfriend is in there, and I'm not leaving until I know she's okay!"

Through the clamor someone called his name. It was Coco.

Mercifully, this time the officer let Joel pass. In the next moment, the young lovers were in full embrace.

Coco melted into the crook of Joel's shoulder with waves of sobs. "It was so awful." She fingered the delicate cross that hung from her neck. "This guy walked into the grille ranting about how he's been selected to purge the human race or something like that." Coco's lip quivered. "Then, all of a sudden, he grabbed my arm! The next thing I felt was a knife on my throat!" Her dark green eyes brimmed with tears, catching glints of gold in the streetlamp light. "And then, like out of nowhere, this stranger walks up and calmly tells the man to give him the knife! The deranged guy hands it over, just like that. I couldn't believe it!"

"It's all right now." Joel cradled Coco in his arms and stroked her silky black hair.

"The officer said I'm free to go." Coco sniffled. "Let's get out of here."

"I'll drive you home," Joel said.

"No!" Coco's reaction was sudden and guttural. She wiped tears from her cheeks and stood straight. "I can't..., not yet."

"You should at least call your parents. They'll probably be worried."

She shook her head. "My mom never watches the news, and I'm sure my dad is asleep by now."

Joel escorted Coco to his Jeep, helped her inside, and drove straight for the Berkeley Marina.

It was after 2:00 A.M. when they arrived. The air was chilly. Joel took his jacket off and wrapped it around Coco's thin shoulders as they strolled along the boardwalk. The night sky was clear and sparkling with bright stars that reflected on the San Francisco Bay. Joel thought of the time they had danced beneath the soft light of the moon. This night, Joel and Coco settled at the end of the pier and quietly listened to the rhythm of the water.

"Do you remember the night we met?" he asked.

"I'll never forget. It was one of the weekly dart competitions at the Seabird, and you were really on point."

Coco sighed. "I remember you drew a crowd, and then that creep started heckling me when I waited on his table."

Joel still felt a rush of anger when he recalled the man's slimy words. "Hey, Barbie Doll, how about taking me for a ride? I'll make it worth your while." The loser had pulled a wad of bills from his pocket and waved them in the air.
"When that slob grabbed your wrist, I saw red," Joel said.
"That's an understatement. My manager had to pull you off the guy. No one's ever stood up for me before," she added, casting a curious look at her boyfriend. "Where did you learn to fight like that?"

Joel recalled the hard lessons he had learned at the Waverly Reform School in Florida. It was a piece of his past he didn't want to think about. "I would defend you all over again just to get your phone number."

"I wasn't sure you'd ever call." Coco gazed at the moonlit water.

It had taken Joel two whole days to work up the nerve, but it was the best decision he'd ever made. Coco was like no one he'd ever met. She was beautiful with her ivory skin and delicate features, but there was so much kindness in her eyes. At the age of nineteen, she possessed an amazing depth of insight and wisdom.

Now, bathed in celestial light, her beauty nearly took Joel's breath away. He reached out and stroked her shiny black hair.

"I feel sorry for him, you know," Coco said.
"Who?"
"That guy with the knife." She swung her legs and looked down at the tide water. "He seemed so tormented."

Joel cupped Coco's face in his hands, and they kissed. Her lips were soft and sweet with hint of cherry gloss. Emotions stirred as he pulled her close enough to feel the beat of her heart.

The ding of a text message interrupted the moment.

Coco checked the cell phone, and her expression changed.

"Let me guess—you've got to go?"

She nodded. "Would it be too much trouble if we stopped by the store on the way?"

It was not the first time she'd made such a request, but Joel had learned not to ask too many questions. "Sure, no problem."

The all-night grocer, a few miles from Coco's suburban home, was like a morgue at 3:00 in the morning. Joel walked the aisles with Coco and watched her load the cart with cinnamon rolls, doughnuts, candy bars, butter, and bread. She took a quick run up another aisle for chips and soda, and then they headed for the checkout counter.

"You must have a super-charged metabolism," Joel joked as she swiped a credit card.

A subtle La Giaconda smile was her only response.

Joel steered his Jeep through the backstreets and rolled to a stop in front of the only house on the block with a weedy lawn. "Thanks for everything," Coco said as she kissed his cheek.

"I'll carry the bags."

Coco shook her head emphatically.

"At least let me walk you to the door."

"No, really. I can manage." She grabbed the groceries

and jumped out. "See you tomorrow?"

"Yeah." Joel watched her make her way up the sidewalk. Before she reached the porch, the front door swung open, a little Asian woman wagged a finger at Coco, and she launched into a shrill lecture. "How could you be so selfish? You know what happens…"

Coco quickly slipped inside and closed the door.

Joel wanted to stride right up that walk, beat on the door, and confront Mrs. Trent, saying "Do you have any idea what your little girl has been through tonight?" He sat a few moments battling frustration. Then he fired up the engine and headed back to the Ozone.

Chapter 3

New York

Tuesday, April 9th

Paige walked down the tree-lined pathway beneath a tender green canopy of new leaves. Springtime in New York was ordinarily crisp and not yet weighted with summer heat and humidity, but today the air was pregnant with moisture. The Bryant Park open-air courtyard, known as Fountain Terrace, was already beginning to fill with the lunchtime rotation of merchants seeking a quiet respite from work.

Paige spotted a table near a planter of red tulips and yellow daffodils. She dusted pollen from a chair's thin wooden slats, draped her jacket over the back, and then settled down to wait for her client.

A few blocks away in Times Square, she could hear cabs honking and imagined the yellow convoys trolling for business beneath the famous square's scintillating electronic signboards and towering skyscrapers. There would be herds of gawking sightseers and fast-walking New Yorkers, who had perfected the art of the tourist dodge while gazing robotically at their smart phones.

Bryant Park, on the other hand, was a small downtown oasis unknown to most sightseers. The locals liked to keep it that way. Paige watched the working class settling in with novels and lunches from the vendors who worked the fringes of the park.

In the distance, thunder rumbled, but no one seemed concerned. *Just another spring storm,* Paige thought as she brushed a swath of red hair from her forehead and glanced at the row of dark clouds forming overhead. *My fair skin will be safe today*, she told herself.

A cell phone trilled at a nearby table. The knick-knack, paddy-whack, give-the-dog-a-bone ringtone caused Paige to stifle a giggle as she watched a stone-faced businessman retrieve the call. *Gotta love the Big Apple,* she thought as she focused her attention on the green space where a small army of groundskeepers were rolling brown logs of sod across the great lawn. It was a ritual that took place twice a year. *I should have checked the weather and the park schedule,* she thought. It was too late to change the plans now.

Squirrels chattered in the treetops, music from the nearby carousel played against the cacophony of city sounds, and the minutes passed. Paige checked her cell phone for text messages.

"I hope you haven't been waiting long!" A young woman settled into a seat across the table. She looked at Paige from behind a huge pair of sunglasses and a hoodie that dwarfed her small, sharp features.

"Not long." Paige smiled. "How are you feeling, Bree?"

"Better." The young woman shook the hood from her head and then pulled the glasses away from her face.

Paige cringed at the sight of the ugly purple bruise on the girl's cheekbone and stifled the urge to say something maternal.

Bree scanned the park with an eye that was swollen and bloodied. She twirled a long strand of dirty-blond hair around her finger as her gaze lingered on the tree-lined paths. "I don't know what would've happened if you hadn't given me the number of the safe house. They've really helped me see things clearly."

"I'm glad to hear that." Paige paused. "Does that mean you're ready for me to file the papers?"

The young woman chewed on her lower lip and clasped her hands tightly in her lap. A minute passed in silence, except for the ominous rumblings overhead. "I just can't. All I have left is my faith, and the church says that divorce is a sin."

Paige felt a swell of sympathy for her young client. "I don't think God wants you to live in fear."

"I agree. That's why I'm going away." Bree pulled a piece of paper from the pocket of her jeans. She placed it in her lawyer's hand. "I'll be living with my aunt in upstate New York. I'll send you a note just as soon as I'm settled." She rose to go, then turned back, and unfastened the clasp on a crucifix. "Someday, I hope to pay you back for all the pro-bono work you did. In the meantime, I want you to have this." Bree pressed the necklace into Paige's palm.

Paige studied the silver cross where Jesus hung in effigy. "I can't accept this."

"Please!" Bree insisted. "It's my way of saying 'Thank you.'"

Worry nagged at Paige as she watched the young woman

head off toward Grand Central Station. *Would a simple legal separation and a restraining order be enough to keep the poor girl safe?*

A lightning bolt streaked overhead, like a camera flash. A clap of thunder immediately followed, echoing through the deep canyons formed by skyscrapers. Paige watched another bolt strike the top the Empire State Building in a blaze of brilliance. Another deafening crack followed and shook the ground. Slate clouds churned above strange striations of white.

Hail! Paige thought, and she launched from the chair. Any moment now, the floodgates of heaven might open in a deluge. She hurried down the gravel pathway at a brisk clip, but it wasn't fast enough. Hail, the size of golf balls, suddenly hurled from the sky and bounced at her feet. Tree leaves and broken twigs rained down around her. Paige held her jacket over her head and raced for the shelter of the children's carousel. There, beside a cheerful painted horse, Paige witnessed a frightening scene. People scattered, screaming in pain as icy projectiles pelted them. Many tried to shove their way onto the carousel, but there was no room. It looked as if a thousand golf balls had been dumped from the sky. Paige, huddled closely with the others, gazed upon the horrific scene. A toddler was crying, mouths were agape and moving, but the sound of hailstones on the roof overwhelmed everything.

Seventeen long minutes later, the storm was over. The city scape was blanketed with balls of ice. Locals moved cautiously at first and then scurried for the nearest subway station. The 42nd Street Entrance was backed up. As far as Paige could see, the streets were jammed with traffic. Sirens could be heard—not one, not two, but many.

In the gutter among the hail stones, she found a bird flailing wildly. Paige stooped to touch its broken wing. There was nothing she could do.

"Repent! Turn away from your evil!" someone yelled.

"That's all we need right now, another New York nut case!" a short pear-shaped woman whined.

Paige, like most, chose to ignore the man, but he continued, "God sends a hail and a tempest to sweep away the refuge!" The street evangelist wore a long, woven vest and tattered jeans. A sudden blast of wind blew his tangled mat of hair, and his crazed eyes darted among disinterested faces. "Turn from your apathy before the destroying waters come!"

The line for the 42nd Street Subway mercifully began to move. Paige anxiously descended the steps and boarded the shuttle for the Red Line. A strange sense of foreboding traveled with her all the way to West Village.

Wednesday April 10th

Sunlight spilled through the skylight and bathed the dark wood floor of the penthouse. Paige, a morning person, busied herself in the gourmet kitchen. As usual, she was up first and dressed for work. She set breakfast foods on the white-marble island and started a pot of dark-roast coffee. The morning routine was fairly predictable, something Paige had grown to value after moving to New York City. *Brody is probably jumping into the shower,* she thought, *and Connor will be waking soon from another restless night.*

Her child had cried out in the middle of the night, shaken

by another one of his nightmares—dreams he refused to talk about. *Residuals of the past,* Paige told herself. Sometimes it was hard to believe that six-and-one-half years had passed since the family's ordeal in Washington, DC. Life had not been easy for the Hays family. Some still blamed the previous administration for the war dubbed "The Third Peril." The stigma of having been the Chief Economic Advisor to the President dogged Brody Hays. *Still, we have our blessings to count,* Paige told herself when her husband finally landed a job as an investment banker with Hensley Capital, a prestigious New York City investment-banking firm.

Paige found the TV remote and powered the flat screen that was mounted above the family-room fireplace. "Freak hail storm pounds New York City," the anchorwoman announced. "The estimated damage could exceed millions of dollars."

"That's an understatement," Brody interjected as he entered the room straightening his tie. "A storm of this magnitude will generate widespread claims."

"Speaking of that, you'll need to check out our roof deck." Paige poured her husband a cup of coffee and handed him the New York Times. "We've lost most of our flowers and some of our Japanese maples, too. The vines growing over the pergola are beat up, but I think they'll survive."

"Maybe later. I've got an early meeting with the Federal Reserve. It's the last day of the State of the Economy Forum." Brody settled at the dining table to skim the newspaper. "Something is killing freshwater fish all across the nation," he read aloud. "Thousands are dying from the Columbia River Basin to the Chesapeake Bay Watershed, and biologists don't know what's causing it."

"Strange," Paige said, but her mind was on other things. She made a mental note to contact the folks at Urban Landscapers. Her eyes were glued to the television on the other side of the room as it scrolled images of the damage left by the golf ball-sized hail. There had been car wrecks, broken windows, and injuries, the worst being an infant who suffered a head wound while in the arms of his fleeing mother.

Connor slipped quietly into the room and punctuated his arrival with a yawn. He poured some milk into a bowl of Fruit Loops and then sat at the table. "We were at recess when the hail came," he said. "Miss Thornton made us all come inside and go to the gym. One of the windows broke." With a hint of a smile, he announced, "No PE until they get it fixed!"

Brody, now engaged with email on his phone, wasn't listening.

Paige mussed her son's red hair. He pulled away and gave her a stern look. "Sorry," she said. "Sometimes I forget you're almost twelve-years old now."

Brody stood, gave his wife a peck on the cheek, and grabbed his briefcase. "Oh, I almost forgot. Could you pick up my tux for tonight?"

Paige stared at her husband.

"You haven't forgotten the Hensley Capital Reception this evening, have you?" Brody said sharply. "We need to be there no later than 7:00 P.M.."

"No, I remember," she fibbed.

Brody turned to Connor and squeezed his shoulder. "Study hard, Son," he said, and he then headed off to his office in the financial district.

"Go get your backpack. It's time to go," Paige

announced, and then she ushered the boy into their private entryway and onto the elevator.

The Chambers Street Subway Station was a short walk from their high-rise penthouse. Paige and her son boarded the rail car and quickly claimed a seat. Connor pulled a tattered sketch pad from his backpack and then studied the subway art that decorated the white tile walls of this particular station— mosaic eyes of every shape and color. Paige watched her child's intensity as he selected a colored pencil and began to draw the blue eye.

"Is that the last one?" she asked.

"Nope," Connor said. "I've got seven more to go."

Paige marveled that her son was gifted in both art and music, talents that he had inherited from neither parent. "You're really very good, you know."

He looked up and smiled. "Thanks, Mom."

Four stations later, the subway operator announced, "Christopher Street." The car rolled to a stop, and the doors slid open. They spilled from the car with dozens of nameless, yet familiar faces that regularly traveled the same route to the street above.

The Tyler Brentwood School was literally just a few steps away from the station; a fact that came in very handy during the frigid Manhattan winters. "Have a great day," Paige said, reeling in her maternal impulse to kiss her son or to say, "I love you." As she watched Connor bound up the steps and slip inside, she felt a sudden rush of emotion. *They grow up so fast...*

When Paige turned to go, she noticed a man standing across the street. His eyes were deeply shaded by the bill of his green ball cap, but Paige had the distinct impression that he was staring at her.

She brushed the notion aside and continued up Bleeker Street. Paige marveled at how quickly the city had returned to normal after yesterday's freak storm. *New Yorkers are a resilient bunch,* she thought as she skirted around scaffolding, construction bins, and the blasts of a jackhammer. The city offered a cacophony of sounds—some pleasant, some annoying. But most urban dwellers seemed impervious, even comforted, by the noise. Paige loved the eclectic architecture of this borough, which included Italianate, Federal, French, and Romanesque Revival. It was reminiscent of some quaint European hamlet. In any case, a stroll through West Village was a great way to ease into her workday at the law office she shared with her partner, Jerry Silverstein, *who,* she reminded herself, *is celebrating a birthday today*!

Paige walked past Perry Street where her office was located and headed for the Honeysuckle Bakery. It wasn't an original idea. As usual, there was a line. Paige checked for messages on her phone while she waited. There was an email from her brother, David, with photos attached. Paige smiled when she opened a picture of her niece, Joy, standing in the shade of a Saguaro cactus. She was just about to open the next one when a text message from her partner popped up on the screen.

"Something's come up. Don't have time to give details. Can you cover for me?"

Paige punched out a quick reply as she stepped up to the counter, "No Problem. I'm minutes away!"

"Hey, Lady, chat on your own time," a customer sniped.

"I'd like a dozen red velvet cupcakes with cream cheese icing," Paige said to the lazy-eyed cashier. As the order was being boxed, she asked for a birthday candle.

"Sorry, don't sell 'em." The young woman shrugged indifferently and shoved the box toward her customer.

A short distance down Perry Street, Paige hurried up the steps of the old brownstone that bore the plaque that read, "Silverstein & Hays, Attorneys At Law."

Their receptionist/legal secretary, Jewel, rose from her desk in a fluster. "I'm glad you're here! I can't handle Jerry when he's in his crisis mode!"

"What's going on?" Paige asked as she headed for the kitchen with the goodies.

"He's meeting with an insurance adjuster." Jewel, a big-boned woman, followed her boss into the kitchen. "His car was pretty banged up by the hail. I swear he talks about his beloved Jag like he was talking about some dead lover."

Paige raised an eyebrow. "Be nice."

"Well, it's true!" Jewel's attention shifted to the box with the Honeysuckle Bakery label. She licked her lips, and said, "What cha' got there?"

"A birthday offering for Jerry."

"Yeah, well, I wouldn't expect it to change his sour mood," Jewel snorted cynically, and then she clomped over the black and white tile floor to the reception area.

Paige headed for her office, stopping briefly at her secretary's desk to collect her partner's case files.

"In my opinion, you shouldn't be covering for Jerry—again," Jewel admonished with an exaggerated eye roll. "You know what an enabler is?" Her editorializing was met with a stern look. "Just saying."

In the quiet of her office, Paige reminded herself that Jewel could type eighty words per minute with no mistakes and spoke legal-ease like it was a second language. Putting up with her histrionic episodes and lack of social skills was the price to pay. She opened Jerry's files to familiarize herself with the cases. Nothing too difficult—a lawsuit, a divorce, and an estate matter.

There was a rap on the door. Jewel poked her head inside the office and grinned. "Must be your birthday, too!" she said as she handed her boss a single blood-red rose.

Paige was puzzled. "Is there a card with it?"

"No. The guy just said to give it to you," Jewel said impatiently. "Do you want me to find a vase?"

"What did he look like?" Paige pressed.

"I don't know. Just some guy wearing a green baseball cap."

Chapter 4

New York

Friday, April 12th

Brody's and Paige's names were checked on the guest list, and they passed into the lobby of the Zena business complex, known to most locals as "the glass tower." The impressive edifice was perched near the edge of the water in Battery Park City. On one side, the mirrored glass surface of the building reflected the Hudson River—on the other three, the slate face of Manhattan.

"Is that a new outfit?" Brody asked as they rode the elevator to the top floor. He was observing her image in the polished bronze. She wore a simple cream-colored cocktail dress, accented with a matching emerald necklace and earrings.

Paige squeezed her husband's hand and smiled. "Most men wouldn't notice, but you're not like most men."

"That's right," he said, leaning close for a kiss as they sped upwards toward their destination. The elevator door pinged and slid open to a stunning circular view. A beautiful brunette dressed in a sparkling gown stepped forward to greet them. "Welcome to The Rounds."

At the far end of the room, a band was playing. It took Paige a few seconds to realize the singer was the Emmy Award winner, Jaylana. A moment later, near a table set with artful gourmet delicacies, she spotted another familiar face—New York Yankees pitcher, Robbie Curerra, recipient of the Cy Young Award last year. *Hensley Capital has spared no expense,* Paige thought.

"Oh, My Dear, you are more stunning than I remember!" The head of the firm, Franklin Rudd, snatched her hand and kissed her fingers, a gesture that seemed a bit too sensual.

"Nice to see you again, Franklin," she said, gracefully extricating her hand. Paige spotted Brody who was speaking with the Chairman of the World Reserve Bank, an impressive figure of a man with short cropped, sable hair, and piercing azure eyes. At six feet, five inches, Alistair Dormin towered over the other guests.

"You're a fine woman, Paige." This time Franklin touched her bare shoulder. "Promise you'll let me know if that husband of yours ever neglects you."

Paige responded with an icy look, but Brody's boss seemed impervious.

He leaned close. "What is that delectable perfume you are wearing?"

"Will you excuse me, please?" Paige said curtly. She wandered over to the floor-to-ceiling window that looked out on the harbor. The Statue of Liberty appeared haunting at night against the black waters, almost lonely in the wash of artificial light.

"Great view, huh?" Robbie Curerra said, shoving a cracker loaded with salmon pâté into his mouth.

"Yes," Paige said, suddenly aware that she shared something in common with this young athlete. Robbie Curerra also felt out of place among the top financial-world powerbrokers.

From a platform in the back of the room, Jaylana trilled a sexy ballad as several men in tuxedos threw money at her feet. There was a time when Paige would have loved rubbing elbows with the rich and famous, but her perspective had changed after her experiences in Washington, DC.

She turned back to the ballplayer and said, "I'm Paige by the way. Congratulations on your award."

Curerra lit up. "Thanks! It's a real honor to receive the Cy Young Award, something I never thought I'd get." He shoveled more goodies into his mouth, set his plate down, and glanced at this watch. "Well, guess I can leave now. 'Just make an appearance' is all they said I had to do."

Paige shook his hand and watched with envy as the young athlete made a beeline for the elevator.

The music stopped. A resonate sound of silver tapping on crystal summoned everyone's attention to the front of the room.

Brody joined his wife as Royce McBride of the International Monetary Fund stepped behind a black marble podium.

"Ladies and Gentlemen, thank you for joining us tonight. I would also like to express my appreciation to Hensley Capital for generously hosting this wonderful reception." He waited for the spattering of applause to die down before continuing. "A little over three years have passed since the Senate ratified the seven-year Global Unity and Economic Recovery Treaty known as GUERT and administered by the World Reserve Bank. This unprecedented international venture has paved the way to identify and address roadblocks to commerce and trade and balance global monetary scales.

"Under the tutelage of one remarkable man, we have witnessed unprecedented economic miracles. And now, we are seeing diplomatic wonders as well." Royce McBride's lips parted in a wide smile. "Ladies and Gentlemen, Alistair Dormin has brokered a peace agreement in the Middle East, and it is my honor and privilege to announce that our illustrious Chairman of the World Reserve Bank has just been nominated for the Nobel Peace Prize!"

Admirers exploded in thunderous applause as Dormin rose to the platform where Jaylana had earlier stood. His intense eyes seemed to gaze past those who were gathered as though they were ghosts. His striking face betrayed no emotion, not even the quiver of a smile, as the audience continued their applause. Dormin waited until the waves of adulation died down. "I am honored and humbled to be invited to speak here this evening." There was a cadence in the Chairman's deep resonate voice that conveyed confidence and captivated the crowd. "But, let us never forget that true peace always comes with sacrifice. Our own interests must be set aside for those of the collective whole. Together as one, we will create a planet where equality and unity reigns supreme!"

Again, the crowd enthusiastically roared.

Paige sensed her husband stiffen and noted that his hands had not left his side. She followed Brody's gaze to a small, dark-eyed man who had entered the room from a door to the left of the podium. "Do you know that man?" she whispered.

Brody nodded, but said nothing.

With a grand sweep of his large hand, Alistair Dormin motioned to the man now beside the podium. "In the spirit of international harmony, please welcome Jean Pierre of the World Fortress Institute, a co-visionary in our quest to build a better world." The Chairman graciously stepped aside to make room for his guest.

"Bonjour," Jean Pierre said. He was a square-faced man who spoke with a thick French accent. "As many of you have, no doubt, heard, the Presidents of the United States and Mexico, and the Prime Minister of Canada have reached agreement. The North American Coalition is now a reality! This night is truly one of celebration—no?" The exuberant response seemed to please him. "I suspect many of you are not here by accident, but rather, fate has brought you to this place in time," Pierre continued. "I look around this room and see the faces of our future—chosen ambassadors for the New Reality. In a world without borders, we can face our common challenges together as we forge this bond of social and economic justice."

Paige was confused. *What, exactly, does this man mean by social and economic justice?*

"The World Fortress Institute has been chosen to assist in the development of unifying strategies," Pierre added. "In cooperation with the World Reserve Bank and other international financial institutions, we will advise in the development of monetary policies that will lead to equitable, world-wide governance."

Brody's hand tightened around Paige's. "That hurts," she whispered.

"Sorry," he whispered. "We had dealings with Jean Pierre when I worked at the White House. I don't trust him or the World Fortress Institute. Empowering Jean Pierre has all the hallmarks of a quid-pro-quo payback by Dormin for all the institute did to get him the chairmanship."

The little Frenchman's talk was soon over, and Royce McBride invited the guests to mingle and enjoy the tables full of fine, catered delicacies. The room quickly morphed back into cocktail mode.

"I'll be back," Brody said as a group of corporate wives approached.

"Darling," Charlene Rudd said as she held out a manicured hand, "it's been too long. We really must make a date for lunch."

After a polite amount of small talk, Paige excused herself and headed for the Ladies Room. There she leaned against the sink, drew in a deep breath, and listened to the classical music that played softly from an invisible speaker. Paige checked her makeup, dotted her lips with color, and then whispered a prayer before emerging.

Paige spotted her husband standing in a dimly lit alcove and was just about to call his name when a blonde woman wearing an expensive suit and stilettos approached Brody. She looked vaguely familiar, but Paige couldn't quite place her.

In the shadows of a coatrack, Paige felt like a voyeur. She intently watched her husband and the blonde, whose conversation appeared cloistered and tense. Brody handed the woman a piece of paper. She slipped it into a handbag and then disappeared down a side corridor.

Brody stood for a moment, squared his shoulders, and

returned to the reception hall.

As the evening wore on, Paige struggled to calm her anxious thoughts. *There must be an innocent explanation,* she reasoned.

On the drive home, Brody seemed unusually preoccupied.

"Where did you disappear to earlier?" Paige asked casually as the city nightscape rolled past.

He gripped the wheel of his BMW. "Oh—I just slipped out to balcony for a little fresh air." Brody fiddled with the radio and tilted his head to listen to the news, "Bartered in exchange for economic goodwill, Alistair Dormin has brokered an historic peace agreement in the Middle East. Israel has agreed to share their holy mount with the Muslim shrine, Dome of the Rock. Construction is advancing on the new temple in Jerusalem…"

"Is there anything that Dormin can't accomplish?" Paige studied her husband's face in the ambient lighting of the dashboard.

"That's exactly what worries me," Brody murmured as he steered into their underground parking garage.

Paige felt uneasy as they made their way to the elevator. Just before the doors slid shut, a dark shadow caught her eye.

Chapter 5

Arizona

Monday, April 15th

David Fillmore flipped the sign on the General Store to "OPEN." He peered through wavy-glass windows decorated with years of collected vintage travel stickers and spotted the newspaper delivery van.

He threw the deadbolt, pushed open the aged door, and stepped onto the porch. "Good morning, Elron. Did you remember to throw a few extra in the bundle?"

The delivery man lifted his head from the back of the delivery van, looked at his client through bloodshot eyes, and slipped a cigarette between his lips. "Yup, put in an extra dozen or so. Can't hardly keep the shelves stocked around these parts." Elron fired up his cigarette and inhaled deeply. "A lot of folks are fit to be tied over what's happening." Smoke poured through his nostrils as he spoke. "The other day, a woman chased after me just to cuss me out. I said, 'Look, Lady, I just deliver the news. I don't write it!'" Elron shook his long horse-shaped face and flicked the ash from his cigarette as he lumbered up the stairs with a stack of newspapers.

"Just put them on top of the soda machine," David said. "I'll do the rest."

"Suit yourself." Elron sighed and heaved the bundle onto the top of an old-fashioned cooler that still hummed with life.

"See you tomorrow," David called loudly as the dusty van began to disappear around the corner headed to the next stop on the route, a local motel called the Tumbleweed Inn.

As the pink glow from the morning sun fanned over the quiet main street of Arroyo Seco, David lingered for a moment, listening to the cooing of the doves that nested in the weathered storefronts. All but a few of the town's commercial buildings sat empty behind windows covered with brittle yellow newsprint or cardboard. If not for the General Store, the Watering Hole Bar, and a few other occupied spaces, Arroyo Seco would be a ghost town.

Just the way I like it, David thought, grateful to have escaped from the pressures of ivy-league protocol and urban demands.

He watched until the brilliant hues of the sunrise faded over the desert. A few minutes later, he grabbed his pocket knife and turned his attention to the bundle of newspapers. He cut the twine and began to read the words that were splashed across the front page of the Tucson Sentinel, "North American Coalition Treaty Signed." An acquaintance of David, a Mexican American named Alberto Vega who had served as a liaison between the US and Mexico, was quoted extensively.

The screen door squeaked open, and David's six-year-old daughter, Joy, climbed into a springy metal chair beside him and bounced with gusto. "Want to see my bug collection?" She held out a mason jar with holes punched in the lid.

David peered through the glass with interest at the moth, a daddy-long-leg spider, and a cricket. "Very nice."

"I'm going to show them to my class today." Joy zipped the jar inside her little lavender backpack as she looked at her father with big brown eyes, a feature inherited from her mother.

"Hey, Baby Girl, it's cold out here! Go get a sweater and tell Mom that they ratified the treaty."

Joy's face lit up. "Like the cupcake treaties Mommy made for my class?"

David laughed. "Yeah, something like that. Your mom will know what I mean." His heart swelled with love as he watched his little Hispanic beauty skip to the door. Sometimes, those dark years from his past seemed like nothing more than a bad dream. It was hard to imagine he had once lived a life of reckless dissipation, rocketing down roads on his motorcycle and braking frequently for biker bars in a feckless effort to escape the memory of his niece's tragic death and the stain of guilt he carried. David thoughts drifted back to the night when he found forgiveness, the night his agnostic views were challenged.

Sitting high upon a rock on Eagle Pass, David retrieved a voice mail from his sister Paige, he recalled. *"It wasn't your fault," she said, "It was an accident." Those words were delivered six-and-one-half years ago, on the night when America was flanked in an unprecedented attack now known as the Third Peril. Looking back, it seemed ironic that personal redemption came on the same night that the United States was under siege.*

David was loading the newspaper vending machine as he reminisced and was startled back to reality by a hand upon his shoulder.

"So, it's true?" Elita reached for a copy of the news and soaked up the headlines. "I never thought I'd see open borders in my lifetime." Her voice cracked with emotion.

David patted his wife's swollen belly and said, "Maybe this baby won't have to experience some of the ugliness we've seen."

The whine of an engine turned their heads as Gordon Spitzer's old Willys Jeep bounced over the cobbled asphalt of the main street of Arroyo Seco. He braked to a hard stop in front of the General Store, raising a cloud of dust. The vehicle's door sprung open with the help of a combat boot with military fatigues tucked in, and Gordon stepped out.

"Be nice," Elita cautioned her husband with a stern look.

The leader of the group known as the Civic Border Guard tipped his fishing hat at the couple and then scanned his surroundings as if he was on some kind of recon mission. His gray gaze fixed on the newspaper vending machine. Wiry and fairly lively for a man in his sixties, Gordon hobbled up the porch steps on his bum knee, a souvenir injury from the Third Peril skirmish that he wore like a badge of honor. "Did either of you get a chance to read any of my letters to the editor?"

David raised an eyebrow. "I always suspected that you were the ghost writer behind all those editorials."

Spitzer scowled. "You lawyers are a suspicious lot! What makes you say such a thing?"

"Well, apart from the fact that they all contain the same rhetoric," David poked, "the real giveaway was the consistent use of bad grammar."

Gordon's face reddened. "What does it matter who wrote those letters? Any idiot with half a brain can see this country is headed for trouble!"

"Aren't you being a little hard on yourself? I'd say you've got a little more than half a brain." David couldn't help himself. Spitzer had served up a fast ball.

"Fillmore, you know what you can do with that Harvard Law School shingle…"

"Gentlemen—that's enough!" Elita held a finger to her lips as the screen door cracked open. Joy peeked out sheepishly and flashed an icing smeared smile. "Oh, Honey, those are for your preschool class!" Elita dashed inside to inspect the damage.

Gordon slapped a couple fives in David's hand and then loaded his arms with newspapers. "I can tell you this much. This open-border policy isn't going to go down without a fight. The American people need to realize what they're getting into." Spitzer thumbed through the editorial section and then announced, "Several TV news stations have asked me for an interview, and I'm expecting more calls. If you're smart, you'll get the General Store stocked up. I have a feeling this little one-horse town is gonna be busting at the seams with outsiders."

The word *carnival* came to David's mind. "That's good advice," he said, making a mental note to increase the store inventory for the next month or so.

Joy, her arms loaded with a box filled with cupcakes, inched her way toward the porch stairs, saying, "I can do it myself!" when her mother offered to help.

"I keep forgetting you're a big girl, now," Elita replied patiently and then grimaced as the box of cakes teetered.

After the last step, the child turned and smiled as if to say, *See, I told you I could do it.*

The adults watched Joy walk two doors down to the old barber shop that now served as the Arroyo Seco preschool.

Gordon shook his head as he hobbled back to his Jeep. "If that was my kid, she'd be homeschooled for sure. No telling what kind of nonsense is being taught these days."

"A conspiracy of reading, writing, and arithmetic!" David quipped, "Oh, and grammar, too!"

Gordon fired up his Jeep, stuck his finger out the window in a gesture, and then roared away.

"How rude!" David said with mock indignation.

"He's not the only one." Elita's dark eyes flashed.

"Oh, Spitzer and I were just having a little fun."

"Well, one of these days, the teasing might go too far," she said and then disappeared into the General Store.

A few moments later, David went inside. Streaming through the storefront window, the morning sun cast warm blocks of light on the antique cash register. David walked past the pickle barrel loaded with sale items and searched the old-style grocery store aisles for movement. The only thing that moved was the oak fan that squeaked overhead. "Elita?" he called. The store was quiet.

At the back near the soda fountain and grille, David looked for his wife. She wasn't there, so he poured himself a cup of black coffee and then trudged up the ancient stairs that led to the two-bedroom apartment they called home.

David spotted Elita standing in front of the living room window looking past Arroyo Seco's gray weathered buildings. Her gaze seemed fixed upon the desert landscape beyond the town.

"I'll try to be more sensitive," David conceded. "It's just

that Spitzer can be such an alarmist..."

Elita didn't seem to hear him. Something in her expression raised David's concern. "Honey, are you all right?"

"What?" She glanced over her shoulder and added, "Oh, I'm fine." The words were punctuated by a forced smile.

"Morning sickness?"

Elita squeezed her husband's fingers. "Actually, there is something wrong. The cooler is acting up again."

"Don't worry about a thing. I'll take care of it." David keyed in a number on his cell phone and listened to it ring and ring, only to hear a generic service-is-not-available message. "When are they going to boost the cell towers around here?" He slid the phone back into his pocket. "I'll take a ride over to Hope Springs and find Randy."

"Well, tell him we need to get it fixed before things spoil." Elita's hand rose to her swollen belly, and she turned back to the window with the same distant look.

David kissed his wife's cheek and said, "I won't be long." He grabbed a set of keys and was off. His motorcycle helmet was in the storage room that doubled as a make-shift law office. David snapped it on, slipped out the back door, and jumped on his Triumph Rocket III. Moments later, he was rumbling down the main street dodging potholes that were big enough to swallow a tire.

Outside of town, David opened up the throttle, leaned into the road, and waited for the exhilaration of speed to free his mind.

The Saguaros were in bloom among a lush carpet of golden Mexican poppies. Subtle scents of spring wafted across the arid terrain and over a gentle plateau, but on this particular morning an ominous feeling of worry needled him.

———

David turned his motorcycle toward a colorful formation of limestone and red shale layers that, from a distance, resembled the rungs of a terrace. Over the crest of the mesa, a strange community of sojourners came into view. It was hard to believe the place was once nothing more than the barn wood remnants of a ghost town. Today, Hope Springs looked like a sprawling camper village nestled in the middle of a desert oasis. *But, it is much more than that,* David mused as he meandered down the dirt road that paralleled a fenced pastureland. Cattle, goats, and sheep grazed among side-roll sprinklers. Further up the road, past the corrals and milking barn, was a garden plot that produced more than enough vegetables, corn, and beans to feed the small village.

The whole thing is incredible! David thought about his late client, Rupert Sims, who'd made provisions in his trust document to set aside a large tract of land for the "People of God." Some suspected that the eccentric rancher was touched in the head, a thought that David himself had once entertained.

Today, however, the manifest vision of the old man was indisputable. The "faithful" had mysteriously begun to show up in Arroyo Seco not long after Rupert's death. People of different colors, church backgrounds, and stations of life—all living and working side by side. Some of the residents had money to invest in the community; others shared special talents or labor.

As the appointed executor of the trust, David had

watched this apparent spirit of cooperation with a judicious eye. The failed hippie communes of the sixties and seventies had imprinted a legacy of cynicism, yet somehow, Hope Springs seemed unique. *How*, he wondered, *can an eclectic mix of people live and work together in such harmony?*

"One word explains Hope Springs," Elita would say. "God!"

Rupert must be smiling down from Heaven, David imagined as he rumbled past several dozen rows of campers—nearly fifty dwellings, some plain, others decorated with flower pots and yard ornaments. It was an unusual mixture: expensive tip-out RV's towered over homemade campers, school-bus conversions, and pop-ups. There were even a few wall tents and a tiny tear-drop trailer. Some of the dwellings had adapted to the extreme temperatures of the desert by erecting an extra roof. Others had added bales of straw or adobe walls for insulation.

David parked his motorcycle beside a large pavilion and waved at Bonnie who was stoking coals in the massive fire pit.

"You're just in time for breakfast!" she hollered and pointed to an oversized frying pan with remnants of scrambled eggs and sausage. "Our hens have been real busy lately. There're more eggs than we could sell at market, so Sue cooked an extra batch this morning."

"It smells good, but I'm on a mission." David waved at Sue, a shy, heavy-set woman who blushed and looked away.

Bonnie wiped her hands on a dishrag. The happy expression she wore on her face made her look younger than her seventy plus years. "I'm glad you're here because there's something I want to discuss. Some of the ladies and I have been making plans. We'd like to throw a baby shower for Elita. What do you think?"

"I'm sure she'd love it, but right now the only thing on my bride's mind is fixing our walk-in cooler."

"Not that again!" The older woman shook her head. "One of these days, we'll be holding a wake for that old dinosaur."

"You're probably right," David said, "but, in the meantime, I was hoping Randy, our neighborhood repairman, could coax it back to life."

"Let's see. Randy might be helping Travis unload some Pinion pine he brought down from the hills, but, then again, he could be off with my husband," Bonnie said. "One of Jim's generators up at the lower dam has been acting up."

David thanked her and then headed along a path to the lower dam. He passed Ziggy Nash, who was adding sawdust to one of the community's self-composting toilets. "I thought you'd be out pumping tanks."

Ziggy, an aging hippie, shook his long, thin hair scraped into a meager ponytail and said, "My honey truck has a flat tire, so I decided to make myself useful around here."

The slang term for a septic tank pumping unit, "honey truck," always made David chuckle. It seemed somehow fitting that Ziggy's wife, Fawn, also an aging hippy, was a beekeeper who sold raw honey and beeswax candles. "I hope you get it fixed soon," David said as Ziggy scooped another bucket full of sawdust from a wheelbarrow.

He passed Travis' wood shop and noted that the flatbed trailer was still stacked with pine. Young Travis Dayton was working up a sweat by tossing adobe bricks into a large pile. "What are you up to?" David asked.

Running dirty fingers through his long mullet, Travis said "Some of the ladies have been complaining about food spoilage, so Randy and I are working on plans for a spring house."

"Speaking of Randy, have you seen him?"

"He went off with Jim 'bout an hour ago," Travis said and then tossed another adobe brick onto the pile.

David headed toward the limestone and shale cliff where a gentle waterfall flowed through a cleft. He followed a footpath over a bridge and passed two aged outbuildings, remnants of the original town. It made him think of the first time he set foot in Hope Springs.

Memories came flooding back… *Zeke clad in shorts, a colorful Hawaiian shirt, and hiking boots, his white beard fluttering in the sweltering hot breeze as he poked about among the ruins. The ancient man found an iron rod and thrust it into the base of a rock. With his own eyes, David witnessed water gush from the spot, pooling in the limestone basins and quenching the thirsty, sunbaked soil. Zeke had tapped into a deep artesian well!*

David's thoughts snapped back to the present when he spotted his friends on the other side of the limestone outcropping. At the base of the lower dam, Randy and Jim were huddled over the generator that channeled electricity into the pavilion. "Having problems?"

"Just a little tune up. She's purring right along now!" Randy slapped Jim on the back. "God knew what he was doing when he sent us a hydraulic engineer."

"I feel the same about having a refrigeration guy in the neighborhood," David interjected.

"Don't tell me—that old cooler is giving you fits again!" Randy lifted his ball cap and fanned sweat from his brow. "I'm no miracle worker, Buddy, but I'll give it a go."

Suddenly, the sound of rapid footsteps slapped across the shale, and the men turned to see gangly Mr. Mike loping up the path in his red Converse running shoes. He waved his twig-like arms in the air and then stooped to catch his breath. A few seconds later, he looked at David through the thick lenses of his heavy framed glasses and said, "You need to get home!" He gulped in another breath. "I just picked up a call on the police scanner. Somebody at the General Store just called for an ambulance!"

⸙

David twisted the throttle and blasted over the county road toward Arroyo Seco. In his rearview mirror, Jim and Bonnie Saunders' Volvo wagon shrank into the distance. Somewhere behind them, Randy Bales struggled to keep up in his repair truck.

Maybe there was an accident in front of the store, David rationalized as blood pounded in his temples. *If anything happens to Elita or Joy...* The thought was too frightening to entertain.

The twelve miles from Hope Springs to Arroyo Seco seemed like fifty. David's mind raced as he turned onto Main Street and skidded to a stop in front of the General Store. Somewhere near the edge of town, the sound of sirens wailed.

David dropped the kickstand on his bike, bolted across the General Store porch, burst inside, and called out his wife's name. No reply! With his heart pumping hard, he launched up the stairs to his apartment.

On the bathroom floor, he found his beautiful wife lying in a pool of blood. "Oh, Honey!" David knelt beside her and tried to process what his eyes were seeing. *This can't be happening...*

Elita's eyes fluttered open and filled with tears. "It's the baby." The words were as thin as a thread. "I'm so sorry..."

David cradled his wife in his arms. "Shhh, now. Everything is going to be okay," he whispered, wishing that what he said was true.

Chapter 6

New York

Tuesday, April 16th

After dropping Connor off at the Tyler Brentwood School, Paige walked by an array of shops and restaurants while checking the calendar on her cell phone. There were no meetings scheduled for today, and Pastor Cedric had asked her to stop by the church to discuss some business. *Probably another pro-bono case,* she figured.

Paige continued two blocks past the Law Office of Silverstein and Hays, turned right on Becker Street, and headed toward a brick building once known to the old-timers as the Grand Muse Theatre. She walked beneath an ornate marquee that now read Urban Hope Church.

On the other side of a set of double doors, Paige spotted Pastor Cedric standing near the former snack counter, now dubbed the "Hospitality Bar." He raised his mug in salutation and said, "Just in time to join me for a coffee break!"

Paige selected a tea bag from a caddy, dropped it into a disposable cup, and added steaming water. "What can I do for you?" she asked as her tea steeped.

The dimples in the Pastor's cheeks deepened. He took a gulp of coffee. "Are you aware of the FAD Act?"

"The Fairness and Anti-Discrimination Act?" she replied.

Cedric nodded, pulled an envelope from his jacket pocket, and handed it to Paige. The return address indicated that it was from the US Attorney's Office—Southern District of New York. "It seems I'm being accused of promoting hate and discrimination against certain classes of people. In other words, the Feds don't like me quoting from what they believe to be offensive texts of the Bible."

"You've got to be kidding!" Paige scanned the letter. After a few moments, she looked up. "This is a warning…"

"That's right!" he cut in. "But if there is another infraction, then our church loses its tax-exempt status and incurs a $5,000 fine!" The pastor set his mug down and began to pace. "Can you imagine paying property taxes on this New York City real estate? We wouldn't have enough left to pay utilities, let alone run any programs."

"Do you have a copy of the statute's regulations?" Paige followed her pastor to his office and watched him rummage through his file cabinet. He produced a thick folder and handed it to her.

"Would you write a response?" Cedric pleaded. "I want to reassure the US Attorney that I will cooperate fully."

Paige flipped to the section that listed the "offensive" passages of scripture and her mouth fell open. "I had no idea the extent of censoring had come to this…"

"Last year, the Supreme Court got involved in a case and ruled that the First Amendment was never intended to promote discrimination. Most people, including myself, thought it was a great idea." Pastor Cedric's brow creased. "Did you know that an abridged version of the Bible is now being recommended to all 'compliant churches?'" He used his fingers to add the quotes. "I guess some scripture is better than none."

Thumbing through the regulations, Paige asked, "But, where will it end? May I take this with me?"

The pastor responded with a nod.

Paige closed the folder. "Maybe I can find a loophole, and we can challenge the law…"

"No, no! Don't do that!" Cedric interrupted. "We can't afford to take the risk."

Paige was disappointed by her pastor's palpable fear and willingness to compromise. "Okay, I'll draft a letter."

"You're a real saint!" Relief washed over Cedric's pudgy face. "Say, how did your last pro-bono case turn out? You know, that young lady with the abusive husband."

Tucked away in her satchel was a cheery postcard. Paige had been happy to hear from her and to know that Bree was doing well in upstate New York. "She's rebuilding her life in a safe place."

Paige's cell phone rang, and she checked the screen. "Excuse me, Pastor. It's my brother who lives in Arizona." She accepted the call. "David, you've been on my mind. How is everything?"

"Something bad has happened." Paige heard anguish in her brother's voice. "It's Elita—she's lost the baby."

"Oh, no!" Paige pressed the receiver hard against her ear and felt the color drain from her face. "Is she okay?" The question sounded trite. *Of course, she's not okay!*

"Elita lost a lot of blood," he paused, "but the doctors say she's out of danger now."

A lump formed in Paige's throat and tears sprouted in her eyes. "Do you want me to come?"

"No, that's not necessary."

"If there's anything I can do—anything at all," she said before David ended the call.

Paige asked her pastor to pray and then hurried for the door on shaky legs.

Outside, the swell of long-buried emotions threatened to swamp her. The news had awakened a sleeping giant of sorrow. The dull heartache had returned. The pain of losing her own little girl, Emily, had left a deep wound that time could never completely heal. Now, Paige's heart broke anew for her brother and his family. "Dear Lord," she whispered, "please send comfort."

Paige suddenly longed to feel her husband's reassuring arms around her. She dialed Brody's private number and waited. The call went straight to voice mail. "Brody... I really need to talk to you. I was hoping we could meet for lunch."

She disconnected and then tried his office. According to her husband's secretary, he had no meetings scheduled for the noon hour, so Paige hailed a cab. She tried to steady her breathing as the driver wove in and out of traffic. She felt calmer when they neared the financial district. The driver pulled to the curb in the shadow of the glass-faced skyscraper that housed the investment-banking firm where Brody worked. "That'll be $8.75," the cabbie said.

Paige leaned forward to check the meter and pulled out some cash. Suddenly, she spotted her husband exiting his building. She froze.

The driver drummed his fingers on the steering wheel. "Look, Lady, I don't got all day."

Brody paused on the sidewalk, fiddled with his phone, and then held it to his ear.

Paige was startled to hear her husband's personal ring tone, and she answered on the first ring.

"Hey, I just noticed you called," he said cheerfully. "About lunch—afraid I can't make it today. I'm looking at a pile of work on my desk that needs my attention."

A blue sports car pulled up in front of the building, and Paige watched her husband step to the curb.

"I'll see you tonight, okay?" Brody said and then climbed into the passenger seat.

Paige couldn't see the driver's face, only that she was a blond!

"What'll it be, Lady?" the cab driver barked.

For a brief moment, Paige considered asking him to follow the blue car. *No,* she thought. *There must be a good explanation.* "West Village." She gave the address of her office on Perry Street.

Paige was putting the finishing touches on dinner when Brody arrived home. He placed his briefcase on the kitchen floor and gave her a peck on the cheek. "You've been crying." Brody wiped a tear from his wife's face. "What wrong?"

"David and Elita lost their baby today."

"I'm sorry." Brody laid his hand on Paige's shoulder.

She stiffened at his touch.

"Are you going to Arizona?"

She shook her head and turned back to the stove. "They don't want me to come."

"It's probably just as well," Brody replied. "Things like this have a way of opening old wounds."

"You always act as though emotions are a sign of weakness. I just happen to hurt for my brother and his family right now, that's all."

"I didn't mean it that way." Brody carried his briefcase over to the family room desk and then settled into his usual place at the dining table. Violin music issued from the formal living room. "Connor sounds pretty good."

Paige stirred alfredo sauce and turned the gas flame to simmer. "We have a gifted son. The music teacher at the Tyler Brentwood School believes he's good enough for Julliard." She cast a quick glance over her shoulder and caught her husband raising an eyebrow.

"I'm not sure that would be in his best interest."

"What do you mean?" Paige pressed.

"Music and art are nice hobbies, but let's face it, very few people ever make a living at it."

Anger surged in Paige's bosom. *Here we go again,* she thought. *Why can't Brody just accept that our son is sensitive?* Paige bit her tongue and then spoke carefully. "The same can be said about sports."

"That's entirely different. A lot of life lessons can be learned in athletics: competition, team work, and resilience, just to name a few." Brody leaned back and folded his arms. "I think playing sports would do Connor some good. Maybe he would even make a few friends."

L.P. HOFFMAN

"He has friends," Paige bristled. "Connor and Josie have been close since we moved into this building, and then there's his Sunday school class…"

"A twelve-year-old boy should be out kicking a soccer ball around with kids his own age, not hanging out with a little girl who is into Barbie Dolls!"

Paige turned to face her husband. "Maybe your son hasn't developed an interest in sports because you're always too busy to show him how!" She expected her husband's usual raft of excuses, but he surprised her.

"Ouch! You're right. I have been remiss." Brody thought for a moment and said, "Maybe I can take him to a ballgame this weekend. Our firm has box seats at Yankee Stadium."

"For real?" Connor, who had been standing in the doorway of their formal living room, ran over to his father. "Just you and me, Dad?"

Brody tussled his son's red hair. "You like the idea?"

"Awesome!"

Paige set plates on the table and was grateful for the excited banter that passed between her husband and their son, but there was something unspoken that still weighed heavy on her mind—something she was afraid to ask about—the woman in the blue sports car.

67

Chapter 7

California

Wednesday, April 17th

Joel discretely checked his smart phone for text messages, wishing he was anywhere but this Barrows Hall section class. Professor Neville Squire's arrogant pontifications about the blunders of the previous administration were getting under his skin.

"Can't wait to see you this afternoon." Joel smiled at the message from Coco that she had sealed with a red heart emoji. His thoughts drifted to his girlfriend's silky black hair and deep green eyes that seemed to gaze into his soul.

"Mr. Meyers, would you care to share your pressing business with our entire class?"

Joel snapped to attention as Neville Squire's shadow crossed his desk. He slipped the phone into his pocket. "No—sorry."

The professor's upper lip grew taut. His eyes peered over the glasses perched on the end of his nose. "Mr. Meyers, perhaps you can tell the class what I was discussing?"

Without hesitation, Joel responded. "Of course, Sir. You were analyzing the negative political strategies of President Thomas Atwood and his cabinet."

The corners of Squire's mouth pinched into a frown. "Young man, do I detect a hint of sarcasm in your tone?" The eyes of everyone in the classroom were on Joel. He felt his face flush. "Well, speak up!" the professor barked.

Pent-up frustration launched Joel to his feet to face Squire. "Are you asking for my opinion, or do you just want me to parrot your classroom rhetoric?"

A burst of laughter popped from Kyle Lobosco's lips. The professor shot the student down with one caustic look and then turned it back on Joel.

"I'm intensely interested in your personal observations. Please, enlighten me!" Neville Squire's words were taut and controlled, but his face quivered with anger.

"I just think there is another side to the story, one that isn't being presented," Joel began. "It seems a little narrow minded to blame every current problem on the former president."

"Narrow!" Squire blew. "Are you insinuating that my insights are somehow lacking?"

Joel stared at his professor, realizing for the first time that the man never once considered that his opinions were anything less than absolute statements of truth. "Why don't you ask the former president to come here and speak for himself?"

Neville Squire erupted in contemptuous laughter. "For one thing, it would be a colossal waste of time to extend such an invitation. Thomas Atwood couldn't possibly defend his actions!"

"Ask him!" The challenge rolled off Joel's tongue before he could stop it.

Neville Squire pushed his glasses to the bridge of his nose and looked at his stunned students. "Well, well…" The gauntlet had been cast down! "Very well. I shall invite former President Thomas Atwood to address an assembly." The professor paused. "I expect a refusal will put an end to such foolishness," he said as the class drew to an end.

Joel rolled to a stop in front of the Ozone beside his roommate's truck and went inside to get ready for his afternoon date.

Finn was sprawled out on the couch with his eyes closed, his mouth open, and drool on his chin. The Dr. Phil show played on their big-screen TV.

Glancing at the time and knowing Coco would be there any minute, Joel asked, "What are you, a bag monster? You haven't moved since I left this morning."

Finn looked at his roommate through half-mast eyes and then rolled over with a moan. "There was a big antler festival over at the Brick House last night, and some bug jumped me." Finn laid the back of his hand over his brow. "Think I got a temperature, Bro!"

"Yeah, it's called bottle fever."

"No kidding, Bro. I'm dying."

Joel spotted his girlfriend coming up the walk "Maybe you should head over to the quack shack and see if they'll give you some antibiotics," he replied.

"Could you drive me over?"

"Sorry, I've got plans." Joel opened to door to leave.

"Bro, would you bring me back a six pack?" Finn affected his best pleading look and added, "Alcohol kills germs."

Joel just shook his head and stepped out on to the porch to meet Coco. Her smile lit a fire in his heart. He laced his fingers behind the nape of her neck and kissed her. In an instant, the dicey exchange he'd had with Professor Neville Squire melted away.

"Dude! Get a box!" Toadie croaked.

The young couple turned to see Joel's other two roommates lumbering up the sidewalk.

Haus hoisted his ample girth up the porch steps and claimed, "Dibs on the leftover ham and beans in the fridge."

"Too late. I flushed it down the john last night!"

"You did what?" Haus grabbed Toadie by the collar of his wrinkled cotton shirt and spun him around. "I oughta flush you down the commode!"

"Have mercy, Dude. I'll make it up to you!" Toadie belched from both ends.

Haus twisted his roommate's collar a little tighter before firing a parting salvo. "Then buy yourself a case of beano, why don't you!" It was more of a suggestion than a question.

Joel chuckled, leaned toward his girlfriend, and whispered, "It's not wise to get between Haus and his food."

"Yes, some people are like that," Coco said without smiling.

As they drove through town, Joel's girlfriend seemed pensive. He watched her silently fingering the amber cross that always hung from her neck.

"Did I say something wrong?" Joel asked.

When their eyes met, Coco's smile returned as suddenly as it had left. "Everything is great! So, where are we going?"

"It's a surprise." Joel headed toward downtown Berkeley and jogged up Hearst Avenue. Coco gave him a quizzical look, but he shook his head. "You'll see." Their destination became clear after Joel drove past the Greek Theatre and continued up Centennial Drive.

"The Botanical Gardens!" Coco clapped her hands together. "It's a perfect day for a walk."

Joel felt giddy with love as fresh air tumbled through the window of his Jeep. The azure sky, dotted with puffy cumulous clouds, capped a green carpet of new grass. *Yes, if everything goes as planned,* he thought, *this will be a day to remember.*

At the gate, Joel flashed his student ID card and paid for Coco's entrance. They parked near the Old Redwood Forest where a bridal party was posing for photos.

Coco's face looked ethereal in the mottled sunlight. Joel took her hand, and they strolled up the trail past the New World Desert. Coco wanted to know the name of every giant cacti and succulent. It was fun watching her take curious pleasure in the wonders that surrounded them. Coco possessed a childlike innocence, always seeing the best in everyone and bringing out the best in Joel. There were times, though, when he caught a flicker of sadness in her old-soul gaze, a vulnerability that made him want to protect her. Other times, his girlfriend seemed to radiate a deep well of inner strength. Coco was the most fascinating person Joel had ever known, and he was hopelessly in love with her.

As the young couple strolled up the South African section of the Botanical Gardens, Coco threw open her arms and exclaimed, "Have you ever seen anything so delightful?"

Each time I look at you, Joel thought.

She was busy reading the names of the spring-blooming flowers. "Cape Cowslips and Marigolds." Coco laughed. "Those purple and white star-like flowers are called Baboon Flowers. What a funny name!"

The trail climbed up as they neared the Asian section. Coco grew quiet when they passed by a pond and bamboo grove.

"I can't believe you've never visited this place."

"My mother and father don't get out much."

"You never talk about your family," Joel said. "I'd like to get to know them. Aren't your parents of Asian descent?" Joel inquired.

"My mother was born in Chinatown."

"What about your dad?"

Coco shrugged. "Irish and Italian, I think." She pointed to a tree loaded with lavender flowers. "I know that one. It's called a Royal Empress."

The earlier pensive mood returned and followed Coco like a shadow as they continued past the rainbow display of bulbs in the Mediterranean Garden.

Joel took his girlfriend's hand and said, "The view from the Old Rose Garden with blow you away."

She stopped in her tracks and looked up with excitement. "Roses? They're my favorite flower!"

Joel squeezed Coco's delicate fingers and said, "I know."

"How?"

"I've noticed the way you look at them."

The couple nearly sprinted up the steepening incline, and before long, they stood in the English Style Garden accented with rock walls.

Joel lingered over the spectacular view of the San Francisco Bay and the Golden Gate Bridge, but Coco ran ahead and climbed a series of steps that led to a pergola.

He joined her there, watching as she leaned close to one of the many white rose buds that graced the trellis.

"White roses are my favorite! Their scent reminds me of violets with a tiny hint of lemon." She traced a tender bud with her finger.

Coco seemed lost in a world all her own, a world that Joel was determined to share. He glanced about the Old Rose Garden, and then, satisfied that they were alone, he reached into his pocket for the ring.

Joel could feel the blood coursing through his veins as he knelt before Coco and watched her eyes widen with surprise. "I'll be graduating in a few months and…" His thoughts raced ahead of his words. "What I'm trying to say is that I don't want to wait. I love you." Joel opened his hand and offered her a white gold ring with a single diamond. "Will you marry me?"

Chapter 8

Arizona

Wednesday, April 17th

David rolled over in bed and reached for his wife. Her blanket was thrown back and her spot was empty. The bedroom was dark, except for the faint glow of dawn emanating from the window. As David's eyes adjusted, he saw Elita sitting in her rocking chair. "Honey, you should be resting," he said.

"Listen," she whispered as the gentle coo—coo—coo of a morning dove issued from outside. "It's almost like she's singing just for us."

David climbed from the bed and stood beside Elita. In the dim light, he could see a tear glistening on her cheek.

Elita looked up with eyes full of sorrow. "He was alive, our little Pajarito. I felt him move that last day." She cried. "Yet, our baby boy never got to take his first a breath."

David knelt and took her hand. "Come back to bed."

A journal fell at her feet when she rose, but Elita didn't seem to care. The spark in her dark fawn eyes were dimmed by sadness. "Go back to sleep," David said as he tucked her back into bed. "I'll take care of Joy and manage the store."

He returned to the window to lower the shade and then tiptoed down the hall to peek into his little girl's room. Joy was sleeping soundly, so David went downstairs to start the day.

With a flip of a switch, the old General Store was bathed in the soft glow of the lights. He moved past rows of rustic pine shelves lined with canned goods and slipped behind the lunch counter to brew a stout pot of coffee. In the stock room, which doubled as David's law office, he unloaded boxes of wholesale merchandise and snack foods that Elita had ordered just before she'd lost the baby.

It was the worst time possible for an influx of outsiders. There would be protesters, activists, and media lured by the controversy surrounding the North American Coalition Treaty. *At least, we have the inventory*, David told himself. They had stocked up on extra perishable items such as lunch meats, cheese, eggs, and bread that had been hastily stacked in the recently repaired walk-in cooler. There was a lot to do before opening, chores the couple normally handled together. Elita usually loaded the shelves and pickle barrels with sale items, while David ran a dust mop over the traffic-worn wooden floor, played general handyman, and managed the books.

David glanced at his watch. *Time to get Joy ready for preschool!*

Back upstairs, he roused his little girl from a dream, plucked a mismatched outfit from her drawer, and tried to be patient when she insisted on dressing herself. Finally, he coaxed her downstairs for a bowl of Fruit Loops.

"Why isn't Mommy up?"

"She's not feeling well."

Joy poked a piece of cereal into her milk and watched it pop back up. "Is the baby sick, too?"

The question took David by surprise. He looked at his child's quizzical face and realized that, amidst the chaos and pain of the last few days, they had failed to explain the situation. He lifted her from the stool and held her close. "Your baby brother lives in Heaven now."

Joy's brown eyes brightened. "What's his name so I can find him when I go there someday?"

David swallowed hard. They had not fully settled on a name. "Pajarito," he said, stroking his daughter's silky brown hair. "It means little bird in Spanish."

"Pajarito," she repeated. "I like that!"

If only we could all accept loss like little children, David thought as he placed her back at the counter.

"Daddy, don't forget to make me a peanut butter sandwich for school," she said, loading her spoon with Fruit Loops.

By 9:00 A.M., Joy was in school, and the streets began to fill with people.

Alberto Vega's early model Toyota Tundra turned onto the main street of Arroyo Seco, followed by a fleet of television news vans.

From the other direction, a caravan of Willys Jeeps could be heard grinding toward the General Store. The Civic Border Guard rolled into town like an army battalion.

From the General Store porch, David waited for the fireworks to begin.

The lead Jeep lurched to a stop in front of the Watering Hole Bar, and Gordon Spitzer, a camo-clad curmudgeon, climbed from the vehicle. Gordon tipped his fishing cap toward the porch and hollered, "Are you with us or against us, Fillmore?"

David shrugged. "I can see both sides of this issue."

"Yeah?" Spitzer spit on the dusty street. "Either they brainwashed you at Harvard Law School, or they syphoned out your brains!"

Arms crossed, stance wide, the CBG militia lined up to make their presence known, gnashing scowling faces at Alberto Vega and the media as though they were spoiling for a battle.

"Somebody get me a glass of milk," Gordon Spitzer ordered.

"I'll get it, Boss!" Tranch, a bald Neanderthal, disappeared through the swinging doors of the Watering Hole Bar and returned with a bar glass full of milk.

Gordon downed it like it was a triple shot of whiskey.

While the TV news crew set up their camera in the street, more vehicles arrived loaded with protestors and picket signs.

The star reporter stepped from the air-conditioned News Cam 4 van and flashed a toothy grin at David. "I love this quaint General Store. It's the perfect backdrop for our cameras. Do you mind?"

"It's fine with me," David said, "as long as they don't block the door."

"Hey, Fillmore, you should learn who your friends are!" Spitzer growled.

The anchorman briskly strode over to the leader of the CBG and thrust out his hand. "The famous Mr. Spitzer, I presume."

Gordon ignored the gesture and wiped milk from his upper lip. "Let me guess. You must be Sherlock Holmes."

The newsman shook his head. "Actually, I'm Jay

Jennings, News Cam 4, and this is my crew," he said, with a sweep of his arm. "Mr. Spitzer, I'd love to interview you. If you're available?"

"Before I agree, Mr. Jennings, I'd like to ask you a thing or two."

"Oh?" The anchorman's eyebrows shot up. "I suppose that would be okay, just not on film. My viewers are used to me being in charge."

"How do you personally feel about open borders?" Gordon set his empty glass on the hood of his Jeep. "Have you given any thought to the impact they will have on our country?"

Jay Jennings fiddled with his tie. "Well, naturally, I'm sure there will be challenges. This is a very complicated issue."

"When are you media types going to wake up?"

"It would help if I could find a Starbucks around here!" The anchorman laughed at this own joke.

Gordon's face remained deadpan as did his steely-eyed troops.

Jay Jennings cleared his throat and then turned back to his crew. "Okay, people, we've got a segment to set up!"

The TV crew tested their equipment while their star preened in front of a hand-held mirror.

Last to arrive was a truckload of Mexican Americans who spilled onto the dusty street with picket signs in hand—words scrawled in crude block letters: F#@% *racism! Stop bigotry! Economic fairness! Freedom!*

Out came the opposition, shouting and waving their signs: *Save America! No Open Borders! Stop the Invasion!*

Someone from the CBG fired a caustic salvo that made

David cringe, "Mexicans Stay Home!" He hoped Elita hadn't heard the hateful slurs through the bedroom window.

The mobs ratcheted up their angry rants as Jay Jennings took his place on the street in front of the General Store and motioned for Gordon Spitzer to join him.

David stepped out of the view of the camera and observed from the porch. *This should be interesting.*

The cameraman's assistant called out, "Five, four, three, two, one."

Jay Jennings lifted a microphone to his mouth and began. "Protests erupted today along the US-Mexico Border in Arizona." The digital camera panned the mob of angry-faced picketers and then returned to Jennings standing beside a camo-clad man wearing a fishing cap. "This is Gordon Spitzer, the head of a vigilante group known as the Civic Border Guard." The reporter asked, "Mr. Spitzer, what is your response to the North American Coalition Treaty that was just ratified by the Senate?"

"It's pure lunacy to open these borders—even anti-American!" Spitzer said firmly. "This nation is still struggling to get back on its feet after the war. The added strain on healthcare, education, and welfare will kill us—not to mention lost jobs and drug traffic!"

"I would like to respond."

The camera swiveled toward a young Mexican American who stepped into the frame.

"Alberto Vega of the Latino Advocacy Group joins us," the reporter intoned. "For those who don't remember, Mr. Vega provided intelligence that helped intercept operatives during the Third Peril. What are your thoughts, Mr. Vega?" Jay

Jennings aimed the microphone toward his newest subject.

"First, I'd like to point out that historically immigrants have been willing to take jobs that most American's are unwilling to do. Legal immigration will not only help US industries to thrive, but it could be a catalyst for policies that will encourage a robust Mexican economy, one that will take my homeland from third-world to first-world status."

"You must be smokin' something if you believe those words flying outta your face!" Gordon Spitzer snorted.

Vega remained calm. "Talks are already underway in Washington, DC, to assess economic and social impacts."

"Ha!" Spitzer's face screwed in contempt. "In all the years me and my boys have been in Arizona, no bureaucrat has ever come close to fixing the problem, but they're good at talk. I'll give 'em that!" Some of the picketers made a ruckus for emphasis.

"Can I ask you something, Mr. Spitzer?" Vega asked.

"Fire away."

"Do you enjoy churning up conflict?"

"What kind of stupid question is that?" Gordon Spitzer returned. "That's like asking me if I've stopped beating my wife! I'm as interested as anybody in finding reasonable solutions to our national problems!"

"Then you will be glad to know that the Mexican government is committed to partnering with the US to address issues such as drug trafficking, terrorism, and welfare abuse. The development of a North American smart currency is being explored to track the movement of money. For several years now, Mexico has been using RFID chips to monitor South American immigrants. This same option is being considered here as well."

Watching from the sidelines, David felt uneasy. *I don't like where this is going,* he thought. Until now, David had never thought of Alberto Vega as a political opportunist.

The head of the Latino Advocacy Group looked professional in his crisp pressed shirt and tie. With his intelligent coffee-colored eyes, Vega looked straight at the camera and continued. "Of course, immigrants to this country will be required to pay taxes, something illegals have avoided in the past for fear of deportation. This revenue will benefit schools, hospitals, and other resources. However, since the long-range goal is to have prosperous neighbors, I have proposed that a portion of these taxes revert to Mexico to help build a healthy economy there, one that will weaken the drug cartels and encourage citizens to stay home."

"Who do you think you're fooling?" Gordon barked. "That's just more fancy rhetoric for wealth redistribution!"

The reporter snatched back control. "As you can see, things are heating up along the border here in Arroyo Seco. Jay Jennings, live for News Cam 4." He stared into the lens until the red light went out and then turned to his crew. "Nice job, fellas. Thanks."

Spitzer wagged his thumb toward Alberto Vega and then turned to the reporter. "You're a weasel for inviting this idiot here today!" he growled. "I bet you'd sell your soul for ratings." Gordon spat on the ground near the anchorman's feet and then hobbled away.

The rabble-rousers and looky-loos soon streamed into the General Store, and by mid-afternoon, David was dog tired. His feet ached from managing the General Store by himself, dashing up and down the aisles, running the lunch counter, filling paper bags with penny candy from the rows of jars, and showing a plethora of novelties like Navajo jewelry and beeswax candles. Even the constant cha-ching of the antique cash register, a sound he usually liked to hear, began to wear on his nerves. David was more than grateful to see his last customer leave. He locked the door, flipped off the switch on the "Open" sign in the window, and glanced at his daughter.

Joy was sprawled on the floor, coloring behind the counter—a box of crayons scattered about.

"How about pizza tonight?"

"Yeah—my favorite!" The child gathered her things and bounced up the stairs as her father trudged behind.

Elita was still in bed. Her long, dark hair laid across the pillow in a tangle, and her face was puffy from crying.

Near the bedroom window, David stooped to retrieve her journal that had fallen at her feet earlier.

She had written: *Mourning comes before the light of dawn. In those dark hours, I wrestle in the cusp of sleep— dreading realization of another day without my son. Emptiness beats in my chest—each stroke—a reminder of the gulf.*

"He lives! He lives!" God whispers. "He lives with Christ forever!"

My soul is comforted in the truth of my Comforter's words. "These arms that hold your child are big enough to hold you, too!"

Mourning comes before the light of dawn.

David gingerly placed the journal on the dresser, and for the first time since his son's death, he let himself cry.

Chapter 9

New York

Thursday, April 18th

"We've been burglarized!" Jewel blurted as Paige walked into the Law Office of Silverstein and Hays. "I just got off the phone with the police!" Jewel fanned her face with her hand. "They should be here any minute!"

Paige scanned the reception area and tried to assess the situation. Aside from a broken side window and an open file cabinet, there didn't appear to be a lot of damage.

"Haven't I always said that we should have a better security system? Maybe you'll listen now!" Jewel plopped down at her desk and rolled her eyes. "I mean, how am I supposed to function as a proper legal secretary if I have to worry about my safety?"

"Was anything taken?"

Jewel launched her amazon body from the chair and clomped over the floor on platform shoes that made her even taller. She threw open the door to Paige's office and said, "You tell me."

Paige gasped at the damage that was done. Drawers had been dumped, and papers were strewn all over the place. She stepped over her printer that was smashed on the floor and picked her way around broken glass. Her family photographs had been ripped from the wall and stomped. Paige's blood ran cold. *Whoever did this was filled with rage.*

"She's right in here," Jewel said as two of New York City's finest entered the room.

"Ma'am, it's best not to contaminate the evidence."

The first uniformed officer suggested that Paige accompany him to the reception area while his partner took photographs of the damage.

He wrote their names down and began taking statements. "Do either of you ladies have any idea who might want to do this?"

Jewel interjected with her usual histrionics. "With such poor security, it could be anybody!" She pressed the back of her hand to her forehead and added, "I just don't know how I'm going to work under these conditions…"

The officer looked at Paige. "No. I can't think of anyone," she said.

"Ms. Hays," he replied, "since you appear to be the target, any suggestions would be helpful. A disgruntled client maybe? Possibly a spurned lover or a sour business relationship?"

"I don't have any enemies that I know of." A chill ran down Paige's spine.

"Have there been any unusual occurrences lately? Suspicious persons?"

Paige chewed her lip.

"The red rose!" Jewel yelped. "I thought that guy was weird when he showed up and asked me to give it to Paige!" She gave her boss a wide-eyed look. "Maybe you've got a stalker!"

The officer pitched forward. "Can you describe this man?"

"He wore a green baseball cap!" Jewel's face lit up under the spotlight. "He was a white guy, medium build, not too tall."

"Can you give me an estimate of his height?"

"I'm a little over six feet, and he came to my chin." Jewel batted her eyes as the officer wrote down the information. "I'll be glad to come in for a lineup if you need me."

"I'm done in here," the other officer said as he emerged from Paige's office. "It appears to be an act of vandalism, but we need you to determine if there's anything missing."

Paige walked the men to the door as her partner, Jerry Silverstein, screeched to a stop at the curb in his Porsche.

"We'll be in touch, Ma'am." The officer tried to sound reassuring. "If you recall anything…"

"There is something," Paige said with growing unease. "The man with the green ball cap—I also saw him last week outside my son's school."

⸉⸊

California
Thursday, April 18th

Joel couldn't believe his eyes! The paper titled Geo-Political Climate and The Third Peril counted for a fourth of his grade, and Professor Squire had given him a D minus!

After more than a week of exhausting research and writing, Joel felt cheated. He had poured over countless interviews with key players in the previous administration, watched hours of news clips, and listened to political pundits until he could stand it no more.

Now standing outside Professor Neville Squire's office, Joel tried to work up courage, but all he could think about were the angry red words marked on the pages of the double-spaced work: *ridiculous premise, implausible, unenlightened, and backward thinking.*

Joel had done his best to present both sides of the issue fairly, and despite his own personal bias, he'd been proud of his work. He drew in a sharp breath, knocked on the door, and waited.

"Enter!"

The professor was leaning over his desk as he flipped through a stack of papers. His gaze briefly flicked over the top of his glasses. "I've been expecting you, Mr. Meyers. Do come in and have a seat."

For several long minutes, Squire ignored Joel while he graded another student's work. Finally, the professor turned the last page, flipped it over, and wrote a bold "A" on the title page. "Fine work—yes—a very thoughtful piece!" Squire's eyes met Joel's, and he added, "Unlike some."

"Sir, I'll get right to the point." Joel cleared his throat. "I don't think this grade is fair."

Neville Squire raised his eyebrows. "I beg your pardon. Young Man, I assure you that my assessments are always fair!" He snapped his fingers, reached across the desk, and snatched the mid-term paper from Joel's hand. Squire thumbed through the neatly typed pages. "My articulations seem quite clear; however, I will attempt to elaborate. Your juxtaposition of contemporary political thought regarding the obsolete philosophy of nationalism was, in my opinion, rather pathetic. A plethora of past political blunders support a more enlightened process, and yet, Mr. Meyers, you have chosen to focus on the potential negatives of globalism, all theories that, in my opinion, cannot be supported."

"I felt it was important to explore both sides of the issue equally," Joel protested.

The professor removed his glasses and rubbed the bridge of his nose. "Frankly, Mr. Meyers, I'm planning to report your conduct to the merit board! While much of your work was adequately referenced, I was quite alarmed that you included unreferenced quotes from former President Thomas Atwood. You cannot fabricate an argument just to drive home a point!" Squire shook his head. "I am extremely disappointed in you."

Joel wanted to defend himself, to say that he had personally interviewed the former president, but who would believe it? No one at the University was ever to know that Thomas Atwood was his biological father. That revelation would violate the agreement made with the Chancellor of UC Berkeley.

Seeing that reasoning with Neville Squire was futile, Joel gathered his papers, thanked the professor for his time, and turned to go.

"I hope you've learned something from our little talk," the professor called out as Joel exited Squire's office in Barrows Hall.

Joel bit his lip and thought of the irony of the situation. *I've learned something all right—Squire's political agenda trumps any expression of free thought!*

Once outside, he took a shortcut between buildings, pausing briefly to check his messages. Still no answer from Coco on his marriage proposal. Though she claimed to love him, Coco had asked for a little time to think. Joel was growing anxious.

He strode briskly toward the Beaux Arts-style arch of Sather Gate. Joel lingered in front of the green patina-covered bronze arch to ponder the sculpted panels on the marble support pillars—images of four nude women that symbolized the disciplines of agriculture, architecture, art, and electricity. On the opposite side, the gate had nude figures of four men who represented the disciplines of law, letters, medicine, and mining.

Higher education, or conformity of thought? In a sudden burst of frustration, Joel tossed his mid-term paper into a trash can and then turned back toward Sproul Plaza to grab a quick bite to eat at the Golden Bear Café. As Joel walked past the Cesar Chaves Center, his cell phone rang. Joel recognized the special ringtone and answered immediately.

"Son," said former President Thomas Atwood, "I've rearranged my schedule and spoken with the University Chancellor. I will be coming to speak at UC Berkeley after all!"

"That's the best thing I've heard all day!" Joel smiled when he thought about how Professor Neville Squire would react to the news.

⚉

Arizona
Friday, April 19th

David squeezed his wife's hand as they stood beside the memorial that marked the spot where their baby boy had been laid to rest.

Joy, who'd picked a handful of wildflowers along the way, dropped the bouquet at the base of the carved stone of a dove and said, "Goodbye, Pajarito! Have fun in Heaven!"

The simple words of faith prompted a tear from Elita. She smiled as she knelt beside her daughter and asked, "Do you know what Pajarito means?"

"Little bird!" Joy answered. "It's a good name, too, 'cause my brother flew away to live with God."

They walked back to town in silence.

Arroyo Seco, for the most part, had been unaffected by the Fillmores' personal tragedy. Throngs of reporters, technicians, and curiosity seekers had poured into the tiny town giving it a carnival atmosphere. But there was something ominous in the air. The streets of Arroyo Seco had become an epicenter of tension, and the media was poised to capture the fight that was spoiling

The North American Coalition Treaty had spawned heated debates. On main streets across the nation, coals of red-hot vitriol were being fanned into flames.

News Cam 4 Anchorman, Jay Jennings, was back. He flashed his pearly smile as the Fillmores approached their store. "Hey, folks, I'd like to stage our cameras on the porch of your marvelous store again, if it's okay with you?"

"Not today!" David said firmly as he led his wife and daughter inside.

The old store looked like a flea market! Jim greeted the grieving family as he rang up sale after sale for shoppers lined up to purchase souvenirs. "Everything's under control," he assured David.

"Don't you worry about a thing," Bonnie called from the crowded lunch counter as the family navigated through herds of customers fingering merchandise.

Priscilla was busy helping out, but she stopped to offer condolences and hugs.

"We are blessed to have such friends," Elita said as they climbed the stairs to their apartment.

Before moving to Arroyo Seco, David's perception of what constituted community had been limited to a tight-knit group of biker friends who would rough someone up as a favor, but things had now changed. In the apartment, the grieving family discovered an outpouring of love in the form of cards, flowers, and home-cooked food.

After reading the cards and shedding a few tears, Elita sat down in Joy's bedroom to read her a children's story. A few minutes later, both mother and child were fast asleep.

David pulled down the window shade and closed his daughter's bedroom door. Near the front of the apartment, things weren't so quiet.

Looking down from the window, he watched as new waves of protesters surged on the street, some waving banners decrying the evils of racism and capitalism and others thrusting signs warning of various conspiracies from communism to one-world government.

While News Cam 4 was busy sweeping the scene for angles, Jay Jennings applied some hairspray and checked his teeth.

On the opposite side of the street, the Watering Hole Saloon had become a stronghold for Gordon Spitzer and his men. The Civic Border Guard membership had exploded overnight with the arrival of a motorcycle club called the Freedom Riders. Together, they puffed and postured, like a menacing army.

Alberto Vega's Latin Advocacy supporters arrived in busloads.

A racial slur sliced through the air, and the crowd surged. In a matter of moments, fists flew, and all chaos broke loose.

David's unease grew as he watched the changing face of his once quiet town. *Is this a portent for the nation?* Somewhere in the back of David's mind, a Bible verse came to mind. *A house divided cannot stand…*

Part 2
The Writing on the Wall

When darkness veils His lovely face,
I rest on His unchanging grace;
In every high and stormy gale,
My anchor holds within the veil.
On Christ, the solid Rock, I stand;
All other ground is sinking sand.

Edward Mote—1834

Chapter 10

New York

Monday, April 22ⁿᵈ

Alone in her office, Paige tried to settle her nerves with a cup of chamomile tea. The recent break in at Silverstein and Hays had everyone on edge.

Just this morning, her husband had accused her of putting their family at risk through her pro-bono work. "The world is full of crazy people, and you practically invite them in!" he impugned.

Brody's salvo had opened a floodgate of internal conflict. *Is it wrong to reach out to those less fortunate? Have I endangered my family? But, what about Christian charity?* "Enough," Paige said aloud. "Pull yourself together."

She forced her attention to the letter and the pressing issues of the Urban Hope Church. Pastor Cedric wanted to reassure the US Attorney for the Southern District of New York that he would fully cooperate with the new rules of the FAD Act. It was a frustrating endeavor for Paige. She had gone over the Fairness and Anti-Discrimination Act more than once, and each time, her spirits sank further. *What ever happened to the separation of church and state?*

The FAD Act, which was initially presented as a safeguard against social injustice, had become a muzzle. Worse yet, the law seemed to be targeted only at people of a Judeo-Christian faith as though they were the only source of social injustice and acts of hate. Few people had foreseen that it could be used as a tool to weaken the doctrinal foundations of the Christian faith. Tax exempt status would be given only to churches that agreed to adopt a plethora of government mandates, even at the expense of core biblical principles.

Paige flipped through the pages of the four-inch-thick FAD file and stopped at the section that flagged offensive scriptures. There were three pages of them! A new abridged bible was recommended to all compliant churches. No other religious texts were cited for promoting hate. *How has our government come to the point of dictating terms of faith?* she thought.

The office door opened, and Jewel approached. She dropped a memo on Paige's desk, flipped her maroon hair extension over her shoulder, and said, "The security guys are almost finished installing the alarm system." On her way out, Jewel paused in the doorway and looked over her shoulder. "Personally, I think we should have bars added to the windows. Just saying."

After thumbing through the document that Jewell had just handed her, Paige found it lacking. Lately, the quality of her legal secretary's work had become sloppy.

In the reception area, she found Jewel leaning back in her office chair, her dreamy eyes fixed upon a workman's tight jeans.

"I found three typos on the first page," Paige said patiently. When her secretary seemed unconcerned, she added, "I need you to focus on your own work—not theirs."

Jewel sat upright and puffed. "Since the break in, I've been a bundle of raw nerves." She laid the back of her hand on her raisin-colored forehead. "I'm sure that's why my concentration has suffered."

"I understand," Paige said. It had taken her the better part of a week to sort through the mess that the vandal or vandals had made of her office. "But we need to press on."

Jewel sighed to show her disapproval and then poised her decorated fingernails over her computer keyboard. "Oh, I almost forgot. The investigator called and left a message."

"What did he say?"

"No leads on that stalker guy." She raised an eyebrow and added, "It gives me the willies to think some creep is out there watching this place."

"That's all speculation. You worry too much," Paige said, but a chill snaked down her spine. "Oh, by the way, would you call Connor's school and tell them I'm on my way to pick him up now."

Jewel flashed a smug smile. "Who's worried now? Just saying…"

Paige tried to shake her annoyance as she walked to the Tyler Brentwood School, but Jewel had touched a sore spot.

Connor was waiting for his mother in the principal's office as instructed. She made the mistake of ruffling his red hair, and he recoiled.

"Mom—don't!" Eager to go, Connor jumped to his feet and slipped on his backpack. As they headed for the

Christopher Street Station, Paige scanned faces looking for anyone suspicious, her eyes keen for the color green.

Paige's cell phone rang as they waited on the subway platform. "Hello?"

"Mrs. Hays, this is Angela Gilbert from the Julliard School. I'm calling to let you know that Connor has been scheduled for an audition."

"That's wonderful!"

"I will send you an email with the date and time. Can I confirm your email address?"

Suddenly there was a commotion on the platform that redirected Paige's attention. As the train approached, she searched frantically for her son.

"Mrs. Hays?"

"I'm sorry. I'll have to call you back!" Paige disconnected and rushed into the crowd calling Connor's name. Relief washed over her heart when she found him. "Honey, are you all right?"

The boy pointed toward the stairs that led to the exit. "Mom, that man took my backpack!"

"Lady, you'd better keep a better eye on your kid," a New Yorker with a thick Bronx accent said. "If I hadn't reached out, that guy would have pushed the kid onto the rails."

Paige began to shake. "What did the man look like?"

"I don't know, just some creep with a baseball cap."

Paige thanked the Good Samaritan as they boarded the subway. "Did you happen to notice what color the cap was?"

"I couldn't say, Lady." The man plopped onto a bench seat and snapped open a newspaper.

"Why would someone want to steal my backpack?" Connor asked as the subway rocked over the rails.

"We'll get you a new one."

"But all my drawings of those eyes are in there!"

Paige realized she was trembling. "Yes, but you are okay. That's the important thing." She stared at the beautiful mosaic tiles that graced the station walls, eyes of every color and shape created by artists, Jones and Ginzel. She rubbed goosebumps on her arms as she pondered, *Why would a grown man want my child's backpack?*

California

Monday, April 22nd

Joel steered his Jeep Wrangler down Madison Street and then turned into the parking lot at the Alameda County Office building.

Seated beside him, Coco looked beautiful in the white gauze and linen wedding dress that she had sewn herself.

"Are you sure you don't mind eloping?" he asked.

"I think it's romantic."

Joel parked the Jeep and hurried around to open the passenger door. He offered his hand.

Coco looked like a fairytale princess as she moved gracefully across the parking lot. When she turned and reached for Joel, sunlight glistened on the diamond engagement ring that he had placed on her finger, and the look in her eyes melted the young man's heart.

In front of the modern facade of the Office of the County Clerk, beneath flags that fluttered overhead, he kissed his bride-to-be.

A few minutes later, the young couple was handed an application for a Marriage License.

"This just doesn't seem real." Coco's eyes brimmed with happy tears.

Joel felt like the luckiest man on earth. With haste, he began to fill out the application. Then his pen froze above the line that required his legal name, the one given at birth, Joel Sutherland, and he recalled when his real identity had been splashed all over the news. First, when he was wrongly charged with the murder of his adoptive parents and later when he was identified as the illegitimate child of US President Thomas Atwood.

"What's wrong?" Coco asked. "You look upset."

Joel chewed his lip and carefully considered his reply. *How do I explain that I've been using an alias, that my last name is not really Meyers, that I'm not who you think I am. And what about my agreement with UC Berkeley?* Joel was legally bound not to divulge his real name. Any breach would result in his immediate expulsion from the University!

He laid down the pen. "I love you, Coco. I really do, but maybe we should put off marrying until after I graduate."

Coco's cheeks flushed. As she looked away, he caught a glimmer of pain in her eyes.

Joel touched her shoulder. "It's only a few months."

Tears rolled down her cheeks. "I understand." She slid the engagement ring from her finger and placed it firmly into the palm of Joel's hand.

"No! I want you to wear this ring. I want to spend my life with you!"

"You have a funny way of showing it!" She bolted into

the hallway and onto the elevator just before the doors closed.

First, Joel searched for Coco in the building, and then he looked for her on the streets that led from the county complex. Every few minutes, he called her cell phone to beg for forgiveness, but his pleas went straight to voicemail.

Finally, Coco responded with a text message. "It's over. Please don't bother me anymore."

Tuesday, April 23rd

Joel sat at the desk in his room staring at his laptop, but thinking of Coco. He had made little or no progress on his assignment in over an hour. *What difference does it make?* he thought. Neville Squire seemed bent on failing him anyway. The professor had been as caustic as battery acid since learning about former President Thomas Atwood's pending visit. But worst of all was the ache in Joel's broken heart.

Music from the other room rattled the wood floor beneath his feet. He pounded the wall with his fist and yelled, "Turn it down!" But it was his housemate's laughter that really got on his nerves. For them, life continued to be one big party. They seemed unaware that yesterday Joel's world had fallen apart. Coco had ignored his calls and text messages. He couldn't eat, sleep, or think about anything else.

Joel closed his laptop and threw open his bedroom door to face a room littered with junk food wrappers, beer cans, and soda bottles.

"Dude," Toadie exclaimed, "it lives!"

Finn lobbed him a football, and Joel caught it by reflex.

"Welcome back, Bro! It's about time you came out of your man cave." He motioned toward the wall where a life-sized cutout of an Oakland Raiders Linebacker had been mounted beside another Fat-Head image of a San Francisco 49er. "What do you think, Bro? The battle of the bay!"

"Sweet," Joel said, but the word fell flat.

In the kitchen doorway, Haus appeared with a heaping plate of hot wings, waved one in Joel's direction, and then skinned the meat off the bone with one bite. He wiped sauce from his chin before settling down in front of the big-screen TV. "Hey, Man, there's a few left if you're hungry."

What little appetite Joel had vanished when he entered the kitchen. Flies buzzed around the sink that was piled high with food-encrusted dishes. The back door was blocked by a mountain of fermenting garbage bags, and the linoleum floor was gritty enough to sprout seeds. Even the ceiling was peppered with fizz and remnants of food fights. Joel considered grabbing a soda from the fridge, but he was afraid to open the door and look inside. *I'm living in a pig sty!* he thought and then headed for the front door.

Toadie cast a quick glance away from the TV screen. "Dude, I was just getting ready to challenge you to a game of your choice."

"Maybe later." Joel fished his keys from the pocket of his jeans, walked onto the porch, and drew in a deep breath of fresh air.

He drove aimlessly for a while as he struggled to come up with another plan to win back Coco's affections. Joel had sent flowers and a bouquet of balloons. Maybe a stuffed monkey holding a sign with the words, "I'm sorry," would work.

Hoping Coco would talk to him, Joel headed to the Seabird Grille. He parked just up the block and glanced at his watch. It was nearly 8:00 P.M. He figured most of the dinner rush would be over.

Inside, he spotted Coco waiting on a table. She chatted with ease as she took the order.

Joel's heart caught in his chest when he saw her smile.

With order in hand, Coco turned his way. Their eyes met, and then she made a beeline for the swinging kitchen door.

Without hesitation, Joel followed.

The cook shot him a look and said, "Can't you read? The sign on the door says, 'EMPLOYEES ONLY.'"

"I just need to have a word with Coco."

The man wagged his thumb toward Joel. "You know this clown?"

"I used to," Coco replied.

The cook set his ladle down. "You need to leave right now!"

"Just give me a few minutes." Joel took a few steps toward Coco, when he felt a heavy hand locked on his shoulder, and he was spun around.

"You don't listen very well!" the cook said as he dragged Joel to the back door.

Before he could respond, Joel was tossed into the alley. "Don't hurt him!" Coco cried out just before he hit the dirt.

Chapter 11

Arizona

Tuesday, April 23ʳᵈ

David returned from the post office with a stack of mail. He slipped behind the register to sort the junk from the bills and called out to his wife, "You missed the excitement. Gordon Spitzer and Alberto Vega were out mugging for the media again."

Elita didn't respond, though he could hear her rattling around near the back of the store.

David was waiting for the laptop near the register to boot up when the News Cam 4 team walked through the door.

"Great footage boys. Are you sure you got it all?" Jay Jennings asked as he followed his camera crew to the lunch counter.

A minute later, Sue Brewster arrived from Hope Springs with a basket full of goods. She glanced around with her usual shy demeanor. "Maybe this isn't a good time?" It was more of a question—with the tone of apology—than a statement. "Should I come back later?"

"No! It's good to see you, Sue." David stepped from behind the counter. "We're almost out of produce, so your timing is perfect." His words seemed to put the shy woman at ease, and he escorted her to the lunch counter and announced, "Look who's here."

Elita looked up from building sandwiches for the News Cam 4 crowd. She smiled warmly, but her eyes betrayed a dark cloud of grief.

"You're busy," Sue muttered. "I don't want to be a pest."

"We always have time for our friends!" Elita turned to Jennings and his crew and said, "You gentlemen don't mind, do you?" Before they could answer, she reached for the basket and gently pried it from the pudgy woman's fingers. Elita unloaded squash, lettuce, tomatoes, and fresh strawberries into the sink to rinse. "What a lovely harvest!" she exclaimed and then peered into the bottom of the basket and pulled out a tissue wrapped item. "What is this?" Elita unwrapped a homemade doll with yarn hair.

"Juanita and her daughter, Pilar, are making these to sell, but they wanted Joy to have this one. Some of the folks at Hope Springs were wondering if you might be able to display goods on consignment." Sue shifted her weight and laced her hands together. "Of course, if you don't have enough shelf space..."

"What kind of things?" David asked.

"Well... Travis is building birdhouses with bent license plates for rooves, and Fawn is weaving tapestries with dyed wool from her sheep."

"I think we have room," David said and then laid a hand on Sue's shoulder. "We've been meaning to ask if you could bake us a few homemade pies? They'd go over well with our lunch crowd."

She looked down and blushed. "If you really think they're good."

"Are you kidding? They're wonderful!" Elita said. "In fact, if we had one now, I bet these gentlemen would eat it up."

Sue made a beeline for the door, apologizing for interrupting the lunch hour business as Jay Jennings turned to David and asked, "What is Hope Springs? It sounds like some kind of sustainable community."

"You could call it that."

The anchorman whipped out his phone and typed in some notes to himself. "I've got to see this place. I'm always intrigued by human-interest stories."

"That's out of the question. They're just a group of people who want to be left alone," David explained cautiously. "Trust me, there's no story there."

Jennings' eyebrows rose, and he barely noticed the grilled ham and cheese sandwich that Elita set before him. "Nonetheless," the newsman said, "my journalistic curiosity is piqued."

By 10:00 P.M., the Watering Hole Bar came alive, drawing night owls and thirsty day workers from miles around.

Jay Jennings and his news crew settled into a booth near the rustic pine bar. "What's your name, Sweetheart?" Jennings asked the cocktail waitress. She fanned her heavy, mascara-laden lashes at the news team and yawned. "Rhonda. So wha'd'ya want?"

"Bring us a couple pitchers of your best draft." He waved his arms in the air to get the attention of the other patrons and then announced, "Drinks for the house on me!"

A buzz rippled through the room, and a few patrons hoisted their glasses to the newsman.

Rhonda ambled back to the table with a basket of peanuts, two pitchers of beer, and some cold mugs.

"Say, Sweetheart," Jennings said, "what can you tell me about Hope Springs?"

"Ain't bothered me none." Rita shrugged. "They mind their business, and I mind my own."

"Well, if you ask me, they're a bunch of nut jobs!" a rough looking character called from the bar. "Some kind of religious cult from what I hear."

"Really..." Jennings popped over to the bar, thrust out his hand, and introduced himself.

The customer downed a shot of whiskey and said, "Yeah, I know who you are. Don't much care much for the media myself."

The anchorman snapped his fingers at the bartender. "Another of whatever this gentleman is drinking. Make it a double!"

The man's previous reserve vanished. He lit up a cigarette, inhaled deeply, and said, "So, what do you want to know?"

A half hour later, Jennings joined his crew at the table. While the boys told tales on one another, he opened his cell phone directory and touched a number. *No service!* "Rhonda, is there a payphone around here?"

The waitress pointed toward the back of the bar near the

restrooms.

Jennings zig-zagged past a rough looking group of pool players and a lone musician who was crooning a crude rendition of "Poncho and Lefty" to the noisy crowd.

In the hallway, Jay Jennings punched some credit card numbers into the pay phone and dialed. "McGuire," he said. "Hey, I've got a lead on a story that is right up your alley."

———∝∞∝———

Joy was sleeping soundly and holding her new yarn doll when David looked in on her. He gently closed the door to his daughter's bedroom and made his way to the bathroom to brush his teeth and get ready for bed.

Clad only in boxers, David peeled back the covers and joined his wife. Elita, propped against pillows, was staring at an open Bible, but her gaze was distant.

David leaned over and kissed her cheek. "What are you thinking?"

She placed the book on her bedside table and said, "I've just got a bad feeling."

"About what?"

She shook her head. "I really shouldn't say. Ever since the baby… Well, I've been so muddle headed. I'm not sure that I can trust my own feelings anymore."

David pulled his wife close and stroked her hair. "Tell me what's bothering you."

"Well, it's Jay Jennings. There's just something about the man…"

"I wouldn't worry much about him. Sooner or later, all

the border media frenzy will die down, and we'll get our sleepy little town back." David kissed her again, this time slow and tender.

"I don't know…"

He held a finger to his bride's lips and pulled her closer, but she turned away and began to weep.

"I'm sorry, I can't" she sobbed as she rolled over.

David heard her whisper a prayer. Such deep faith puzzled him, and for the first time since they had lost the baby, David realized that his own heart had become hardened toward God.

Chapter 12

New York

Sunday, April 28th

It felt strange walking beneath the old marque and through the double doors of the Urban Hope Church without Connor, but seeing the excitement on her son's face this morning had made it all worthwhile. Even after Connor's sleep had been wrecked by a string of nightmares, he'd bounced out of bed excited to spend the day with his father at Yankee Stadium.

Paige spotted Pastor Cedric at the hospitality station surrounded by parishioners. He gave her a little wave.

Not a good time to visit about the FAD Act, she thought and then slipped into the sanctuary for some quiet reflection.

Before long, people began to trickle into the cavernous room and settle into the old velvet-covered theatre chairs.

Right on schedule, the music ministry team took their places on stage and opened with a song that electrified the atmosphere. The mood in the room grew celebratory. Worshipers clapped and danced with abandon.

Are we taking such freedom for granted? Paige wondered. After a while, the music slowed to a more reverent tempo, which gave way to church announcements. Finally, Pastor Cedric took his place behind the podium, bowed his head for a silent prayer, and then motioned for the ushers to come forward.

Something seemed different, but Paige couldn't put her finger on what it was.

"Beloved, this morning we have a special gift for each of you." The Pastor beamed. "If you'll look beneath your seats, you will find a Bible. This is a new version, and it is yours to keep and treasure!"

As Paige thumbed through the book, her heart sank. Numerous scriptural texts had been omitted! She placed the book back under the seat, while others all around accepted the offering without question. *This is so wrong...*

Pastor Cedric uttered a quick prayer and then instructed the congregation to open their adulterated Bibles to 1 Samuel, Chapter 8. He read the scripture—a story that had not been altered—and then began his sermon. "Long ago, the people of Israel demanded that a king should rule over them. Their trust in God was shallow, and they wanted a figurehead in the form of a man. Even the judges were willing to compromise their faith for personal gain, saying, 'Give us a king!'

"However, one man stood alone. The Prophet Samuel warned them of the cost of rejecting God. The people were in danger of going into bondage under the tyranny of a wicked ruler, but they refused to listen. 'Give us a king!'" Pastor Cedric repeated. "Samuel foretold how a king would rule over them in 1 Samuel 8:15-17. 'He will take a tenth of your grain and your grape harvest and distribute it among his officers and attendants. He will take your male and female slaves and demand the finest of your cattle and donkeys for his own use. He will demand a tenth of your flocks, and you will be his slaves.'"

This story mirrors today's headlines! Paige thought about Alistair Dormin and his appointed position of power. *How can Pastor Cedric and so many others be blind to the irony?* A shiver ran up her back.

The pastor bowed his head in prayer. "Thank you, Lord, for showering your people with blessings and providing for all our earthly needs." He uttered a blessing over the congregation and then dismissed the service.

As Paige rose from her seat, she suddenly realized what was missing—the old wooden cross that always hung behind the altar. Someone had taken it down!

When the service concluded, Cedric headed straight to the hospitality station to connect with his flock.

Paige caught up with him there and asked, "What happened to the cross?"

"Oh, that… We're in the process of modernizing," Cedric explained. "We must move with the Spirit or get left behind, you know."

Which Spirit? Paige wondered with a heavy heart.

"Wait a minute," Pastor Cedric said as she turned to leave. "I have something for you!" He grabbed a manila envelope from under the counter and handed it to Paige. "This was left here for you earlier this morning."

Paige stepped outside, drew in a fresh breath of air, and looked at the envelope. Someone had written her name on the outside. She opened the flap with her fingernail and looked inside. The contents made Paige's blood run cold!

It was one of Connor's mosaic-eye drawings from the subway! "I'm watching you," was scrawled near the bottom with a thick black marker.

—∞∞—

California

Sunday, April 28th

What am I doing here? Joel wondered as the found himself in the UC Berkeley Commons. The place was overrun with groups protesting the arrival tomorrow of former President Thomas Atwood.

A group thrusting signs shoved past. "ATWOOD GO HOME! WE AREN'T LISTENING!" Joel stepped over a mass of students who were theatrically sprawled upon the steps pretending to be dead. They wore blood colored banners across their chest that read, "FRUITS OF ATWOOD." The crowd grew more raucous by the moment, hurling accusations, "ATWOOD—KILLER OF THOUSANDS!" *How,* Joel wondered, *can so many people still believe that the former President was to blame for the Third Peril?* It wasn't him, but a coalition of other nations who had masterminded the attack, yet, somehow, Atwood had become the scapegoat!

Joel longed for Coco. At this moment, if he could do things over, he would gladly trade his Berkeley education for her love.

A parade of nudes marched through the commons flying

an upside-down American flag. The police stood aloof on the fringes like tin soldiers.

The throng surged. Suddenly, feeling claustrophobic, Joel searched for an escape route. He pressed against the flow, inching slowly toward Sather Gate. There, he came to a sudden stop. Hanging in effigy from the center of the gate was a stuffed dummy with a Halloween mask bearing his father's face!

Joel stared upward, barely aware of the jogger who knelt in front of him to tie his shoe. *This is a strange time and place for a run,* Joel thought.

The runner stood, stretched, and casually slipped a note to Joel. "Read it in private," he said before jogging away.

Arizona

Monday, April 29th

At around 10:00 A.M., Travis Dayton's flatbed truck rolled to a stop in front of the General Store. "They're here!" David called.

Joy shrieked with delight and skipped over the old pine floor with a page torn from her favorite coloring book. "I made this for Hari." She held it up for her dad's approval.

"It's a work of art!"

Elita, who'd been arranging canned goods on the shelf, came to the window and watched as Travis jumped from his truck and hurried to the passenger side to open the door.

David chuckled. "He acts like a love-struck teenager."

"Well, I think it's sweet." Elita smiled as the young man held out his hand to help Priscilla and Hari, her six-year-old son, from the cab. "Priscilla doesn't have a clue how he feels about her. Sometimes, I don't think she even sees him."

"It might help if he changed his hairstyle. I mean, who wears a mullet these days?"

"It's the man underneath that counts," Elita said. "Travis Dayton is always the first one there when anyone needs help. He's a hard worker, too."

David couldn't disagree.

Hari blew through the screen door just ahead of Priscilla and showed Joy his new wooden truck. "Look what Mr. Dayton made for me!"

Travis tipped his head toward David's wife and said, "Mornin' Ma'am"

"It's 'Elita' to all my friends. Besides, 'Ma'am' makes me feel so old."

"Sure thing, Ma'am... I mean, Elita." Travis hooked his thumbs in his belt loops and said, "Figure I'd better head back to Hope Springs."

Priscilla scrapped a stray strand of her blond hair into a clip. "I thought you needed to pick up a few supplies?"

"Yeah, I almost forgot," Travis said sheepishly. "Let's see, I've been needing some..., baked beans! Yeah, that's right!" He hurried to the shelf and grabbed four cans and returned to the check-out counter.

"Oh, we could use several dozen more farm eggs," David said as he rang up the sale.

Travis' gaze shifted to Priscilla. "It just so happens I'll be coming back through town around half past twelve. Can I give you a lift?"

"That would be nice." Priscilla waited for him to leave before turning to Elita and giving her a hug. "I've been praying ever since you lost the baby. How are you doing?"

"I'm all right," David heard his wife saying, though he knew she wasn't. Still, he was glad Priscilla had stopped by to offer her friendship and support. Across the room, the happy sounds of their children lightened the mood.

"You two go catch up on things," he said. "I'll take care of things around here."

Elita kissed her husband's cheek and then wandered to the lunch counter to pour a couple glasses of iced tea. "We'll be out back watching the kids, if you need us!" she called.

David stocked shelves, ran a dust mop over the floor, and balanced the books. The morning passed slowly. It was nearly lunchtime, the kids were hungry, and David joined the women at the counter.

"It's quiet in town today," Priscilla noted.

"I'm grateful," Elita said, slapping together some peanut butter and jelly sandwiches. "The constant media frenzy was beginning to get to me."

"Well, don't get too comfortable," David said. "That news crew van is still parked over at the motel."

The screen door opened, and David rose from the stool. Beyond the rows of shelves, he spotted a new face. "Can I help you?"

"I'm looking for camping supplies." The thirty-something stranger strode forward with squeaky hiking boots and parked his hands on utility trousers that looked like they'd just come off the rack of a trendy sporting-goods store. "Think

I'll need a can of Sterno, a Swiss army knife, maybe a tarp, and some bear spray?"

David cracked a smile. "Bear spray?"

Priscilla giggled. "You're funny!"

"No, I'm Beck." He looked at her through rectangular rimless glasses, "And, you're stunning. I've never met anyone with violet-colored eyes before."

The young mother's cheeks pinked. "Thank you."

"Say, do you peeps know of any good places around here to set up my tent?"

David's radar went up. The guy looked like the type that would be more comfortable at a spa resort. "The desert can be pretty harsh. Most people opt for hard-sided camping because of the scorpions and rattlers."

"Snakes? I suppose they don't make snake repellant?" Beck shuddered. "Actually, I heard about an awesome community of people…"

"Hope Springs!" Priscilla volunteered.

Beck's face lit up. "Yes, that's the one! Do you know any of the people?"

"Actually, I live there." Their gaze connected for an awkward moment before Priscilla said, "How did you hear about Hope Springs? Was it a dream or maybe a vision?"

The stranger looked momentarily confused, and then without missing a beat, he said, "Oh, definitely a vision! Do you think they have room for one more?"

"No one's ever been turned away," she said.

"My car is outside," Beck cooed. "Would you take me there?"

Elita looked concerned for her friend. "Isn't Travis

stopping by to pick you up?" she asked as Beck raced around the store tossing supplies into a shopping basket.

"Oh, I'm sure he'll understand," Priscilla said as she gathered Hari and his toys.

Gordon Spitzer hobbled into the store and passed Priscilla as she left with the newcomer. He pointed toward the window and said, "So, who's the granola driving the Prius? Don't tell me those Jesus fishes snagged another convert?"

"It's always wonderful to see you, Spitzer," David said.

Gordon dropped a couple quarters onto the counter to pay for the newspaper he'd picked up on the way in. He opened the Sentinel and began to read. Spitzer's ears turned crimson, and he bellowed, "So it's official! The Chairman of the World Reserve Bank has appointed Alberto Vega to a special panel! Listen to this…" Spitzer read a quote from the Latin activist: "'Long-term economic benefits outweigh any downward pressure on wages caused by open borders,' said Vega. 'US agriculture and construction sectors will thrive and taxable income generated by migrant workers will offset economic stress to US social/welfare programs.'"

The head of the CBG shook his ashen face and slapped his fishing cap onto the counter. "I can't believe this! Vega recommends the immediate use of mandatory RFID implants for immigrants, claiming it will address fraud and drug trafficking issues!"

Purple veins bulged near Gordon's temples, and he quivered with rage.

"Take it easy," David said.

Sweat glistened on Spitzer's forehead, and a strange slack look came over his face. He turned to the couple and tried to speak, "Whaaa… Ca…"

"Are you okay?" Elita cried.

A string of drool ran from the corner of Gordon's mouth.

He's having a stroke! David thought as Spitzer wobbled, tried to take a step forward, and then fell over.

Chapter 13

California

Monday, April 29th

Only one sentence had been written on the message given to Joel by the mysterious jogger. *Go to the nearest BART station.*

As Joel headed to the downtown Bay Area Rapid Transit station west of campus, the sound of protests faded behind him. He didn't know what to expect when he arrived. *A second cryptic note? A meeting?* Joel didn't have to wait long to find out.

A dark suburban rolled up beside him as he walked and the door opened. "Quick! Hop in."

Joel recognized Lance, a member of his father's Secret Service detail. Joel did as he was told, and the vehicle promptly pulled away. "Where are we going?"

"To an undisclosed location." The man flashed a micro smile, and the Suburban zigged and zagged through a residential neighborhood. Finally, on the edge of Berkeley, they turned down an older, tree-lined avenue with stately vintage homes. *Not quite Atherton,* Joel thought, *but close.*

The ornate gates of one residence parted, and without stopping, Lance steered the vehicle up a narrow driveway that ran alongside the Spanish-style mansion. The Secret Service agent announced their arrival on his lapel radio as he pulled around the back of the building and into what was once a carriage house.

Thomas Atwood was waiting in the doorway with a cane in hand. He greeted his son with open arms and said, "I've been looking forward to seeing you!"

"Me too." Joel felt a bit saddened as he watched his father struggle to walk the short distance to the dining room.

After taking their seats, Atwood said, "So, tell me all about your studies? Particularly political science?"

Joel pondered confessing that he was about to fail the class, but he didn't want to see the disappointment on his biological father's face. "Uh, I've been working hard. Actually, I'm still having trouble with my professor, but it's nothing to worry about."

Thomas Atwood poured himself some coffee from a silver service. "Neville Squire, I presume? I've read some of the man's work. A lot of ivory-tower rhetoric if you ask me." The former president's hand shook noticeably as he sipped from the china cup. Parkinson's Disease was beginning to take its toll.

Joel unfolded his napkin, and the silverware fell out. "I'm beginning to think it was a mistake asking you to speak at UC Berkeley." He placed the linen on his lap and waited for his father's reaction.

"Don't tell me your worried about all the protestors on

campus!" Thomas Atwood laughed and then leaned forward lacing his fingers together. "It's never easy to take a stand for the truth. Remember that, Son." The former president looked earnestly at Joel. "You are a fine young man, Joel. Your adoptive parents must have been remarkable people. I just wish somehow you could have been spared all the hardships you've suffered."

"It wasn't really so bad." Joel shrugged.

"I suppose your struggles made you stronger." After a protracted silence, the former president spoke again. "Son, I've been thinking…" he began. "I would be honored if you called me 'Dad.'"

Joel stared out the window. "Sir, I will always be grateful that you helped to clear me of murder charges. And I will always be indebted for the college tuition, which," he added, "I intend to repay, but…"

"You needn't say more—I understand." Atwood tried to hide his disappointment by shifting his attention to the wait staff carrying lunch plates. "Something smells wonderful! Shall we eat?"

New York
Monday, April 29th

Feeling a bit anxious, Paige walked toward a massive tan building with sharp jutting lines. Inside the Julliard School at 60 Lincoln Center Plaza, her son was just finishing up the with the audition committee. She kept her fingers crossed, hoping all went well as she pushed open the glass doors. Paige made her way through a cavernous foyer that was bathed with natural light and paused outside the room. A few hours earlier, she had left Connor there with his violin. Parents were discouraged from attending the auditions.

Inside the audition hall, Paige ran a hand through her recently clipped red hair and glanced around. Ms. Ackerman, an anorexic looking woman, spotted Paige, rose to her feet, and strode forward with hand extended.

"Mrs. Hays, you have a very gifted son." The woman's thin lips parted to show her tiny teeth and a gummy smile. "We are pleased to announce that Connor has been invited to join our upcoming Pre-College Division." She ushered Paige to the back of the room where Connor was being shown the proper way to hold his bow. "We encourage next year's students to take lessons during our summer break, so I have taken the liberty of introducing young Master Hays to one of our best violin instructors, Horatio Montanegro."

A short man wearing a vest bowed his head and said, "Mrs. Hays, Connor has great potential, if properly channeled." Horatio flipped his head and then tucked a long oily swath of hair behind his ear. "Despite a full schedule, I would be willing to work with the boy." Mr. Montanegro handed Paige a business card and strode off.

A few feet away, she watched Connor fasten his violin case, unaware that his mother was about to burst with pride. On the sidewalk in front of the angular building, she threw her arms around her son and kissed him.

"Mom, stop!" He wiped his cheek. "Don't embarrass me."

"I can't help it," she gushed. "I was really worried that you wouldn't be up to the audition."

The child looked puzzled. "Why?"

"Did you forget about those nightmares you had last night?"

Connor shrugged.

"It might help if you talk about them." Paige paused as he shook his head. "Well, anyway, it's not every day my son gets accepted into the Julliard School, so I think we need to celebrate!" She hailed a taxi cab and told the driver to take them to the Hungarian Pastry Shop on Amsterdam Avenue.

Connor rattled on about the audition as the taxi moved through the Morningside Heights traffic. "They're all really nice there," he said. "I had fun."

After paying the driver, Paige and Connor stepped onto the curb in front of an old-style, Parisian-looking café. Red awnings shaded students and professors from nearby Columbia University as they relaxed at outdoor tables. Inside the Hungarian Pastry Shop, they walked past scores of customers nibbling on strudel and sipping coffee. Nearly every wooden table was occupied. Beneath soft lighting, Paige waited in line and admired the 1960's artwork that decorated the walls.

"Mom, would you order for me?" Connor shifted from foot to foot and handed her his violin case. "I need to go," he yelped and then hurried toward the bathroom.

When her turn came, Paige said, "A couple of cherry-cheese strudels and two hot chocolates. In a bag, please," she added.

Connor returned describing the graffiti decorated walls. "It's like they let people draw anything they want and write poems, too!"

"I knew you'd appreciate this place." Paige received the order and suggested they have a picnic on the manicured church lawn across the street. Instead, they settled in a spot of sun on the steps of the grand cathedral, a towering gothic edifice known as Saint John the Divine.

As mother and son leisurely finished their pastries, Paige said, "I've never been inside this church." She brushed crumbs from her hands and stood. "Shall we take a peek?"

Paige led Connor to the immense bronze-paneled double doors where she pointed out the workmanship on the panels. "Beautiful, aren't they?"

There was no reply. Her son was staring up at one of the dozen relief columns, six on each side of the door. Connor's eyes were wide with fear!

"What's wrong?"

He pointed to a fresco at the base of one of the columns. It was a carving of New York City with toppling skyscrapers. The image depicted a colossal tidal wave curling over the tops of the buildings. "My dream!" Connor cried out. "That's what happens in my nightmares!"

Arizona

Tuesday, April 30th

Something roused Beck from his slumber, and he opened his eyes. His nylon tent was aglow with late-morning sun.

"Hello? Anybody home?" It was a man's voice.

"Just a minute!" Beck quickly tossed his sleeping bag

over his voice recorder and laptop that he kept charged with a small solar panel. Before unzipping his tent flap, he ran a comb over his hair and rubbed his teeth with his index finger.

Randy Bales was standing a few feet away. "I'm sorry. Were you asleep?"

"I must have drifted off," Beck said, slipping on his rimless rectangular glasses.

"That sun will warm a tent pretty fast," Randy said. "Heat stroke can pose a real danger."

"I'll try to remember that." Beck slid his feet into a worn pair of Birkenstocks, pushed his way through the flap, and stretched.

"Now that you're settled in, I thought you might like a tour of Hope Springs."

"Fabulous!" Beck flashed a perfect smile. "Just give me a second or two to get gathered." He dove back into his tent, slid a little recorder into his vest pocket, and emerged.

"We don't see you much at our mealtimes," Randy said as they neared the Hope Springs communal gathering place. "There might be some leftover breakfast if you're hungry."

"No thanks. I had a granola bar." Beck stopped and stared at the pavilion. "Is that some kind of mist I see coming from the ceiling?"

Randy chuckled. "It's an evaporative cooling system that I set up. In an arid climate like this, mist makes you feel more comfortable. When it gets really hot, that's where everyone hangs out."

"Good to know." Beck followed Randy up a trail that led to the reservoirs and fixed his attention on the generators that serviced the pavilion.

"We use every drop of water around here. Water from the communal bath house is funneled to the livestock watering tank," Randy explained. "Even the gray water from washing the dishes all gets recycled to the green house and gardens. Did you know that soap is also a natural pesticide?"

"Really?" Beck slipped his hand in his pocket and turned up the microphone on his recorder. "What a tremendously evolved eco-conscience you all have."

Randy laughed like Beck had just told a joke. "It's just a matter of working together and conserving our resources." He pointed to the rows of eclectic dwelling places: some trailers shaded under reflective tin roofs, wall tents, and motor homes skirted with bales of straw. "See those trees on either side of the street? Those fruit trees are sustained by a drip system set up to use the gray water from each camper. In turn, those fruit bearing trees provide both shade and nourishment!"

"How do you know the water supply won't run out?" Beck asked. "And, is it really safe for human consumption?"

"The whole thing is fed by a deep artesian well that is probably cleaner than most big-city systems," Randy countered. "And, so far, no one has gotten sick around here."

Beck flung his arms wide and spun around. "You have gardens, beehives, herbs, poultry, and livestock. You even have composting toilets and a bath house! Not to mention all those marvelous cottage industries, like Fawn's textile art and those fabulous little crosses that Priscilla makes from repurposed molding. I'd love to hear each and every intriguing story—like yours for example."

Randy gave him a quizzical look. "Maybe later. I offered to help Travis make some adobe bricks. You're welcome to lend a hand if you don't have anything better to do."

"Oh, I wouldn't know the first thing about that."

"A little mud, a little straw, and the hot sun. There's nothing to it."

"Perhaps some other time," Beck said as they neared the sawmill. "There are a few things that need my attention." As he headed back to his tent, Beck slipped the recorder from his pocket and spoke into it, "A mysterious and curious mix of people. Still looking for the proverbial 'glue' that binds them."

Chapter 14

California

Tuesday, April 30th

Joel arrived early at UC Berkeley Zellerbach Hall as instructed.

The sound team was testing equipment on stage while the local news crews were busy setting up cameras in the media booths that hung below the upper balconies.

Zellerbach Hall was a venue for large concerts and popular speakers because of its size and acoustics. Joel was impressed as he looked around. It was the first time he'd seen the place when it wasn't full of people. This massive multi-tiered room, equipped with curved rows of blue and purple seats, was also where most UC Berkeley graduation ceremonies took place. Joel imagined himself stepping up onto the stage to receive his diploma. *I'm ready to leave this town*, he thought, *as long as I can convince Coco to come with me.*

A text message popped into Joel's cell phone and his heart leapt. *Maybe that's her now!*

It was from Lance, his father's personal Secret Service

agent, instructing Joel to take a seat on the front row. "No personal contact with the advance team," the agent had advised.

Two local police officers entered from the stage with a German Shepherd in the lead. *Bomb sniffing dog, no doubt.* In the upper balcony, Joel spotted a suited team of Secret Service personnel doing their sweep of the place. Joel didn't recognize their faces, though they were never hard to spot. *Probably brought in for this specific event,* he concluded.

Time ticked slowly for the Joel as he waited. He checked his email, sent Coco another text, and waited some more. Finally, the first students began trickling in, and the massive hall began to fill.

A few seats away, Kyle Lobosco plopped into a chair and nodded in Joel's direction. "Can you believe it?"

"What?" Joel asked.

"The ex-president coming here!" Lobosco snorted cynically. "Squire said it would never happen. I'm looking forward to seeing the professor with a crow feather hanging from his smug mouth." He cracked the joints of his fingers and muttered something else under his breath.

Joel directed his attention to a ruckus near the auditorium entrance. Screaming protestors had surged on the building only to be turned away.

Handbags and backpacks were being checked at the door. "No food, drink, picket signs, or projectiles allowed in Zellerbach Hall," Lobosco mocked as the ground-floor seating began to fill up.

Joel was grateful when a couple of girls took the seats between him and Lobosco. There was something about the kid that was unnerving. *Maybe it's the way he talks to himself,* he mused.

Before long, the balconies were jammed with locals, students, and faculty who had turned out to hear what former President Thomas Attwood had to say for himself.

Banter filled the atmosphere, and Joel tugged at his collar. *What kind of reception will my father receive?* he wondered.

At 5:00 P.M. sharp, Professor Neville Squire strolled onto the stage. With hands clasped behind his back, he waited for the buzz to fade to a few whispers. Then, after introducing himself with a brief academic pedigree, he began, "Ladies and Gentlemen, I'm delighted that so many of you turned out. Welcome, welcome, one and all!" Squire swept his arm to the side of the stage and said, "This should be an illuminating evening, so, without further ado, please welcome Mr. Thomas Atwood!"

Applause reverberated around the auditorium as the former President of the United States, cane in hand, slowly made his way to the podium on legs ravaged by Parkinson's Disease.

One of the girls seated beside Joel leaned toward the other and said, "He looks so old."

It was true that Atwood had aged since the war. Though his salt and pepper hair had faded to dull gray, and the creases of his face had deepened, Atwood's eyes still held a fire.

The former president began by thanking Professor Squire for the gracious introduction before addressing the students and guests.

"I am here today to talk about the events that led up to

the Third Peril, why I took the actions that I deemed appropriate at the time, and more importantly, why I believe many of the policies that have been adopted since the Third Peril represent worse threats to the future of American democracy and the US economy.

"Let me begin by saying not a single day goes by that I don't remember that millions of Americans were killed, injured, or substantially impacted by those tragic events on that fateful October day when our Nation was ambushed on several fronts. The fact that the Third Peril happened on my watch has driven me to my knees in prayer almost daily, and it is a burden that I will carry with me to my grave."

Atwood paused for a moment, struggled for composure, and then pressed on.

"Perhaps a little perspective on the state of the nation and the policies that were implemented prior to the Third Peril will help us to better understand. When I took office, the United States of America was in a deep recession that was further exasperated by three years of drought. Our agricultural economy was devastated, and food prices were escalating. These catastrophes fueled inflation even more, compounding our systemic economic problems.

"Now, we are all gifted with 20-20 hindsight, and I am well aware that there have been more than a few critics of the administrative actions we chose to take. However, these myopic viewpoints fail to acknowledge that a coalition of nations collaborated to attack the US. Since then, in our zeal for diplomatic solutions, we have linked arms with the international community at the expense of our sovereignty." The former president shook his head.

"I remember clearly meeting with the World Fortress Institute in the Oval Office, along with my Chief Economic Advisor, when they proposed that the United States join the smart card coalition. We declined their offer for a variety of reasons. We had already seen how much difficulty these multi-national economic unions were experiencing. The European Union has had many significant challenges as they strive to reconcile differences in socio-economic policies among diverse nations and peoples. More to the point, the American people have a historically strong disapproval of intrusive government information gathering as well as centralized power and control over everyday lives. And, perhaps most important, we felt that America had much more to lose than it would gain from a proposal to level the global economic playing field.

"But, the people have spoken. Their votes were cast for Ira Corbin who promised to embrace the global economy and woo the international community." Atwood drew in a deep breath. "Today, President Corbin's handpicked Chairman of the World Reserve Bank has been granted unprecedented power, and indeed, some say the United States, along with the rest of the world, has recklessly ceded our sovereignty to a man who is not accountable to anyone! Willingly, I fear, we are marching down the road to perdition."

The former president glanced briefly to the side of the stage where Neville Squire stood and then returned his gaze to the audience.

"This may appear to the ivory-tower elitists and idealists to be the perfect utopian dream, but I assure you, it is a path filled with hidden snares. It is all good and well to say 'nationalism is limiting' and 'revolution is evolution,' but such trite phrases ignore the economic reality and cultural risks we take when we throw our hat into the global community ring. There are certain economic principles at play here that are as incontrovertible as the laws of physics. There is no such thing as a free lunch. Somebody, somewhere has to pay for that lunch. When it comes to equalizing the global playing field, which country do think has the most to lose? Of course, it is the United States, the largest economic engine in the world, whose coffers will be drained in order to lift weaker nations out of poverty. As Margaret Thatcher famously said, 'The problem with socialism is that eventually you run out of other people's money.'

"Imagine a global revolution that seeks to create a homogenous utopian society by mashing down cultural differences with the club of tolerance, where free thought and speech are forbidden. Imagine, if you can, a world without American exceptionalism. The United States, once known as a force for good and the protector of the oppressed, reduced to third-world status. Yes, imagine no religion, or belief systems of any kind, in a world where school children recite the Pledge of Allegiance to the World every morning before class. Imagine no worries whatsoever; the state-run mental health system has a pill for that, too. Imagine an RFID chip embedded under your skin that enables the global government to track all of your purchases, all of your movements, and even your pulse, blood pressure, and brain waves. Yes, imagine, if you can, that you have ceded all authority to Big Brother, and now you are completely and utterly dependent on the global state for everything you need or want."

Thomas Atwood clasped his shaky hands together and

stared earnestly at the faces before him.

"Is this the kind of world you want to live in? History books, even the Bible, are full of stories about how mankind has tried to establish our own kind of utopia, but we have always failed. We have chosen to be ruled by judges, monarchs, ruthless dictators, benevolent dictators, and, yes, even democracy. History demonstrates that human-run institutions, despite our best intentions or a well-planned organizational structure, seldom result in peace and goodwill toward mankind, but always collapse under the burden of bureaucracy, waste, fraud, and abuse. History tells us that when people turn away from God and resort to philosophies, such as moral relativism or secular humanism, we lose the blessings of God. Culture and civil society collapses, and humanity devolves into self-absorbed hedonism."

A chorus of boos issued from around the auditorium followed by synchronized finger snapping.

The former president forged on. "I fear this once great nation is headed over a precipice. It is imperative that you keep an open mind and question the status quo, before it is too late. Your futures and freedoms are at risk!"

Atwood closed, saying, "Thank you for inviting me to Berkley and for listening to an alternative point of view. May God bless each of you, and may God bless the United States of America."

The naysayers' protests were offset by a weak smattering of applause.

Neville Squire bound across the stage, motioned the crowd to settle, and then thrust a hand toward the former president. "A very interesting speech, Mr. Atwood, very interesting indeed!"

Suddenly, a gunshot echoed throughout the cavernous room and then another, quickly followed by three more. A second of profound silence followed, and then the girl to the right of Joel screamed, "He's going to kill us all!" Chaos filled the void as she and her friend both dove over the back of their seats.

Kyle Lobosco stood and looked straight ahead. His expression was beyond calm, it was emotionless. In stunned disbelief, Joel watched Lobosco raise a semi-automatic pistol to his own head and pull the trigger.

All around Zellerbach Hall, pandemonium erupted. There were cries of fear, and humans stampeding to the nearest exit, but Joel's thoughts were straight ahead. He didn't recall standing or climbing onto the stage. He only remembered the shocked look on Professor Squire's face as he clutched his wounded shoulder. A few feet away, Thomas Atwood was lying in a large and spreading pool of blood.

Without warning, Joel was slammed to the stage. A small brigade of Secret Service agents disabled him.

"Dad!" he called out, but there was no answer.

Chapter 15

Arizona

Tuesday, April 30ᵗʰ

Within the hour, a crowd was clustered near the General Store lunch counter staring at the flat screen TV that was mounted nearby. They stood silently, transfixed by the tragic news. Former President Thomas Atwood had been assassinated after giving a speech at UC Berkeley!

Scenes of pandemonium were played over and over by the California news outlets that now thought the appearance of the former president at the university was newsworthy. Amateur cell-phone videos were still coming in, graphic images of the shooter's last moments, and Thomas Atwood lying motionless in a huge pool of blood.

Some footage captured a young, mysterious man scrambling onto the stage toward the fallen president. Seconds later, the kid was violently wrestled to the floor by the Secret Service. TV talking heads bantered back and forth. Some suggested that this young man might be Thomas Atwood's illegitimate son, yet no officials had confirmed it. Old press photos of Joel Sutherland were compared to the grainy news footage and speculation was rampant.

Ziggy and Fawn Nash walked into the General Store, followed by Raymond Lee and Mr. Mike.

"Is it true?" Ziggy asked as his wife, Fawn, floated over to the counter in her gauzy dress and took a seat. The aging hippy straddled the stool beside her and tightened his pony tail.

"I'm afraid so. How did you hear?" Elita asked.

Mr. Mike raised a finger. "I picked up chatter on my ham radio." The electronics geek removed his black-framed glasses, rubbed grime from the lenses, and said, "I probably know more about this whole sad event than the press does."

The TV anchorman announced that the current president, Ira Corbin, would be addressing the nation within the hour, and the story shifted again to the shooter who had taken his own life. He was identified as a UC Berkley student named Kyle Lobosco. Multiple witnesses on campus had been interviewed, though few personally knew the young man other than to say he was a loner who was failing most of his classes and had anger issues.

"What a waste." David shook his head.

Quiet as usual, Raymond Lee sank his long fingers into the pockets of his baggy slacks and nervously jiggled change.

No one spoke as the group stared at the TV screen.

The Whitehouse Press Room doors swung open, and the President of the United States was announced. The Commander in Chief, Ira Corbin, took his place at the press podium. His square chin was taunt, and every hair on his head was in place.

Somehow, David thought, *he appears smaller than*

normal behind the podium.

Shutters clicked and reporters' hands shot up. "Mr. President! Mr. President!" their voices echoed frantically.

"I have a brief statement about our nation's tragic loss, and then I will take a few questions," the president said. "I was shocked and saddened to learn about the assassination today of former President Thomas Atwood at the University of California at Berkley. Though we were political opponents, I always knew Thomas Atwood to be a kind and caring man who put his country ahead of himself and someone who remained committed to his ideals and principles. My thoughts and prayers are for Thomas Atwood's family as well as the family of the disturbed young man who carried out this horrific act."

Ira Corbin looked solemn as he gazed upon the sea of faces. He pointed to a reporter.

The woman rose and identified herself as Piper Tweedy from the Washington Tribune. "Thank you, Mr. President," she began. "It is widely known that Thomas Atwood was actively opposed to many of the policies advanced by your current administration. It has even been suggested that the shooting might have been a political assassination. How do you respond?"

"This is absolutely ridiculous!" A look of righteous indignation flashed across Corbin's face. "These incredulous notions are nothing more than conspiracy fantasies that I refuse to dignify, except to say that the shooter was nothing more than a severely disturbed young man with a gun!"

Ira Corbin turned and nodded to a male journalist from the Chronical.

The older man with a goatee rose from his seat. "Sir, in

the wake of today's shooting, do you have a plan to address gun violence?"

The President seemed pleased. "Excellent question, Sam! Gun violence is a growing threat to our citizens, and it is an issue that must be addressed. I have directed the Department of Justice to draft legislation calling for the immediate registration of all firearms. I am assured by key members of Congress that this legislation will be favorably received."

David's thoughts turned to Gordon Spitzer, who had been progressing steadily in his recovery since suffering a stroke. *The last thing he needs right now is another fight.*

California

Tuesday, April 30ᵗʰ

Joel was ushered down the hospital corridor by his father's personal Secret Service agent. "The upholstery on the side of the auditorium seat had been cut," Lance explained, "Kyle Lobosco had stashed the weapon there sometime before the event. Ordinarily, the dogs would pick up the scent of a gun, but this one had never been fired." The man stopped just outside a room marked "Private." Lance looked deeply anguished as he opened the door. "There are no words to tell you how sorry I am."

Thomas Atwood was laid out on the examining table partially covered by a sheet. He looked as though he was asleep. A few feet away, an attending physician stood by silently.

"Did he suffer?" The whole thing didn't seem real to Joel.

"No. The bullet severed the aorta just above the heart. We believe he died instantly."

Joel began to weep for the man who had given him life. "Dad," he whispered as regrets swamped his soul. *If only he could hear me now.*

"Take as much time as you like," the doctor said.

There is no point—no reason to stay. "He's not here," Joel said under his breath and then looked one last time at the face of Thomas Atwood, a man who had literally given himself for the nation. "My dad is in a much better place."

The University Chancellor was waiting for Joel in the hallway to offer his condolences. "I know this is not a good time, but there is another pressing matter." Dr. Bentley laid a hand on Joel's shoulder. "I'm afraid the media has identified you as Atwood's son. Your photograph is all over the news. It would be too disruptive to allow you to continue here as a student."

Joel nodded, but said nothing.

"You will, however, receive your diploma."

"What about finals and my political science class?"

"Under these mitigating circumstances, we have chosen to wave your final exams. As for Neville Squire, he now realizes that you neither plagiarized nor fabricated the interview cited in your last paper. You will receive a Bachelors Degree in Political Science." The Chancellor offered a limp handshake and then added, "I wish you the best, Young Man."

Joel was numb with shock and grief when he headed for the main entrance. The sun was setting over the Pacific, but there was just enough light to make his movements conspicuous.

He spotted a cluster of news people with cameras in place and quickly detoured down a driveway. Past the emergency room entrance, he paused to make a call on his cell phone.

Toadie answered on the first ring. "Dude! We've been living with a celebrity all this time and didn't even know it!"

"Is Finn there? I need to ask him a favor." Joel listened as Toadie yelled for his other roommate.

After a brief wait, Finn came on the line. "Hey, Bro— that's rough about your old man…"

"Listen," Joel cut in, "I'm at the hospital, but my Jeep is still parked near Zellerbach Hall. I need a lift home."

"Yo, I'm not sure that's such a good idea, Bro. I mean, there's a gang of reporters here, and they're all waiting to pounce on you. If I were you, I'd lay low, at least until things blow over."

Joel thanked his roommate for the heads up, ducked down an alley, and slipped away unseen. It was a long hike to the university campus, but night was falling, and his chances of being spotted lessened. More than anything else, Joel just wanted to be with the woman he loved.

New York
Tuesday, April 30th

Paige watched her husband pacing back and forth in the family room with his cell phone pressed against his ear as he gathered details about the assassination from Atwood's West Wing staff. Brody had been more than the late-president's

Chief Economic Advisor—he had been a friend.

The landline trilled and one glance at the caller ID told Paige it was Irene Moyer who had served as the White House Press Secretary. She let the call go to voice mail.

Brody ended his conversation and then sank onto the sofa. He sat hunched over with his face in his hands.

Paige joined her husband, letting him feel her presence. Seasons of sorrow had taught her that words alone could bring no comfort. The TV was playing in the family room, muted scenes that would never be forgotten. Brody turned up the sound as a photo of the shooter appeared on the screen—just another troubled young man.

"I don't understand what's happening…" Brody's words trailed off.

Paige rubbed her husband's shoulders. "We live in a fallen world."

New information came across the newsfeeds. "So it was Joel Sutherland who ran up on stage!" Brody said.

The reporter went on to explain that Joel was a student at UC Berkeley registered under the last name, "Meyers."

"His birth mother's maiden name." Brody shook his head in anger. "That poor young man has been through a lot and now this." His cell phone rang again, and Paige heard him say, "Delmont, North Dakota? Yes, we will definitely be there! Just get back to me with the date and time."

"I'm so sorry," Paige said. "Thomas Atwood was such a decent man."

Brody reached out and stroked his wife's short red hair and then looked at his young son. Connor was leaning over the coffee table engrossed in his newest drawing. "Sometimes I worry about where this world is headed."

"I know where you can find answers."

"Don't start with all that preachy religious nonsense!" Brody withdrew his hand in anger. "Have you forgotten that all your Christian charity work with street people nearly got our son killed?"

Trying not to raise her voice, Paige said, "That's not fair! The detective has been unable to connect the stalker to any of my pro-bono cases!"

The telephone rang again, this time the landline. Brody launched to his feet and hurried to the desk to answer the call.

Left alone with her thoughts, Paige had to face the terrifying truth. Someone out there had threatened her family.

The worried mother watched Connor work on a detailed sketch of a tree. "That's a beautiful picture."

"Thanks Mom." Connor looked over his shoulder and smiled. "You can have it."

Paige thanked her sensitive red-headed boy and invited him to join her on the couch.

Bloody images from the UC Berkeley shooting kept playing on the screen that was mounted above the family-room hearth. "I think it's time to turn off the TV," Paige said as she grabbed the remote from the coffee table.

"Wait!" Connor pointed to a news anchorwoman, "That's Dad's friend! She sat with us at the Yankees game."

Paige studied the flawless olive complexion and brown-almond eyes of Katrina Katz. Even the sound of her voice that streamed from her full cherry lips was soothing, but it was the hair that gave her away. The same color and length of the woman Paige had seen talking to Brody at the Hensley Capital

Reception. *Is that the woman with the blue sports car?* she wondered. Paige felt her throat tighten. "Did this lady stay for the whole ballgame," she asked.

He shook his head. "No, but they are really good friends. They talked a lot."

Trying to sound casual, Paige asked, "What did they say?"

Connor shrugged. "Secrets, I guess. They whispered most of the time."

Paige swallowed hard and looked at her husband, wondering, *Can it be true? Brody is having an affair!*

Chapter 16

California

Tuesday, April 30th

    Joel knocked on the door of the suburban home where Coco lived. He could hear someone moving around, so he knocked again. A tiny Asian-American woman answered the door. She took a long sweeping look at Joel and said, "So you're the rat who broke my daughter's heart."

    "Mrs. Trent, may I come in?" Joel ran a hand through his ash brown hair and realized how disheveled he must look.

    She folded her arms. "My daughter's not here. Coco's still at work."

    "Who's out there?" a man's voice bellowed from somewhere inside the house.

    "Nobody!"

    "Please, I really want to talk with Coco," Joel pressed. "There are things I need to explain."

    Mrs. Trent's lips tightened, but she unfolded her arms. "Coco promised to stop at the grocery store on the way home from work. Maybe you could come back later."

The little woman started to close the door, but Joel held it in place with his foot.

"Please…"

A flash of temper erupted, and then to Joel's surprise, she softened. "Well, I suppose it wouldn't hurt, but you'll have to wait in this room." Mrs. Trent stepped aside and ushered Joel to a sterile looking living room that reeked of lemon oil. "Sit there." She pointed to a plastic covered couch, turned on her heels, and disappeared down a hallway.

Joel's mouth was dry, and his palms were moist as he relived the horror of his father's assassination. It seemed unreal, like his own eyes had betrayed him, but the spots of dried blood on his shirt told the true story. A clock on the mantel ticked away the minutes.

Somewhere in the house, he heard a man raise his voice. "I want to meet this kid."

Mrs. Trent's response was shrill. "He's trouble if you ask me!" They continued in hushed tones.

Any other time, Joel would have bolted for the door, but today had been no ordinary day.

The front door opened, and he launched to his feet. "Coco," he said.

She whirled around, dropped the bags of groceries, and ran to him with arms held open. "I've been so worried about you ever since I heard the news." Coco kissed a salty tear track on Joel's face and gazed into his nut-brown eyes. "I don't know what to say."

He pulled her closer. Joel could feel his heart pounding inside his chest. "I wanted to tell you everything about who I really am, but I'd signed a contract with the University."

She held a finger to his lips, "It doesn't matter now. You're safe, and that's all I care about."

Mrs. Trent appeared and hissed and growled like a Tasmanian devil about the groceries that were spilled on the floor. "The eggs! You better not have cracked any because that's what your father wants for dinner tonight."

Coco cowered under her mother's rage. "I'm sorry. I'll clean it all up."

Joel knelt to help.

"Never mind! Never mind! I'll do it myself!" Mrs. Trent opened a carton of two dozen eggs and found one cracked. She glared at her daughter, and then her sharp gaze turned on Joel. "Your father wants to meet this heartbreaker."

Coco seemed stunned. "Are you sure?"

"That's what I said, isn't it?"

Joel felt Coco's delicate fingers clutching his hand. Slowly, she led him down a long hallway to a set of double doors. There, she hesitated.

Sensing her unease, Joel asked, "What's wrong?"

"I really love my dad. I just want you to understand that before you meet him." Coco knocked softly on the door and then pushed it open.

The first thing that struck Joel was a wall of putrid air, a mixture of body odor and decay. Then he saw him. A man of massive proportions was sprawled across a large bed. One of Mr. Trent's legs was wider than a linebacker's torso! *He must weigh over six hundred pounds!* Joel thought.

"Please forgive the mess." Coco's dad waved a hand toward a nightstand littered with junk food wrappers.

Joel smiled. "It looks a lot like the place I share with my

college roommates."

A gelatinous roll of laughter rippled over Mr. Trent's belly, and Coco seemed relieved.

"Dad, I'd like you to meet Joel."

The crane man—a term reserved for people who are so obese that they require special equipment to get them out of a house—raised his eyebrows. "So do you go by 'Meyers' or 'Sutherland' or maybe 'Atwood?'" He nodded toward the news that was playing out on his oversized big-screen TV.

"It's kind of a long story," Joel said. "Thomas Atwood offered to have my name legally changed, but I prefer Sutherland out of respect for the family who raised me."

"Yeah, I know all about it!" Mr. Trent smiled. "Heck, when the news gets through analyzing you, the American public will know more about your life than you do." He chuckled and then scratched at the folds of flesh that hung around his neck. "I can only imagine what you've been through today. Of course, you're welcome to sleep here on the couch tonight." The big man turned toward Coco abruptly causing his jowls to wag and said, "Hey, Baby, I'd like to speak privately with your young man if you don't mind."

After a few seconds of hesitation, Coco nodded and left the room.

When he was alone with Joel, Mr. Trent beckoned him to come closer. "I want to know what your intentions are concerning my little girl?"

"I love Coco, and I want to marry her, that is, if she'll still have me."

"I believe you." With considerable effort, Mr. Trent rolled to his side and opened the top drawer of his bedside table. He fumbled around for a pen and an envelope. He slid out some ruled, yellow paper and unfolded it to reveal handwriting. Mr. Trent clicked his pen and added a few lines, slid the letter back into the envelope, and licked the seal. "Are you a man of your word?"

"Yes, Sir," Joel said without hesitation.

"Then, before you and my little girl leave together, I need you to promise me two things." As footsteps approached from the hallway, the big man handed Joel the letter then quickly gave his instructions. "Promise?"

"I promise, Mr. Trent," Joel said just before Coco entered the room.

⸺⸱⸺

Arizona

Wednesday, May 1ˢᵗ

With his car loaded with bottled water, granola bars, Twinkies, peanut butter, paper products, batteries, and hand sanitizer, Beck carefully steered his Prius over the bumpy road that led to Hope Springs. He was still unconvinced that the community water and food supply was safe for human consumption.

Beck passed a field where cattle and goats grazed. Beyond the tiny village, the hills were dotted with white-fleeced sheep foraging for desert grasses. He switched on the wipers and squirted cleaning fluid on his dusty windshield. "Just my luck to take an assignment in a one-horse town without a car wash!" he grumbled.

157

Ziggy and Fawn Nash's grown offspring was busy at the milking barn. The barefoot man-child with dreadlocks turned on his stool, lifted a hand from a cow teat, and offered as peace sign as the newcomer rolled past.

"That went out in the sixties, you moron," Beck said under his breath as he pushed up his polarized sunglasses and flashed a toothy smile. "Note to self—stay away from the dairy products!"

Beck turned onto a road that ran between the eclectic assortment of Hope Springs dwellings.

Carlos Ortega and his twin boys, Miguel and Manuel, were busy pruning fruit trees and barely noticed their newest neighbor rolling to a stop beside his campsite.

Before unloading his water and groceries, Beck glanced around for prying eyes, and then he quickly hid the food in his tent. *Sooner or later, I'll have to eat from their communal trough,* he told himself, but the thought made his sensitive stomach churn.

Beck's tent was partially shaded by a small tree and a large rock, but by late afternoon, it was already unbearably hot. He took a big swig from a bottle of water and pulled a travel mirror from his Dopp Kit to admire his chiseled features and salon-tanned face, now peppered with whiskers. *Not bad for a guy who hasn't shaved in days.* Stepping out, Beck thought about Priscilla's big violet eyes, willowy frame, and sweet nature. *Not the brightest creature,* he figured, *but I can teach her a thing or two.*

Beck popped a breath mint into his mouth, zipped the flap of his tent, and headed for the communal pavilion to do a little research. The more he studied the people of Hope

Springs, the more questions he had. *How did such a diverse mix of people find each other? Some are simple folk, some complex. A few of the community residents are even highly educated, like Jim, an engineer. Others,* Beck suspected, *are barely able to read. Yet there is some mysterious bond they all possess…* The investigative journalist found himself struggling for words to describe what made them so peculiar, but came up short.

"Good afternoon!" Bonnie Saunders called from the large brick grill in the corner of the communal center. "We were beginning to wonder if you'd ever join us."

"Just a little tired from my travels, but I'm all rested now." Beck passed beneath the mist of the evaporative-cooling system and walked over the flagstone floor to join Bonnie. "Something sure smells delicious," he lied. "What culinary delight are you preparing tonight?"

"Stewed chicken with fresh tomatoes and basil," Bonnie said, "but that heavenly aroma you smell is homemade bread."

At the brick, wood-fired oven, Sue Brewster's cheeks turned crimson. "Now, really, these aren't my best loaves."

"Don't sell yourself short, Gorgeous," Beck tapped the side of his nose, "My smeller never lies."

The little round woman lowered her head and said, "I'm making apple cobbler for dessert."

"I'll be sure to save room!"

A child giggled, and Beck turned to see Priscilla with her little boy, Hari, making their way to the pavilion from the west side. The sun hung low, showing the young mother's silhouette through the light cotton dress.

Holding a bouquet of fresh flowers, she said, "I picked

these from my garden."

"They're lovely, Dear," Bonnie said. "There's a vase in the pantry shed."

"Can I help?" Beck volunteered.

Priscilla politely declined.

Beck licked his lips as he watched her glide gracefully toward the wood hut they used for dry-good storage. *Yes,* he thought as his imagination roiled. *There are things I'd love to teach that girl.*

California

Wednesday, May 1st

Joel helped Coco pack her belongings into a suitcase. She didn't take much: makeup, toiletries, three pair of jeans, seven dresses that she had designed herself, some tunic blouses, skirts, shorts, sandals, tennis shoes, and a pair of boots.

"Avert your eyes," Coco said as she opened the top drawer and pulled out her undergarments.

Joel was facing the door when it suddenly swung open.

Mrs. Trent stood in the threshold, scowling, as her eyes zeroed in on the suitcase. "So, it's true then!"

"Mom," Coco pleaded, "please try to understand."

The tiny woman strode across the bedroom and slapped her daughter. "How can you be so selfish?"

Joel stepped in between them and postured protectively. "Mrs. Trent, it seems to me that you're the one being selfish!"

"Both of you, get out!" Her voice was as shrill as a skill saw.

Coco's hand covered the crimson fingermarks left on her cheek. "But I want to say goodbye to Dad."

The woman bolted down the hall and returned with an aluminum baseball bat. She raised the weapon. "Leave now!"

Joel quickly zipped the suitcase, ushered Coco from the house, and loaded her things in his Jeep.

"You're no daughter of mine!" Mrs. Trent shrieked before slamming the door.

Coco wept softly as they traveled through the suburban neighborhood.

"Your mom didn't mean that last comment," Joel said.

"I wish that was true." Coco wiped her eyes and blinked as the Alameda County office complex came into view. "Where are we going?"

"There's something we need to do before we leave town." Joel pulled in front of the Alameda County Clerk's office and killed the engine.

He opened the glove compartment and pulled out the velvet box that still held her wedding ring. "We can be married today by a justice of the peace." He held out the ring. "I love you with all my heart, Coco. Will you be my bride?"

"Yes."

That one simple word sent a rush of elation through Joel, and they hurried into the building to fill out the necessary forms.

"We want to be married today," Joel said as he pushed the completed application back across the counter.

"Sorry, Young Man." The clerk pointed to a clock that hung on the wall. It was 4:05 P.M.. "No civil ceremonies are preformed after 3:45 P.M.."

"Just this once?" Joel protested. "We're leaving town this afternoon."

"No exceptions, but an Alameda County marriage license is good anywhere in California." The clerk scratched her curly mop of hair. "Maybe you can find a pastor or somebody else who can perform the ceremony."

Wednesday, May 1*st*

"My sunglasses are in the glovebox," Joel said as they headed east on I-80.

There, beside a pair of Ray Bans, was a well-used Bible. Coco pulled it out along with the sunglasses. "Is this yours?"

Joel slipped on his shades. "It once belonged to an old roommate of mine." He hadn't thought about Daryl Capps in years. The memory of how the poor kid died always brought a surge of anger.

"We've never really talked about our beliefs," Coco said, quietly fingering her amber cross necklace. "Do you read it?"

"Sometimes." Joel reflected on how the wild college years had dulled his faith, at least, until Zeke showed up again with a timely warning. *"Things are going to get a little rough from here on out."*

Joel plugged in his iPhone, turned on his music, and they moved through traffic without talking.

Nearly an hour and a half later, Joel spotted a mega church on the outskirts of Sacramento and made a quick detour. "I bet we'll find a pastor here!"

With license and ring in hand, Joel escorted his bride

inside the multilevel building. From a modern reception desk, a well-dressed woman gave the couple a friendly wave and said, "Greetings, where can I direct you?"

The lobby was white with rich wood accents. Overhead, a stylized mahogany cross hung from a vaulted ceiling. "We're looking for a reverend or a pastor. We'd like to get married."

"Oh, then you're here for counseling?" She consulted her appointment book and then looked up, "We don't seem to have a session scheduled."

"No, you don't understand." Joel held up a marriage license. "We just need someone to perform the ceremony."

"This is highly irregular." The woman punched a number on her switchboard, drew in a breath, and said, "Pastor Garland, there's a young couple at reception who would like a minute of your time." She hung up and smiled. "He will be right out."

After five minutes with Pastor Garland, Joel knew it was a waste of their time. Six weeks of marriage counseling at the minimum, but first they had to complete a church membership class.

As they left Sacramento behind, Joel said, "It's doesn't make sense to me."

"What?"

"If we had arrived at the Clerk's office an hour earlier, we'd be married by now. You'd think a church would be in the business of blessing marriages in the eyes of God rather than playing God."

Wednesday, May 1st

By the time Joel and Coco reached Placerville, California, they were hungry. In the shadow of a tall bell tower, they found a quaint town center with an unusual mix of shops and eateries.

They settled into a booth at a local grill and ordered burgers and sodas.

"How long will it take to get to North Dakota?" Coco asked.

Joel reached across the table and held her hand. "A couple of 12-hour days, maybe more." Their eyes met, and feelings were stirred.

Putting a couple glasses down, the waitress said, "Here're your sodas. Your order will be up soon." She slipped a bottle of ketchup and mustard from her apron pocket, set them on the table between the couple, and then moved to the next booth.

Coco picked at her meal when it came. "I was just thinking about your father's funeral. There will probably be a lot of people there to pay their respects. Your dad was a great man."

"Yes, I believe he was." Old regrets began to surface, but Joel pushed them from his mind. "Nora says that the Presidential Library won't be ready for the memorial service for a while, so we've some time for short honeymoon."

"Aren't you forgetting something?"

Joel smiled. "Don't worry. I'm not leaving California until you're my bride."

They ate the rest of their meal in quiet reflection.

After placing a nice tip on the table, the couple continued their quest, stopping at random churches along the way.

"I can't believe how many churches are abandoned!" Coco marveled. "I wonder why?" As they headed northwest on US Route 50, she grew more anxious.

Joel reassured her, "We'll find some place. Don't worry."

Near the El Dorado National Forest, Coco pointed out a golden eagle soaring toward some snow-covered peaks and gasped at the sight. Among the hardwoods, pines, and shrubs, she spotted a red fox scampering off and yelped like she'd found a pot of gold. "It's so beautiful!" she exclaimed.

Joel agreed as he looked her way. "This view is outstanding."

Thunder rumbled, and a few minutes later, dark churning clouds rolled over the snowcapped mountains.

"Hey, there's a church!" Coco leaned forward eagerly and then frowned. It was just another abandoned house of worship with un-kept grounds, peeling paint, and broken windows.

Joel checked his watch. It was nearly 8:00 P.M.. At this hour, what were the chances of finding a minister willing to marry them? Feeling frustrated, he pushed on the throttle as a few drops of rain began to hit the windshield.

"Where are we going to sleep tonight?"

It was something Joel hadn't considered. "I guess we'll push on to Lake Tahoe."

Overhead the sky darkened and began to spit out fat droplets. The windshield wipers slapped hard as buckets of rain began to fall.

"Boom!!!" The sound sent shockwaves through the Jeep, and Joel jerked the wheel to the right, fighting to keep the vehicle under control. They came to a stop on a narrow pull out.

"What happened?"

Adrenaline pumped through Joel's veins. "I think one of the tires blew." Sheets of water drenched Joel as he stepped out and confirmed his suspicions.

"What are we going to do?" she asked as he slogged back inside.

Good question, Joel thought as he struggled to form a plan. They were practically out in the middle of nowhere. His Jeep was too compact to sleep in comfortably, and there was no one they could call for help.

"I think we should head back to that old church," Coco suggested. "At least, we'll find shelter from the storm."

Joel offered no argument. He grabbed a wool blanket and an emergency candle that he always kept behind the driver's seat, and they sprinted back to the abandoned building.

It didn't take long to find a way inside. Half of a stained glass window near the back had been broken out. Joel made sure the sill was free of jagged shards before lifting Coco through the opening.

Inside, they lit the emergency candle and huddled together beneath the damp blanket. Joel pulled Coco near and felt her shiver. He rubbed her arms and then kissed her softly. "This is kind of romantic," he whispered in her ear while nuzzling her neck. "I know a way to keep you warm." He leaned over her trembling body.

"Stop!" Coco pulled from his embrace. "This isn't right."

"We're engaged," Joel pleaded. "That's practically married."

"Not here." Coco looked beyond the rickety pulpit to a primitive, barn-wood cross that hung on the wall. "This is a house of God."

"But…"

Coco held a finger to her fiancé's lips. In the soft flickering candlelight, her eyes sparkled.

"At least, let me hold you."

She nestled contentedly into his arms. Listening to the rhythm of Coco's breathing and the patter of rain on the tin roof, Joel drifted off to sleep.

Chapter 17

California

Thursday, May 2nd

Something roused Joel from his slumber, and he opened his eyes. It took him a moment to remember that he and Coco had taken refuge from the storm in an abandoned church. She was sleeping soundly beside him; the warmth of her back was cradled against Joel's body. Coco stirred, and the tangle of her black hair mingled with the scent of mango shampoo tickled his nose.

A click of metal sent a chill down Joel's spine. He turned to face the barrel of a shotgun. Instinctively, he tried to shield Coco from the threat. "Please, don't shoot!"

"So, I finally caught you vandals!" the man bellowed. "You young folks ought to be ashamed of yourselves!"

Joel sat upright and held out a hand defensively. "We didn't do anything wrong."

"What about all those stain glass windows you've been breaking? And, I don't even want to think about what you two were doing in here last night!"

"Sir, he's telling you the truth!" Coco protested. "Nothing happened."

"Yeah? Have you ever heard of breaking and entering?" His bushy eyebrows kissed. "This is private property you're on!"

"Look, we're really sorry about that," Joel explained. "We had a flat tire last night and didn't have anywhere else to take shelter."

The man's scowl began to soften. "That storm was a real doozy." He lowered his weapon. "So that must be your Jeep back up the road."

Joel nodded.

"My place is about a half mile farther. If you would have kept going straight, then you could have slept together in a real bed."

"Oh, we're not married," Coco blurted.

"We'd like to be," Joel quickly added, "but we're looking for someone to perform the ceremony."

Rubbing the stubble on his chin, the man said, "You'll need a license for that."

"We've got one!" Joel pulled the folded document from his pocket and held it up.

"It looks like you came to the right place." The man smiled. "I'm a minister; at least, I used to be before the church got fleeced by regulations." He thrust out his hand and introduced himself as Pastor Eli White. "I refused to let the government strip me of my faith and principles."

"I don't understand. What does the government have to do with churches?" Coco asked. "I thought there was a separation of church and state."

"Things have changed, Young Lady. Have you kids ever heard about the FAD Act?"

Joel and Coco exchanged a look and then shook their heads.

"That's part of the problem." Pastor White ran his fingers through a thin crown of hair. "Most folks don't pay attention to what's happening right under their noses with all that twittering and face paging and what not. Anyway, I'm afraid you young people are gonna wake up one day and suddenly realize that your freedom is gone."

"We did notice a lot of small churches that were closed," Joel said.

"It's ironic when you think about the whole thing. Our government is using an anti-discrimination law to discriminate! Take this little house of worship, for example. We were threatened with fines for non-compliance, so we finally had to shut our doors." Eli White slowly shook his head and looked discouraged. "Folks are all flocking to larger government-subsidized churches, so they can write off their tithes. From what I hear, it's happening all across the country. Guess that's why our Lord called us sheep."

"But surely there are Christians who still love the truth," Coco said.

"You're right, Young Lady, but a lot of these good folks are meeting in homes because they're worried about persecution."

"Unbelievable!" Joel said. "It's like real Christianity has become a counter culture."

"Well, now," Pastor White rubbed his hands together, "it's time we talk about your wedding plans. You've got the license, but what about a ring?"

"In my pocket," Joel returned.

"We're gonna to need a witness." Pastor White headed for the door. "Why don't you two get ready while I call a few of my neighbors." He paused in the threshold of the church and looked back at the young couple. "I'm so excited! We're going to have a wedding here today!"

Joel jogged up the road and retrieved Coco's bag from his disabled Jeep and waited for her to change her clothes in the backroom.

"Don't look!" she called as her groom paced nervously in front of the altar. "Ordinarily, you're not supposed to see the bride before the wedding begins, but I'm not superstitious." After a few moments, she announced, "Okay, you can turn around now."

Coco was wearing a repurposed, mid-length dress that she had created from a white, linen table cloth. It was trimmed with delicate lace.

Her beauty literally took Joel's breath away, and he gasped.

"What do you think?" she asked expectantly.

"That you look amazing, and I'm the luckiest man on earth!" Joel's heart beat faster as he cupped her face in his hands and tenderly kissed her. "Sorry I don't have something more appropriate to wear. I couldn't go back to the Ozone because of all the media."

"I wouldn't care if you were wearing a bathrobe." Coco laughed. "All I see is the man I love."

Pastor White returned wearing a suit that was a bit tight around his middle. He looked somberly at the couple. "I've tried every neighbor and friend I know. Nobody is around to stand in.”

"What are we going to do?" Joel queried.

Coco took his hand. "Let's pray." Together with Pastor White, they asked God to send them a witness.

Moments later, their heavenly petition was answered!

The door of the old church squeaked open, and a little man with long, white beard poked his head inside and said, "Am I too late?"

New York
Thursday, May 2nd

Paige walked into the Unified Broadcasting Corporation New York studio. The waiting area looked swank and modern with colorful pops of art and white leather furnishings. The sleek lines were arranged around a massive flat-screen TV that played the morning news show.

From behind her glassed-in reception area, a bronzed beauty smiled as Paige approached. "Are you here for an interview?"

"I was hoping to have a word with Katrina Katz," she replied.

"Is Ms. Katz expecting you?" The young woman's smile seemed frozen in place as she spoke.

"No, but I believe that she will make time." Paige summoned courage. "Will you tell her that Brody Hay's wife is here to see her?"

"She has a very busy schedule," the receptionist warned, "but if you will have a seat, I'll relay the message to her."

Paige sat down on one of the stiff, white couches and stared at the TV screen. A local philanthropist was discussing an upcoming fundraiser in Central Park, something about a bicycle rodeo. Paige's thoughts were a million miles away. She still couldn't believe that her husband was having an affair.

"Mrs. Hays?" The look on the receptionist's face spoke volumes. "I'm sorry, but Ms. Katz is in the middle of a project."

"I see," Paige mumbled. She stood, swung her satchel over her shoulder, and headed toward the door. She had worked up the courage to confront the "other woman" only to be turned away. On the sidewalk out front, her cell phone rang, and anger rose like a volcano. It was Brody. *Katrina Katz didn't waste any time!* Paige thought as she drew in a breath and answered.

He jumped right to the issue at hand. "It's not what it looks like."

"I don't know what to think anymore."

"Do you remember that little coffee house we used to go to?" Brody asked.

Paige fought the urge to hang up. "The one on the West Side?"

"I'll meet you there." After a brief pause, her husband added, "We need to have a talk."

The words sounded ominous. Somewhere Paige had heard that most men chose to end their marriages in public places in order to avoid an emotional scene. Her heart began to pound as her former anger turned to fear. "Okay," she said to herself. Instinct kicked in as Paige hailed a cab. She reflected on her marriage and her love for Brody. *What about Connor and Emily, the precious little girl they had lost? Such fond memories of a lifetime are worth fighting for!* Paige thought.

At the designated meeting place, she ordered black coffee and cupped her shaky hands around the mug, but she couldn't drink it. Her stomach was turning cartwheels as she waited.

Finally, when Brody walked through the door, she mustered courage and fought back a swell of tears. Paige searched her husband's face as he sat down. "Are you having an affair?"

"Absolutely not."

"Your husband is helping me," came a female voice from behind.

Paige spun around in her seat to face the woman in question—Katrina Katz.

Without being invited, the anchorwoman sat down. "I've been working on an important news story." Katrina's tone was ominous. "It's an exposé that could signal the fall of this great nation."

⸺∞∞∞⸺

Arizona
Thursday, May 2nd

At his makeshift desk in the General Store stock room, David scrolled down the internet news page, reading about current events. "Alistair Dormin, dubbed an 'economic savior' by some, has been awarded the Nobel Prize for brokering peace in the Middle East…" The next few articles hit closer to home. "According to Alberto Vega, the North American Coalition Treaty was moving toward the goal of open borders. And, now, in response to the assassination of former President Thomas Atwood, Congress has passed a mandatory gun registration bill. Strict penalties would be enforced against anyone who refused to register their firearms." David leaned back in his chair and tried to process the rising swell of social and political change.

An unusual aroma wafted through the heavy tapestry curtains that hung in the doorway, coaxing David back from his concerns. He shut down his computer and went to investigate.

Elita stood behind the lunch counter stirring a large pot of stew.

"What in the world are you cooking?" he asked.

"It's a Mexican soup made with a broth and red-chili-pepper base. It also has lime, chopped onions, cilantro, and oregano."

David watched his wife add two cans of white hominy to the pot.

"This is my special variation on the recipe, so don't tell anyone," Elita cautioned.

"For a kiss, your secret will be safe with me." He straddled a vinyl covered stool and leaned across the well-worn countertop to collect. "Smells great," David said as his wife returned to stirring. "What kind of meat are you using?"

"Beef," she replied. "Cow stomach, actually."

David's appetite suddenly vanished. "Why such a big batch?"

"Menudo is the Mexican equivalent of chicken soup."

Elita turned off the burner and placed a lid over the stew. "Gordon is coming home from the hospital today, so I was just about to ask you to help me deliver this to the CBG compound."

"I can't believe they are releasing him so soon."

Elita carried the cutting board to the sink and scrubbed it. "Thankfully, it was a minor stroke. The doctors believe he'll make a full recovery."

"Spitzer is just too stubborn to stay down!"

"If you don't have anything nice to say…"

David grinned. "I really don't mind the old goat, except for that abrasive personality of his."

Elita shook head and gave her husband "The Look."

"Right, something nice." David thought about it. "Okay, I've got it! All those endless debates with Spitzer challenged me to rethink some of my populist viewpoints."

"That's better!" Elita tossed David some oven mitts. "We've got a couple hours before Joy gets home from preschool, so let's get going."

With the pot full of menudo in the back of the pickup, David carefully dodged the growing craters in the crumbling asphalt of Main Street and turned down the highway.

Gordon had already arrived back at the compound, and the couple found him slumped in an easy chair, staring blankly at a news program.

"We come bearing gifts!" Elita announced as her husband delivered the stew to the kitchen.

"Maybe the boys are hungry." The head of the CBG mumbled a few more words under his breath as David returned. "Have a seat."

Gordon's attempt at gratitude was feeble, at best, but David chose to let it slide.

"You're looking well," Elita said cheerfully.

Spitzer looked her way, revealing a drooping mouth on one side of his face. "Darlin', you'd never make it as a poker player." He turned his lifeless eyes back to the TV.

A few awkward seconds passed.

"So, what do you think about the new gun registration law?" David asked.

"It's probably not a good time to talk politics," Elita cautioned. "Gordon really shouldn't get upset."

Suddenly, Spitzer came to life. "I don't appreciate being treated like a china doll!"

Tranch slapped Gordon on the back and said, "That's the fighting spirit, Boss! We ain't gonna let those Feds push us around!"

Gordon let out a long sigh.

"Isn't that right, Boss?" Tranch pressed.

Spitzer shrugged and sank back into his chair. "What's the point in resisting the inevitable?"

David couldn't believe what he was hearing. The shocked faces of the rest of the Civic Border Guard told him he wasn't alone.

Tranch and the boys exchanged perplexed looks. "You're messing with us, aren't ya, Boss?"

The leader of the Civic Border Guard pointed the remote control at the TV and killed the news. "Everybody knows we've got ourselves an arsenal here. It's just a matter of time before they come for us!"

"What about all the things you stand for? All those

speeches you've made, like gun registration leads to gun control, and an armed citizenry can't be oppressed by its government?" David pressed.

"I'm tired," Gordon said flatly. "I need to rest."

He rose on wobbly legs, leaned hard on his cane for a moment, and limped toward his private quarters.

Angry outbursts erupted among the CBG members as their leader hobbled away looking old and worn out.

"You can be a quitter if you want," Tranch bellowed, "but me and the boys ain't gonna let this one go down easy!"

Chapter 18

California

Thursday, May 2nd

Birds were singing in the churchyard trees as Joel watched his bride-to-be gliding gracefully toward him down the church aisle in satin slippers and her white linen and lace dress.

Mottled light from the stained-glass window remnants bathed the room with color, while Zeke—dressed up in pressed trousers and his best Hawaiian shirt—escorted Coco down the aisle.

Joel's eyes misted with happiness as his soulmate, holding a delicate bouquet of wild flowers, took her place beside him. In all of his life, he had never felt such a depth of joy.

Pastor White opened his Bible and began to read from 1 Corinthians, Chapter 13. "Love is patient and kind. Love is not jealous or boastful or proud or rude. It does not demand its own way. It is not irritable, and it keeps no record of being wronged. It does not rejoice about injustice but rejoices whenever the truth wins out. Love never gives up, never loses faith, is always hopeful, and endures through every circumstance." He paused to let the words settle, and then he instructed the groom to repeat a vow.

Joel spoke the words as though they were imprinted on his soul. "I take you, Coco, to be my wife, to stand beside you whatever comes, both in times of light and times of darkness, to love you faithfully with all my heart from this moment forward."

Then Coco spoke with the same conviction.

"May the Lord bless this union and bind you together with the cord of His love for as it says in Ecclesiastes 4:12, '...a triple-braided cord is not easily broken.'" Pastor White smiled at the couple. "It is my great honor and privilege to pronounce you man and wife!"

Joel swept Coco into his arms, kissed her, and said, "You've made me the happiest man on earth." Through a fractured stained-glass window, a shaft of sunlight shined down on the young lovers as if it was sent from Heaven above.

Zeke let out a joyous praise and did a little happy dance. "This is the nicest wedding I've been to in years, though I have to admit that the party at Cana was a real hoot!"

Pastor White fished a handful of rice from his pocket and tossed it. "I almost forgot to tell you that I called up my roadside service people to fix your tire. You should be good to go."

Joel reached for his wallet, but the Pastor held up a hand in protest. "Consider it a wedding gift."

After a round of hugs, Joel and Coco headed out the door.

"Hold on a minute! Not so fast!" Zeke hurried over to his

old Rambler station wagon and lifted the back hatch. "I've got a little something for you two."

As the old man rifled through boxes, Coco leaned close to her new husband and said, "I get the strangest feeling that I've met Zeke somewhere before."

Joel laughed. "He has that effect on people."

Finally, the bearded gent emerged from the Rambler and presented the couple with a framed photo of a beautiful log home that was overlooking a lake. Zeke paused, and his pale blue eyes locked on Joel. "Before I give you my gift, I wanted to say how sorry I was to hear about your dad—such a terrible thing."

"Thanks," Joel said solemnly as the old man pressed a key into the palm of his hand. "What's this for?"

"The address is on the back. This place is on the west side of Lake Tahoe and has a view that's out of this world. I figure you two lovebirds need a proper honeymoon, and the folks who own this summer cabin are out of the country. They are good peeps! The place is all stocked and ready for you. They said to make yourselves at home. Just leave the key on the dining room table when you leave."

Coco looked at the picture. "They call this a summer cabin? It's more like a mansion. These people must be billionaires!"

A puff of laughter blew through the old man's downy beard. "Everybody needs God, even rich people! Some folks just don't know it yet."

The newlyweds found a note on the kitchen table that read, "Welcome! Make yourselves at home!"

"Are you sure we can stay a full week?" Coco asked.

Joel nodded. "My father's memorial is still in the planning stage, so we can take our time." He threw open the doors of a large stainless-steel fridge and said, "I'm starving."

"Wow!" Coco marveled, "That thing is big enough to live in!"

Joel smiled. "We'd have fun trying to keep warm."

"You're impossible!"

They found a loaf of French bread and a dish of freshly prepared lasagna. "This is my absolute favorite meal!" she said. Coco located the switch for the range hood and fired up the gas oven.

The kitchen was equipped with rustic cabinets of knotty pine and a massive farm sink set below windows that showcased a pristine meadow.

Joel settled in at a long, ornately carved table and watched his bride as she explored the cupboards.

"I've never been in a kitchen like this before!" Coco said as she located the plates and silverware. It didn't take long before the aroma of warm lasagna filled the room. "Can you believe the architectural details in this house? Like that hand painted cabinet in the entryway and those amazing antler chandeliers!"

"Yeah, and those heavy beams and the wrought iron work on the doors," Joel noted as his stomach growled. "But the view is what really gets me."

Coco looked out the window and smiled sublimely. "Yes, definitely not made by human hands."

The young couple lit a candle on the table.

Joel took a bite of their first meal as husband and wife and was about to take another when he noticed that Coco had her head bowed. After a brief pause to give thanks, Joel devoured his meal.

As he helped Coco wash the dishes after dinner, she asked about his mother. "What did she say when you told her about me?"

"Nora was thrilled. Said she can't wait to meet you!" Joel dried a plate and returned it to the cupboard.

"I'm afraid she won't like me."

"That's impossible. Nora is one of the kindest people I've ever known. I'm lucky that she's in my life."

Coco cast a sideways glance at her new husband. "There are some things in your past that you never mention."

"Why should I? The news has it covered." Joel put the last dish away.

"Former President Thomas Atwood was assassinated while speaking at his illegitimate son's university…" He felt a gentle touch on his shoulder and turned.

"The media may have revealed some secrets, but they don't really know you."

The couple retired to the deck and snuggled in a lounge chair made for two. The setting sun behind them glistened upon the waters of Lake Tahoe, and the treetops, brushed with the soft dusky light of alpine glow, swayed in a gentle breeze.

"Tell me everything. What were you like as a boy? Your family?" Coco inquired as Joel pulled her closer.

"They were good loving people, except for my sister." Joel fell silent and drew in a deep breath.

"You have a sister?"

In his mind, Joel drifted through painful memories of murder and betrayal. "I don't like to talk about that part of my life. The only good thing that happened back then was a road trip with Zeke that changed my life."

"Hey, I just remembered where I've seen that old man before!" Coco exclaimed.

"Why don't you tell me later." Joel took Coco in his arms and kissed her. "Right now, I want to concentrate on you." Enraptured by the delicate outline of Coco's profile, Joel felt his heart flood with desire as he traced the outlines of her palm. "It's getting chilly here on the deck. We should go inside."

Coco seemed distracted. "Wait! It was him," she blurted. "Zeke was the old man who took the knife away from the deranged guy who tried to attack me!"

"Are you talking about that incident at the Seabird Grille?"

"Yes, but he left before I could thank him!"

Joel thought back to the night when he spoke with Zeke at the Ozone. *The old traveler said he couldn't stay long—there was someplace he needed to be!*

"It's like Zeke was there for a reason!" Coco rubbed the goosebumps on her arms. "And it wasn't chance that brought him to the church at the exact moment when we needed a witness either."

"When it comes to Zeke, nothing surprises me. I'll tell you some stories, but right now, I've got other things on my mind." Joel stood and coaxed Coco from the lounge chair.

When the massive lodge door closed behind the couple, Joel felt his heart beat quicken. "You are so amazingly beautiful."

She looked up. Her dark jade eyes reflecting light from the chandelier. Joel cupped Coco's face in his hands, and they kissed slowly and tenderly. He ran his fingers down her spine and felt her quiver. Her body leaned into his as Joel nuzzled her neck with utterances of love and whispered, "It's time for bed."

Chapter 19

Arizona

Sunday May 5th

Joy scrambled across her mother's lap as soon as David put the old pickup truck into park. "There's Hari!"

They watched their little girl leap from the cab of the truck and dash off toward the Hope Springs pavilion.

Elita squeezed David's hand and said, "Thanks for coming."

David scowled as she gathered a plastic tub filled with oatmeal cookies. "You make it sound as if I've never attended a Hope Springs fellowship dinner before."

She raised an eyebrow. "'Never' would be a slight overstatement."

"I'm just not into organized religion, that's all."

"Look around," Elita challenged as they approached the gathering. "I see a bunch of individuals from different religious backgrounds who share a common love for God and each other."

David shrugged and said, "Maybe you married a rebel."

Elita laced her fingers through her husband's hand. "I can see the seeds of your faith, even if you can't."

David thoughts went back to all the unexplainable graces he had witnessed. *The vision of a dying rancher named Rupert Sims, the arrival of a mysterious old man named Zeke, the birth of Hope Springs, the happenstance of all the events surrounding the Third Peril. It's hard not to believe that the hand of God is in all of it.*

"Well, if it isn't the Fillmores!" Jim Saunders waved them over to a large table.

David took a seat beside a young man, who was twirling a dreadlock. "How are things with you, Cosmo?"

The young man looked up through half-mast eyes and said, "Cool and breezy, man, 'cept for this bummer." Cosmo lifted a bare foot to his lap and began to pick at a planter's wart on his heel.

Wade Michaelson, affectionately known as Mr. Mike, leaned over the table and in a somber tone said, "I picked up some chatter on my ham radio this morning."

"Oh? Anything interesting?" David pictured the techno geek in his converted school bus that was jammed from floor to ceiling with electronics. Even the cot where Mr. Mike slept was equipped with a high-tech set of head phones.

"Yeah, might say so." The gadget man drummed his dirty fingernails on the table and adjusted his glasses. It was a wonder he could see through the smudges on the thick lenses. "The ATF is planning a little visit to our neck of the woods. Didn't catch a date, but there was mention of the CBG compound."

A few feet away, Raymond Lee took his place on a tall

stool and began to tune his guitar. The sound echoed over the flagstone flooring. "Did you know he used to play backup for some big-name blues artists?" Jim Saunders asked.

"I'm not surprised," David said, grateful to extract himself from Mr. Mike's secret world. "In fact, I might have heard him play once back when I was living on the road."

On the other side of the table, Travis Dayton stood up abruptly. His chair fell over, causing heads to turn.

David followed the young carpenter's gaze to Priscilla and the newcomer, Beck McGuire.

A few yards from the pavilion, they stood, engaged in an animated conversation. Priscilla threw her head back in laughter. Beck flashed his perfect white teeth, brushed a strand of blond hair from her forehead, and then ran a finger down her arm.

Travis Dayton's lips tightened, and his fist curled as he watched his rival making his moves. "Priscilla, I saved a seat for you!" In a flash, the smitten young carpenter was at her side offering her an arm.

"Trouble with the new guy?" David asked.

Jim Saunders ran a hand across his clean-shaven chin. "We hardly know the man. It's rare that Beck joins us for a fellowship dinner, and he never attends Sunday morning service."

"Well, the guy's not starving," Elita said. "He's always at the General Store using our Wi-Fi and stocking up on food supplies."

Raymond Lee began play his guitar, and the community members all took their places to sing some songs of praise. Finally, Randy Bales asked a blessing, and the feast began.

"Mind if I join you?" Beck McGuire asked and then plopped down beside the Fillmores. "I understand that you're the executor of the Rupert Sims estate. What can you tell me about that old rancher?"

"What do you want to know?" David replied cautiously.

"Like, tell me about that vision thing. Was it for real, or was the old guy a bit loco?" McGuire poked at his food as he waited for a reply.

"Look around. You should be able to answer that question yourself."

"Yeah, sure, the people of God and all that, but did Sims have any religious quirks?"

"I knew Rupert Sims since I was a child," Elita cut in. "He was a kind man who read the Bible and loved God. What's wrong with that?" She gave the newcomer a curious look. "Why did you come here, Mr. McGuire?"

"I guess you could say that I have a reverent respect for nature—that's my religion." Beck set his fork on his untouched plate of food as the others at the table fell silent. "Actually, I was led to believe this was a community of forward thinking eco elites."

"You must have been shocked to learn that you were among regular hardworking people," Elita said.

"That's putting it mildly!" Beck used his butter knife to separate his food. "When I heard about the Rupert Sims angle, I wondered if Hope Springs was actually some kind of isolate cult!" he said as laughter rippled around the table.

Elita, however, crossed her arms and said, "Maybe this isn't the right place for you."

"Oh, I'm in no hurry to leave. There are still a few things

that I'd still like to check out." Beck's gaze shifted to Priscilla who was seated at the next table. He wiped his lips on a napkin, used it to cover his wasted meal, and excused himself from the table.

Elita leaned in close to her husband and whispered, "There's something about that guy that I don't trust."

David nodded in agreement as he watched Beck saunter away.

———

New York
Sunday, May 5th

Paige checked the roast that was braising on a bed of sliced carrots and onions. It had another twenty minutes to go. She poured a splash of Merlot over the meat, added a sprinkling of sea salt and fresh ground pepper, and slipped the pan back into her gourmet oven.

In the warming oven, Paige checked a dish of new potatoes with sour cream and chives along with a bowl of fresh peas and pearl onions.

"More wine?" she offered.

Katrina Katz accepted another splash.

Paige joined her husband and their guest at the table and nibbled from a tray garnished with an assortment of cheeses and olives. "Brody also believes that our nation may be headed for trouble, but I would love to hear your viewpoint."

The anchorwoman nodded. "But, first, let me say that I think your husband has shown a lot of courage putting his career on the line. Brody has been an invaluable source in helping me piece together my story that, I hope, will serve as a wake-up call to America. I believe the public should be aware that national sovereignty and even their personal freedoms are in jeopardy."

"Katrina, I'm curious. Why are you able to see what others are blind to?" Paige asked. "Most people feel that our nation is on the mend, at least, economically. How can any of us really foresee the future?"

"Simple—by looking back at history. I've been noticing some disturbing parallels." The anchorwoman hesitated. "Maybe I should explain my point of view. I come from a long line of Russian Jews. My ancestors fled to Poland after the Bolshevik Revolution and later wound up in the Warsaw Ghettos. My great grandmother, Sophie, survived, and she vowed to make sure that the historic events that preceded those times would not be forgotten. Both Russia and Germany used propaganda through educators, film, and other media to marginalize religion and to build a new society with altered moral values."

"The economy is a huge social agent for rapid change," Brody interjected. "In Russia, communism rolled in on the Trojan Horse of class warfare. In Germany, Hitler first gained his cult following by building a robust economy. Today, multiple nations, ours included, have ceded economic sovereignty, which makes me very uneasy."

"If you laid a historical template over today's trends, the similarities would shock you." Katrina said. "Where will it end?"

"How do you plan to break this story?"

"Ordinarily, that would be a challenge. UBC policy prohibits news anchors from making personal editorial statements without prior approval. My station manager has the power to quash the whole piece, so I've been waiting for the right moment, and then, something wonderful happened! This year I am receiving the Empire Media Award! As the recipient in a room full of journalists, I'm expected to make an acceptance speech, so…"

Brody chuckled, "I'd love to see their faces."

Katrina shook her head. "And risk being outed as one of my sources? Not a chance. In fact," she added, "I feel it would be prudent to end all contact when this thing goes mainstream."

The timer on the oven signaled that the braised roast was ready. As Paige rose, her thoughts drifted to the FAD Act and the recent compromises she had seen in church. She quivered. *Is it true that the tragic lessons of history are being ignored?*

Chapter 20

New York

Friday, May 10th

At the office of Silverstein and Hays, the morning had sped by in a flurry of calls and casework.

Jewel poked her head through Paige's office door and said, "I'm going to the deli. Jerry wants an onion bagel with lox and smear of cream cheese. Want anything?"

"No thanks," Paige said without looking up.

"Are you sure? Jerry said he's buying, and you know that doesn't happen often."

Paige glanced at her secretary, who was examining the polish on one of her long nails, and said, "I'm too busy to think about food."

"Suit yourself." Jewel shrugged.

A few minutes later, the phone rang. Her law partner didn't seem inclined to answer, so Paige plucked the phone from the cradle. "Silverstein and Hays."

"Mrs. Hays? This is Jane Pike at the Tyler Brentwood School."

Paige pitched forward. "Is something wrong?"

"Connor is fine, just a little shook up." The school secretary paused. "Let me explain. It seems that someone has displayed some artwork in our lunchroom. Connor claims they are his drawings and that they had been stolen."

Paige began to tremble. "Are they mosaic eyes?"

"Why, yes."

"Mrs. Pike, I think you should call the police," Paige said. "I'm on my way!"

Arizona

Friday, May 10th

A media van rolled past the window of the General Store, followed by another. "They're back!" Elita called.

David emerged from the storage room just in time to spot Alberto Vega cruising down Main Street in his chauffer driven Cadillac Escalade. The newly appointed government liaison emerged along with his entourage of assistants.

Elita unfolded a newspaper and pointed to an article on the front page. The headlines read. "Alberto Vega to Receive the First RFID Chip."

Right on cue, a battalion of Civic Border Guard Jeeps turned onto the town's main street. David watched as the caravan parked in a row and the troops stepped out to make their presence known. Their leader was conspicuously absent.

"I'm glad Gordon didn't come," Elita said. "This event would not help his recovery."

Out front, Jay Jennings snapped his fingers and ordered his crew to set up the cameras on the General Store porch. "I'm sure they won't mind," the anchorman said with an air of presumption.

"He's got some nerve," David grumbled.

Elita sighed. "Let's not make an issue of it," she suggested. "I'll just be glad when this circus is over, and we can get on with our lives."

It wasn't the media hype or the disruptions that worried David; it was something broader.

The couple watched from the window as Jennings and Vega posed for the camera. "Three, two, one," said the production manager as he pointed his finger to cue up the video feed.

Jay Jennings stood before the lens looking polished and primed. "We're back in the tiny border town of Arroyo Seco with Alberto Vega, this time to witness a historic occasion." His resonate voice was choked with emotion. "Today, the dividing walls that have evoked such racial fervor are about to come down!" The anchorman tilted his microphone toward Vega.

"Though I have become a naturalized citizen of the United States, my love and respect for Mexico and her people has not diminished." His deep brown eyes courted the camera lens with passion. "As a government liaison between two great nations, I am proud to pave the way to our future." Alberto Vega opened the palm of his hand and the camera man zoomed in to show what appeared to be an oblong piece of metal. "This RFID chip, no bigger than a grain of rice, will allow me free access to all countries that border the US. It is the promise of new economic and social hope for our peoples. This miniscule device will be a deterrent to terrorism and crime, but its applications can also help to safeguard our medical and social programs against abuse."

Vega slipped the chip that he'd used as a prop into the pocket of his blue blazer. "I'm ready Dr. Grice," he announced to a man standing by in a white coat.

The former Mexican national removed his jacket and rolled up the cuff of his expensive silk shirt.

The doctor stepped forward with an applicator that resembled an oversized hypodermic needle. He instructed Alberto Vega to hold out his hand, palm down. Moments after numbing the injection site, the RFID chip was injected into the flesh between his thumb and forefinger.

Without flinching or missing a beat, Alberto Vega proclaimed, "This new mandatory visa signals an unprecedented day of international freedom and brotherhood!"

The Civic Border Guard crowd began to heckle as the cameras shifted back to the anchorman. "Jay Jennings, reporting live for News Cam 4."

"Did he say mandatory?" Elita asked as they watched the team dismantle their equipment. "I still have cousins living in Mexico. Is Alberto saying that I can no longer see them without a chip?"

"I don't think they can do that," David said with mounting concern. "We have constitutional amendments that protect us and our personal property from unwarranted intrusions."

By late afternoon, the couple was exhausted from feeding the news crew and cleaning up. After closing early, Elita took

Joy upstairs to rest while David retreated to his office to immerse himself in constitutional law.

Around dinner time, someone pounded on the General Store door, jarring David's thoughts from his case-law books. The "CLOSED" sign on the door was obvious, but the knocking grew more insistent.

David went to investigate, feeling more than a little annoyed when he spotted Beck McGuire peering at him from between the travel stickers on the window. "Can't you see we're closed?"

"Let me in. It's urgent!"

David turned the latch. McGuire pushed his way inside and looked out the window. "I knew he'd follow me. Quick, lock the door!" he yelped as Travis Dayton's flatbed truck skidded to a hard stop on the other side of the street peppering Beck's Prius with gravel. The young carpenter jumped from the truck and stormed into the Watering Hole Bar, only to emerge a few seconds later. Travis' face was purple with rage as he strode toward the General Store.

"He's crazy, I tell you!" McGuire took cover as Travis burst through the door, his fists curled for action.

"Where is he? Where's that weasel?" He spotted Beck cowering behind the cash register and dragged him into the open.

Travis drew his fist back and got in one good shot before David stepped in and held the men at bay. "What's going on here?"

Beck retrieved his bent glasses from the wood floor, cupped his bloodied nose, and shrieked, "You'll be sorry! You and all those loonies you live with! You're going to regret this!"

David restrained Travis as McGuire fled out the door, jumped into his Prius, and sped away leaving a cloud of dust behind him.

"Okay, start from the beginning."

"He tried to violate Priscilla, that's what!"

"Are you sure you didn't misread the situation?" David calmly asked.

"What are you insinuating?" Travis quivered with redirected rage.

"Look, I'm not your enemy," David cautioned. "It's obvious that you like Priscilla, but it's possible that she had feelings for Beck."

Travis shook his head emphatically, ran sweaty fingers through his mullet, and blurted, "That animal jumped Priscilla when she was taking a shower. I heard her in the bathhouse crying and begging him to stop!" Dayton cracked his knuckles. "I should have kicked his bony…"

David held up his hand. "I get the picture."

Elita came down the stairs from their apartment. "I couldn't help over hearing you two. Is Priscilla okay?"

"She's shook up and a little bruised." The young carpenter's face softened. "I'd best get back just in case she needs me."

When they were alone, Elita reminded her husband of her feelings. "I told you that guy was trouble. I'm glad he has left town."

David threw the bolt on the front door and said, "I'm not sure we've heard the last of Beck McGuire."

Chapter 21

North Dakota

Sunday, May 12th

The newlyweds arrived in Delmont, North Dakota, to find a large banner hanging over the porch of Nora's Bargain Bin that read, "CONGRATULATIONS!!!"

Before Joel could park his Jeep Wrangler, a middle-aged woman of average build swooped from the porch with arms held wide. After a round of hugs, she stepped back to gaze at the new bride.

"Coco, this is my…" Joel stopped himself. "This is Nora."

Nora looked at her new daughter-in-law with smiling brown eyes and welcomed her to the family.

Gertie Bell's rotund frame filled the doorway of the grand old building. "Well, don't just stand there yacking! There're more introductions to be made."

Joel laced his fingers through his wife's hand and led her across the oversized porch of the repurposed building that was once known as the Delmont Hotel.

The blue-haired woman stepped aside as the young couple entered a room filled with racks of used clothing and other wares.

"This is Grandma Gertie," Joel said. "At least, she's the closest thing I've ever had to a grandmother."

"She does most of the cooking around here." A large man wearing a beanie twirled the end of his handlebar moustache, and added, "But don't let that scare you! She hasn't killed us, yet."

"Mind your manners, you big Huckleberry!" Gertie bellowed. "I don't see you complaining whenever you help yourself to seconds!"

"You'll get used to these two," Joel whispered to his bride. "Coco, this is J. J. O'Shay."

The older man removed the cap from his balding head and thrust out his hand. "Former weightlifter and circus clown, at your service. Heavy lifting and juggling are just a few of my specialties!"

"You forgot to mention lounging around in front of the TV and rifling through the fridge!" Gertie quipped. "Which reminds me…" The elderly woman disappeared through the swinging door into the kitchen and returned with an odd-looking cake. I baked a special eighteen-layer Norwegian wedding cake for the occasion. It's called a Kransekake."

"It's shaped like a traffic cone!" J. J. laughed. "And, with a name like Kransekake, it's a wonder anyone in Norway gets married!"

"I think it looks delicious," Coco said.

Gertie seemed pleased. "Well, then I'll set Mr. O'Shay's portion aside for you."

"Now children!" Nora cautioned her adult friends. "Play nice. I'm not going to let anything spoil this beautiful day."

"Why don't you have a seat, and I'll serve the cake," Gertie said.

Near a massive unlit fireplace was a large rug and a curious mix of mismatched furniture.

Joel and Coco sat on a loveseat, and he pointed to a flat-screen TV that was mounted on the wall beside the fireplace. "Wow, that's new!"

"It was on clearance at Walmart," Nora said.

"Gertie and I pitched in, too," J. J. volunteered. "Figured it was time to join the twenty-first century."

"Nice," Joel replied.

"Now, tell me all about your trip!" Nora settled into a vintage rocking chair that was upholstered in plaid and leaned forward in anticipation.

"It was wonderful," Coco said. "We stayed at an awesome cabin near Lake Tahoe and then went sightseeing near Idaho Falls."

Joel slipped his iPhone from his pocket and showed the group some photos. "These are the Twin Falls in the Snake River Canyon."

Coco leaned forward and pointed to one of the pictures. "There! If you look closely, you can see the rainbow in the mist. That's the part I loved the most."

"I see you visited Yellowstone," Nora said as her son scrolled through shots of Old Faithful, buffalo, and numerous selfies.

"We stopped at Mount Rushmore, too, but we didn't stay long." Joel's thoughts drifted to the email he'd received from

Thomas Atwood's secretary, who asked if he would give a brief eulogy in honor of his late father. "Is a date set for the memorial service yet?"

"Not yet, but I hear they're making progress." Nora leaned over and laid her hand on her son's arm. "I'm so sorry for your loss." The atmosphere grew somber until Gertie entered the room, balancing plates of cake in her hands—one for everyone except J. J.

Undaunted, O'Shay slipped into the kitchen and helped himself to a double portion. "So, where are you two love birds going to stay?" he asked when he returned.

"You are both welcome to stay here," Nora interjected. "In fact, Joel, I've been fixing up your old room."

O'Shay nearly choked on a large bite of cake. "Wait a minute! Are you talking about that room next to old Earl Crakenbush with Gertie on the other side? Those two snore like a couple of offbeat jack hammers. This young couple won't get any rest!"

"I do not snore!" Gertie bristled. "However, J. J. does have a point when it comes to Mr. Crakenbush."

Nora rubbed her forehead. "Oh, dear. At times like this, I miss the farmhouse." She paused to explain that the family home was destroyed during the Third Peril and that her insurance company wouldn't cover Acts of War. "Since then, I've been living here in a tiny apartment off the storage room."

"What about your rental?" Joel asked.

"I'm afraid it's being leased."

"Hey, I've got an idea!" Gertie blurted. "A bit unconventional maybe, but with a little imagination and some elbow grease, it could be the perfect spot for an adventurous couple to begin their lives together!" The old woman clapped her mottled hands together and said, "What do you say we all take a little ride in the country?"

⸙

Gertie's minivan bounced down a dirt road that cut through fields of new corn. "Where are we going?" Nora asked from the front passenger seat.

"You'll see soon enough!" The old woman took a fork in the road that ran alongside a cottonwood-lined stream. Gertie glanced in her rearview mirror at Joel and Coco seated in the back. "You two won't hurt my feelings if it doesn't suit you. Just keep an open mind. That's all I'm asking."

Joel and his bride exchanged a quick look, but said nothing.

Gertie continued along the streamside embankment. As they crested a gentle hill, she pointed to a small barn and a wood shed and said, "This piece of land belonged to my late husband's people. They were descended from the Basques."

After another quick glance in the rearview mirror, the old woman added, "I see by the look on your face, you've never heard of a Basque."

"No, Ma'am," Joel replied.

"They were a wandering bunch of sheepherders, especially after being displaced from their homeland in the Great Pyrenees Mountains between France and Spain. Some of them immigrated to the western United States. There are pockets of Basques in Nevada, Idaho, and Wyoming, but my husband's people were among a small handful that settled here in North Dakota."

Gertie parked beside an old wooden outhouse and cut the engine. "If you gotta go, there's no time like the present. The plumbing still works," she added with a wink.

"You drove us out here to look at a toilet?" J. J. twirled his index finger near his temple. "Now, I know you're a half-a-bubble off level, and I've got witnesses!"

The old woman shot O'Shay a look as they all climbed out of the van. "That's only part of it. The rest is just up ahead. Follow me," Gertie said and then led the march along a wall of willows and up a short path. Soon, they approached a vintage sheepherder wagon that was shaded beneath the massive bows of a cottonwood tree. She looked at Joel and Coco and asked, "What do you think?"

Joel was stunned. An antique caravan with no electricity and no running water, except for the pebbled creek that flowed a few yards away, stood in front of them.

Coco raced over to the wagon and threw open the door. Inside, sunlight poured through small dusty windows. "It's perfect!" she gasped as Joel stepped inside, unable to take his eyes off the stained bedroll that had been placed across a platform.

"I'm not sure..."

"No, really!" his bride insisted. "Look at all the storage drawers under the bed and this adorable little kitchen." She lifted an enamel coffee pot that sat on top of a compact wrought-iron stove.

Joel sat down on a bench near a compact, collapsible table. "We should think about this."

Coco didn't seem to hear him. She was busy exploring

the contents of the handcrafted shelves.

"There's no place to wash up," he reasoned. "What about electricity and food storage?"

When Coco turned his way, her face was aglow with excitement. "Oh, that," she said with a little wave of her hand. "We can go to your mom's place to shower and buy a cooler."

Joel offered his bride a hand as she stepped from the wagon.

"It's a very interesting place," Joel told Gertie as they headed back to the van, "but we need to think about it."

"Very sensible," Nora agreed as they discussed the pros and cons.

"Well, I think it's the most adorable place I've ever seen!" Coco countered. "All it needs is a new mattress and a woman's touch."

"It just so happens that someone recently donated a full-sized, pillow-top mattress," O'Shay said as the van rocked over a rut in the dirt road. "It's propped up in the Bargain Bin storage room."

Coco gave her husband a hopeful look, but his thoughts were fixed on more practical issues like a power source for his laptop and iPhone. He remained quiet during the rest of the ride back to town.

After dinner and a homemade dessert, Gertie yawned, excused herself, and headed up to bed. Joel and his bride stayed downstairs to visit with Nora.

Joel was glad to see that the bond between Coco and her new mother-in-law grew deeper with each passing minute, but road weariness was beginning to take its toll. He stood, rolled his neck, and said, "It's been a long day…"

Nora glanced at her watch and exclaimed, "Oh my, is it really after midnight?"

In Joel's old room, his birth mother had placed a new comforter on the bed and brightened the space with a vase of fresh flowers.

"Your mom is so sweet!" Coco said. "I already love her."

Joel smiled, peeled back the sheets, and said, "You're the only one I'm thinking about right now."

A sudden noise rumbled from the room beside the young couple, and then a loud snort and chortle issued from the other side. Ranging from a trumpet to a snort wheeze, the sounds continued through the long night.

Sleep was fitful at best, laden with a variety of strange dreams from a walrus mowing a lawn to a bear sawing wood. At the first light of early morning, Joel awoke to find Coco reading a Bible that had been sitting on the bedside table.

She kissed the tip of her finger and touched her husband's forehead. "Good morning, My Love."

Joel propped his elbow on the pillow and said, "I've been reconsidering that sheepherder wagon…"

North Dakota

Saturday, May 18th

Joel and his bride spent most of the week transforming the caravan into their private, honeymoon oasis.

With the help of a ladder borrowed from J. J. O'Shay, Joel was busy securing a waterproof canvas awing to the bows of the cottonwood tree that shaded a weather-worn picnic table. When he was finished, Joel rolled their grill under the shelter, dumped a pile of charcoal inside, and doused it with fire starter. "I'll be ready for those brauts in about thirty minutes!"

Coco threw open the door of the sheepherder wagon and stood on the narrow landing above the steps. "Come see what I've done!"

Wearing her red bandana and loose-fitting layered t-shirt, she reminded Joel of an exotic gypsy girl.

Inside, the tiny space smelled of pine and wood cleaners. All the cobwebs and dust were gone.

"It looks really nice," Joel said.

Coco smiled. "Thanks to your mom." She drew her husband's attention to the cheerful bedding on the pillow-top mattress. Nora had encouraged her new daughter-in-law to select curtains, throw pillows, and any other decorations she wanted from the Bargain Bin.

The little window behind the bed was now adorned with off-white curtains that cast a glow of warm light. Coco pointed to the large throw pillows she had placed on either side of the window. "I figure that would be a good space to read or just hang out."

"That too." Joel punctuated the sentiment with a tender kiss.

"You've got a one-track mind." Coco redirected her husband's gaze to the shelves that were now stocked with canned goods, jars filled with grains and pasta, and a few decorative tins. Directly below, on a blue gingham table cloth, Coco had placed a glass vase with a yellow-silk rose.

Joel took Coco into his arms and pressed his lips close

to her ear. "There are no words to tell you how much I love you…"

"Anybody home?"

The startled couple opened the door to find Nora, Gertie, and J. J. O'Shay wandering up the path lugging some shopping bags.

"We come bearing gifts!" Gertie hollered.

"I had a little solar charger rattling around my closet," J. J. said. "With the adapters, you can charge both your phones and a laptop."

"Sweet!" Joel said. "That'll come in handy!"

Coco invited the women inside to admire her decorating while Joel took advantage of J. J.'s muscle. Together, they centered the picnic table under the awning.

Soon, the coals were ready for the brauts, so Joel invited everyone to stay for lunch.

O'Shay chuckled and rubbed his belly. "I've never been one to turn down a free meal!"

After admiring the homey touches to the sheepherder wagon, Nora and Gertie helped Coco set the picnic table with a brand new set of dishes and cutlery. There were other gifts for the newlyweds, too. Gertie brought some of her handmade dishtowels, and J. J. gave the couple a solar shower that he said was left over from his hippy days.

"All you have to do is fill it from the stream. The sun and gravity do the rest," O'Shay explained.

"Well, I've never heard of such a thing!" Gertie bristled. "These kids would have to be nudists to go in for that sort of nonsense."

"I've got the perfect solution," Nora said. "Somebody

just dropped off one of those antique shower rings. Add a new curtain and problem solved!"

"Lunch is ready," Joel announced as he placed the sizzling sausages on the buns.

Beating a fast path to the picnic table, J. J. said, "Ketchup, mustard, pickle relish, chips, and beef brauts! What more could a man want?"

Joel exchanged a longing look with his wife, and the corners of her mouth curled into a subtle smile. "What more indeed?" he said.

They bowed their heads, asked a blessing, and then watched J. J. attack his food.

"Slow down, you big Huckleberry!" Gertie admonished. "The good Lord gave you teeth so you could use them."

"How are you coming on the speech for your father's memorial service?" Nora asked.

"It's not really a speech," Joel said. "They just want me to say a few words."

Nora reached across the table and touched her son's hand. "It's going to be a tough day, so I want you to know that I'll be praying…"

The solemn silence that punctuated the moment was broken when an odd-shaped vehicle rolled into view. Pocked with primer and rivets, it looked like a cross between a military Humvee and a rusty Range Rover. The driver slowed down long enough to take a hard look through heavily tinted windows at the gathering. Suddenly, the vehicle jerked forward, sped up the dirt road, and disappeared over the hill.

"What in the world was that?" Coco asked.

J. J. poked Gertie in the ribs and said, "I see you

neglected to mention their crazy neighbor."

The old woman snorted and shot O'Shay a disapproving look. "Sergeant Rudd. He's harmless. A little eccentric is all!"

"Is he ex-military?" Joel asked.

"No, just a sad case who thinks he's fighting world war three! His elevator doesn't go to the top if you ask me," J. J. said and then shoved another bite into his mouth.

"No one asked you!" Gertie turned to the newlyweds to explain. "His mother named him Sergeant, but that's about all that woman ever gave him. Poor Mr. Rudd has had a hard life. He prefers to keep to himself, that's all."

"Just don't go near his bunker." O'Shay wiped a dribble of ketchup from his chin. "Word is he's got the place rigged with booby traps and is stockpiling weapons of mass destruction!"

Joel rose from the picnic table and stared up the road. "What kind of bunker?"

"Rudd's built himself a wall of shipping containers. No telling what's behind them," J. J. said.

"That's enough, you big Huckleberry!" Gertie barked. "You're gonna scare these young folks with all your foolish talk."

"I'm not worried," Coco said cheerfully. "Does anybody want seconds?"

Chapter 22

New York

Friday, May 24th

"I don't like leaving you at a time like this," Brody said as they pulled up to La Guardia Airport.

"We'll be fine," Paige reassured her husband. "Detective Rowland said he's following a lead."

Brody popped the trunk on his BMW and retrieved his travel bag. "I'd still feel better going to North Dakota if there wasn't some deranged madman stalking my family."

Paige kissed his cheek. "It's important that you attend Thomas Atwood's Memorial and the Presidential Library Dedication. Don't worry. We live in a high security building, and you'll only be gone a few days?"

Slipping through the airport doors, her husband looked back and waved. Paige waited until he was out of sight and then pulled away from the curb. The truth was she did feel uneasy. They were being watched by someone who had been able to sneak into her son's school!

Paige jumped when her cell phone rang. She glanced at

the screen. It was the Manhattan Precinct calling. "Hello."

"Mrs. Hays, this is Detective Rowland. I think we may have apprehended a suspect. Can you come in for a lineup?"

"Of course! I'll be right there." Paige hung up, called her neighbor to ask if Connor could stay through dinner, and then headed straight to the police station.

Once there, time seemed to drag as Paige waited hopefully for an end to her nightmare. Finally, she was led into a room to look through a one-way mirror.

"Do you recognize any of these men?" Detective Rowland asked.

Paige stared at their features searching for familiarity. Other than the green ball caps worn by all the men, she was uncertain. A lump formed in her throat. "I only saw him once."

"Take your time Mrs. Hays," the detective pressed.

Unable to contain her frustration, Paige snapped. "I want that monster caught more than anybody, but I just can't be certain!" She offered an apologetic look. "I'm sorry. I know that you're doing the best you can."

"I understand." Rowland signaled to a guard, and the men filed from the lineup. "We'll keep turning over stones."

Paige's hands felt clammy as her mind replayed the stalker's psychological games. "Why Connor?" she asked. "I mean, he's just a boy. What would possess someone to steal a backpack and then terrorize a child with its contents?"

"Sometimes a person's logic gets twisted."

"As in deranged?" Paige felt herself go cold.

"All we really know is that the perpetrator is trying to intimidate you," the detective said carefully. "His motive and intention remain unclear, so until we catch this guy, a little extra caution is warranted."

It was almost dark when Paige left the precinct. For the first time since this awful ordeal began, she felt raw fear. *Who is this mysterious stalker, and what does he want?* A few months ago, Paige would have called her pastor and asked for prayer, but now, even the church had changed. *Nothing makes sense anymore.*

In the parking lot, Paige approached the BMW, opened her purse, and grabbed her keys.

Suddenly, footsteps slapped from behind. In the dusky light, Paige saw a blur of green just before something cracked across her skull. In pain, she dropped to her knees and squeezed the panic button on her key fob. The shadowy figure jerked her satchel from her arms and bolted off as the shrill sound of the car alarm sliced through the evening air.

The next thing Paige remembered was Detective Rowland and some uniformed officers standing over her. "Are you okay, Mrs. Hays? How many fingers am I holding up?"

Arizona

Friday, May 24th

The sun had set an hour ago, but David's eyes were on an eerie glow emanating from the south of Arroyo Seco. *Something's wrong,* he thought and went outside to investigate. As he stepped onto the General Store porch, a soft breeze carried the answer. *Smoke!*

"I think there might be a fire at the CBG compound," he

yelled through the screen door. "I'm going to check it out!"

"I'll call 911. Be careful!" Elita cried out as her husband raced for their old pickup truck.

Bumping down the dirt road that led to the compound, David could see thick columns of smoke billowing from the old mission that was now used as a bunkhouse by the members of the CBG. As he got closer, it erupted into an inferno! Beyond the chain link fence, David spotted flames through the Quonset hut windows. The Civic Border Guard headquarters was on fire, too!

Suddenly, a movement in the headlights of the truck caught his attention. David swerved hard, jammed on his brakes, and barely missed a human form.

Gordon Spitzer hobbled toward him.

"What's happening?" David called to him.

"Mutiny, that's what!" Spitzer said as he climbed into the cab of the pickup. "We got word that the ATF was arriving tomorrow to register our inventory. I tried to reason with the boys, but those darned fools said they'd rather burn the whole place down than let the government have its way. They built a huge bonfire out back to melt all the guns, and then they piled all the ammo in the middle of the hut, stacked furniture on top, and torched that too!" Spitzer removed his fishing cap and wiped beads of sweat from his scalp. He looked old and tired in the eerie glow of the blaze. "After setting fire to the that old historic building, all the boys drove off and left me behind, yelling, 'Mission's over!'"

"Help is on the way," David said. "In the meantime, maybe there's something we can do."

Spitzer shook his head, pointed to the Quonset hut and

said, "That building has a thick coat of spray-on insulation. When the flames reach the ceiling, it'll be too late. Besides, you don't want to be anywhere near when that pile of ammo starts to cook off!"

David turned the truck around and drove a safe distance from the CBG compound.

Sounding defeated, Gordon said, "Pull over here. We need to warn the emergency response units about the danger."

David backed onto a dirt road, and they watched the scene unfold. The metal building glowed orange and began to sag. It didn't take long for the structure to collapse into a heap of red liquid.

Soon, the sound of firetruck sirens screamed closer, washing the dark landscape with strobing red lights. From the CBG compound, projectiles flashed across the night sky like fireworks!

In a few short hours, Gordon Spitzer's life work was burned to the ground while everyone stood by helplessly and watched.

New York

Saturday, May 25th

The telephone was ringing. Paige opened her eyes, rolled over, and grabbed the receiver on her bedside table. "Hello," she said weakly.

"Are you okay?" Brody sounded concerned. "I tried your office, and Jewel said that you left a message saying you were sick."

Paige sat up. Her head was racked with pain as she touched the goose egg on her scalp. "Maybe a touch of the flu, that's all." *No sense worrying him,* she told herself. *The details about the assault will keep.* "So, how was your trip?"

"The usual red-eye flight," he said. "You wouldn't believe the turnout here in Minot. The Presidential Library Committee blocked an entire hotel just to accommodate Atwood's former staff and cabinet. We'll be traveling over to Delmont in the morning on chartered buses. They're expecting that little town to be one massive parking lot. It's refreshing to know that so many people still respect Thomas Atwood."

"Will you extend my condolences?"

"Of course." He paused. "Feel better soon. I love you."

After hanging up, Paige slipped on her robe and padded down the hall to check on her son. Connor, who would ordinarily be in school by now, was still sleeping soundly.

Paige's protective instinct surged as she made her way downstairs. With a violent stalker on the loose, she wasn't going to take any chances with her child's safety. From the built-in desk in the open-concept family room, Paige reached for her cell phone, only to recall that it had been in the satchel that her attacker had ripped from her hands. Anger welled in her bosom as she thumbed through the massive Manhattan phone book. Her finger stopped on the listing for the Tyler Brentwood School, and she dialed using their land line.

"This is Mrs. Hays. Connor won't be in for a few days. In the interim, I'll be sending a courier to collect his assignments."

"If this has anything to do with the recent lunchroom incident, I want to assure you we've taken steps to elevate security."

"It's a personal matter," Paige said. And it was! The perpetrator's actions were escalating. His next move was anyone's guess. ·

Chapter 23

North Dakota

Sunday, May 26th

Joel and Coco stood outside the new Presidential Library admiring the architecture. It was graced by gently sloping rooflines and stonewalls designed to complement the North Dakota countryside. The front of the building consisted of floor-to-ceiling windows that reflected the quilt-like patches of the surrounding farmland.

Wearing a stunning gold suit with matching pumps, a woman approached the young couple with purpose. Her hair, swept up and lacquered, didn't budge in the breeze coming off the Great Plains.

It was the moment that Joel had dreaded, and he felt his ears go hot. *What does former First Lady Heddy Atwood think of her husband's illegitimate son? Does she blame me for the assassination?*

She stood looking reflectively at the building before she turned to the couple and said, "Thomas wanted his Presidential Library to be unpretentious."

"It reminds me of him—quiet, solid, and unwavering," Joel replied.

"I've looked forward to meeting you for some time. Your father was very proud of you." She smiled at her husband's only child before turning to Coco to offer an equally warm greeting.

"I'm sorry that things turned out this way," Joel said with a suddenness he hadn't intended.

The former First Lady nodded. Tears brimmed briefly in her eyes, but she steeled her emotions as a man approached. "Joel and Coco, I'd like to introduce you to Brody Hays. He served in the White House as your father's Chief Economic Advisor."

Brody reached out for a brisk handshake and added, "Thomas Atwood was a great man."

"You're the one with a little boy that knows Zeke," Joel said and then added, "My Dad told me the whole incredible story."

"Yes, I have a son, Connor. He's twelve now," Brody replied as his gaze followed another string of busses rolling into the parking lot like train cars.

"Please, excuse me," Heddy said, "but I must head inside and prepare to greet our guests."

Brody Hays offered his arm and escorted the First Lady back to the Presidential Library.

"She's lovely," Coco said as men dressed in silk suits and women adorned in dark finery emerged from the charter buses to pay their respects to the late Commander in Chief. "What's the story about the little boy and Zeke?"

"It's complicated." Joel reflected on his incredible

journey with the mysterious old man. "Someday, I'll tell you about my road trip with Zeke, but this is not the right time," he said as they fell in among the throngs.

The crowd was directed to the garden out back, a simple landscape, where the memorial service was to be held.

After offering their condolences to the former First Lady, who stood near the back door, the guests were led to their seats by ushers.

Lastly, Heddy Atwood took her place beside Joel and Coco who, at her request, had been seated with the family.

A few yards in front of them, Thomas Atwood's body lay in state.

Finally, the service began with the mournful wail of a cello. Joel glanced skyward, almost as if he was expecting to see the musician playing in the clouds.

With her back to the onlookers, Heddy allowed a tear to escape. The late morning sun caught it glimmering as it rolled down her cheek.

Joel swallowed hard, but the bitter taste of guilt was on his tongue. *If only I hadn't asked Dad to come to Berkeley... If only we had never met...*

Heddy Atwood reached out with a gloved hand and squeezed Joel's fingers. "It wasn't your fault," she whispered as the music played. "God is in control."

A reverent silence settled over the crowd when a man of the cloth stepped to the podium. "Many who are here today are unaware that our former President was a man of deep faith." The pastor lowered his eyes to an open book and continued.

"This is Thomas Atwood's Bible. Its pages are well worn and the binding is bent, but there is one chapter that is particularly dog eared. I am told that Psalm 139 was one of Thomas Atwood favorite passages." The man paused, and then he began to read.

"O LORD, you have examined my heart and know
everything about me.
You know when I sit down or stand up.
You know my thoughts even when I'm far away.
You see me when I travel and when I rest at home.
You know everything I do.
You know what I am going to say even before I say
it, LORD.
You go before me and follow me.
You place your hand of blessing on my head.
Such knowledge is too wonderful for me, too great
for me to understand!
I can never escape from your Spirit!
I can never get away from your presence!
If I go up to Heaven, you are there; if I go down to
the grave, you are there.
If I ride the wings of the morning, if I dwell by the
farthest oceans, even there your hand will guide me,
and your strength will support me.
I could ask the darkness to hide me and the light
around me to become night— but even in darkness
I cannot hide from you.
To you the night shines as bright as day.
Darkness and light are the same to you.
You made all the delicate, inner parts of my body
and knit me together in my mother's womb.
Thank you for making me so wonderfully complex!

Your workmanship is marvelous—how well I know it.
You watched me as I was being formed in utter seclusion, as I was woven together in the dark of the womb.
You saw me before I was born.
Every day of my life was recorded in your book.
Every moment was laid out before a single day had passed."
    —Psalms 139:1-16 NLT

Then the pastor laid the Bible down and motioned for Joel to come forward. He introduced him as the late President's son and then stepped to the side.

Joel clutched the podium and silently battled nerves as he looked across the rows of people who had come to pay their respects. *This is the least I can do for my father,* he thought and then summoned his courage.

"I was conflicted when I was asked to speak about my father," he began, "because many of you had the benefit of knowing Thomas Atwood much longer than I. What can I possibly say that you haven't already witnessed? Would I tell you that he was a man of integrity, who stood strong during a time of national crisis? That he was a selfless soul who carried the truth even in the face of social slander and vitriol? Would it be a revelation to any of you if I said that that Thomas Atwood had the courage to speak out against the current political trends? No, I think that all who truly knew my father understand that he was a man of conviction who cared deeply about the path we're on. Thomas Atwood died with a warning on his lips. Let us all pray that he did not die in vain!" Joel let the words settle over the silent sea of faces. "Though I am not the man that Thomas Atwood was, I can tell you this. Somehow, I will strive to carry on my father's legacy by speaking out against a cultural tide that threatens our country." Joel stepped down from the podium, and to his surprise, the former First Lady stood and began to clap. The crowd followed her lead, and feeling overwhelmed by the response, he sank into his chair.

The pastor returned with a heartfelt petition from 2 Chronicles 7:14, "Then if my people who are called by my name will humble themselves and pray and seek my face and turn from their wicked ways, I will hear from Heaven and will forgive their sins and restore their land."

"Sometimes I think that our nation can't turn back now, that we've gone too far," Joel whispered into Coco's ear.

"Then why did God put such a fire in your heart?" Coco replied.

Two uniformed soldiers stepped forward to fold the flag that had been draped across the casket. After presenting it to the former First Lady, they accompanied her back into the presidential library.

In front of onlookers, Heddy Atwood placed the American flag into a glass case and handed it to a volunteer. The gesture signaled that the dedication was officially underway.

Inside the Thomas Atwood Memorial Library, guests milled around glass-encased artifacts unique to the late President's term. The walls were lined with words of wisdom spoken by the President, along with displays of mementoes reminding visitors of Thomas Atwood's numerous humanitarian contributions to the country's heart and soul, such as the farm aid that was extended to the drought-ravaged areas.

An entire wing had been dedicated to the act of war that had become known as the Third Peril. There was the tail section of the Canadian fighter jet that crashed in North Dakota, ironically, into the yard of Joel's birth mother. There was a piece of the nuclear submarine that leveled Norfolk, Virginia, and the surrounding Hampton Roads area. Also on display was a go-kit carried by a cabinet member who had been sequestered at a Continuity of Operations Site during the war.

Along the walls were framed satellite images of the invasion in progress, including the US Navy battle group as they were ambushed in the Formosa Straights. Some visitors settled onto bench seats to watch a video of the President's heartfelt address to the wounded nation; others lingered nearby as Thomas Atwood solemnly expressed his resolve for justice along with grief for all who had lost their lives.

After the tour, Joel took his bride by the hand and navigated toward the food buffet. There, he loaded his plate with delicacies while Coco admired an ice sculpture that was centered on the linen-covered table.

Staring up at the clear image of an American eagle, she said, "Look at those details! How can an artist put so much work into something knowing that it's just going to melt?"

"This food is going to disappear fast if you don't get a plate." Joel bit into a smoked-salmon canapé and was still chewing when two men approached.

A short, billiard-ball-shaped man, wearing a maroon jacket with an emblem, thrust out his sweaty palm for a handshake and said, "My name is Sam Quince, Chairman of the Thomas Atwood Foundation, and this is Harold Dansforth, Director of the National Archives and Records Administration."

A knock-kneed, Lincolnesque man looked down on the young couple, blinked his droopy eyelids, and said, "The pleasure is all mine." He made a few feeble attempts at small talk before excusing himself.

Sam Quince lingered, awkwardly rocking back and forth on his sensible shoes. "Young Man, I like what you said during your father's service. Something tells me you've got a lot more to say, so I would like to make a proposition."

"Oh?"

The round man's head bobbed up and down. "Here at the Library, our board has been discussing the creation of a blog. More to the point, I feel that you would be the perfect person to spearhead the project."

Setting his plate down, Joel asked, "What would I be expected to do?"

"Analyze current political actions, policies, cultural trends, and such. You would, of course, receive a salary." When Mr. Quince was met by silence, he raised an eyebrow. "I assume you meant what you said about carrying on your father's legacy?"

Arizona

Monday, May 27th

"Are you sure that you heard correctly?" David asked his wife Elita.

"I couldn't believe it either! Imagine Gordon Spitzer staying at Hope Springs!" Elita squirted ketchup in the shape of a smiley face on Joy's hamburger, added a handful of cheese puffs, and called her little girl to the lunch counter. "After all the horrible things he's said about those people, they've welcomed him with open arms. It's a miracle if you ask me!"

Those were the same words that Elita had used over six years ago when David was exonerated from a legal malpractice charge. His thoughts drifted to past unexplainable events, from Rupert Sims to Zeke and, finally, to the chance jailhouse encounter with Alberto Vega that helped deflect an invasion across the Mexican border. Looking back now, David realized that these mysterious divine appointments had formed a fissure that began to fracture the bedrock of his atheist beliefs. Still, questions remained to shake his new-found faith. *Where was God*, David wondered, *when my little niece, Emily, died tragically in my arms? And what about my stillborn son?*

The telephone rang, stirring David from his thoughts. He strode across the wood floor of the General Store to the counter and saw his sister's number illuminated on the caller ID. He plucked the receiver from the cradle. "I was just thinking about you. How is everything?"

"It's been better," she began. "I'm a bit under the weather."

"Nothing serious, I hope."

"Just a slight concussion, but Brody's on his way home after attending the Thomas Atwood Memorial." Paige drew in a deep breath. "How are you all doing after…"

"Elita takes flowers to the grave almost daily," David said quietly, so Elita would not hear. "She cries a lot when she thinks no one is looking."

"And you?"

David swallowed hard, but said nothing.

Paige gracefully changed the subject. "Listen, I'm calling about an article I just read in the New York Times. Your name is mentioned."

He laughed.

"David, I'm not kidding."

"Let me guess—it's something to do with the NAC Treaty."

"No, this is something else."

On the other end of the line, David could hear the sound of a newspaper rustling.

"Have you ever heard of a freelance writer named Beck McGuire?"

David leaned against the counter. "I can only imagine the lies that man has written about Hope Springs."

"He calls the residents 'a controlling fringe sect' and names you as the executor." Paige hesitated. "I'll email you the story, but by now, it's all over the wire. I'm afraid this piece was picked up by the AP."

Not long after they said goodbye, the article popped into David's email inbox. It read as a scandalous exposé filled with spiteful and damning insinuations. Beck described the residents of Hope Springs as a ridged cult of religious bigots who were squandering and polluting natural resources. The punchline of the article named David Fillmore as the group's executor who regularly turned a blind eye to their anti-government practices.

Such utter nonsense! Beck McGuire is a vindictive liar! David was busy formulating a legal response when a stranger walked through the door of the General Store.

"Are you David Fillmore?" The man straightened his tie and slipped some papers from the pocket of his suit jacket. "My name is Morgan Sawyer. I am from the Internal Revenue Service, and I'd like to ask you a few questions."

"What's this about?"

The agent leveled a stone-cold look at David and said, "Your fiduciary tax return for the Rupert Sims Trust and Hope Springs is being audited."

Chapter 24

New York

Tuesday, May 28ᵗʰ

Paige checked on her son who was sleeping soundly. Ever since their visit to the cathedral of Saint John the Divine, Connor's bad dreams had turned into night terrors. The boy had been deeply affected by the images on the church columns, especially the one depicting huge waves of water crashing over skyscrapers. Paige brushed a strand of red hair from her son's forehead and whispered a prayer before returning to the family room.

It was past 11:00 P.M., and Brody should have called by now. His plane was scheduled to land an hour ago.

Feeling restless, Paige made herself some chamomile tea and settled on the couch to thumb through a magazine. Something caught her ear, and she sat upright.

The sound was coming from the penthouse door. Someone was fiddling with the lock! Fear, bordering on terror, caused a shudder to run down Paige's spine, and her heart began to pound. "Who's there?" she called. When the door opened, she felt a rush of relief.

Brody set his suitcase down just inside the entryway and held out his arms as Paige rushed to greet him.

"How did you get here?"

"Have you ever heard of a taxi?" Brody teased. "They love to hang around La Guardia."

"I expected you to call."

"You've been under the weather, so I didn't want to bother you." He leaned in for a kiss and added, "I missed you."

The tenderness of the moment made Paige feel ashamed of her deception. "Honey, something happened while you were gone..."

Brody's concern turned to alarm as she told him about being attacked by the stalker. "You could have been killed!" he exploded.

"But I wasn't."

Brody began to pace the penthouse family room. "Why didn't you tell me about this on the phone?"

"Because I knew that you would catch the next flight home." Paige positioned herself in front of her husband and laid her hands on his shoulders. "Honey, Detective Rowland is looking into the attack, Building Security has been notified, and Connor's school has posted a guard."

"Maybe so, but until they catch this madman, we are not going to take any chances. I'm hiring a driver for you and Connor."

Paige didn't argue. The incident at the Tyler Brentwood School followed by the assault had left her rattled. The terror was escalating!

When Brody's cell phone began to ring, he seemed annoyed by the intrusion. "Whoever it is can wait until morning."

As they headed for bed, a voicemail message came in.

"Maybe it's important," Paige said.

Brody removed his jacket, loosened his tie, and checked his phone. "It's Katrina Katz. What does she want at this late hour?"

"I thought the goal was for her to end all contact with you," Paige muttered as her husband listened to the voicemail. The expression on Brody's face raised an alarm. It was a look that she hadn't seen since he worked in the White House with the Atwood Administration. "Is something wrong?"

Brody put his phone on the charger and went into the bathroom. Paige followed him and stood by as he splashed water on his face. His reflection in the mirror was grim. He rubbed a towel over his graying five-o'clock shadow and then said, "It's probably nothing to worry about, but Katrina's computer was hacked this evening. The IT Department reports that her email was breeched along with the story she's been working on, the one about Alistair Dormin and the World Fortress Institute. Jean Pierre and the World Fortress Institute have always done Dormin's bidding and they work quietly in the background to advance Dormin's agenda."

"So, someone hacks into a reporter's computer and steals a story," Paige reasoned. "They would have to expose themselves to go public with it. Besides, you work for Hensley Capital. What can Dormin do to you?"

Brody fell into a brooding silence as they readied themselves for bed. "That's a good question," he said just before turning out the light.

North Dakota

Monday, June 3rd

Feeling Coco's warmth beside him, Joel awakened with the first light of dawn. Staring at the shadows of morning sunlight advancing across the arched ceiling of the sheepherder wagon, he wished he had not agreed to meet with Sam Quince to discuss a job. *What did he call the position? Policy Analyst—that's it!* In the shadow of his late father, Joel's insecurities were multiplied. *What could I possibly say that would interest anyone?* He slipped out from under the comforter and felt the cold plank floor under his bare feet.

Quietly, he opened one of the built-in drawers under the platform bed and began to dress. *What does a blogger wear?* he wondered, and then he chose his best blue jeans, a button down shirt, and a pair of loafers.

Coco arched her back and stretched beneath the covers, stirring fresh memories of the soft feel of her skin against his. She opened her dark green eyes and smiled. "Why didn't you wake me up?"

"What? And disturb my sleeping beauty?" Joel loaded the sheepherder stove firebox, struck a match, and put it to the kindling.

Coco, wearing an oversized lacrosse jersey, climbed down from the bed. She rubbed goosebumps on her skinny arms and shimmied into a pair of leggings. "A good wife would make breakfast for her husband on his first day at work."

"Who told you that? Your mother?" Joel regretted his words as soon as they left his mouth. He watched his wife turn pensive.

"Mom sent me a text yesterday. She told me that Dad's health has declined rapidly since I abandoned him." Coco chewed her lip. "Maybe I should go home for a visit."

Joel's thoughts flashed to the promise that he had made to Mr. Trent regarding his daughter. "That's not a good idea!" Coco looked shocked by her husband's emphatic response. "I'm sure your father is fine," he added. "Besides, you've only been gone a few weeks. Maybe you and he can Skype or something."

"You're probably right. Still…, I worry." A familiar look of guilt shadowed her brow.

Joel grabbed a griddle and placed it on the stove. "How about some French toast?"

Coco's mood lightened, and she volunteered to retrieve the supplies from the cooler that they kept underneath the wagon.

After whisking eggs in a bowl and adding cinnamon, nutmeg, and a splash of canned milk, Joel was ready for the next step. He dipped several slices of bread and dropped them onto the sizzling griddle.

"What are you going to call your blog?" Coco asked as the smell of breakfast filled their cozy love nest.

"Beyond the Fall," Joel said as he flipped the French toast. "When my Dad gave his speech at UC Berkeley, he warned us that our country was headed over a precipice."

"I like it!"

Joel sprinkled powdered sugar on the toast, handed Coco her plate, and together they headed outside to the picnic table to enjoy the cool morning air. "Now, I need to come up with a topic to write about."

"You'll think of something." Coco smiled as she used her fork to cut through the toast. Her face looked sublime as she fixed her gaze on cornrows swaying in the gentle breeze. "It is so peaceful here."

Suddenly their quiet moment was shattered by a hail of gunfire!

"What was that?" she shrieked.

"Sounds like our neighbor, Sergeant Rudd."

"Well, I think it's rude!" Coco's eyes flashed with anger. "How do we know that he's not shooting toward us? As far as I'm concerned, the sooner the government does something about guns the better!"

Joel shook his head emphatically. "You don't know what you're talking about. The Second Amendment is explicit about our right to own firearms, and it is intended to safeguard citizens against government oppression."

Coco parked her hands on her hips and scowled. "I doubt that our founding fathers envisioned a country full of gun-toting, paranoid, militia types!"

"If we compromise the Second Amendment, what comes next? The right to free speech?"

Joel's wife seemed stunned by her husband's position. "After watching your father being shot, I thought you, of all people, would be against guns!"

Joel bristled. "Thomas Atwood died defending our nation's freedoms, and I swore to carry on his legacy." He paused and added, "I believe I've just found a subject for my first blog post."

Arizona

Monday, June 3rd

David found the documentation he was looking for in the back room of the General Store and carried it to the lunch counter.

Elita was making a batch of potato salad at her workstation, and Joy was playing happily with some plastic animals.

David sat down on a stool, emptied a file box onto the counter, and began to sort its contents.

"Hey, you'd better leave some room for the lunch crowd," Elita warned. She glanced at the wall clock and noted it was nearly 11:30. A.M.

"This shouldn't take long." David shuffled through papers. "It's all here—everything I need to get the IRS off my back and prove my fiduciary integrity regarding Hope Springs. I am getting these documents in the mail today, so that this tax case can be closed."

Elita stopped dicing potatoes and turned to her husband. "I still don't understand how Beck McGuire can get away with writing those lies." She slipped into the walk-in cooler and returned with a new jar of mayonnaise. "Isn't there a law against that kind of thing?"

"Yes, but in order to make a case for slander, you have to prove damages. I'd say that his motives have more to do with character than journalistic integrity. Beck McGuire calls his hatchet job an 'editorial.' Different codes of conduct apply to opinion pieces and editorials."

"Do you mean to say that editorials don't have to be fact checked?"

"That's right. Even liars have the right to free speech. Unfortunately, once something appears in print, most people believe it is true." David organized his papers and was returning them to the file box when Kay Bales arrived looking anxious.

Her honey-brown eyes locked on David, and she rushed across the room saying, "We've got problems out at Hope Springs, and some of the guys sent me to get you."

"What's going on?"

"There are a couple of men from the regional EPA office poking around the place this morning." A strand of mousy-brown hair had fallen from Kay's ponytail, and she threaded it behind her ear. "They seem to think that Hope Springs is in violation of the Clean Water Act!"

Elita wiped her hands on a towel. "What in the world is going on?"

Kay shook her head. "Those EPA guys said that we need to comply with their regulations or face stiff penalties. In the meantime, our drinking water is off limits."

David shoved the rest of his IRS documentation back into the file box and told Elita not to hold dinner. *More backlash from Beck McGuire's piece*, he told himself as he followed Kay out the door. *There's no telling where this will end...*

Chapter 25

Arizona

Saturday, June 8th

It was gearing up to be another beautiful day in the Arizona desert. The Mexican poppies, though past their peak, formed pops of gold against a backdrop of layered rock formations.

Just over a gentle mesa, Elita drew in a sharp breath as nearly forty acres of vibrant green Timothy grass and hay came into view. The contrast was startling, like an oasis among the muted Sonoran landscape.

"First one to see the cows!" Joy announced as she bounced in her big-girl car seat. "I win!" she declared with a clap of her hands.

David drove between fields where black and white Holsteins were grazing among the pigs, goats, and free-range chickens. On the other side of the milking barn, they spotted a corral full of sheep ready for sheering.

The old pickup rolled down the rutted road past the eclectic mix of Hope Springs dwellings, from massive RVs to tiny tear-drop campers. There were bus conversions and wall tents, all with homey touches and gardens. "Wow, I can't believe how fast the fruit trees are growing!" Elita leaned out the truck window to get a better look at the greenery planted on either side of the residential road. "It's a good thing the EPA ban doesn't affect their drip system. Just imagine having to water all this with buckets." She looked at her husband and added, "I know you've told me about their water delivery system, but I've never been able to wrap my brain around it."

"They planted those trees downhill from their homes and dug trenches to make use of the gray water from each camper," David explained. "They got the idea from an ancient system developed by the Persians that uses gravity and conserves water in one of the world's driest places. All the water from Hope Springs flows through generators to produce electricity as it comes out of two reservoirs. After that, it is divided into two channels. One fills cisterns that feed the lines that deliver drinking water to the campsites. The other is diverted for use near the pavilion, such as cooking, washing dishes, and the solar shower hut. The waste water from the pavilion is then channeled down to the barn and corrals to supply the irrigation sprinklers, greenhouses, and livestock tanks."

"The first half is what the EPA shut down, right?"

"Actually, both—any water used for human consumption," David said with a nod. "But we have to continue to run water through the hydroelectric generators, and we can use wash water that then supplies the downstream non-human uses. The whole system was brilliantly designed to make use of every drop of water."

"I sure hope this meeting goes as well, and this situation

gets cleared up as quickly as that IRS audit did. Thank goodness that's behind us!" Elita said as they parked alongside a government vehicle.

As they neared the pavilion, it became obvious that the whole community had turned out for the inspection. Jim Saunders waved at the young family and explained, "I was just telling Agent Potts about the new cold-storage facility. The whole thing works through evaporative cooling. Randy designed it, and Travis constructed a springhouse with three-foot adobe walls over the stream that flows from the base of the lower dam. The springhouse has got slotted floors that allow air flow," Jim added. "Anyway, on top, we've added a stovepipe chimney capped with a spinning fan. Right now, we're working on building an adobe cover over forty feet of the stream. This should create a refrigeration tunnel using a convection current to draw air over the water and then up the chimney. Between the chilled temperature of the water and the evaporative effects, we estimate that the springhouse could be as much as thirty degrees cooler than the outside temperature, even on the hottest days."

Agent Potts glanced at his watch. "Yes, well, it's all very fascinating, I'm sure, but as you know, that's not the reason for my visit today."

"Ah, yes," Jim Saunders said. "Water quality!" He led the group up the hill to the spring that fed the first reservoir. "We drilled a special well to be used solely for human consumption purposes." He pointed to the location they chose then pulled a folded paper from his pocket. "Here are some figures you might find interesting. The elevation of the well is above our self-composting toilet, solar showers, and gray water uses down below."

"Saunders here is a handy fellow to have around." Randy Bales slapped a hand across the older man's back. "In fact, he used to work with the Army Corp of Engineers."

"Oh?" Mr. Potts raised his eyebrows as he studied the paper. "May I keep this?"

"By all means," Jim said as the EPA agent slipped the figures into his vest pocket.

The agent then unzipped his field satchel, produced a testing kit, and proceeded to collect samples of water into a couple of small beakers. With a dropper, he added some chemicals, swirled the vials, and waited. A few seconds later, a fleeting look of disappointment flashed across the bureaucrat's face. "Well, gentlemen, it appears that you have met EPA requirements," he said, returning his testing tools to their case. "I will, however, have to perform periodic compliance inspections."

The men invited the Field Rep to join them for lunch, but he declined and briskly walked off toward his vehicle.

"Drive cheerfully!" Randy called as they watched Mr. Potts pull away.

"That went smoothly!" Jim Saunders announced when they joined the others back at the pavilion and gave them all the thumbs up sign.

After a round of hoots and cheers, Kay Bales clapped her hands together and said to the group, "It's time to celebrate!" She directed everyone's attention to a table spread with homegrown delicacies: barbecued chicken legs, fresh baked cornbread, and apple fritters.

After a prayer of thanksgiving, the friends and neighbors

fell into the buffet line.

Soothed by the aroma of comfort food and the sound of children laughing, David felt peace as he inched along the chow line with the others. Finally, as everyone settled beneath the communal pavilion, they all broke bread together, like one big extended family.

Even Gordon Spitzer, who had once derided the Hope Springs crowd as a bunch of religious nuts, seemed at home. He sat chatting with Mr. Mike, no doubt discussing the latest electronic innovation.

After lunch, Raymond Lee had just begun picking his acoustic guitar when the former Civic Border Guard Leader hobbled over and interrupted the music. "Hey, everybody, can we have your attention?" Gordon waited a moment then raised the musician's microphone to his lips. "I've been having an interesting talk with Mr. Mike over here. It seems he's been picking up some interesting chatter on his ham radio." Spitzer's voice conveyed a sense of urgency. "As you all know, the US Government has recently relaxed the requirements for work visas for our North American neighbors, and we are now aware that there is a mass gathering of migrant workers gearing up to cross the Mexican Border."

"Isn't that a good thing?" Sue Brewster blurted with uncharacteristic brazenness. She quickly averted her gaze and apologized, "I didn't mean to interrupt… Sorry." A flush of crimson spread across her chubby cheeks.

"She's got a point," Bonnie Saunders agreed. "At least, those poor women and children don't have to risk being robbed by criminals or abandoned in the desert anymore."

Looking mildly annoyed, Gordon adjusted his fishing

cap. "Go ahead, take the Pollyanna approach that all those bleeding-heart spin doctors have been peddling to the public, but mark my words, things are about to change around here. What about drug runners, terrorists, and murderers? Ever think of that?" Spitzer warned as he handed the microphone back to Raymond Lee and hobbled back to his table.

The gathering went quiet for a few moments and then returned to friendly banter.

David spotted Travis Dayton strolling near the gardens with Priscilla. *A good match,* he thought. Travis with his southern pride and chivalry, and Priscilla, a young, single mother whose guarded nature hinted of a scarred past.

It didn't take long for Joy to finish her meal. "Can I go play now?" She waited for her parents' permission and then bolted off with little Hari.

Elita was chatting with Fawn Nash, who was sitting yoga style in loose fitting linen pants and a sleeveless denim shirt.

Cosmo, Fawn's adult offspring, plopped down on the bench across from the women and began to devour his second helping. He ate prison style, hunkered over his meal like it might be snatched away. His long brown dreadlocks nearly touched his plate.

"Boyd!" Fawn shook her head, letting her loose gray braids swing free. "Where're your manners?"

With his cheeks full of fritters, the man-child mumbled something unintelligible and gulped down his bite with a cup of apple cider.

"How many times have I told you? Don't talk with your mouth full!"

Boyd pulled a dirty bare foot onto the bench and began

picking at an ingrown toenail. "My name is Cosmo!"

"Isn't my Boyd a handsome young man?" Fawn crooned and blew him a kiss. "I don't care what you call yourself. You'll always be my baby 'Boyd.'" She stood and waved as her husband's pump truck, called a honey wagon, rolled to a stop in the pavilion parking lot. "Your father's back!"

Ziggy Nash, an aging hippy with long hair that surrounded a shiny scalp dome, ambled over to the food table.

"We've been approved by the EPA!" Fawn yelled. "Now you can wash your hands!" She leaned over to David and Elita and said, "It's such a relief to have access to water again. It's not easy living with a guy who cleans sceptic tanks for a living."

"Hey, people, looks like we've got company!" Gordon Spitzer snapped his fingers and pointed to a vehicle that was winding up the road. "Looks like another Fed, if you ask me."

After parking, a young man stepped from his car and approached the group. He wore ordinary jeans and a plaid shirt, but Gordon Spitzer's instincts proved correct. This man was anything but ordinary.

"My name is Anthony Plume, and I am with the US Fish & Wildlife Service Ecological Services Office in Tucson. I'm here to discuss this development. Our records indicate that there has never been any consultation with the Fish & Wildlife Service about potential impacts on endangered species and other resources under our jurisdiction."

Stepping forward, David asked, "Is there a problem?"

"Sir, if this issue is not resolved, it could result in a violation of Section 7 of the Endangered Species Act and other laws protecting wildlife.

Really?" David couldn't believe what he was hearing. "We weren't aware of these requirements. Are there even any endangered species around here?"

"Oh, yes," said Plume. "There are eleven species protected in this area, including endangered jaguars, ocelots, and the Lesser Long-nosed bats as well as several threatened and candidate species."

"Candidate species!" Spitzer bellowed. "Are those anything like these yahoos who line up to run for president every four years?"

Visibly irritated, Plume pressed on, "The Fish & Wildlife Service also protects 48 migratory bird species, Bald and Golden Eagles, and wetland resources in this part of Arizona."

"Okay," David drew a deep breath and cautioned Spitzer to remain quiet. "Tell me more about what we need to do."

Plume seemed happy to explain. "Basically, you need to work with the local Ecological Services Office to establish whether your activity may result in adverse impacts and, if possible, come up with a conservation plan that will outline ways to mitigate any potential issues. We try to work cooperatively with people, but ignoring these laws can result in prosecution by the US Attorney's Office for Arizona."

David ran his fingers through his thick crop of hair. The whole thing made his eyes glaze over. "I heard you mention 'wetlands.' Do we get any credit for expanding what's here?"

Plume smiled. "Ordinarily, yes. However, since these wetlands have already been created, a plan is now required in order to conserve them. Also, because these new wetlands potentially create habitat for a number of protected species... " He paused to gather his thoughts. "For example, your livestock may attract jaguars and ocelots, therefore, you must create a plan to mitigate potential conflicts with protected species."

"The lunatics have taken control of the asylum now!" Spitzer crowed.

David shot Spitzer another look and turned back to Plume. "How long is this process and how much is it likely to cost?"

The young ecologist rubbed his chin. "A lot depends on your willingness to cooperate and what our biologists have to say. If they believe that potential impacts cannot be mitigated, then there is no telling how long it will take to resolve. On rare occasions, these matters have to be litigated."

"Okay," David said, "let me have your business card, and we will be in touch to initiate this 'consultation.' I think you will find that the people of Hope Springs also want to conserve what they have here."

Plume and David exchanged cards and shook hands, and the people of Hope Springs watched another bureaucrat drive off in a cloud of dust.

"Well, now, I've seen everything!" The spark in Gordon Spitzer's eye was back. "Next, they'll want us to control the dust, too!"

"Let's all relax a little," David said in his most soothing tone, even though he too, was growing frustrated by the recent waves of government intrusion.

New York
Thursday, June 20th

Paige and Connor walked through the door of their Tribeca Apartment, her arms loaded with groceries from the fresh market. "Honey, can you get the door?" she said.

Nearly two weeks had passed since Brody had hired a private driver to chauffeur his wife and son to and from school and work. There had been no sign of the stalker recently, and Paige was beginning to feel as though she was under house arrest. No jogging down near Battery Park, no subway excursions, and no shopping trips.

Connor pushed the door shut behind his mom and dropped his new backpack in the entryway as he made a beeline for the TV in the family room.

"Shouldn't you be practicing your violin?"

The boy scrolled through the channels and then threw himself onto the couch. "I recorded a program on the DVR that I want to see."

Paige placed the bags on the granite counter, but kept a curious eye on the program that had captured her son's attention. Ordinarily, Connor was indifferent to television, but this time, he sat transfixed by a documentary about past natural disasters and the potential for future ones. Some of the footage was disturbing.

"I'm not sure you should be watching this," Paige cautioned as she laid out carrots and onions to chop for a bed for the braised beef bourgeon.

"Why, Mom?" Connor said. "It's only the History Channel."

"I don't want you to have any more nightmares." Anxiety fluttered in Paige's chest as she watched clips of an F-5 tornado slice through an Oklahoma town. Next came a series of earthquakes in Virginia and a freak windstorm known as microburst in Wyoming that snapped a whole forest of lodge pole pines like they were toothpicks. A panel of biologists suggested that dangerous weather patterns and geological events might be a contributing factor in the alarming rise of fish and bird mortalities. When they began to predict the potential for future cataclysmic events, Paige's heart skipped a beat.

Connor shot to his feet and pointed to a computer-simulated projection of a landslide in the Canary Islands. Massive volumes of the island mountainside sluffed into the ocean causing a catastrophic tsunami. "In a matter of hours, New York City could be devastated," the experts warned.

"Honey, you've got a recital coming up. Time to practice!" Paige strode across the family room, grabbed the remote, and turned off the TV.

Soon, the sweet melody of violin music issued from the formal living room, but Paige could not shake her restlessness. She rolled out dough for homemade noodles, ran them through her pasta machine, and set them aside.

The music stopped abruptly, and Connor poked his head through the living room threshold. "Mom, do we have any more violin strings? I broke one."

"Don't you have some spare ones in your case?"

"I used them all."

"Just a minute." Paige made a mental note to pick up more at the music store as she moved to the built-in kitchen desk, where she kept her favorite cookbooks. Paige opened the drawer and rummaged among the clutter. No matter how many times she organized the space, it always ended up being a catchall of pens, notes, and various items. "Ah, ha! We're in luck!" She found an unopened package of violin strings and tossed it to her son.

Paige was just about to close the drawer when something caught her eye—a silver crucifix and chain. She took it in hand, recalling that day in Bryant Park when she had accepted it as a gift from one of her pro-bono clients. Bree had sought counsel regarding her abusive husband, and Paige had helped her obtain a restraining order. Her thoughts shifted to the stalker and her stolen briefcase. *The letter from Bree was in there!* she realized.

Paige sank into the desk chair and reached for the phone to dial Detective Rowland at the Manhattan Precinct. "I may know who the stalker is," she said, hoping her hunch was wrong.

North Dakota
Monday, June 24th

Joel followed Sam Quince down a set of stairs at the Thomas Atwood Library.

"I think you'll find your office space quite comfortable," the little round man said as they walked past a series of rooms. "The computer lab is right next door, so feel free to access our resources if you need to research anything about your father's presidential term.

In the basement, they walked down a long gray hallway that was lined with framed photos taken by the presidential photographer.

Quince stopped at a door, presented Joel with a key, and waited for him to go inside. The space looked austere beneath the harsh glow of florescent lights, but it had everything he needed: a modern desk and chair, a file cabinet, a coat rack, and most importantly, a new laptop computer.

Joel nodded to show his approval. "I've decided to call my blog 'Beyond the Fall.'"

Sam's round face scrunched as he pondered the words. "Hmm, interesting name," he ventured, "but what does it mean?"

"It's a metaphor," Joel explained. "A warning of America's potential decline and what may lie ahead."

"Of course. I see it now!" Mr. Quince's head bobbed, and he fidgeted with the pockets of his maroon blazer. "Very clever, Young Man, very clever indeed! Well, I'd better let you get on with it then," he said before slipping back out into the hallway.

Joel settled at the desk and drew in a deep breath. After spending time on the design and layout of the blog, he pushed back waves of insecurity and began working on his first blog post.

"As the citizen of a free nation, I act on my right to free speech by examining current political trends that may contribute to the erosion of our constitutional foundations. I open this blog by urging dialogue regarding the current administration and the recent challenges to the Second Amendment," Joel wrote.

That dreadful day at UC Berkeley replayed in Joel's thoughts as he continued to type. "Thomas Atwood's life ended violently, yet the governing principles that our late president believed in are still alive! My father fought to maintain the constitutional foundations of the United States of America, which includes the right of the people to keep and bear arms."

Joel's fingers hovered over the keyboard for a moment as words formed in his mind. "Gun registration has now become a reality, political consensus is building, and the ideological divide is widening. I implore us all to study those countries that have chosen to tread this path before us. All too often, mandatory registration has led to the confiscation of guns. Do we want to live in a nation where political agendas and media-fueled biases drive policies that erode personal liberties? What will be next?" he asked. "Will we ban kitchen knives, ropes, or baseball bats?" Joel ended his first editorial piece by stating, "More government regulation is not the cure for violence. Our problems must first be addressed by an honest analysis of the rapid breakdown of social mores." After a quick proofread, Joel posted his first blog opinion and stared at the screen wondering if anyone would respond.

A half hour later, Joel gathered his things, said goodbye to Mr. Quince, and headed for Delmont to pick up his wife.

Coco barely noticed when he walked through the door of Nora's Bargain Bin. She was sitting at an antique treadle sewing machine near the massive fireplace. Pieces of colorful fabric lay all around her. He walked up behind his bride and kissed her neck. She turned, removed a couple straight pins from between her lips, and smiled. "How was your first day as a blogger?"

Joel shrugged. "Time will tell if anyone is interested in what I have to say."

"Of course, they are!" Coco said with a smile.

"It looks like you've been busy." Joel stepped over a pile of remnants and asked, "What are you up to?"

"Your mom gave me this old sewing machine and free access to all the clothing racks. I've been having so much fun!"

Entering from the kitchen, Nora said, "Coco is a very creative seamstress. Look at all the unique pieces she's put together in just one afternoon!" Joel's mom motioned to a portable rack of colorful repurposed dresses and tunics.

"Nora believes that I could market these items on the Internet," Coco said. "What do you think?"

An email pinged on Joel's phone. "You'd be wonderful," he said before directing his attention to the message. Another popped in, followed by another. Soon, he was overwhelmed by the responses to his editorial on the Second Amendment. "I've opened a floodgate," Joel muttered as he read a string of vitriolic anti-gun diatribes.

Chapter 26

New York

Tuesday, June 25th

Paige looked out the window of her West Side law office and let her mind wander. She could not decide which was worse: waiting for a report from Detective Rowland, or worrying about her husband.

Brody's brooding silence had always signaled trouble and only made his wife's anxiety worse. Last night, as they lay in bed Paige had asked, "How are things going at work since Katrina's computer was hacked?"

"Don't worry. Everything's fine." Brody fluffed his pillow and rolled over only to toss restlessly throughout the night.

Now, sitting at her desk, Paige forced her attentions back to the stack of work that needed her focus. She was halfway through the folders when her law partner walked into her office.

Jerry Silverstein sat down, folded his arms, and gave Paige a long sympathetic gaze. "Whatever happens, I want you to know that I'm here for you." The words dripped from his tongue. "If there's anything that I can do during this difficult time, anything at all…"

She'd spoken to no one about her troubles. "What are you talking about?"

Jerry's mouth dropped open. "I just assumed… I mean, Brody's name is all over the news!"

Paige was shocked as she accessed the Internet and typed her husband's name. The breaking news seemed unreal.

"The Securities and Exchange Commission Investigates Insider Trading by Wall Street Investment Banker, Brody Hays," one headline read.

"This is ridiculous!" Paige blurted.

"Of course, it is." Jerry reached across the desk and gave her hand a fatherly pat. At the door of her office, he turned and said, "I'm sure this whole thing will blow over."

Alone in the office, Paige felt her heart pounding in her chest. She had lived in New York long enough to know that allegations like this never just "went away." Careers in the world of high finance were built on trust.

The intercom on the desk crackled. "Phone call on line two," Jewel announced. "It's someone from the Manhattan Precinct."

Paige snatched the receiver. "Detective Rowland?"

"Yes," he said. "I just got off the phone with the Albany PD."

The pause that followed seemed eternal. "Well?"

"I'm afraid your hunch was correct Mrs. Hays." The detective's tone was ominous. "A patrolman was dispatched for a welfare check and found Bree's aunt. She had been shot, but is expected to make a full recovery."

"What about Bree?" Paige clutched the receiver so tight her fingers went numb. "Is she all right?"

"We have reason to believe that the young lady has been abducted by her estranged husband."

Paige sent up a silent, but urgent, prayer for her former client. Judging from what this crazed man had put her own family through, there was no telling what he might do next.

⌇

Arizona

Friday, June 28th

Word among the border communities spread fast. Everyone in Arroyo Seco was talking about the murder of a group of Mexican immigrants, mostly young men. These unfortunate souls had been killed execution style. Before setting the corpses on fire, the assailants had removed each of the victim's newly implanted RFID chips!

"Gordon Spitzer was right," David said.

Elita's soft brown eyes brimmed with tears. "Whoever did such a thing is heartless and cruel."

Joy skipped into the General Store waving a sheet of light-blue construction paper. "Look what we made in preschool today!" She placed her masterpiece on the lunch counter and waited as her parents admired the concentric arches of Fruit Loops she had glued onto the page to form a rainbow. "We made the clouds out of cotton balls," Joy announced.

"That's so beautiful!" Elita said as she leaned over to study her daughter's latest creation.

"I think we should hang it on the wall behind the lunch counter so all our customers can admire it!" David said, smiling inwardly as his little girl puffed with pride.

Elita threw some tortillas onto the grill and sprinkled them with grated cheese. She had just folded the quesadillas and set them on plates when the screen door opened and closed with a bang.

Two strangers entered, scanning the General Store with their dark eyes. "Buenos dias, Amigos" the taller one said as he locked eyes on the family.

David gave the strangers a friendly nod as the short, stocky man grabbed a shopping basket and followed the other man who swaggered between aisles.

Since the borders had officially opened, the General Store had become a thoroughfare for legal migrant workers seeking staples such as rice and beans, but these men seemed different. They filled their baskets with luxury items like jerky, candy bars, soda, and chips.

They approached the lunch counter and lingered. "Something smells good. We'll take two of what you're having and a couple of cervezas, too."

"We don't have a liquor license here. You'll have to go across the street to the Watering Hole for beer," David replied.

The shorter, blocky man set the shopping basket on the lunch counter and lowered his stout frame down beside Joy. "Hola, Bonita!" he said.

David tensed as the stranger reached out to touch the child's head. Joy pulled away and slipped around the counter to stand behind her mother.

"Ah, a shy little one!" he said as the taller man sat and stared at Elita who was busy at the grill.

After lunch, David followed the men to the register and rang up their purchases. The tall stranger added a few cartons of cigarettes to the order and slapped some crisp twenty-dollar bills on the counter. "Keep the change," he called as they walked out the door.

From across the room, David and his wife exchanged a concerned look, but said nothing.

More customers came and went as the afternoon wore on. Joy worked on a puzzle, and Elita was busy at the lunch counter when a well-to-do American couple made an entrance asking for a lawyer named "Fillmore."

David looked up from stocking shelves, and said, "That would be me. How can I help you?"

The man, wearing a golf polo, ran his ring-covered fingers through his neatly clipped hair and seemed startled by a lawyer dressed in jeans and a black t-shirt. "I don't mean to be rude, Young Man, but where did you get your law degree?"

"No offense taken." David walked over, brushed dust from his hands, and said. "I graduated from Harvard Law School."

The man blinked and announced, "I'm Charlton Bennett, and this is my wife Vanessa." He thrust out a hand, shook David's, and said, "Well then, I'll get right to the point. We own property in Mexico—have for years. Yet, suddenly, we're told we cannot enter the country unless we receive an RFID chip!"

"Surely, you've been following the news regarding the

NAC Treaty," David said patiently.

"Of course," the gentleman bristled. "However, I assumed that it applied only to migrant workers, not to US citizens who have valid passports!"

"This is total nonsense if you ask me!" Vanessa Bennett clutched her designer handbag, tossed her hair, and punctuated her statement with an indignant huff. "I refuse to let them violate my person with that—that little chip thing!"

"You raise an interesting argument," David said. "It's very possible that Constitutional protections may apply here." After jotting down their names and contact information, he agreed to look into the matter.

"I do hope this issue will be resolved quickly," Vanessa pressed. "Charlton is in need of a rest." She turned to her husband and said, "Darling, maybe we should just receive the implant. I mean, what could it hurt?"

"Absolutely not! It's the principle of the matter!"

The couple continued their bickering as they headed for the door.

"I'll be in touch!" David called as they climbed into their Lexus.

Elita turned the sign in the window to "CLOSED" and locked the door. "Do you think they'll be back?"

"Depends on who prevails," David said as the evening shadows crept across the old pine floor.

The young family headed up the stairs to their apartment. There, Joy climbed on her father's lap to watch cartoons from a DVD.

Across the room, Elita stood looking out the window. The glow of the sunset outlined her silhouette. Soon, the veil of a moonless night would blanket the sleepy town. *Would more faceless monsters come out?* David wondered with a shudder. "Elita, why don't you join us?" he suggested as protective love for his wife and family filled his heart.

Later, when everyone was safely tucked in bed and sleeping, David tiptoed back downstairs to re-check the window latches and door bolts. Something about those Mexican strangers who had earlier patronized the General Store left him feeling edgy.

North Dakota
Tuesday, July 2nd

"I made an online clothing sale today!" Coco announced as the Jeep Wrangler turned down the country road that led to their love nest. "Remember that tri-colored tunic, the one with the big pockets?"

Joel nodded, though he was uncertain as to which one of his wife's clothing designs she was referring. "That's great!"

Coco smiled. "I've been waiting for you to talk about your work at the Presidential Library. Do you like the job?"

The question stirred a strange mix of conflicted feelings in Joel. "My first post is still going viral on social media, and now, some of the comments are trending," he said, dodging a series of ruts in the road.

"You're kidding! The blog post about gun rights? Why didn't you tell me?"

"Because I know how you feel about the issue." Joel

braced himself for another round of debate with his wife regarding her dislike of guns. As Joel was quickly learning, the alarming truth was that Coco was not alone. All across the country, anti-gun rhetoric was building enough mass and momentum to steamroll over the Second Amendment of the Constitution. Ironically, the name of his blog, "Beyond the Fall," might soon be a prophetic reality for the nation.

"So, what did you write about today?" Coco asked.

"The advance of globalism and the denigration of nationalism." Joel feared the subject was way over his head.

"Sounds interesting."

Joel bit his lip and battled a surge of insecurity. The truth was that trying to defend the late-president's ideologies was proving to be more difficult than he had ever imagined. The comment strings were turning uglier. One responder had referred to Joel as a stunted ideologue, another called him an ignorant capitalist hack, and worst of all, someone labeled him a brainwashed, bastard son. The white gloves of civility had turned to brass knuckles. Adding to Joel's distress, the discouraging slurs kept trending!

Joel parked under the cottonwood, and the couple walked along the willow path that paralleled the creek. Near the bottom of the sheepherder wagon steps, Joel took his bride in his arms, kissed her, and whispered in her ear, "I'm so lucky to have you."

Dinner was later than normal. Coco fixed a box of macaroni and cheese, while Joel grilled a ham steak. As usual, they ate at the picnic table, brushed by a gentle breeze and the smell of wildflowers.

Sinking below the horizon, the sun cast an orange glow

upon the rushes and reeds. "I love this time of the evening," Coco said as she gathered the dishes. "Let's go for a walk."

Joel laced his fingers through his bride's, and they strolled along a footpath that ran along the creek. They spoke no words as they walked together; there was no need. The couple paused where the gurgling creek swirled around a deep hole. "My dad used to take me fishing when I was little."

"Thomas Atwood?" Coco asked.

"No. The dad who raised me. I still miss him."

Something rustled in the bushes, and Coco gasped. "What was that?"

"Probably just a squirrel."

She cocked her ear. "I don't think so. Squirrels don't whimper." Coco approached the willowy bramble and parted the branches. There, a speckled creature with scraggly fur and oversized floppy ears peered at them with bulging eyes.

It was the ugliest puppy Joel had ever seen!

Coco scooped the little mutt into her arms and exclaimed, "Isn't he beautiful?"

Chapter 27

New York

Friday, July 5ᵗʰ

The minute Paige saw Brody's face, she knew things were bad. "What's wrong?" she asked as he dropped his briefcase by the desk chair.

"Hensley Capital has asked me to take a leave of absence while the investigation is active. At least, I will still get paid—for now."

Paige left mushrooms and scallions sautéing above a gas flame and hurried to her husband's side. "But you're innocent! I can't believe that anyone who knows you could believe that you're guilty of insider trading!"

"My face is all over the tabloids. In the court of public opinion, I've already been convicted." Brody took hold of his wife's shoulders and their eyes locked. "You need to understand that these trumped-up charges aren't going to just disappear." His tone was serious. "It's obvious that someone set me up. There's a carefully planted paper trail that points directly at me."

"But why?" Paige's thoughts were a whir of speculation, and then in a flash, she knew. "This is because of the story that Katrina Katz has been working on about the World Fortress Institute! If her source can be discredited, then…"

"That's right." Brody loosened his tie and draped his jacket over the chair. "I'm sure that Alistair Dormin is behind this whole thing, but I just can't prove it."

He moved to the family room and flipped through the news channels. All clips of Brody showing him surrounded by paparazzi. He had become the new Bernie Madoff.

Paige's cell phone rang, and she glanced at the screen. It was the Julliard School. *Probably a reminder of Connor's upcoming recital,* she thought and let it go to voice mail. "What does our lawyer say?"

Brody rubbed his weary face. "I don't need anyone to tell me how bad things could get! Next, they'll probably freeze all our assets!" He walked to the liquor cabinet. "Do we still have that bottle of brandy someone gave us for a Christmas present?"

"I'm sure it's in there somewhere."

He found the bottle, broke the seal, and poured a stiff drink into a crystal bar glass.

Hopping down the stairs two at a time, Connor asked, "What's burning?"

Paige raced to the stove and killed the gas flame under the sauté pan. The mushrooms and scallions were shriveled and burnt. "Good thing we have some leftovers." She summoned a smile and stooped to kiss the top of her son's head. "What have you been doing?"

"Memorizing a Bible passage from the book of

Matthew," the child said. "Want to hear it?"

"Sure," Paige said with forced cheerfulness.

"It's from the Sermon on the Mount," Connor said before reciting the scripture. "God blesses you when people mock you and persecute you and lie about you and say all sorts of evil things against you because you are my followers. Be happy about it! Be very glad! For a great reward awaits you in Heaven."

Paige listened to the words and blinked back a swell of tears.

"Blessed? That sounds like a bunch of nonsense to me." Brody swirled his brandy.

"Dad, God wants us all to trust him, even when people do bad things to us."

"No offense, Connor, but at your age, I don't think you've had enough experience to know what you're talking about."

"God said it, not me," the child replied.

A few feet away, Paige listened to the voicemail message and felt the color drain from her cheeks. She laid the phone on the granite countertop and turned to her son. "Connor, that was the Julliard School…" She knelt and pulled her child close. "Honey, they have decided that you no longer meet their academic criteria. You've been dismissed."

Brody downed his brandy, slammed his crystal glass into the fireplace, and leaving a trail of expletives in his wake, he stormed from the room.

⸎

Arizona

Monday, July 8th

David had spent the morning immersed in Constitutional Law books. The strongest angle was the common law right of bodily integrity. It seemed wrong to force law-abiding citizens to undergo implantation, even though not everyone was opposed to the idea. Migrant workers streaming across the border had embraced the RFID chip. For the first time, they were free to come and go legally.

But what about people like the Bennetts who viewed the implant as a violation of their personal rights? He wondered, *Why haven't they returned to challenge the matter? Have they decided it is too much trouble to fight it?* David's thoughts drifted to the darker side of the NAC Treaty. *In light of the recent murders along the Mexican border, are RFID implants putting people at risk? How,* he pondered, *will the North American Coalition respond to this criminal activity? Will they propose adding tracking capability to the device further infringing on personal privacy?* David leaned back in his chair and further reasoned. *Even if the RFID chips are capable of tracking, it won't stop cold-blooded killers from pirating the device to sell on the black market!*

As a young law student at Harvard, he had excelled at Constitutional Law, but this issue—and the challenges it created—was multifaceted and complicated.

Elita poked her head between the tapestry curtains that separated David's law office/storage room. "I thought you could use a break!" She placed a brass platter on the file cabinet and poured them each a cup of coffee from a thermos.

"I made a fresh batch of oatmeal cookies, too."

David stood and pulled Elita in for a kiss. "How did I ever find someone like you?"

"You didn't have to look. God had the whole thing arranged."

"I wish life was that simple," David said and selected a cookie.

Elita looked up, her velvety brown eyes searching his. "All you have to do is believe."

David turned his gaze to the steam rising from his mug and fell into a contemplative silence. He recalled the undeniable moments when he had called out to God and witnessed divine intervention. Still, the logical and educated side of reason needled David. *Where is the proof that God exists?*

"I just read a fascinating article," Elita said. "Did you know that the human ears and nose continue to grow throughout a person's lifetime?"

David grinned. "Lucky for you, I'm not Cyrano de Bergerac!"

Elita parked her hands on her hips. "Laugh if you want, but what about the human eye and its amazing ability to focus or to let in different amounts of light?"

"What's your point?"

"Darwin's Theory of Evolution couldn't even explain such complexities!" She sighed. "All I'm saying is this—if you want to see evidence of God and His wonders, open your eyes!"

David was mentally preparing a response when the phone on his desk rang.

The caller ID told him that it was his brother-in-law. He plucked the receiver from the cradle and said, "Hey, Bro, what's up?"

"I need your help."

Coming from the lips of Brody Hays, such words startled David. "I'm listening."

"We've got major problems brewing here in New York City." David listened quietly as Brody outlined the recent allegations of insider trading along with the swells of media harassment. "It's a bad situation." He paused and then added, "There is something I need you to do for me..."

North Dakota

Monday, July 8th

"Well, if it isn't the Blog King!" J. J. O'Shay bellowed when Joel walked through the door of the Bargain Bin.

The big man knelt and removed his beanie in mock submission.

"Just ignore this big Huckleberry!" Gertie said and waved her hand in the air. "He's just jealous 'cause nobody has ever even taken a peek at his dumb blog!"

J. J. shot to his feet and pointed a finger at the blue-haired woman. "Aha! If that's true, how do you know I have a one?" A grin spread across the man's face. "I always suspected you were my secret fan!"

Gertie huffed, and her cheeks turned crimson as she stomped into the kitchen.

J. J. O'Shay pulled his beanie over his ears, twisted the end of his handlebar mustache, and said, "Seriously, Joel, you're the tweet-meister! Last time I checked, your Twitter account had over a thousand followers! So, what controversial subject did you punch out today? How 'bout giving me a little hint?"

"I wrote about how the Ivory Tower is nurturing intolerance and fostering a culture of victimhood under the guise of political correctness." Joel thought about his own college experience, where free thought was often discouraged and sometimes penalized. "If our nation keeps traveling down this path, then self-determination and individuality will be seriously compromised. We could end up with a society of homogenous drones."

"Wow, College Boy, those are some big words your using!" J. J. said. "Let me see if I can translate. Are you saying that old-school, moral values are in trouble?"

"That's right."

"Keep stirrin' the pot, Man. That's how the stew gets cooked and counter-culture movements are started!"

Nora appeared carrying the ugly puppy that Coco had rescued from the rushes.

Stroking its wiry, speckled fur and scratching its mismatched ears, she said, "You've got a smart little dog here. I think Moses is nearly housebroken already!"

"Moses?"

"That's the name Coco picked out." Nora smiled and handed her son the short-legged mutt with bulging eyes. "Moses in the bulrushes! Don't you think it suits him?"

"Where is Coco?" Joel asked.

"We moved the treadle sewing machine into the back room so she could concentrate. Your bride is finishing another one of her extraordinary creations. Did you know she sold two more dresses online today?"

From the kitchen door, Gertie called out, "Hey, kids, soup's on if anybody's hungry."

Joel politely declined the invitation. It had been a long day. All he wanted to do was spend a quiet evening with his bride.

On the drive home, Coco cuddled with their new puppy and chattered about her day. "We should take Moses for a walk before dinner," she said as they parked near the willows. "He's been inside most of the day. Did you know he's housetrained already?"

"I heard."

They followed behind as the little dog waddled about sniffing. Suddenly, Moses lifted his floppy ears, cocked his head, then dashed up the road, and disappeared from view.

Joel made a mental note to get a leash as the couple jogged after the mutt.

Just over the rise, Coco scanned the inhospitable terrain for her puppy. "Do you see him?"

They looked for movement among Sergeant Rudd's crudely painted signs. Red splotchy words slapped on pieces of fiberboard, "WARNING! STOP! NO TRESPASSING! DANGER!" Near the end of the washed out road was a fortress of end-to-end shipping containers that were buffeted by coils of military razor wire.

"Have you ever seen anything like it?" Coco marveled. "I thought J. J. was exaggerating when he described this place."

Joel counted at least forty shipping containers that walled the property. What was behind them was anybody's guess. Small, square holes, like gun turrets, dotted some of the containers. In the center of one of the containers, a garage door had been installed.

"It's not a very inviting place. Maybe we should leave." The words had just left Joel's lips when a pack of deep-throated dogs began to bark.

Scanning the area nervously, Coco then pointed, "There's Moses!"

Suddenly, a gunshot cracked the calm. A spit of dust exploded a few yards from where the couple stood.

"This is private property!" a raspy voice croaked. "Can't you read?"

Joel spotted the barrel of a rifle jutting from one of the square, turret holes.

"We'll leave as soon as we gather our puppy," Coco said firmly.

"I'll let it go this time, but if that flea-bit dog of yours makes trespassing a habit, then I'll feed him to my Rottweilers!"

"You'll do no such thing!" Coco shrieked. She strode forward, scooped the pup into her arms, and stood defiantly. "Bullies like you don't scare me!"

"You're a mouthy little thing, ain't ya?"

Joel tugged at his wife's arm and said, "Let's go."

She refused to budge. "What kind of a person hides behind a wall of steel and fires shots at unarmed people?" Coco demanded. "It seems to me that the least you could do is talk with us face to face!"

A few seconds later, the garage door shuddered and rumbled upward. Sergeant Rudd stepped onto the threshold. Rifle in hand, he stood as if his presence would be a menace that would send the couple scurrying. Finally, he set the gun aside and stepped into the evening light. "Speak your piece and be done with it!"

"Like it or not, we are your new neighbors, and I don't appreciate your threats!" Coco scolded. "While we're on the subject, I don't like listening to you blowing things up all the time either."

Sergeant Rudd's stormy slate-colored eyes shifted to Joel. "Ain't you the one that does that blog called 'Beyond the Fall' about the Second Amendment? Why don't you educate your little gal there about the right to bear arms and all those other personal freedoms you write about."

"Like the right to free speech?" Joel returned. "My wife is entitled to her opinions, just like you."

"Well, ain't you a classic metrosexual!" Sergeant Rudd cleared his throat and spat on the ground. His gaze shifted back to Coco. "Okay, Little Lady, just to prove that I can be neighborly, I'll only fire my ordinances a couple of times a week, instead of every day."

"Thanks, I appreciate that."

"I was thinkin' about cutting back anyway," Rudd said with a shrug. "The price of ammo is goin' up." Grabbing his rifle, he headed back, but then he stopped and turned to issue a warning. "Next time, mind those signs and stay the hell away!"

Chapter 28

New York
Wednesday, July 10ᵗʰ

At the law office of Silverstein and Hays, Paige caught a flash from the corner of her eye and looked up from the case she was working on. A man, with camera in hand, stood brazenly outside her office window! Paige launched from her desk and quickly closed the blinds against the intrusion of a cluster of reporters who had gathered for a glimpse of the woman whom the tabloids had dubbed "The Socialite Wife of Wall Street Villain, Brody Hays."

Paige's veins surged with righteous anger when her desk intercom crackled.

"Your son's school called," Jewell said. "They said there's some kind of trouble."

Paige began to shake. In an instant, wrath had turned to fear, and she found herself standing at her legal secretary's desk. "What did they say?"

"'Trouble'—that's all they told me."

"Why didn't you transfer the call to my office?!"

Jewell sighed as she stared at her newly painted fingernails. "I'm sorry. They asked me to let you know and that's exactly what I did. By the way, have you seen that circus outside?"

Paige brought up Brody's speed dial on her cell phone and retreated to her office. "I need you to pick me up—immediately!" she said. "I'll explain when you get here. Just hurry!"

A crowd had gathered on the steps of the Tyler Brentwood School. Someone pointed and yelled as Brody pulled up to the curb. "Wait here," Brody told Paige as he stepped from his car.

She watched with mounting concern as her husband picked his way through the media firewall, deflecting a barrage of inflammatory questions with each step. Finally, he pushed through the double doors of the school.

The reporters waited, their cameras poised for action.

How has it come to this? Paige's frustration grew as she waited behind the dark tinted glass of the BMW. The media had publically convicted Brody, and now, their voyeuristic sights were set on destroying his family!

Paige prayed as each anxious second passed. Finally, the double doors opened. The school administrator, accompanied by a guard, admonished the press in a feeble attempt to mitigate the situation.

Stepping away from the building, Brody sheltered Connor beneath his suit jacket from a lightning storm of photographs.

Paige's eyes filled with tears as her husband and son buffeted through the tangled frenzy of chaos. Through the glass, she could hear reporters yelling, "Has this investigation affected your family? How long have you been defrauding investors?"

Brody and Connor climbed inside the car, locked the doors, and the BMW screeched away from the curb. They drove in stunned silence through the busy streets of Manhattan only to find another media swarm waiting at their Tribeca apartment. Cameras clicked when Brody leaned from his car window to swipe the parking garage card. And then, in the bowels of their building, they finally escaped the onslaught.

Paige began to cry, and Brody took her in his arms.

"It's going to be okay," Connor said as his parents struggled for composure. The child held their hands as they rode in the elevator.

"We'll get through this together," Paige said as they entered the safety of their apartment.

Without responding, Brody headed for the computer in the family room and sat down at the desk.

"What are you doing?"

He waited for the machine to boot up and then said, "I'm booking airline tickets for you and Connor. I want you to start packing."

"Don't be ridiculous!"

Brody looked at his wife with worried eyes. "Listen to me, Paige. This scandal is getting uglier by the minute. I'm afraid it's only the beginning." He paused to check the airline schedules on the screen. "There's a flight available this evening."

"But we can't leave. Our place is with you!"

"I've already wired your personal funds to an account in Arizona. David has been helping me with the arrangements." He paused.

"Wait just a minute! You've been planning this?" Paige exploded. "Don't I have a say?"

"We've always worked as a team, but this is different," he said firmly. "Someone with a lot of power has framed me! I don't know what else they are capable of doing, but I'm not willing to risk my family!"

North Dakota

Wednesday, July 10th

Joel sifted through the landslide of responses to his last blog post and began to notice something amazing. The political and social subject matter of his blog posts was beginning to resonate with a growing number of Americans. Many young people were weighing in, those who felt robbed of the opportunities and the freedoms enjoyed by previous generations. Some feared they were witnessing the death of the American Dream. The social media hashtag, #BeyondtheFall, was trending in record numbers.

J. J. O'Shay had referred to Joel's followers as a new counter-culture movement. *Maybe he's right,* Joel thought. It seemed ironic that old values and morals, once rejected, were now being reclaimed by his own generation.

Joel studied and began to Retweet some of the concerns raised by followers and added a link back to his blog.

"Has political correctness muzzled free speech?" one Tweet said.

"Are religious freedoms being compromised?" said another.

"Does victimhood outweigh truth on the scales of justice?" was his last Tweet.

The response was immediate! The analytics software indicated a landslide of hits on his blog, and Joel's Twitter account exploded with activity. Retweeting the questions, followers added their own answers, and the retweets prompted more and more interest. By late afternoon, Joel Sutherland was being tagged on social media sites all across the country. Not all responses were positive, yet the debates that were sparked gave voice to many young and disenfranchised Americans. *Maybe it's not too late to turn this nation around,* Joel concluded.

His iPhone chimed with his mother's unique ringtone, and he picked up.

"Gertie is driving your wife home," Nora blurted. "She's very upset, and I think you should be there."

"What's wrong?"

"Coco's mother called from California with some very bad news."

Chicago
Wednesday, July 10th

"Wake up, Honey," Paige said as the plane landed in Chicago.

Connor yawned and rubbed his eyes. "I'm hungry, Mom."

"We've got time to grab some dinner before our next connection," she said as the jet taxied up to the gate.

A few minutes later, with carry-on luggage in hand, they entered the terminal and found a restaurant.

Paige poked at her salad as Connor ate his cheeseburger and fries. She thought about her husband trying to handle this crisis alone and felt a swell of guilt. *So many friends and business associates are turning their backs on Brody,* she thought. She laid down her fork, bit her quivering lip, and took a sip of water. "Waiter, we'll take the check, please." Paige handed a pimply-faced, young man her credit card as Connor dipped his last French fry into ketchup.

The waiter returned with a sheepish look on his face. "Excuse me, Ma'am. There seems to be a problem with your card."

"There can't be." Paige waited for him to run it again.

"Sorry. It's been denied."

"That's odd," she said, fishing another card from her wallet. "Try this one."

He reappeared with the same message and added, "Maybe you'd like to pay in cash?"

Paige fished through her wallet and gave him enough money to cover the bill and a tip. Feeling a bit embarrassed, she said to Connor, "Honey, our plane will be boarding in about a forty minutes. Let's go wait for it."

"Sounds good!" Connor said enthusiastically. "I can read my Bible."

Mother and son easily found Gate C-3 and settled into some chairs among the other passengers. As the minutes passed, a ticket agent announced their flight would be delayed, and Paige made her way to the counter. "Will it be a long delay?" she asked. "We've got a tight connection in Denver."

The woman flashed an officious smile and held out her hand. "Ticket, please?"

Paige waited patiently as the woman's fingers danced across the keyboard. A curious look appeared on the agent's face. "Wait here. I'll be right back," she said as she strolled over to a uniformed man standing near the boarding ramp.

The man's eyes were locked on Paige as he followed the agent back to the counter. "Do you have identification, Mrs. Hays?" he asked.

"Yes, but why?"

The guard offered no explanation as Paige opened her wallet and handed him her driver's license. After studying it with great interest, he handed it back. "Mrs. Hays, I'm afraid you won't be traveling this evening. Your name has been added to the No-Fly List."

Paige couldn't believe what she was hearing. "What? How could that be? I mean, I flew here today."

He crossed his arms and shrugged.

She returned to her seat and tried to think, but her thoughts were racing.

"What's wrong, Mom?" Connor asked.

"I'm not sure." Paige dialed her husband's cell and was startled to hear that his account had been deactivated. Next, she phoned the penthouse landline. "This number is no longer in service." Suddenly, Paige recalled Brody saying they could freeze all their assets! Reality began to settle in as she realized that it was not only their credit cards that had been frozen. *This can't be happening at a worse time!* Paige and Connor were stranded in Chicago with nothing, but their carry-on luggage and less than fifty dollars in her wallet! The only piece of luck Paige had going was that her cell phone still worked, an account paid for by her law firm.

Darkness had descended over the Chicago skyline, but it was two hours earlier in Arizona. Paige phoned her brother who was probably on his way to Tucson to pick them up by now. "There's been a complication...." Paige explained the situation when David answered.

"Try not to worry," he told his sister. "I'll pick up your luggage at the Tucson airport and then wire funds to a Western Union in Chicago. I'll send a text to let you know where."

"It will be dark here soon, and I don't have enough money for a hotel." Paige glanced at Connor who was reading and then whispered into the receiver, "What if the funds can't be wired until morning? David, I'm scared."

"Stay put for the night," her brother said calmly. "O'Hare is probably the safest place to be right now."

Paige ended the call, summoned courage, and mustered a smile. "Guess what, Connor? You and I are going to have a sleepover here at the airport!"

Chapter 29

Arizona

Friday, July 12th

    David felt weary as he made his way home from Tucson. It had been a long day of driving, but his tasks were done. The money had been successfully wired to his sister, Paige, and he had collected the luggage from the Tucson airport.

    Now, David's thoughts turned toward home. *It won't be long now.* The setting sun cast a twilight glow on Eagle Pass, and he imagined Elita in their little apartment over the General Store reading a book to Joy, while a cast iron skillet of stew and biscuits simmered in the oven.

    Treasured moments rolled through David's mind as the old truck downshifted and ground up Eagle Pass. Just over the rise, the tiny border town came into view with squares of light from house windows dwarfed by the bright porch lamps of the Watering Hole Bar.

    An odd feeling came over David as he descended from the pass. Something was missing, and then it hit him. The large rectangle silhouette of the General Store building should have been half lit this time of night. Elita would have closed the store and headed upstairs with Joy by now, yet the apartment windows were dark!

Something's not right! David thought. His breathing quickened. Tires squealed as the old truck descended a series of modest switchbacks. At the bottom, he challenged the old engine to move him faster. In Arroyo Seco, David pounded over the potholes in Main Street, skidded to a stop, and launched himself up the steps. The front door of the old General Store was wide open, and the space inside looked like an ominous black hole! Across the street, the usual Watering Hole revelers whooped and hollered, but David's heart thundered in his ears. He groped for the light switch. The fluorescent lights hummed and flickered to life revealing an open cash register. The glass display cabinet of authentic Native American jewelry was broken and empty. "Elita!" he screamed, feeling light headed. Silence. "Joy?"

David uttered a prayer as he bound upstairs two steps at a time. He threw open the door to another dark space. When light flooded the apartment, David staggered with fear. Terrifying thoughts flashed through his mind as he looked around. Drawers had been dumped and furniture overturned. Someone had stubbed out a cigarette on the coffee table, burning a hole in the wood. In the kitchen, the refrigerator door was open, and sandwich material was scattered across the countertop. A kitchen knife with mayonnaise residue had been tossed on the linoleum floor.

"Elita! Joy!" A lump tightened his throat, and his mouth was dry. "Where are you?" A faint noise issued from a back room. Suddenly, David was standing in the room he shared with his wife, not knowing how his feet had propelled him there.

"Is it safe to come out?" Elita whispered. Her muffled words came from the closet.

Relief washed over David as he yanked open the closet door and shoved clothes aside. "It's okay. I'm here now."

In the corner near the back of the closet, there was a hidden cubby where Elita stored bedding. When he heard his little girl whimpering, David dropped to his knees and opened the little hinged door.

"Daddy, some bad people were here. We heard them breaking things in the store, so Mommy said we had to hide quick. We were brave, weren't we?"

"Yes, my sweet girl." David fought back grateful tears as he scooped his wife and child into his arms. "You and Mommy were very brave."

North Dakota
Friday, July 12th

Joel turned down the dirt road and pushed the gas pedal to the floor, spinning his wheels. In the rearview mirror, he saw a cloud of dust settling across the fields of corn, but all he could think about was Coco.

He slowed just enough to make the turn safely down the country road that led to their sheepherder wagon. Then, Joel stomped on the throttle again, bouncing over ruts as he sped along the cottonwood-lined stream that led toward home.

Gertie's vehicle was parked alongside the willows. He skidded to a stop, threw open the door of his Jeep, and bolted up the trail.

The old woman was sitting alone at the picnic table. She turned and said, "Oh, thank heavens you're here! Coco wanted to be alone, but I just couldn't bring myself to leave her in such a state."

The door of the sheepherder wagon opened, Joel's bride descended the steps, and sobbing, she flew into his arms. "Dad is gone!"

"I'm so sorry," Joel said softly, cradling Coco's head close to his chest. He nodded to Gertie as she tiptoed away and then turned his attention back to his wife. "What happened?"

"It was a massive coronary, but Mom says he died of a broken heart because I abandoned him." Coco gulped a breath of air. "She says I killed my father!"

"That's not true!"

"But, what if it is?"

The look of guilt on his bride's angelic face angered Joel. "Your mother was cruel to say that to you!"

"Don't talk about Mom like that," Coco cried. "Now, she's got nobody left, but me. I should go back to California and be there for her."

Joel took her hands in his, and their eyes met. "Your place is here with me."

"But, you don't understand…"

"Coco, do you remember the day you left with me, and your Father wanted to speak to me alone? There is something I need to show you." Joel led her back into the sheepherder wagon.

Inside, Joel lifted the mattress and produced an envelope that was hidden underneath.

"Your dad wrote this letter to you. He made me promise to give it to you if anything happened to him."

"What does it say?"

Handing it to her, Joel said, "I've never read it."

She looked at her father's handwriting on the sealed envelope. "To my darling Coco…"

Tears flowed like a river as she slipped the seal open. "Would you read it for me?"

Joel took the letter, cleared his throat, and began…

Hey, Baby Girl, if you're reading this, don't be sad for me. I can finally get out of this bed, and all my struggles are over! You taught me about God's love and acceptance, and you brought me so much joy. Without complaint, you have put up with your mother and selflessly tended to my needs. Now, it's time for your dad to take care of you.

My heart aches with hopes for your future. I long to see you free from the shackles of this house. Go with my blessing and don't look back! This is my gift to you. Nothing would make me happier than to know that you are free and happy.

The color of the ink changed from blue to black, and Joel looked up from the note. "Your dad wrote the last few lines before he gave the letter to me," Joel said.

"Go on," Coco said, choking back tears.

Joel nodded. "Your father added this…"

Now, I've met your future, and I like him. This honorable young man has made two promises that have brought great comfort to my heart. If you're reading this letter, he's already fulfilled the first one.

Coco lowered herself to the kitchenette bench and said, "What is the second promise?"

Joel sat down beside his bride, put his arm around her shoulder, and continued reading.

Baby Girl, because you were born with a tender and giving nature, you will find my wish difficult, but I'm asking you to honor me. Don't come home—not for the funeral—not out of guilt—not ever! Don't look back. Go forward and build your life, and one day we'll meet again in Heaven!
With love,
Dad

Part 3
The Third Woe

His oath, His covenant, and blood

Support me in the whelming flood;

When every earthly prop gives way,

He then is all my Hope and Stay.

On Christ, the solid Rock, I stand;

All other ground is sinking sand.

Edward Mote—1834

Chapter 30

Chicago

Friday, July 12th

It had been a long, exhausting night at O'Hare Airport. While her son slept peacefully beside her, Paige had watched weary passengers trudging through the terminal, coming from or going to another red-eye flight. She dozed sporadically in the early morning hours, only to be chased awake by anxious dreams. One young woman, who sat reading at an adjoining gate, resembled the pro-bono client, Bree, who had been abducted by her estranged husband. In comparison, Paige's troubles seemed small. *Is she alive?* "Please Lord, keep Bree safe," she prayed as the endless minutes ticked past.

Finally, the sun rose, spreading a wall of light through the terminal windows, and Paige rubbed her son's shoulder until he stirred. "Time to go, Honey." With carry-on luggage in hand, Paige and Connor left the airport, hailed a cab, and directed the driver to take them to a Western Union Station in downtown Chicago, according to instructions provided in David's text message.

Fatigue weighed heavily on Paige's shoulders as the car headed toward an impressive cluster of skyscrapers. She rubbed a kink in her neck and tried to smooth her wrinkled skirt. Paige glanced at her image in the rearview mirror, not surprised by the disheveled red hair and sea-foam green eyes framed by dark circles. She was too tired to care.

Connor pressed his face against the window and took in the sights while his mother tried to contact Brody again, to no avail. Feeling frustrated, Paige ended the call.

The cab driver wove in and out of lanes of traffic among the morning commuters, then zig-zagged through the city center, and finally stopped at a curb. "Here's the Western Union Station, Lady." The cabbie tapped the meter, announced the figure, and held out his hand. "I'd prefer exact change if you got it."

After settling up, Paige joined her son on the sidewalk.

Connor pointed to the sign in the window. "They're not open yet, Mom."

She checked her watch. It was 6:30 A.M.. They had half an hour to kill before Western Union opened. "Are you hungry? Let's go find a place to eat."

"We just passed a restaurant." Connor took his mother by the hand and led her down the block and around the corner to an eatery called Lou Mitchell's. A sign that boasted "The World's Finest Coffee" was enough for Paige. *If anybody can use a cup, it's me,* she thought as they went inside.

Even at this early hour, the place was bustling with patrons. A hostess, dressed in a white top and black skirt, led them to a booth near the corner of an angled breakfast counter. The young lady handed Paige and Connor a couple of menus and then sauntered back to her post for the next wave of morning customers.

"This is a busy place!" Paige said over the clamor of dishes, order calls, and chatter.

From the nearby counter, a little, old man wearing a Hawaiian shirt spun around on his golden stool and jumped into the conversation. "You're right about that! Lou Mitchell's is a local icon. Even a few US presidents have stopped in for some grub! Come to think of it, the last one was Thomas Atwood, God rest his soul."

"Oh?" Paige said, not letting on that they knew the late Commander in Chief.

The old man winked at Connor and said, "Bet you've never had one of their famous Milk Dud pancakes before!"

The boy's mouth was agape as he stared at the man's white beard. "Hey, don't I know you?"

"Well, come to think of it, you look mighty familiar to me, too!" The elderly gent snapped his fingers and hopped from his stool like it was a springboard. "Connor, isn't it?" Thrusting out his hand, he offered a hardy handshake. "Why, you were just a little squirt when I last laid eyes on you."

This is surreal, or is exhaustion taking its toll? Paige wondered as she watched the elderly man and her child speaking as though they were lifelong buddies. "I don't understand…"

"Don't you remember, Mom? We met at Valley Forge!"

That family outing to General Washington's headquarters, when Connor was only five-years old, had been hard to forget. "Yes, I recall that day. Your name is Zeke!" Paige suddenly found herself inviting the stranger to join them.

"I'd be honored!" The old man plopped down and added, "But breakfast is gonna be on me, and I don't just mean my shirt."

Connor began to giggle, and Paige was astonished. Somehow, this odd man was able to bring out the child in her usually serious little boy.

When their orders came, Paige nibbled on a bagel while her son wolfed down a plate of Milk Dud pancakes and then asked for more.

Zeke plowed through a stack of Belgian malted-pecan and bacon waffles and leaned back to pat his round belly. "There goes my girlish figure," he groaned and then snatched the check as it arrived.

"Thank you," Paige said, feeling her usual Eastern reserve melting away. "You've been so kind, but we really must be going."

Stifling a belch, Zeke said, "So soon? We're just getting reacquainted!"

"We need to stop by the Western Union and then catch a bus to Arizona."

The old man's hoary eyebrows arched. "What a small world! It just so happens that I'm headed that way, too! Got some friends that live in a little town called Arroyo Seco."

"Cool!" Connor said, "That's where my cousin, Joy, lives!"

Paige felt her reserve return. "What a coincidence…"

"Don't much believe in chance meetings myself." Zeke twirled the tip of his beard. "Could it be that we're all here because we're not all there? Come to think of it, my friends in Arizona have a little girl named Joy. Her last name wouldn't be Fillmore, would it?"

Paige was dumbstruck.

Zeke clasped his wrinkled hands together and said, "Why don't we all ride together? I've got plenty of room, and I'll be traveling down what's left of Route 66, America's Main Street! Some stretches of that old highway crumbled away, some got swallowed by progress, but there's still a lot of reminders of the way things used to be."

"Can we, Mom?"

Paige shook her head. "No, I'm afraid that would be too much to ask."

"No trouble at all!" Zeke insisted. "Hey, I'll bet you didn't realize that some folks consider Lou Mitchell's to be the starting point for the Mother Road herself. What are the odds of running into each other at this restaurant?"

Paige shook her head. "I don't understand…"

Giving his mother a pleading look, Connor interrupted, "It's like a sign from God!"

"Taking a bus across the country is no way to see the sights!" Zeke added. "Besides, I always say that friends don't let friends drive on Interstates!"

Paige struggled to come up with another reason to turn down the invitation, but the truth was she was worn down. She looked from face to face. Old and young, they both looked like kids at Christmas. "Okay, but only if you let me help with expenses, like motels and gas."

"You've got a deal!" Zeke said. "But just so you know, my car gets great gas mileage!"

Up the block and around the corner, Paige collected the money that David had wired. Then she and her son followed the strange little man to a nearby parking garage.

With a go-bag full of doughnut holes, just in case they wanted a snack, Zeke loaded his passengers into an old Rambler station wagon that was pocked with rust and patched with duct tape. "Here's a little bit of trivia I'll bet you didn't know," the old man said as he turned the key and the engine sputtered to life. "Chicago is both the beginning and the end of Route 66!"

Less than an hour later, they left the heart of the city and puttered through suburbs to a village called Plainfield, Illinois. Zeke backed into a parking space and suggested they all take a moment to stretch their legs. "Besides," he added, "there's a curiosity I want you to see." He directed their attention to the road signs that marked the intersection of Route 66 and the historic Lincoln Highway. Zeke wagged his downy beard in wonder. "Just think, two crumbing national byways. Brings to mind something my best friend once said, 'Stand at the crossroads and look; ask for the ancient paths, ask where the good way is, and walk in it... You will find rest for your souls.'"

"Your friend didn't make that up," Connor challenged, "because it's in the Bible!"

"Ah, but God is my best friend!" Zeke retorted as they piled back into the Rambler to continue their journey.

"Who knows the lyrics to that famous song about this old road?" Zeke waited a few seconds and then said, "I'll start things off and before you know it, we'll all be singing along!" He tapped a beat on his steering wheel and began,

"If you ever plan to motor west
Travel my way, take the highway that's the best

Get your kicks on Route Sixty-six.
It winds from Chicago to L.A.
More than two-thousand miles all the way
Get your kicks on Route Sixty-six..."
Zeke paused, "This is the fun part so pay attention...
Now you go through Saint Louie
Joplin, Missouri
And Oklahoma City is mighty pretty
You'll see Amarillo
Gallup, New Mexico
Flagstaff, Arizona
Don't forget Winona,
Kingman, Barstow, San Bernardino..."
By the time they got to Wilmington, Illinois, Connor had memorized all the words and joined in with childlike enthusiasm.

"I got a surprise for you, Little Man," Zeke said as they rolled through the Chicago suburb. "Ever heard about Giants in the land?"

"I've read the Bible story about Joshua," Connor replied.

"Hang onto your eyeballs, so they don't fall out of your head!" The old man pointed out the window. "Meet the Gemini Giant!"

The boy spilled from the car as soon as it came to a stop and hurried over to massive piece of folk art. Paige snapped photos with her phone of her delighted son posing at the base of a twenty-foot-tall green space man.

"Wait until I tell Dad about this!" the boy puffed as they piled back into the Rambler and continued on their way.

Connor sketched pictures of the massive space man while

the old car chugged past fields of low grass and rows of corn.

Zeke passed around his bag of doughnut holes and pointed out neglected remnants of the historic asphalt that had long ago been swallowed up by grander thoroughfares.

For miles, the Rambler loped along stretches of the old Mother Road that paralleled Interstate 55. It seemed odd to see big rigs, vans, and even smart cars whizzing past the old station wagon, while Zeke, un-throttled and unhurried, noted relics leftover from the golden age of America.

Paige spotted a green sign that indicated Springfield, Illinois, was twenty miles down the road. "Maybe we should stop for gas and get some lunch."

"Nope, the gauge reads full," the old man said, "but I know a great place to grab a bite to eat. First, I want to stop and get a hospitality gift, some famous Funk's Grove Mapel Syrup. They may not know how to spell 'maple,' but they sure do make great syrup."

They turned down a dirt road and stopped by an old barn. Zeke went in and soon returned with a jug of the sweet elixir. A short time later, they motored up to an old-school drive-in called the Cozy Dog. "This is one of my favorite watering holes, and it just so happens to be the birth place of the corn dog!"

Connor pitched forward on the Rambler's old bench seat and said. "For real?" He looked at his mom. "This is going to be the best trip ever!"

Chapter 31

North Dakota

Friday, July 12th

Joel chose to work on his blog for the next week from home so he could stay close to his grieving wife. Coco had cried most of the night over the sudden death of her father. By mid-morning, he was ready to proofread his latest musings.

The topic of the day was one that had concerned many of his followers, but Joel chose to take his thoughts a step further. "Political correctness," he postulated, "is being used as a tool to chip away at any belief system that threatens social non-compliance. The recent Fairness and Antidiscrimination Act has loosened another brick in the crumbling wall that is the US Constitution," Joel wrote. "We must consider the cost of ceding our individual rights to think, speak, and worship freely without the threat of reprisal." He ended his post by calling for action. "It's time to actively resist new regulations and take a stand against the swelling cultural tide of social engineering!" he declared.

After tweaking a few sentences and correcting some typos, Joel was ready to publish his post. Using the touch of a finger and a satellite Internet connection, Joel launched his thoughts into the hinterlands.

The sound of Coco weeping softly brought Joel to his feet. He himself was no stranger to tragedy. He ached knowing that there were no words or an easy way around such pain. "Baby, I'm here..." He touched her back and felt the shudder of a silent sob. "You're doing the right thing. Remember, it's what your dad wanted."

Coco rolled over and her damp mottled face reflected shame. "But don't you see? I've lost both my parents now."

Mrs. Trent's battery of guilt trips had been relentless, but the phone call last night had dropped her daughter to her knees. "If you don't come back for the memorial service, then you're dead to me!" she had threatened.

Joel wanted to tell his bride that her mother was heartless and cruel, but he bit his tongue, tenderly wiped a tear from her cheek, and said. "We've got each other."

Coco sat up, smoothed her hair, and offered a weak smile. "I'll make us some tea." She climbed down from the sheepherder wagon platform bed and lit the burner under the kettle.

Even in wool socks, sweats, and a baggy t-shirt, she took Joel's breath away. He pulled her close, and they swayed together as though dancing to some silent song.

"What subject did you write about today?" she asked.

Joel kissed her ear and whispered, "Nothing as interesting as what I'm thinking now."

A few feet away, Joel's cell phone rang, but he made no move to answer it.

"Aren't you going to get that?"

"If it's important, they'll leave a voice mail." He latched the door, closed the curtains, and took his wife's hand in his.

Outside a breeze blew, and the afternoon sun projected dancing shadows of cottonwood leaves on the soft white curtains. For a while, all worldly cares melted away. Nothing mattered, but the love that passed between them. Then, the phone rang again, and everything changed.

—∞—

Route 66

Friday, July 12th

Paige checked her wrist watch as Zeke's Rambler chugged down the old road. It was almost 4:30 P.M.. "Where do you think we will stay tonight?" It had been a long eventful day full of photo-ops, but after hours of travel, she was exhausted.

"Just a few more miles," the old man said. "I know of a great place to stay just outside of Rolla, Missouri."

Paige slipped her cell phone from her purse. There was still no word from Brody.

"Can I look at the pictures again?" Connor asked eagerly and then reached for his mother's phone.

She watched her son scrolling through photos taken earlier in the day. The boy posing beside massive statues, the Gemini Giant, Paul Bunyan, Cow in the Corn, and the world's largest covered wagon. "Wouldn't it have been awesome if you had taken a picture of me climbing that big Catsup Bottle Tower we saw?"

"I don't think my heart could take it!" The smile on her son's face brought a rush of joy to Paige's heart. *The child in Connor is finally coming out to play!*

"This is one of my favorites." He pointed to a serene photo that could have been a postcard. Connor stood in the middle of the Sugar Creek Covered Bridge with arms open and a bright smile on his face!

"I am partial to all those vintage gas stations along Route 66," Zeke volunteered. "Can't get more Americana than that! Have you ever seen so many candy-colored gas pumps in all your life? Yellow, blue, red, and orange! Say, that reminds me…" The ancient man popped the glove box open and pulled out a bag of M & Ms. "Any takers?"

"I want some!" Connor cupped both hands, and Zeke filled his trough.

Paige thought about all those gas stations they had driven by along the way. "Shouldn't we be filling up soon?" she asked.

Zeke popped a piece of candy into his mouth and then tapped the Rambler gas gauge that still registered full. "My old rattle trap might not be much to look at, but like I said, she gets great gas mileage!"

Paige's phone rang. It was an unknown New York City number, but she answered immediately. "Brody?"

"Listen Paige," Brody cut in. "All my phone services have been cut off. I had to buy one of those burn phones just to call you. Every time we talk, your general location can be traced, and I don't want the media hounding you and Connor." After a long pause, he continued, his voice taut with emotion. "I love you. Please don't worry. Everything will be okay…"

306

After Brody hung up, Paige felt a mixture of relief and conflict. Brody's career and reputation were spinning out of control. As a woman of faith, she should have been the one to offer reassurance, not the other way around. *Lord, help my unbelief and protect my husband,* she prayed silently.

Zeke handed the rest of the candy to Connor and then turned left down a country lane. He drove by mobile homes and metal-roofed houses and took a zig and a zag that led to a long driveway that cut between fields of milk cows grazing in knee-deep grass.

They passed a huge milking barn, and Zeke pointed out a two-story brick farmhouse, "That's the place! My friends here run the best bed & breakfast in the whole country! Wait till you taste their famous buttermilk biscuits and gravy!" The old Rambler rolled up to the farmhouse and sputtered to a stop in the circular driveway.

Looking like they'd just stepped out of a Norman Rockwell painting, a couple emerged from their dwelling. The woman, as round as she was tall, waddled from the porch with flabby arms open wide. "Zeke, I had a dream last night that you were coming. The good Lord don't disappoint!" She swallowed the little man in a suffocating, billowy embrace. Finally, she threw back her head, swaddled with silver braids, and took a look at Zeke. Her chubby cheeks shook with joyful laughter. "You haven't changed a bit!"

"Neither has Funk's Grove. Here," Zeke said, handing her the jug of maple syrup.

A lanky, bowlegged man limped over, took hold of both of Zeke's hands, and pumped them vigorously. "Welcome, welcome, Old Traveler!" he drawled. "Always good to see you,

Zeke, and to meet your friends." He raised a bony ledge of eyebrows as he turned his attention to their other guests.

Zeke made the introductions. "Paige and Connor, it's my pleasure to introduce you to Homer and Harriet."

In the next moment, mother and son were flanked by a flurry of heartfelt welcomes and ushered inside.

Directing her guests to a sturdy, Amish-made couch, Harriet said, "Make yourselves at home."

Pointing to an intricate lace doily that was placed in the center of the coffee table, Paige said, "This is beautiful."

"I made it myself!" Harriet said. "If you like it, you can have it."

Paige felt her face flush. "I couldn't, really."

"Nonsense. Nothing would please me more." The bowling ball of a woman scooped up the doily and placed it in Paige's hand. "Besides, it gives me an excuse to crochet another."

On the other side of a braided rug, Zeke settled into a matching chair. He laced his hands behind his hoary head and sniffed the air. "Is that fresh-baked cherry pie I smell?"

Harriet's apple cheeks puffed with delight. She wiped her hands on the gingham apron she wore and wagged a finger at the old man. "Nothing gets by you, Zeke! Told you I had a feeling you were coming. But first things first! I've got a big pot of chicken and dumplings simmering on the stove."

Paige followed the older woman into the kitchen and was promptly put to work placing dishes and cutlery on a heavy farmhouse table with bench seats.

After saying grace, they ate and swapped stories of blessing and praise.

"Did Zeke tell you about the big pickle he got us out of?"

Homer asked.

"Was it a costume?" Connor asked. "Did the zipper get stuck?"

Laughter erupted around the table as Paige explained the figure of speech. "It's another way of saying that they were having difficulties."

"I'll say we were! It was the worst drought in years, and our cows weren't producing. We had to drop our farm policy just to make ends meet," Homer explained. "And then, one of my milk cows decided to throw herself a tizzy. She stomped all over me, and by the time the paramedics arrived, I thought I was a goner. But that's not the worst of it."

Harriet swallowed a dumpling, forked another, and said, "Homer was rushed to surgery for a ruptured spleen. While at the hospital, we learned our old barn burned down." She spooned another generous helping onto her plate.

"Yup, there I was, laid up, our livelihood was reduced to a pile of ashes, and we didn't have two nickels to rub together!"

Taking a sip of milk, Connor asked, "So what happened next?"

"Out of the clear blue sky, Harriet finds a check in the mailbox. Some anonymous donor wanted us to build ourselves a new barn!" Homer's eyes began to water. "Chokes me up whenever I think about it. I was sitting on my porch recovering from surgery when I see this old Rambler grinding up the road with a caravan of cars and trucks following behind. About a hundred people showed up to help, mostly strangers from some church over near St. Louis. Before we knew it, our new barn was raised!"

Harriet dabbed her mouth with a cloth napkin, looked at

Zeke, and said, "I can't count the times you went rooting around in the back of your wagon and found some tool that was needed for the job."

"I'd still like to know what kind of paint you used," Homer cut in. "It's lasted all these years!"

"Don't recall," Zeke said, then patted his stomach and yawned. "I hate to be a party pooper, but I think it's time to put my food baby to bed."

Upstairs, the sojourners were shown their rooms located on either side of a shared water-closet equipped with an old-fashioned elevated toilet tank complete with a pull chain.

Paige and Connor said their prayers and nestled into a feather bed. She laid her head on a crisp embroidered pillowcase and pulled the chenille bedspread up around her chin. As her son drifted off to sleep, Paige reflected on her family's tenuous future and a strange feeling came over her. Warmed by an evening of unconditional love, she was overcome by the notion that, somehow, Brody was right—everything would be okay.

New York
Saturday, July 13th

Katrina Katz quietly slipped out of her office and into the elevator. The New York Affiliate of the Unified Broadcasting Corporation employed thousands, but as co-anchor of the weekend morning show and also the eleven-o'clock news, Katrina's face was easily recognized. On the seventh floor, the elevator door sliced open, and a couple stepped inside. "Morning Ms. Katz," said the young woman with a pixie haircut as the young man punched a number and sidled close to his companion.

Katrina nodded politely. *New interns and another budding romance,* she thought as they descended to the ground floor. Pulling a scarf over her head, the anchorwoman did her best to scoot through the lobby unnoticed. Outside, she hailed a cab.

After giving the cabbie directions to a little Italian bistro in Midtown, Katrina listened again to the voicemail on her phone. It was an unfamiliar number. "Can you meet me at the usual place?" Brody asked. "I think we're being watched."

She asked the cab to drive around the block once and then instructed him to turn down the alley behind the restaurant. Katrina grabbed a handful of cash and passed it to the driver before stepping outside.

"Hey, Lady, don't you want change?" the man called out as she slipped through the back door of the bistro.

Brody was sitting in the usual booth staring into a glass of red wine. He lifted his head when Katrina approached, and she saw the effects of discouragement.

Feeling responsible for his condition, she asked, "How are you?" Brody looked as though he'd aged ten years.

"They've frozen all my assets," he sounded flat. "Even my phone account. Can you believe that? I bought one of those throwaway phones this afternoon, so I could speak with Paige. In Chicago, they refused to let my family board the plane. We've been put on the No-Fly List!" Brody shook his head. "If I go to prison, what's going to happen to my family?"

"It won't come to that," Katrina said firmly. "There's got to be something, or someone, who can tie this whole thing to Dormin. As soon as I find it, I'm breaking this story!"

"Are you sure that's wise?"

"It's a matter of principle. The only way to deal with this level of arrogance and presumption is to call it out."

The waitress arrived to get their order. "Just a glass of water for me," Katrina said, then she looked at Brody. "I've got to be back at the station before they miss me."

"Understood." Brody rubbed his forehead. "I'm being questioned by an investigator from the Securities and Exchange Commission tomorrow morning."

"Do you have a lawyer?"

Brody shook his head. "I'm not sure who I can trust anymore."

"Keep your eyes open. Maybe something will turn up." Katrina stood. "It's getting late, and I need to prepare for the eleven-o'clock news."

They left the restaurant pretending not to know each other. On the sidewalk, Katrina stood and stared at what was known as a New York City phenomena.

A crowd had gathered and were pointing at the golden-orange ball of the sinking sun as it channeled it rays of light between the skyscrapers. "Look, it's the Manhattanhenge!" A group of young people manically began clicking photos with their cell phones.

Within minutes, the vibrant spectacle of light bled into the evening grays of the city and faded away. Wondering just how she could straighten out the mess she'd made of things, Katrina hailed a cab and headed back to work.

Chapter 32

Arizona

Saturday, July 13ᵗʰ

A full morning with Gordon Spitzer was almost more than David could bear, but he had to admit, when it came to security, the former Civic Border Guard knew his stuff. With Gordon's help, the General Store was now fully equipped with warning signs, security lights, and a silent alarm system that would alert the law enforcement of a security breach. Unbeknownst to David, Spitzer had also set the system to alert himself on his cell phone.

"Lunch is on us," Elita called out from behind the counter. "I've made some fresh chicken salad and cottage fries."

Gordon limped over to a stool, leaned heavily on the counter, and lowered his frame. "There's one more security measure I recommend," he said as David took a seat beside him. Spitzer fished his wallet from his hip pocket and retrieved a business card. "There's an ol' boy I know over in Kirby who can give you a sweet deal on a pistol."

David shook his head. "You know how I feel about guns."

"Yeah, yeah, I know how you metrosexual types think, but when it comes to defending your wife and kid, I thought you'd man up, especially, when you consider that the bad guys don't think twice about pulling a trigger."

Elita set the lunch plates down in front of the men and weighed into the conversation. "Joy's out back playing, but she'll be in for lunch soon. I don't want any more talk about weapons. There will be no handgun in this house as long as there's a child around!"

Gordon grumbled under his breath and cast a sideways glance at David. "Ever heard of a gun safe? Just sayin'."

Trying not to think about what could have happened during the recent intrusion, David brooded silently as he ate. He shuddered and then picked at his meal. The truth was that the whole frightening event left him feeling as though he had failed his family.

The General Store screen door banged, causing heads to turn. Randy Bales walked in across the pine floor and slapped a hand onto David's shoulder. "Everything's ready over at Hope Springs," he announced as he straddled a stool. "Travis finished building a wood-framed shelter yesterday and worked on the plumbing. Today, we added the solar panels and a satellite dish." Randy lifted his ball cap and ran a hand through his hair. "Yes, Sir, I'd say your sister and nephew will be very comfortable."

Route 66

Saturday, July 13th

Feeling humbled by the couple's generosity, Paige waved goodbye to Homer and Harriet. They had treated her and Conner like family and refused all her attempts to compensate them for their down-home hospitality.

"We've been blessed by the Lord's bounty, and it's a privilege to share," Harriet said just before placing an intricate lace doily in Paige's hand. "Remember, Dear, our door is always open."

"What'd I tell you about that country breakfast?" Zeke asked as the old Rambler rocked down the country road and turned back onto Interstate 44. "If the genuine affection in that home doesn't bring you back, those melt-in-your-mouth pancakes smothered in Funk's Grove Mapel Syrup will!" With a sigh, Zeke added, "Contentment is a great place to be!"

"Is that where we're going next?" Connor asked.

Zeke hooted with joyful laughter. "It's a state of mind, Little Man, not a place. You'll know it when you get there."

"But, how?"

"Simple," Zeke answered as he tapped the steering wheel of the old car. "If you've learned to sit back and enjoy the detours in life, then you've arrived!"

As they cruised through Lebanon, Missouri, without stopping, Paige let Connor take moving snap-shots of remnants of Route 66—motels flagged by ancient neon signs, historic markers, old stores, and retro service stations.

In the next city, Paige pointed out an artistic mural painted on the side of a building. "Look at that, Connor."

"Awesome!" The image was inspired by the Trompe l'oeil rendition of old store fronts and pedestrians dressed in vintage clothes. Zeke pulled over to the curb, and Connor fished out his set of colored pencils and sketch pad from his new backpack and began to draw.

Paige leaned back and closed her eyes, wondering what would become of her family. Her hopes and dreams had begun to crumble, like the old road they traveled. She whispered a silent prayer for their tenuous future.

"Next stop, Fantastic Caverns!" Zeke announced as the Rambler wound up the northern edge of the Ozark Highlands, prompting another group sing along.

"Get your kicks on Route 66. Now you go through St. Louie, and Joplin, Missouri, and Oklahoma City looks mighty pretty…"

Soon the old car traveled beside a blue-green river that sparkled in the sunlight, and Zeke hollered, "First one to spot the old red mill wins a vintage, smiley-face button!"

Connor popped up and eagerly scanned the scenery. A few miles later, he pointed toward a limestone bluff. "There it is, near that big white rock."

"By golly, you're right." Zeke raised a bushy brow. "Say, you haven't been here before, have you?"

"Nope, honest. I just spotted a speck of red between the trees."

"I was just foolin' with you, Little Man! Why anybody with any sense can tell you were born with eagle eyes!" Zeke grinned and pointed to the glove box. "You'll find your prize in there."

Paige felt unusually happy as she watched her son

proudly pinning the badge on his t-shirt, and the feeling remained as the old Rambler puttered past patchwork fields of corn and soybeans.

Zeke cranked down his window and drew in a breath of fresh air. His long, white beard fluttered in the breeze as he chattered on about wild critters they might catch a glimpse of along the way.

A short while later, they spotted a sign for Fantastic Caverns, and with a jerk of the wheel, the car squealed into the parking lot and braked to a hard stop.

Five minutes later, the threesome found themselves loitering with a group of tourists at a bus stop. They didn't have to wait long. From a narrow road and through a tunnel of trees, a Jeep arrived towing a long, red wagon.

The driver collected the tickets and yelled, "All aboard!"

Zeke elbowed Connor and asked, "Ever been on a hayride?

"I bet it's a lot like this!" the child said as the Jeep entered the mouth of the cave.

The driver chugged slowly through the caverns, and Paige was in awe. Above and below, stalactites and stalagmites shined with an iridescent rainbow of colors. Few words passed among the travelers while they rolled through the caverns.

Walking back to the Rambler, Zeke, Connor, and Paige quietly reflected on the beauty of God's jewel-toned creation.

"Shotgun!" the child said and scrambled for the front passenger seat.

Paige didn't mind. As they continued on their way, she checked her phone. There was a text from her legal partner, Jerry, asking a question about one of her cases, which he had agreed to take on, and a voicemail from an unknown number. She felt the blood drain from her face as she listened to the trembling words. "Please help?" Bree pleaded. Paige's former client was crying, and her voice was filled with fear. "I think he's going to kill me." Next, came a brief silence followed by a hasty whisper. "He's coming." The disturbing call ended abruptly.

A lump formed in Paige's throat, and with trembling hands, she dialed Detective Rowland at the Manhattan Precinct. To her surprise, he answered on the second ring.

He took down every word along with the number that Bree had called from. "I'll have the phone company run a check and see what they can come up with. In the meantime, let me know if you receive any more calls."

Paige hung up feeling swamped by guilt. *If only, I hadn't been so careless with Bree's address... If only....*

In the rearview mirror, Zeke's pale eyes locked on Paige. "I was just thinking about something your husband's old boss once said."

"Thomas Atwood?" she asked.

"Yup. The President of the United States rubbed elbows with a lot of important people, but he never let it go to his head. Nope, that man reckoned his greatest privilege was getting on his knees and talking to the Creator of the whole universe, something even the simplest person on earth can do any time they have a mind to." The old man's eyes turned back to the road ahead. "Kinda puts things in perspective, don't you think?"

Paige nodded in agreement and prayed quietly while Zeke and Connor launched into another round of singing Route

66. Before long, they passed a sign that read, "Welcome to Kansas, the Sunflower State." Immediately, stunning fields of gold came into view.

"These are one of my all-time favorite flowers," the old man said. "Did you know that their faces are always turned toward the sun?"

Paige snapped photos as the Rambler sputtered across a fourteen-mile slice of the state.

"We're not in Kansas anymore, Toto!" Zeke exclaimed as they crossed into Oklahoma. "Next stop on the agenda is the famous Blue Whale of Catoosa," the old man said. "Some guy built it as a birthday gift to his wife who collected whale figurines. I'd love to have seen her face when she unwrapped it!" It wasn't long before they pulled off the road and the structure came into view—a big blue whale that was built over a pond.

"Awesome!" Connor bounced on the bench seat, then spilled from the car, and ran to the blue creation. "Can I go swimming?"

"Once upon a time, you could, but not anymore, I'm afraid. Folks are too worried about germs these days." Opening the back hatch of the wagon, Zeke retrieved a rattan basket and a table cloth and made his way to a picnic table.

"Look at me! I'm Jonah!" the boy called from the smiling mouth of the blue whale.

Paige took a few pictures and then helped Zeke with the spread. "When did you get all this?" There were fresh cold cuts, cheeses, red grapes, and even some goldfish crackers—Connor's favorite.

Zeke grinned. "Just a few things I dug out of my cooler."

Trying in vain to recall a grocery store stop, Paige said, "I'd be glad to reimburse you."

The old man sliced a hunk of cheese and summer sausage. "I've got more goodies in the back end of that old rattle trap than I can eat!" He bowed his head for a little prayer and took a bite. They ate beneath the warm noon sun and then packed it all back into the car to continue what Zeke called, "Their Big Adventure."

By the time they got to Arcadia, Oklahoma, Connor was an expert at iPhone photos. He scrolled through an eclectic assortment of pictures, ranging from a notable round barn and a towering neon soda bottle to fields of cows and flowers. Paige did her best to give her son her undivided attention, but she soon found her mind drifting. There had barely been enough time to process all the events of the last few weeks. The mysterious stalker that terrorized her family, the recent compromises by her church, her husband's criminal investigation, the abduction of her client, and now, a completely unexpected Americana road trip with this mysterious little man.

North Dakota
Saturday, July 13th

"I can't imagine why they wanted you to come in on a Saturday," Coco said as she and her husband approached the receptionist at the FBI Field Office in Minot, North Dakota.

"My name is Joel Sutherland," he said to a woman

wearing oversized glasses.

"Of course. Agent Pollard is expecting you." Her magnified eyes shifted to his bride. "Mrs. Sutherland, I presume?"

Coco nodded. "Yes, can you tell us what this is about?"

Without answering, the receptionist lifted the receiver, pressed a button, and spoke quietly to a person on the other end. "Someone will be with you shortly."

The couple took a seat beside a coffee table lined with outdated magazines. Joel's leg jiggled nervously as the minutes ticked away.

Finally, the door opened, and a man wearing a gray suit and matching tie approached. His hair was clipped short, and his face and eyes were stony. Skipping polite formalities, he said, "Joel Sutherland. Follow me."

Agent Pollard thrust open the metal door and led Joel down a corridor lined with framed documents and newspaper articles. In a room containing only a table and a few hard chairs, Joel was instructed to sit.

The agent paced the floor, turned abruptly, then he placed both hands on the table and leaned forward. "Mr. Sutherland, do you admit to authoring a blog called 'Beyond the Fall?'"

"Yes, Sir."

The agent slid a memo from his vest pocket and briefly consulted it. "Is it true that, in your own words, you encouraged your readers to '…to actively resist new regulations and take a stand against the swelling cultural tide of social engineering?'"

"I believe that's what I wrote."

"Are you aware, Mr. Sutherland, that your inflammatory

blog has spawned protests all across the country?"

"You're kidding, right?" One look at the man's sharp, stony features made Joel realize he wasn't. "Why are you asking me these questions?"

"During one of these protests, a police officer was injured. At another rally, a storefront was damaged, and items were looted."

Joel shook his head. "But, I never encouraged reckless or illegal behavior."

"On the contrary, Mr. Sutherland, the US Government is preparing to indict you for inciting a riot and sedition."

"What? This is totally outrageous!" Joel launched from his chair and faced the agent. "Am I free to go?"

"Yes, Mr. Sutherland, but I must caution you not to leave the country."

In the waiting room, it took Coco only one look at her husband's stunned expression to know the meeting had not gone well, and she quietly followed him out the door. In the shadow of the Minot Federal Building, Joel punched out a tweet alerting all his followers about the pending charges.

Chapter 33

New York

Monday, July 15th

Katrina Katz knocked briefly before entering the office of the UBC executive producer. "You wanted to see me, Sir?"

Ed Blankenship looked up from his cluttered desk. "Come in, but don't get comfortable."

She approached her boss and waited for instructions.

"Have you heard that Thomas Atwood's kid has been indicted by the US Attorney in North Dakota for inciting a riot and sedition? What am I saying? Of course, you've heard! Every media outlet in America is buzzing about Joel Sutherland! The Civil Justice Union practically fell all over themselves scrambling to represent this young man. Shares and tweets are through the roof right now! And, thanks to every major network in America, this kid has become a household name. Some are even calling him a folk hero and rightfully so!"

Katrina had never seen Ed Blankenship so enflamed. He jumped to his feet. "You know what all this means, don't you?

It's a total affront to the First Amendment, free press, and all that!" he muttered. "After all the bones that the media has thrown to this administration, you'd think they would show a little respect. Ira Corbin practically owes his landslide election to the press, and this is the thanks we get?" Blankenship lurched to a sudden stop and turned to his lead anchorwoman. "Well, what do you have to say about it?"

Hoping that this was the opportunity she had been waiting for to finally break her story, Katrina replied, "Plenty. Actually, Sir, I have been working on a piece about other, yet similar, government abuses."

Ed sank back into his desk chair, folded his hands together, and said, "I'm listening."

"Well, it's not just the First Amendment that's under attack. If Alistair Dormin has his way, our national sovereignty along with our freedom could be compromised!"

"Has his way?! You're talking about a man who has worked economic miracles and even brokered peace in the Middle East! Some are calling him a 'political savior!'"

"More like a Svengali if you ask me," Katrina countered.

"Really, Ms. Katz, that's a bit histrionic, don't you think?" Ed Blankenship scowled. "Where did you come up with such a notion?"

"I've been working on a story and using an anonymous, but credible source, one who was recently outed," Katrina explained. "Since then, this man's career has been sabotaged by trumped-up charges, and his family has been persecuted."

Blankenship leaned forward and clasped his hands together. "If you're talking about Brody Hays and his insider trading, what makes you so sure these allegations are false?"

"I don't think it was a coincidence that he suddenly became the subject of a Securities and Exchange Commission investigation right after my computer was hacked."

"Wait just a minute. Are you saying that Hays was framed just to discredit him as a source?"

"Yes, Sir," Katrina said firmly, "that's exactly what I'm saying."

Her boss flicked his wrist, stared at his watch, and said, "I'm late for a meeting." "Bring me some proof, and maybe we'll continue this conversation. Until then, concentrate on the story about the late president's kid. Our First Amendment rights need defending!"

Route 66

Monday, July 15th

After spending two nights in a nice hotel in Oklahoma City, Paige felt rested enough to join in with another chorus of "Get your kicks on Route 66…"

Outside of Amarillo, Texas, Zeke surprised Connor with a row of brightly painted cars jutting from the Texas farmland, their front ends buried in the sunbaked soil. "No trip down the Mother Road would be complete without stopping at the Cadillac Ranch!" Zeke parked the Rambler behind a minivan and said, "You two go on ahead. I'll be rooting around the back of my wagon for a few minutes."

When he joined Mother and Son, he had a little gift for Connor. Handing him several cans of spray paint in variety of colors, Zeke said, "You got work to do, Little Man! Go make your mark!"

They wandered around the strange farmland icon, admiring the art contributions left by countless visitors. Several other people were making their marks, and the air was permeated with the smell of spray paint. There was hardly a space on any of the buried Cadillacs that hadn't been decorated with graffiti—some primitive, some worthy of a frame.

Connor selected a spot and went to work with an intensity and enthusiasm that Paige had rarely seen. She took pictures as her son painted sets of eyes that seemed to follow you with their gaze. He painted until the colors ran out on the last buried Cadillac.

"Nice job!" Zeke said. "But why did you choose to paint eyes?"

"Because, I want everybody to know that God is watching over them!" Connor said, skipping back toward the car.

As they climbed back into the Rambler, Paige longed for faith like her child. "Please, Lord, help Bree," she prayed.

The next stop, 40 miles east of Amarillo, was no surprise. For miles and miles, they had seen the gigantic steel cross, looming larger and larger, as the old car chugged closer to the tiny town of Groom, Texas.

Just past an ancient leaning water tower emblazoned, "Britten USA," Zeke steered for the 190-foot cross and came to a stop at the popular site for tourists.

A series of the life-sized bronze statues of Jesus with other Bible characters surrounded the gargantuan Christian symbol. "These sculptures are called Stations of the Cross," Zeke explained. "They tell the visual story of the Lord's crucifixion."

A woman, wearing jeans and a t-shirt, stepped forward with a clipboard in hand. "Would you join the petition to save the cross? We need as many signatures as we can get because there is a movement underway to have this whole thing torn down."

"Why?" Connor asked.

"I don't know," she said. "Some people think it's offensive; others think that old religion impedes progress."

"Kinda like that old Mother Road we've been traveling. She's been left to crumble, replaced by interstate highways, so a lot of folks who have no idea where they're going can get there faster." Zeke scribbled his name on the paper, passed it on, and gazed upward, his fingers contemplatively twirling the end of his long, white beard.

Paige was about to respond when her cell phone rang with a now familiar number. She answered immediately. "Bree!"

"I can't talk long," the young woman said under her breath. "He just went outside for a minute."

"Quick, just tell me where you are!"

"Vermont, I think, in some abandoned shack near Lake Champlain."

"Think hard, Bree. Are there any landmarks nearby?"

"We crossed a bridge, and I saw a sign—Windmill Point…" The conversation ended abruptly.

Paige pressed her ear to the phone and could hear breathing. "Are you there?"

A man's icy voice replied, "Bree can't play right now. She's all tied up." The line went dead.

Tears streamed down Paige's face as she called Rowland

to pass on the new information.

"Windmill Point is a lighthouse on Lake Champlain. If I remember correctly, it's just a few miles from the Canadian line. When Bree was abducted, her husband was put on the Interpol list. With or without RFID chips, this couple will be detained at the border, so I'm betting they'll head north on foot."

Paige's temples throbbed. "I'm so worried about Bree. What if…"

"Let's not think the worst. We may have lost the element of surprise, but time is still on our side," Detective Rolland said. "If they're out there, we'll find them."

As Paige slipped her cell phone into her bag, she felt a warm hand on her shoulder. Zeke's pale-blue eyes were filled with love and compassion. He directed her gaze to the white cross that kissed an azure sky. "Connor is right, you know," the old man said with a smile and a wink. "God is watching over us."

Arizona
Monday, July 15th

"Have you caught the men who robbed us?" David asked as the Sheriff walked into the General Store with his deputy.

Sheriff Griff shook his flattop. "I'm afraid we're here on a different matter."

"Oh?"

The deputy flipped open a small notebook. "We

understand you spoke with a couple a few weeks back." He paused, consulted his notes, and continued. "Charleton and Vanessa Bennett. Can you tell me about the nature of that visit?"

"It was a legal matter," David said. "Though I haven't been formally retained, I have been consulted, so it would be a breach of ethics for me to comment further."

"Yeah, we know, lawyer-client privilege!" Griff sank his hands into the pockets of his tan uniform. "Would it help you to know that this couple may be in danger?"

"What do you mean?"

"According to the Border Patrol, they passed through their station last week and updated their passport status," the Sheriff explained, "but they never made it to their property in Mexico."

"Are you saying that they took the RFID chip?"

"That's right," the deputy interjected. "It's our understanding that the wife was okay with the injection, but the husband gave the border agents an earful before taking his."

"They never arrived?" David muttered. "This changes everything about lawyer-client confidentiality. Charleton Bennett felt that being forced to have a chip imbedded in his body was a violation of his civil liberties, and after looking into the matter, I tend to agree."

Griff handed David his business card. "The Bennett's daughter has filed a missing-persons report, so if you hear from them, please let us know."

David glanced at his little girl with her box of crayons spread out on the lunch counter. A few feet away, her mother pressed burger patties. "About those men who robbed us, do you think they might be connected with the group of migrant workers who were recently murdered?"

The lawmen exchanged a look. "That's a possibility, but we can't do anything until the victims are identified."

"So, in the meantime," David said, "innocent people, like the Bennetts, might be targeted by bandidos who want to steal their identities."

⸙

Route 66

Monday, July 15ᵗʰ

By the time they reached Albuquerque, New Mexico, Paige was sick with worry. If there had been any good news about Bree, Detective Rowland would have called by now.

America's main street ran right through the heart of the Sun Belt city. The Rambler slowly cruised by—without stopping—old-style diners, a wall of eclectic road signs, and vintage gas stations.

Outside the sprawling southwestern town, the travelers encountered the vast arid flatness of the landscape, but Zeke drew their attention to a sandstone mesa in the distance. "I've got a buddy who lives halfway to El Malpais. You'll get a hoot out of Kibby's place! It's a real curiosity!"

Forty minutes later, Zeke's Rambler was bouncing down a dirt road and collecting a layer of fine dust on the windshield. They drove along a barbed wire fence decorated with an assortment of battered pots and pans, colorful enamelware, and rusty cast iron. "You should hear this place when the wind blows!" The old man let out a whistle.

"Why are all those pots there?" Connor asked. "Does your friend like to cook a lot?"

Zeke laughed with delight. "Didn't I say? His last name is Potts! The way Ol' Kibby explains it, he hung these out here so that the mail man would know he was on the right road."

Connor giggled, but Paige began to wonder what they were getting themselves into.

"Is that a ship?" The boy pitched forward and motioned to a large wooden boat propped upright in the dry landscape.

"That's what you call a tug boat! It's something you don't lay eyes on every day out here in the desert."

"Awesome!" Connor yelped. "Look at all those doors!"

Just beyond the boat was a line of old doors that had been hinged together to form a wall. Their baked and crackled paint popped with color.

"Did I say that Ol' Kibby is a collector of sorts?"

"What does he collect?" Connor asked

"He sorta collects everything!"

Paige was stunned when they passed under an arched gate of antlers and parked alongside a row of old school-bus bodies that had been crudely welded together.

Kibby Potts stepped up to the car as his visitors emerged, and two grossly obese Dachshunds waddled up with tails wagging. "Well, I'll be a round monkey's uncle!" he chortled. Then he grabbed Zeke's hand and pumped so vigorously that his plump cheeks jiggled.

Noting the man's black, brillo chin and navy-blue cap with gold braiding, Connor said, "You look like a captain of a ship. And, you've got lots of medals, too."

Mr. Potts responded with a laugh so hearty that his vest

covered with lapel pins began to jingle. There were airline pins, club pins, sports pins, police pins, and too many others to identify.

After proper introductions, Mr. Potts invited them all inside. He slapped a hand onto Zeke's back and said, "I was beginning to think you'd forgotten about your old friend. How long has it been? Fifteen years or so?"

"It's taken me that long to find something unique to add to your collection!" Zeke brushed his long, white beard aside and reached into the breast pocket of his Hawaiian shirt. He pulled out an antique, gold skeleton key adorned with intricate etched patterns. "I'm told this is one of a kind."

Kibby's eyes widened as he studied the new addition. He wiped the trace of a tear away with cuff of his sleeve. "You didn't have to bring me nothing, you Ol' Coot!" Mr. Potts grinned showing a rack of bad teeth and said, "Thank you, Jesus, for Zeke and these new friends that he brung me!"

The man's belly rumbled like an old steam pipe. "Hey, bet you're all as hungry as I am!" He and his Dachshunds led them through a maze of connected bus bodies that had been stripped of the bench seats. The first bus displayed a collection of license plates, the next an assortment of travel spoons, the following one showcased an eclectic mix of eyeglass frames that had been glued to the walls. Finally, they entered a round room that had been constructed of concrete encased with old bottles that let in colorful shafts of light. White, green, blue, and amber light fell across the floor from the direction of the setting sun.

"This here is what I call my sitting room," he announced, pointing to a childish-looking sign near the entrance made with a wood burner. It read, "Sometimes, I sits and thinks, and sometimes, I just sits."

Kibby invited his guests to sit on the old bus seats that had been placed haphazardly. "Make yourselves at home, while I toss the dogs in the deep-fat fryer."

Connor's face turned pale. "I'm not hungry!"

Zeke patted the boy's shoulder. "Kibby's talking about hot dogs, not the Dachshunds. Best splitters you'll ever sink your teeth into," he added with a wink. "Trust me, you're gonna love 'em!"

After dinner, Kibby wanted to show off his garden. They strolled by cosmos flowers that were growing in the center of vintage iron-bed frames. The odd fellow came to a stop and with a sweep of his hand, he said, "These are what I call my container plants!"

Paige couldn't help but smile. She snapped pictures of the bright flowers that sprang from the bowls of a dozen porcelain toilets.

As twilight settled over Kibby's treasure land, he loaded his arms with quilts and pillows and then instructed the group to follow him up some rickety stairs that led to the roof above the sitting room. "Time to count the stars," he announced before placing bedding on a row of cots. "I'll have a pot of stout coffee and a skillet of hash ready in the morning."

Paige tucked blankets around her son then she laid down on her cot and looked up. Soon Zeke's breathing turned to a subtle snore, and she could hear Connor trying to number the stars above. Before long, everything and everyone grew quiet.

The deep-fried hotdog Paige nibbled for dinner wasn't sitting well, and the canvas cot felt hard against her back. She thought about her life: born into a family of money and privilege, her education at an ivy-league college, and the comforts of her penthouse. Suddenly, conviction swelled in her heart. *Am I a hypocrite?* Paige wondered. Many times since her conversion, she had reached out to the underprivileged, but until now, she had been unable to relate fully. *My life is in shambles.* She thought about people like Zeke, Harriet and Homer, and Kibby Potts; people who on the surface had little, yet they had opened wide their hearts and homes to strangers.

Tears streamed down Paige's cheeks as she reflected on her latest pro-bono case, a young woman now fighting for her life. "Help her, Lord!" she whispered.

The response came almost immediately by text message! "Bree is safe! Husband killed by Canadian Mounties trying to run the Border," Detective Rowland wrote.

Paige felt a rush of relief mingled with a strange sense of sadness for the tragic end of the life of a young man who had terrorized so many. She turned her eyes to the blanket of stars that shined down upon a world that seemed to be spinning apart. An inexplicable sense of peace settled over Paige's soul as she drifted off to sleep.

Chapter 34

North Dakota

Tuesday, July 16ᵗʰ

Joel slipped through the door of the Thomas Atwood Presidential Library and hurried downstairs to his office. His mind was in a whirl.

Thanks to the Civil Justice Union and the indignation of the mainstream media, the charges of inciting a riot and sedition had been dropped. There was so much to say, but this time, Joel decided to draw from the wisdom of those patriots who had gone before him.

After booting up his computer, Joel was stunned by the avalanche of responses to his recent legal issues. He scrolled through hundreds of blog comments, most expressing outrage and encouragement. "Stand against tyranny! Don't give in!"

Joel consulted his notes and began to type:

"If freedom of speech is taken away, then dumb and silent we may be led, like sheep to the slaughter."—George Washington

"I believe there are more instances of the abridgment of

the freedom of the people by gradual and silent encroachments of those in power than by violent and sudden usurpations."—James Madison

"Whoever would overthrow the liberty of a nation must begin by subduing the freeness of speech."—Benjamin Franklin

There was more at stake than just being right. As former Supreme Court Justice Oliver Wendell Holmes Jr. warned, "We should be eternally vigilant against attempts to check the expression of opinions that we loathe. If there is any principle of the Constitution that more imperatively calls for attachment than any other, it is the principle of free thought—not free thought for those who agree with us, but freedom for the thought that we hate."

Former President Harry S. Truman agreed, saying, "Once a government is committed to the principle of silencing the voice of opposition, it has only one way to go, and that is down the path of increasingly repressive measures, until it becomes a source of terror to all its citizens and creates a country where everyone lives in fear."

Joel paused over the keyboard to reflect upon his own thoughts. "This 'fear' that Truman mentioned is confirmed by every mute voice that has been silenced by the unbridled march of political correctness," he wrote. After thanking his supporters and promising to continue the fight, Joel posted the newest addition to his blog and sat back in his chair.

There was a soft rap on his office door, and it slowly swung open. Sam Quince, Chairman of the Foundation, entered. He paused to place a box on top of a file cabinet and stood expectantly. His manner was tense.

"Is something wrong?" Joel finally asked.

Mr. Quince brushed a glistening bead of sweat from his clean shaven upper lip, and said, "Well, yes, now that you mention it. Our voicemail boxes are jammed with calls from reporters. There are messages from talk show hosts, morning show hosts, and radio personalities—all inviting you to be a guest." Avoiding eye contact, Sam sank his hands deep into the pockets of his maroon blazer. "The fact is…" He paused before finishing. "We just feel that this arrangement is not working out."

"We?"

"The Executive Committee of the Board of Directors has met several times regarding your ordeal." The little, billiard ball of a man paused to gulp a breath of air, then he continued. "This kind of kerfuffle is simply not what we envisioned for your father's presidential library." Sam Quince motioned to the package that he had placed on the top of Joel's file cabinet. "To show our gratitude for your efforts, we've decided to present you with a brand new laptop."

"What about my blog domain?"

"Beyond the Fall? Oh, that is entirely your creation! Yes, please feel free to transfer all your files." Mr. Quince hesitated for an awkward moment and added, "It's been a pleasure working with you, and I do hope there are no hard feelings." Without waiting for a response, he offered a sweaty handshake and then hurried out the door.

⸺∞⸺

Arizona
Tuesday, July 16ᵗʰ

Before loading the newspaper machine on the General Store porch, David scanned the headlines, "American Couple Missing." He read on, "Charleton and Vanessa Bennett disappeared after recently updating their passports and receiving RFID chip implants at a border crossing. They never arrived at their resort property in Mexico. The US State Department is investigating the disappearance as a possible abduction."

Or worse, David thought.

Elita returned from the Arroyo Seco Post Office with a handful of mail. "You finally got a letter from the US Fish & Wildlife Service," she announced.

David laid the newspaper on the stack of others and opened the official looking envelope. "We have reviewed and approved your conservation plan pursuant to requirements of Section 7 of the Endangered Species Act. However, substantial alterations to existing infrastructure must receive prior approval. Failure to meet regulatory requirements will result in further review." He folded the letter and slipped it into his pocket. *One more skirmish won,* he thought. Still, David had a feeling that the battle wasn't over.

New York
Tuesday, July 16ᵗʰ

From her desk at the Unified Broadcasting Corporation,

Katrina Katz waited by the phone for Joel Sutherland to return her call. *Unlikely*, she thought. *Every journalist in the country is probably hounding this poor young man!*

Across the nation, the media was strutting their victory. The Fourth Estate, as they were known, had collectively flexed their muscle, battled the government, and won! Joel Sutherland's First Amendment right to maintain his blog without fear of prosecution was now secure. *At least, for the time being,* Katrina speculated.

The phone rang and after glancing at the caller ID, Katrina snatched the receiver from the cradle. "Yes—have you found something?" she asked.

"Whoever hacked your computer is good. I'll give 'em that," said Oggie from the IT department.

On the other end of the line, Katrina could hear the techie punching over his keyboard. "So, are you telling me there's no way to trace them?"

"Naw!" Oggie balked, "I've still got a few tricks up my sleeve when it comes to sleuthing slippery IP addresses."

"I'm glad to hear that," Katrina said, trying to mask her disappointment. "Listen, Oggie, this is really important. I appreciate all your help."

"Hey, no problemo! When it comes to a tech challenge, I'm in the game!"

"Will you let me know if anything comes up?"

"Wait a minute—hang on! I do believe the winning lottery numbers are beginning to line up!"

Katrina pressed her ear to the receiver.

"Hello! Sweet Hal—I think I've nailed down the smoking IP!"

"What?" The anchorwoman held her breath in anticipation.

"And the winner is…, Drum roll please…" Oggie rapped on his desk for effect.

"Just tell me!" Katrina pressed.

"Oh, alright. The offending computer resides in an office of the World Fortress Institute in New York."

"I knew it!" The anchorwoman slapped the desk with the palm of her hand. "Can you tell whose office?"

"Gregory Flout, Administrative Assistant to somebody named Jean Pierre. I'll shoot you an email with all the details."

"I could kiss you, Oggie. You just earned yourself a bonus!"

"Just make it a fat gift card for Starbucks, and we'll call it even," he chuckled. "Well, it's been fun, but I'd better do some real work here before they fire me."

After receiving the email from the IT department, Katrina gathered her folder in arm and marched down the hall to the executive producer's office.

Ed Blankenship was just on his way out the door when she arrived. "I'm off to another board meeting. Can this wait?" He looked at his reflection in a glass partition and straightened his tie.

"No, Sir, I'm afraid it can't." Katrina followed her boss to the elevator. "Remember when you told me to find evidence that Dormin's people might be involved in the hacking of my computer?" She held up her folder. "I've got it! Now, about my editorial?"

Ed stepped into the elevator and held up a hand. "Okay, fine, just lay a copy on my desk when you're done working on it."

When the elevator door closed, Katrina headed back to her office with a renewed fire in her belly.

⸺⸎⸺

Arizona
Tuesday, July 16ᵗʰ

The sun had long ago set when Zeke's Rambler pulled up to the General Store in Arroyo Seco. David and Elita practically flew down the steps of the porch to welcome the travelers.

Paige left her son sleeping in the back seat and emerged for a round of family hugs.

Elita peeked at her nephew slumbering in the station wagon and turned to her sister-in-law. "Joy tried her best to stay awake, but her dad finally carried her upstairs and tucked her into bed."

"We expected you earlier and were getting a bit worried," David interjected.

"What? With me at the wheel?" Zeke said with a wink and a grin.

"If anybody is hungry or thirsty, there are refreshments inside," Elita announced.

"Got any toothpicks to prop my eyelids open?" the old man said with a yawn. "Just cause I'm not asleep, doesn't mean I'm awake either."

"Why don't we catch up tomorrow after everyone's rested," Paige suggested. "I understand everything is set up for us at Hope Springs."

"Do you want to follow me there?" David asked.

"Don't bother. I know the way," Zeke said. "I'll be poking around a while this time, so we'll have time to do some catching up."

After giving Paige directions to her new trailer, David pulled his sister close for another hug. "It's good to have you here. We'll see you tomorrow morning around 9:00 A.M.."

"I can't wait," Paige said as she slipped back into the old station wagon. The Rambler rolled across the desert highway under a star-sprinkled veil of darkness. As much as Paige enjoyed the road trip, she was grateful it was mostly behind her. The battle between fear and faith had left her so exhausted that even her bones felt heavy. A good night's sleep and a place to settle was just what she needed.

The old man steered toward lights that shined in the distance like illuminations from a miniature city. Zeke turned down a rough dirt road and rocked over the ruts. Under the moonless night sky, they drove along fenced pastures and past the barn. "Welcome to Hope Springs!" he announced.

Dashboard lights twinkled in Zeke's eyes as he turned up a tree-lined drive that ran between rows of various mobile dwellings. "This is no ordinary place," he said.

"At this point, I am not particular. I just want to wash away some road dust," Paige replied.

"Here it is—Home Sweet Home." The old man pulled up beside a silver pickup that was parked in front of an Airstream trailer nestled under a shelter.

"Wake up, Honey." Paige reached in back to stir her sleeping boy. "We're here."

Connor popped up like a jack-in-the-box, rubbed his

eyes, and said, "Awesome!"

The travelers passed beneath a striped awning and found the door unlocked. "Mind if I take a peek?" Zeke said.

"More than that! I'd like you to make yourself at home. There's room on the couch," Paige said as she looked around the brand new camper with all of its modern amenities.

"Nice digs you got here, if I don't say so, myself." The old man checked out the fully stocked fridge, Corian counters, and the flat screen TV. "I appreciate the invite, but I've got one of those fancy pup tents. All I have to do is slide it out of the bag, give it a flick of the wrist, and it springs into action!"

As he headed out the door, Zeke turned toward the mother and child. "Remember, just because you're here doesn't mean you're there yet! Your journey is far from over."

Chapter 35

Arizona

Wednesday, July 17ᵗʰ

Paige awoke to the faint sound of a rooster crowing. It took her a few seconds to orient herself in the new trailer that her husband had arranged to be delivered to Hope Springs.

She threw back the covers on her bed and padded across the floor to check on her son. Connor was gone! A quick glance out the window calmed her panic.

Zeke and the boy were kicking back in some folding lawn chairs just beyond the striped trailer awning. "We're just catching a few morning rays!" the old man said. "Want to join us?"

"I must have slept in." Paige glanced at her watch. It was half past eight. *Just enough time for a quick shower,* she reasoned.

A gaunt man with heavy-framed glasses emerged from his school-bus conversion next door. He nodded at Paige and ambled over to Zeke, holding out an enamelware coffee pot. "Refill?" he asked.

"Don't mind if I do!" Zeke said. He stretched out his arm, cup in hand, and cast a glance toward Paige. "Mr. Mike is a handy neighbor to have around. If you have any electronic-gadget problems, he's the guy to call."

"Nice to meet you!" she said and then excused herself. After her shower, Paige threw on some clothes, dabbed on a touch of makeup, and emerged from the trailer feeling refreshed.

"Missed a doozy of a sunrise a couple of hours ago," Zeke said as she took a seat beside them. "But this coffee, on the other hand, is strong enough to make you wanna slap your grandma!"

Connor began to giggle. "Mr. Mike is really awesome, Mom. He can take a whole radio apart and put it back together again!"

Paige spotted a cloud of dust in the distance and recognized the old pickup truck that had been parked at the General Store the night before. She stood and waved as it approached and rolled to a stop next to Zeke's old Rambler.

Joy scrambled over her mother's lap, jumped from the truck, and ran straight to Connor. "This is a fun place," she said, taking her cousin by the hand. "It's got a swimming hole and everything! Come on, I'll show you around."

As the children dashed off to explore, David suggested that they all make their way to the pavilion where a big breakfast had been prepared in honor of the travelers.

As they walked along the path, Paige's brother put his arm around her and said, "Brody called the General Store last night."

"Why didn't he phone me?" she asked.

"Hope Springs has spotty cell service, but Mr. Mike is working on a device that should solve the problem."

Paige searched her brother's face. "Is Brody okay?"

"I'm afraid he's been evicted from the penthouse, but don't worry," David quickly added. "Brody wanted you to know that he's got a place to stay—housesitting for a friend of someone you both know, Katrina Katz."

"What about our belongings?" Paige found herself saying, though her mind was elsewhere.

"He didn't say."

"Look around! You've got more treasures than you can count." Zeke threw his arms wide and drew in a deep breath of fresh air. "No rust or moths to worry about here."

Paige mustered a smile for the unique crowd that had gathered to welcome them. The cheerful residents of Hope Springs held a homemade banner printed with the words, "Welcome Home!"

One by one, the people approached with arms outstretched and faces aglow. Paige felt her eastern reserve melting under the outpouring of love and acceptance. It was almost as though she had known these people all her life.

"A little glimpse of heaven on earth," Zeke said as though he'd read her thoughts.

"We are so glad to have you with us." A small woman with short, silver hair invited everyone to form a line to a bountiful buffet they had prepared.

After filling their plates and finding a seat at one of the many tables, an older gentleman who introduced himself as "Jim" bowed his head, gave thanks for the newcomers' safe arrival, and asked a blessing on the meal.

"Do you think you got enough?" David teased Zeke whose plate was piled high with a little bit of everything.

The old man tucked his beard into the collar of his Hawaiian shirt and then snapped open a napkin. "This is only my first helping," he replied. "Gotta save room for seconds!"

After the meal, David stood to make a few announcements. He began by formally introducing his family and thanked everyone for the warm welcome they'd received. Next, David announced that the endangered species conservation plan had been approved.

Hoots and cheers rippled around the pavilion.

Paige kept an eye on Connor who seemed drawn to a lanky man tuning a guitar.

"That's Raymond Lee," David leaned over and told his sister. "He leads worship around here. Wait until he finds out Connor is also a gifted musician."

It didn't take long. Connor dashed off and returned with his violin case.

"Bring it on, Little Dude!" the former blues man said with a high five. Their music blended as though they had played together for years.

Finally, David called Zeke up front and stood beside him. "Hey, everyone, I'd like to introduce the special character that helped make Rupert Sims' vision become a reality. It was Zeke who first brought me here. Without this amazing man, we would never have discovered the artesian well that makes Hope Springs sustainable."

A collective gasp issued from the group that was gathered, and applause echoed throughout the pavilion along with words of appreciation.

Zeke's cheeks flushed pink. He poked at the ground with the rubber toe of his Converse tennis shoe and said, "You good folks are pointing your eyeballs in the wrong direction. I'm not the source of living waters!" The old man turned his sage face skyward and said, "Every good and perfect gift comes from above."

<hr />

North Dakota
Thursday, July 18th

Lying next to Coco's warm body, Joel listened to her soft and steady breathing. Carefully, trying not to wake his sleeping bride, he slipped out of bed. *If only we could hitch this old sheepherder wagon to a draft horse and steal away for a few weeks,* he mused. Things had been crazy lately. Joel's mailbox on his iPhone was filling up faster than he could reply. Every major media outlet in the country was clamoring for an interview. Joel suddenly found his quiet life, once protected by anonymity, had been catapulted into the national spotlight, the last place he wanted to be!

He pulled back the homemade curtain above the bed and looked outside. Judging by the positon of the sun, they'd slept in. It didn't matter, at least, for the moment.

Joel leaned over Coco. When she stirred, he kissed her ivory cheek and said, "Good morning, Sleeping Beauty."

Coco turned and looked over her shoulder. The window light reflected specks of gold in her dark green eyes. "Every morning I wake up with you is good," she replied.

Crawling back into bed, Joel snuggled close until he could feel their hearts beating as one. He whispered, "I love you," and then gently turned her until they were face to face. "What do you say we stay in bed all day?" Joel leaned in to taste the sweetness of her lips.

Coco responded with a sublime smile that drove him wild. "What would our neighbors think?"

"That we're newlyweds?" Joel drew her even closer until time melted away. The couple lay content as the morning shadows passed across the canvas top of the sheepherder wagon. Joel felt a peace he'd never known before. All the turmoil and heartache grew dim in the light of such powerful love. Beside him, Coco lay still in the tangle of damp sheets, her eyes staring out the little window as if she were looking into another world. "What are you thinking?" he asked.

Her fingers traced the amber cross that hung around her neck. "About God," she replied. "Did you know that those who love Him are called the Bride of Christ?"

Joel didn't know how to respond, so he said nothing.

"It's such a great mystery when you think about it," Coco mused. "I mean, it's hard to comprehend that our love is just a foreshadowing of the love God has for each of us."

"I think it's time to get moving," Joel said, wanting to change the subject. He rose and quickly dressed.

"How come you never talk about what you believe?"

Feeling a bit uncomfortable with the path the conversation was taking, Joel said, "It's complicated." Discussions about faith always had a way of resurrecting his painful past. He raked a comb through his dark ash hair, sensing Coco's eyes upon him. "I've seen a lot of bad stuff, that's all—things that make me wonder if God is real."

"The murder of your adoptive parents wasn't your fault," Coco said.

"Wish I could say the same about Thomas Atwood's assassination," Joel returned. "I mean, if it wasn't for me..."

"You've got to stop blaming yourself! What happened to President Atwood at Berkley could have happened anywhere!"

"Right now, I need to be thinking about a job." Joel grabbed his cell phone along with a pen and paper and settled down to listen to voice-mail messages.

Coco slipped on a summer dress, lit a fire under the tea kettle, and prepared tuna sandwiches for lunch.

"This sounds interesting!" Joel said after listening to one of the messages. "It's from the Patriot Review. It's a national weekly online magazine, and they're offering me a salaried position for my 'Beyond the Fall' editorial opinions." Joel was jotting down the contact information when he was interrupted by a knock.

"I didn't hear anyone drive up," Coco said as she opened the door to find Sergeant Rudd dressed in army fatigues.

He shifted his squinty eyes toward Joel and growled, "I've got something to say to you, Sutherland."

Joel stepped up and positioned himself between Coco and their unbalanced neighbor. "We can talk outside."

"What I have to say won't take long." Rudd unfolded his arms, thrust out a beefy hand, and said, "Keep up the good work! Anyone with the guts to fight the Feds is all right by me!"

Arizona

Friday, July 19th

The afternoon heat had settled over the desert community of Hope Springs, and Paige, along with the other residents, had begun to ease into siesta mode. A few yards away under the watchful eyes of their parents, the children giggled and splashed around the sandstone kiddie pool. Zeke shed his high-top tennis shoes, rolled up his big baggy shorts, and joined the fun.

Priscilla brought Elita and Paige a glass of cold tea and then pulled up a chair. Soon the other women joined the gathering while the men congregated nearby.

"I see you've met Kay and Randy Bales and Bonnie and Jim Saunders," Elita said. "These two couples keep things organized around here."

"Oh, I wouldn't say that," Kay said, pulling her honey-brown hair into a pony tail.

"That's right," Bonnie, an older woman with short spiked hair, agreed. "Everyone at Hope Springs contributes in one way or another." She reached across the table and patted Priscilla's youthful hand. "Like this young lady, who does a fine job of helping Kay teach our children."

"Priscilla also builds stunning crosses from architectural salvage materials," Kay added. "She sells out every time we got to market."

"I'd love to see them," Paige said.

Priscilla looked at Paige with smiling violet eyes as Fawn Nash joined the group.

"I raise sheep, shear their fleeces, dye, spin, and weave

the wool," Fawn volunteered. She lifted her wrinkled bohemian dress and scratched an itch on her thigh. "Yup, I make vests, purses, tapestries, even slippers for the craft fairs. You name it; I can weave it." She laced her fingers behind her long gray hair, looking older than her fifty years. The smell of patchouli oil mingled with body odor hung in the air. Fawn nodded in the direction of a young man with dreadlocks who was sitting at a nearby table. "That's my son, Boyd. He milks the cows, and the rest of the time, he likes looking for images in the clouds. Guess you could say he's lazy, unlike his dad who's in the sceptic tank business."

Fawn Nash was drawing a breath when a petite, brown-skinned woman approached, held out a hand, and introduced herself. "I'm Juanita Ortega. I take care of the green house, and my husband tends the fruit trees. Of course, our children help, too."

"The Ortega's have four fine children," Kay added.

After the appropriate greetings, Paige directed her attention to a heavyset woman, who hadn't said a peep. "I don't think we've met."

The woman mumbled her name, but the words were inaudible, and she quickly averted her gaze.

"Sue is a very gifted baker." Bonnie Saunders jumped in. "She works with me in our communal kitchen."

"Really? I love to cook, too," Paige said. "Maybe I can help." Judging from the brunch that was served, it was obvious to Paige that these ladies had mastered the art of preparing large meals over coals and in a brick oven.

Zeke sloshed to the center of the pavilion, leaving a trail of wet footprints in his wake. "Now, that is what I call refreshing." The old man shook water from his long, white beard, slipped back into his high-top tennis shoes and tied the laces. "I really like what you've done with the place! It's a far cry from the little spit of a town where Rupert Sims was born." Zeke spun around for a panoramic view. "Where can I find a tour guide to show me around these fine facilities?"

Randy Bales, Jim Saunders, and David quickly volunteered. A few of the ladies tagged along, including Paige who marveled at the depth of the small sustainable community of Hope Springs. They strolled past pig pens and a chicken coop and lingered at the milking barn to hear about plans for a solar-powered pasteurization machine.

Zeke rubbed his chin. "Is it true that pigs can eat cow manure, and chickens can eat pig manure?"

"Yes," Randy said, "so I've heard."

"Well, then," the old man quipped, "if you could just get the cows to eat chicken feathers, you'd give new meaning to the idea of sustainable ranching!"

Stunned, they all looked at Zeke before bursting out into laughter.

As they strolled back toward the pavilion, Jim Saunders, their resident engineer, pointed out the stack of reservoirs filled from the deep artesian well from which Hope Springs got it name. "Every drop of water is used. Wash water is funneled to the greenhouse, and any excess is directed to the fields for irrigation. We rely on gravity to move it and water wheels along the way help generate power," Jim said, and then he directed their attention to their new cold storage facility.

Randy stepped up to explain the function of the thick adobe structure with what appeared to be a long tail on one end. "I built this springhouse over the stream that flows from the base of the lower dam." Randy motioned to the attached tunnel with hinged hatches that covered a long section of stream. "Air is cooled as it is drawn up the tunnel, and it keeps the meat, fruit, and vegetables cool in the adobe hut," he explained. "Food is stored on built-in wooden grates where the circulating air helps preserve our meat."

"I'm a vegetarian," Fawn Nash announced. "Personally, I think it's a healthier lifestyle."

Zeke raised an eyebrow. "I've always wondered, can a vegetarian eat animal crackers?"

After the tour, the old man announced it was time to hit the road. Zeke shook hands with Connor first. "Little Man, it's been a pleasure traveling with you. You keep that ear of yours tilted toward Heaven."

Paige stepped forward for a long hug. "I'll never forget you," she whispered.

"And I'll remember you, too. That way, we'll recognize each other the next time we meet," Zeke said with a wink. He fired up the Rambler, hung his hoary head from the window, and waved to the group. Just before he drove away, he pointed at Connor and Paige and said, "Thanks again for giving me those photographs from our road trip together. Good memories!"

Chapter 36

New York

Wednesday, July 24th

One hour before the evening news was set to air, Anchorwoman Katrina Katz got the call that she had been hoping to get. After going over her proposed editorial piece, Ed Blankenship, UBC's Executive Producer, had given her the green light!

Tonight, the issues that had been burning in her bosom for so long could finally be spoken. Katrina emailed the file over to the control room to be loaded into the teleprompter, but there was really no need. She knew the words by heart.

At 11:00 P.M., she was sitting in front of the cameras feeling relaxed, like the calm before a storm. There was no telling what kind of backlash her opinion piece would unleash. Katrina, however, was willing to take the risk. She felt no fear and had no butterflies in her stomach. It was as though this moment in time had been foreordained.

The countdown began. "Five, four, three, two..." The director then pointed to Katrina, indicating that she was on the air.

"Good evening, viewers," Katrina began, "Tonight, I am breaking our station's regular protocol to bring you a personal appeal.

"In Washington, DC, there is a statue named 'Future' near the corner of the National Archives building. On this work of art, a profound statement is inscribed, 'What Is Past Is Prologue.'

"Like a great Irish statesman once said, 'Those who don't know history are destined to repeat it.' I also believe that."

Katrina looked directly at the camera. "I'm sure that you are all aware of Joel Sutherland's recent battle with our present administration, simply because he dared to question new restrictive policies and promises to build a 'better' society." She had used her fingers to put the quotes around the word and then paused to punctuate the seriousness of her message. "This new story is really an old one. Stalin and Hitler both promised to build a utopian society. Each leader garnered a cult-like following of citizens who gave them unquestioning trust. These men surrounded themselves with elite loyalists who helped implement their reigns of terror. Under these tyrants, free thought and speech were strictly forbidden, weapons were confiscated, and religious ideologies that threatened the sterile teachings of the State Church were punished."

The anchorwoman leaned forward. "It's time to wake up America, for the same trends are forming under our watch! Again, I quote from Edmond Burke who warned, 'The only thing necessary for the triumph of evil is that good men do nothing.'

"My unease about the direction this nation is going is shared by others. Several months ago, a brave private citizen approached me with concerns about the sovereignty of the United States. This man was particularly distressed by the power that has been willingly ceded to the World Reserve Bank, and by extension, to its Chairman, Alistair Dormin."

Katrina shifted in her chair before continuing. "Recently, my computer was hacked, and the man of whom I speak, Brody Hays, was outed as my source. Since that time, Mr. Hays has been framed for a crime he did not commit. This innocent man and his family have suffered persecution after he was wrongfully charged with insider trading! How do I know that Brody Hays is innocent? The breach of my computer has recently been traced to the office of the World Fortress Institute, an ally of Alistair Dormin, Chairman of the World Reserve Bank. I am convinced that this smoking gun ties the trumped up charges of insider trading against Brody Hays to Alistair Dormin."

Across the room, a light blinked, signaling the approach of a commercial break. "Trust no mortal words that promise either economic prosperity or monetary equality," Katrina pressed. "Pride and presumption often lead to abuses of power. The lessons of history warn us to be cautious of pledges given by men who want control. Again, I implore the good people of the United States of America to wake up before it's too late!"

⸻

North Dakota
Thursday, July 25th

"It's official! I've been hired!" Joel announced as he and

Coco walked through the door of the Bargain Bin. Nora threw her arms around her son's neck and gave him a big hug. "This calls for a celebration!"

J. J. O'Shay poked in his beanie-covered head from the storage room, "Did somebody say party? I'm in!"

The kitchen door swung open, releasing the aroma of home cooking. Gertie stood on the threshold with her wrinkled hands parked on her round hips and said, "You're just in time for lunch! I've got a big pot of beef stew simmering on the stove, and it just so happens that I made an extra batch of lefse, too!"

Raising an eyebrow, Joel asked, "What is lefse?"

Beaming with pride, Gertie explained, "Lefse is a traditional Norwegian flat bread made with potato flour. It's sort of like a Scandinavian tortilla," she added.

"Now that the culinary class has ended, I'll provide the entertainment!" J. J. twisted the waxed tips of his handlebar moustache and started for the stairs.

Blue-haired Gertie stamped her foot and bellowed, "If you get out those juggling pins of yours, I'll whack you over the head with one! Remember the last time you brought those things out? You dropped one and darn near broke my toe!"

Joel leaned close to Coco and whispered into her ear, "Mr. O'Shay is a retired circus clown."

Nora weighed in as peacemaker. "Maybe later we can watch J. J. preform his act from the front porch. Right now, I want to hear all about my son's new job."

All eyes turned to Joel who said, "My Beyond the Fall blog has now become a regular editorial column for the Patriot Review!"

"How wonderful!" Nora puffed. "I'm so proud of you!"

"I've always wanted to be a writer myself!" Gertie interjected.

"So, what's stopping you?" J. J. jabbed. "Talent?"

Ignoring the remark, Gertie announced, "Lunch is ready."

Before long, they were all sitting around the large fireplace enjoying steaming bowls of beef stew and telling humorous stories.

After a pleasant afternoon, the young couple left with their hearts and bellies warmed by the affection and food, but on the ride home, Coco grew sullen.

"What's wrong?"

"It's just…" She swallowed hard. "I've never really felt like I belonged to a real family until now."

Joel reached over and took his wife's hand. "Everybody loves you, especially me."

Suddenly, up ahead, a convoy of dark vehicles crested a rise in the main highway and turned down the dirt road that led to the couple's love nest. "I wonder what's going on?" Joel said as the Jeep was engulfed in a wake of dust.

The cavalcade rolled past the sheepherder wagon, picked up speed, and then disappeared over the hill.

"They're headed to Sergeant Rudd's place!" Coco said. "Who are they?"

"The ATF, I'd guess," Joel said with growing concern as he parked the Jeep and quickly ushered his bride toward their home, adding, "This may get nasty."

Inside the sheepherder wagon, their new puppy, Moses, had chewed up one of Joel's slippers and left a puddle, but the dog mess was the least of their worries. From over the rise, an explosion shook the ground, followed by the staccato sound of gunfire.

"What should we do?" Coco clutched her quivering puppy.

"I think we should just stay put," Joel said with forced calm. "At least, we have the terrain between us."

There was another explosion, followed by another, and then more gunfire. Joel stepped outside to listen. What he heard sounded like a war zone!

"Maybe we should head back to your mom's place," Coco called out from the door.

Joel returned to the wagon, and from there, the couple watched the sky near Rudd's shipping-crate fort fill with billows of black smoke and sparks. "No, I think we should pray." Those words coming from his lips surprised him.

Without hesitation, his wife curled her fingers around his and began to cry out to God for their neighbor, their nation, and finally themselves.

For a few moments, things grew quiet, and then a strange, yet familiar, sound met Joel's ear.

"The sky looks so strange," Coco said as it darkened from light gray to shimmering black. "Is that smoke?"

"I don't think so." Joel felt his pulse quicken, and he pulled his wife so close that their heartbeats thundered as one.

Like dark sinister fingers, the apparition moved closer. The noise grew louder. Outside, the atmosphere was thick and hazy. Speckled dots of light shimmered in the shadow that pummeled the canvas roof of the sheepherder wagon.

"It's a swarm of locusts!" Joel said as they listened to the whirr of a million gossamer wings.

North Dakota

Friday, July 26ᵗʰ

Sometime after midnight, the bumping, chewing, and whirring subsided. The dense cloud of locusts seemed to have left as quickly as it had descended. Only a few insects remained behind, scratching the top of the sheepherder wagon as they crawled across the canvas.

Under the moonless sky, the night was as dark as ebony. Peering out between her white curtains, Coco said, "There's something going on over at Rudd's place."

Joel joined his wife at the window just in time to see lights coming from the direction of their neighbor's compound. "I'm going to check it out," Joel said, grabbing the flashlight that hung from a nail beside the door.

"Don't!" Coco cried. Her eyes were wild with fear. "What if the locusts are just hiding?"

As quickly as they had appeared, the lights went away. Joel put his arms around his bride and stroked her hair. "Don't worry. I'm sure the locusts have moved on, too." He did his best to sound reassuring, but the truth was the whole thing had creeped him out. The swarm was just like the nightmare he'd had while still in college.

Finally, at dawn, the sun fanned golden rays across the sky, pushing back the darkness to reveal a battered and bruised landscape that had been stripped of greenery. Former fields of corn had been reduced to jutting spears of yellow, and even the leaves of the willow trees, which had once given the couple's dwelling some privacy, were gone! Other trees and a few shrubs were left untouched for reasons known only to the locusts. After a night of terror, an eerie silence had settled over the once pristine countryside.

Hand in hand, Coco and Joel started up the road and silently took in the devastation. Even the grass that once grew along the old country road was chewed to the soil. In just a few hours, the grasshopper-like insects had eaten a ten-mile-wide strip through the heart of North Dakota.

Their puppy, Moses, waddled beside the newlyweds as they topped the hill.

"Oh, Sweet Lord, no..." Tears streamed down Coco's cheeks and dropped to the ground as she gazed upon another horrible sight.

Sergeant Rudd's place had been reduced to a pile of charred and blackened remains. Response units surrounded the place, and police tape fluttered near a tangle of melted steel. A few shipping containers had survived the blaze. Joel watched as men with hazmat uniforms collected samples, and then he saw three body bags lined up in a row! Something told him Sergeant Rudd was one of the fallen.

Chapter 37

New York

Friday, July 26th

From the studio at UBC, Katrina Katz shared the news. "In North Dakota, a locust invasion of biblical proportions has devastated regional crops that provide much of the wheat and flour for the nation. The loss of income from crop damage and the negative economic effects on the farm economy will be felt all across the Great Plains. The swarm came after a fatal skirmish that erupted between a local man and the Bureau of Alcohol, Tobacco, and Firearms. The ATF said the conflict with the civilian began because Mr. Sergeant Rudd had allegedly refused to register his arsenal of weapons. Rudd and two agents were killed in the clash."

The camera view shifted to the White House where Ira Corbin made a statement about the tragedy involving the ATF. "As law abiding citizens, we must take a stand. The time is at hand for further measures. We must put an end to gun violence!"

Strange, the anchorwoman thought, noting that the

President had made no mention of the locusts and the resulting impacts on the agricultural economy.

Katrina Katz reported the rest of the news, feeling preoccupied by all that was going on—not only in the world—but in her own nation.

After the weatherman gave his report, the Off-Air lights flashed, and Katrina headed for the elevator. Since giving her editorial a few days earlier, her inbox had been flooded with replies, some good, others threatening.

On the top floor, the doors slid open, and Katrina Katz was surprised to see her Executive Producer standing there. "Ed, I was just coming up to have a word with you." She looked at the cardboard box in his arms. "Are you going somewhere?"

"I've been fired." Mr. Blankenship's face was pale. "Actually, they used the politer term, 'Let go.'"

"But, why?" Katrina was stunned. "Did my editorial have anything to do with it?"

"It wasn't mentioned as the reason for my termination, however…" Her former boss raised an eyebrow in a cynical gesture before stepping onto the elevator. "If I were you, I'd watch my back," he warned. "You may have opened Pandora's Box."

Arizona
Wednesday, July 31st

Paige gripped the wheel of the brand new Ford F-150 as

she steered down the narrow highway that led to Arroyo Seco. She had grown used to New York City's public transit system, and compared to Brody's BMW, the powerful four-wheel drive felt like a tank.

"This is an awesome truck!" Connor said from the back seat as his mother rolled along using every inch of the asphalt on the lonely road.

"It's for moving the Airstream if there is a need," she explained.

Connor leaned forward and rested his chin on the back of Paige's seat.

"You're not buckled!"

"I want to ride up front with you!"

"It's safer in back," Paige countered.

"Mom! You're treating me like a baby! There's an on/off switch for the passenger airbag. I know because I read the manual, and besides, you're only going forty miles per hour."

"We're almost to Uncle David and Aunt Elita's place," she said as Connor dove over the bench seat, turned off the airbag, and fastened his seatbelt.

Paige left the country road and turned onto the main artery of the sleepy town. She rocked over potholes big enough to swallow a tire. There were tumbleweeds resting in front of boarded-up doors, and storefront windows were covered with yellowed newspaper. *If the remnants of Route 66 are nicknamed America's Main Street, then this must be America's crumbling back alley,* Paige thought.

Joy hopped down the steps of the old country store when they arrived and took her cousin by the hand. "Mom baked blueberry muffins, and I'm hungry."

David was behind an empty oak display case that was once full of Navajo jewelry. He smiled as they walked inside and said, "I'll join you all for breakfast just as soon as I sort through this stack of mail."

"Good morning, campers!" Elita called from the back of the store. She waved them over with her hand that was covered with an oven mitt.

Paige followed the children to the lunch counter and offered to help her sister-in-law.

"Heavens, no!" Elita pulled a large tin from the rack. She set the muffins down to cool and then pointed to a stool. "Make yourselves comfortable."

"I wish we lived in a cool place like this!" Connor grinned as his little cousin spun him around on a red vinyl stool.

"This place is like a museum!" Paige glanced around the large vintage building noting the worn pine floors and the antique light fixtures that hung from the decorative tin ceiling.

"Yup, it's pretty much like it was when I grew up here." Elita nodded, "And that's what my dad said, too. Of course, back in my grandfather's day, they had an ice house out back instead of a walk-in cooler." She set a stack of plates on the lunch counter marked by generations of pocketknife graffiti and cigarette burns. "The only thing that changes around here are the items we stock on the shelves. We're the closest thing to a grocery store around these parts."

Paige admired the ancient Wonder Bread and Bottled Coca Cola signs that hung on the wall behind the grill while her sister-in-law loaded plates with muffins and set them down in front of the children, along with silverware rolled in a paper napkin. "No breakfast for me, just coffee," Paige said. She took a sip and watched Elita visiting with Connor. Normally reserved, the child chattered happily about his art and music. Paige felt a swell of affection for the woman her brother had chosen for his wife. Brown-skinned and earthy, she was beautiful inside and out!

David approached and straddled the stool beside his sister with an envelope in hand.

"What have you got there?" Paige asked as he laid out the contents.

"The latest government assault on Hope Springs." David shook his head in disgust.

Paige set her mug down. "What do you mean?"

The incandescent light that hung overhead illuminated the discouragement in her brother's nomadic eyes.

"It all started when some poser, named Beck McGuire, showed up at Hope Springs."

"You've met Travis, right?" Elita asked Paige.

"Yes, he seems like a very a nice young man," Paige replied.

"He is," David agreed, "but when McGuire tried to take advantage of Priscilla, Travis bloodied his nose. Turns out, Beck McGuire was a freelance, investigative reporter, and he got his revenge by writing a scathing indictment of the folks at Hope Springs."

Paige gasped. "Is he the person who wrote the story that the AP picked up?"

"That's right, the one you emailed to me, but it didn't stop with an article. As trustee for the Rupert Sims estate and Hope Springs, I've been audited by the IRS. Then the EPA had everyone jumping through hoops to comply with the Clean Water Act. Finally, the US Fish & Wildlife Service threatened to fine the community because of possible impacts on endangered species."

"This sounds like harassment!" Paige was insistent.

"I think it's gone beyond that," David said, handing his sister the latest letter from the government.

Paige glanced at the familiar-looking letterhead from the Department of Justice—this time the Arizona Office of the US Attorney. The first two lines told her everything she needed to know. "They are saying that Hope Springs is a church community and is in violation of the Fairness and Anti-Discrimination Act! This is unbelievable."

"It seems that Beck McGuire claimed that they shunned him because he's an agnostic." A puff of cynical laughter blew across David's lips. "Those people took in Gordon Spitzer, and I'm pretty sure he's an atheist!"

"Well, this time the government picked the wrong battle," Paige said emphatically. "It just so happens that I know a thing or two about the FAD Act!"

New York

Monday, August 5ᵗʰ

Katrina's first meeting with her new Executive Producer, Otto Benedict, was anything but pleasant. She rose to greet him as he approached her desk, but the large blocky man with fleshy-hooded eyes and thick-framed glasses thrust a memo into her hand. "These are some stories that I want you to cover, including that locust thing on the Great Plains. Maybe you can sniff out a human interest story there, you know, the plight of the downtrodden farmer and all that."

"Yes, Sir." Katrina hesitated. "I would also like to follow up on the ATF standoff that occurred in the same region. A civilian and several agents were killed in the ensuing skirmish."

Benedict waved his hand dismissively. "No story there. Just some right-wing nut looking for his fifteen minutes of fame! You can work the gun control angle though."

Katrina watched the odious man schlump back to his office, and then she turned her attention to the news memos. Along with the story about the locust plague, there was a piece about the future dedication of the temple in Jerusalem that was liberally sprinkled with religious metaphors. Katrina's heart sank. World Reserve Bank Chairman, Alistair Dormin, was being hailed not only as an economic miracle worker, but also as a prophet of world peace.

Whoever was pulling Otto Benedict's strings was obviously demanding Katrina's atonement for her sin of reporting the truth, yet the seeds of her editorial had already been planted and were beginning to grow! *No amount of bullying is going to dampen my spirits!* she told herself. Just this morning, she had learned that an in independent investigation regarding Brody Hays and the false allegations of insider trading was underway. If all went well, the world might come to see that Alistair Dormin had feet of clay!

Chapter 38

Arizona

Thursday, August 8th

By late afternoon, David was still hunched over a binder in his makeshift office in the General Store storage room when Paige walked in.

"Why don't you buy one of those abandoned buildings on Main and make that your law office?" she asked. "It would do wonders for the economic development of Arroyo Seco."

"Arroyo Seco is a no-growth town," David said with a wry grin. "Besides, Joy isn't old enough to wander the streets by herself."

Paige shook her head and laughed. "You were always different!'"

"What do you have?"

"I worked out a draft response for the US Attorney's office." Paige pulled a stack of papers from her shoulder satchel. "I've addressed most of their concerns about Hope Springs being a 'religious institution,'" she said. "This whole thing is frivolous as far as I'm concerned! We've got

Presbyterians, Baptists, Catholics, Charismatics and Independents. You can't get more ecumenical than that!"

David carefully scanned the document that his sister had put together. "This is good. However, according to the US Attorney's complaint, communal worship at the pavilion constitutes a religious activity, thus making Hope Springs a religious institution. But the only verbiage in the Rupert Sims trust that hints of religion is the use of the phrase, 'people of God,' but it doesn't specify any particular religion," he noted.

"The point is that no one is forced to attend," Paige countered. "In fact, many of the artisans travel to festivals on Sundays to sell their goods." She produced a letter from a resident and handed it to David. "I'm hoping this will clear the whole thing up. Gordon Spitzer states that, as an atheist, he has never attended a single service."

"True. He just shows up for the brunch afterwards." David ran a hand through a tangle of dark hair. "I'm beginning to believe that our government is more interested in having control than finding solutions. It's ironic that, if a complaint of sexual assault had been filed against Beck McGuire, he would never have gotten away with the claim that he was persecuted for being agnostic. But because the good-natured people of Hope Springs chose to overlook the offense, they left themselves open to these charges!"

"That's exactly right!" Paige said. "We should include this background information in our response, along with the letter from Gordon. If the US Attorney refuses to listen to reason, then we may have to fight this charge in court."

"Let's hope it doesn't come to that." David stood, stretched, and rubbed the stubble on his face. "This was a free country the last time I checked."

His sister sighed. "That's one of the problems. People are too busy with their own lives to pay attention to what's happening around them. I'm guilty of the same thing myself. I heard about the FAD Act on the news a few times, but I was more concerned with what herbs would go best with my latest gourmet dish."

"You're not alone," David said as he followed his sister to the front of the store. "I used to think that the North American Coalition Treaty was a good idea. Now, I've come to realize that the solution might be worse than the problem."

Paige turned. "What do you mean?"

"People are being murdered for their RFID chips. Somewhere out there, thanks to our new technology, coldhearted killers are now able to come and go as they please."

"Oh! I almost forgot," Paige announced. "Hope Springs has cell service now, thanks to Mr. Mike! In fact, I phoned Brody last night, and he said that some promising leads have turned up regarding the bogus charges of insider trading."

After seeing his sister safely to her truck, David returned, locked the General Store's doors, and activated the new silent alarm system that he and Spitzer had recently installed.

In the upstairs apartment, Joy was lying in a patch of evening light watching old cartoons. She looked up from the braided rug and smiled, sending a rush of love through her father's heart.

Seated on the couch nearby, Elita turned a page of the book she was reading. Without looking up, she said, "I'm almost done with this chapter." A few minutes later, she placed a marker in the novel and set it on the coffee table. "What would you like for dinner?"

David leaned over and kissed the top of his wife's head and then wandered over to the refrigerator. "Why don't I heat up the leftover spaghetti and meatballs?"

Suddenly, the family was startled by the sound of breaking glass!

Elita grabbed Joy by the hand, and they tiptoed to the cubby in the back of the closet where they had hidden before. "Come on—there's room," she whispered, but David shook his head. Near the door of the families dwelling, he picked up a baseball bat, turned the knob, and crept down the old stairs.

The floor near the lunch counter creaked, and David could hear voices—low and unintelligible. He crouched behind a coat rack, clutching the bat.

Figures moved past. *Two—possibly three,* he thought. A pair of heavy boots paused, and David could hear the flick of a lighter. Cigarette smoke wafted through the room.

One of the intruders tossed a bag of chips to another and laughed as they ripped it open and began to consume it.

David moved with stealth alongside a shelf, drew closer, and caught only a momentary peak. He looked at the bat in his hand and tried to formulate a plan. Near a rack of camping gear, he crouched for a better look. *It's the same men who showed up after the migrant workers had been slain,* he realized. He watched them sauntering through the General Store like they owned the place! *Where is the sheriff?* David wondered.

The bandidos took their time fingering goods, helping themselves to whatever they wanted, and laughing as they rifled the place. At the front of the store, they paused for a brief conversation, and then one of them smashed the recently replaced glass of the showcase near the checkout counter that was full of new curios.

Propelled by sudden anger, David bellowed, "Stop!" and, with bat held high, he rushed the men.

Suddenly, one of them produced a pistol with a barrel nearly as long as a ruler. The bandido's mouth spread open in a mocking grin, and his partners began to laugh.

David felt the blood rush from his head. He dropped the bat and held up his hands. *I'm going to die*, he thought as he saw the blue flash of the gun.

What happened next was something right out of a movie. Gordon Spitzer burst onto the scene from the back of the General Store with his gun blazing. The intruders fired back. A hail of bullets and expletives ricocheted throughout the room. David saw blood spurting from Gordon's tactical vest, but the old man kept blasting away until the last intruder fell. Clutching his chest and sputtering blood from his mouth, Spitzer dropped to his knees and said, "That should put an end to this little crime wave." Just before he died, he lamented, "Looks like I won't get to finish that cold glass of milk I left over at the Watering Hole."

North Dakota
Saturday, August 10th

Scrolling through his iPhone, Joel followed Coco through

the door of the Bargain Bin.

"No p-phubbing allowed! I don't like it when people snub other people in favor of perusing their smartphones," Nora said, causing her son to look up and acknowledge the crowd of locals who had gathered.

"I was just looking at the responses to my latest blog post, "Joel explained. "The Patriot Review says that their readership has nearly doubled since they featured Beyond the Fall. People are really stirred up over the shootout at Sergeant Rudd's place, calling it another Waco. Incredibly, most of these posts are coming from my generation, young folks who are concerned about the future of liberty."

"That's wonderful," Nora pressed, "however, I called this meeting to discuss the locust damage that hit our community last week."

Joel switched his phone to silent, slid it into his pocket, and took a seat beside his young bride who had pulled some sewing from a tote bag. "No s-phubbing either," he whispered into her ear, and she put the sewing away.

"As you're all aware, the harvests have been devastated, and we all know what this means." Heads nodded, and Nora continued. "Five years ago, during the drought, we passed out care packages to supplement farm families until their insurance claims were settled."

"Maybe they have locust insurance?" J. J. O'Shay interrupted.

"You big dumb Huckleberry!" Gertie bellowed, "The last time our country had a locust plague was back in the late 1800s!"

"Really?" O'Shay goaded, "What was it like?"

The old woman wagged her finger. "I'd rather eat nails than swallow insults from the likes of you!"

"I heard the Governor is asking our President to declare the area impacted by the locust plague a national disaster," Coco said.

"Yes, that's true." Nora ruffled her short brown hair and sighed.

"In the meantime, we'll just have to roll up our sleeves and get busy with another food drive," Gertie said. "Folks around these parts are tough. We've seen hard times before and always come out stronger for it! With the good Lord's help, we'll get through this, too."

Arizona
Sunday, August 11th

Elita drove their old pickup along the US-Mexico Border, while David, his left arm still in bandages from the flesh wound he had received during the gunfight at the General Store, sat on the tailgate, dropping ashes from a plastic coated cardboard box as they crept along. Gordon Spitzer's last wishes were written in a note found among his few belongings. "Don't want no fuss. Just scatter what's left of me along the border and let the wind take me away."

When the box was empty, David gathered up the lid, got in the cab, and they headed back to town.

"Mr. Mike said that he and Gordon had a serious talk about God last week. I don't think he was the atheist he pretended to be." Elita dabbed her forehead with a bandana in the sweltering heat and said, "I can't believe he's really gone."

A tangle of emotion caught David by surprise, and he choked back a tear.

"Gordon went out with his combat boots on," Elita said as if she sensed her husband's internal conflict. "I think that's the way he would have wanted to go."

David forced a smile, but remained silent until they pulled up to the store. "I think I'll take the bike for a spin."

Elita stood on her toes to kiss her husband's cheek. "What about your shoulder?"

"I can ride," he said. "I'll just take it easy."

"Be careful!" she admonished.

Behind the General Store under a wooden lean-to, David carefully pulled the plastic cover from his Triumph motorcycle and brushed a little dust from the leather seat. It had been a while since he'd felt the urge to ride. He straddled the bike, rolled up the kick stand, and turned the key. The engine rumbled to life. David motored slowly around the potholes of Main Street and steered toward the highway. There, he twisted the throttle gingerly. Soon, he was flying past the desert landscape of saguaros and yuccas until it all became a blur.

Spitzer died, so I could survive. It was a humbling thought that carried a wave of guilt, a familiar feeling that had dogged David throughout his life.

Chapter 39

New York

Monday, August 12ᵗʰ

Katrina had just drifted off to sleep when the telephone rang in her Manhattan apartment. The clock beside her bed indicated it was after midnight. *Who's calling at this hour?* She leaned over to check the caller ID. It was a private number, her boss at UBC! Katrina cleared her throat and snatched the receiver from the cradle. "Hello."

Mr. Benedict wasted no time. "All hands on deck."

"What's going on?" She swung her legs from the bed and slid into her slippers.

"You'll be briefed when you arrive at the station," he snapped. "Just get your butt in here, now!"

There had been times, like the aftermath of the attack on the twin towers on 9/11, when the staff had been called in to work overtime. This time, something about the tone her new boss used raised a similar alarm.

Katrina threw on a suit fresh from the cleaners, did her best to tame her blond hair that had been disheveled by her pillow, dabbed on some makeup, and dashed out the door.

In the elevator, she tried to calm her nerves. After all, she hardly knew Otto Benedict. *Maybe he is given to histrionic power drills,* she thought.

Though the streets of Manhattan never slept, Katrina noted an unusually large presence of New York City's finest. Their lights strobing and intermittent siren blasts meant something major was underway.

At the entrance to the UBC parking garage, Katrina swiped her card and waited for the automatic gate to open. A co-worker pulled up behind her, bathing her blue Porsche in its headlights. She took the first parking spot she could find and fell in with a cluster of anxious-looking employees. "Does anyone know what's going on?" someone asked.

One by one, their phones began to sounding off, and the area was filled with the shrill tones of multiple emergency warning alerts. Bleary-eyed UBC staffers stared in disbelief at their lit phone screens. "Tsunami threatens East Coast. Seek high ground. Evacuation orders to follow."

One woman pushed her way onto the elevator and began manically punching buttons. "Calm down!" one of the assistant producers shouted. "If this is true, we've probably got some time."

"My husband is at home, and I've got a son taking classes at Hudson!" cried the ashen-faced woman. Tears streamed from her eyes as the rest of the group crammed into the elevator.

Otto Benedict was waiting for the staff to gather in the large UBC lobby. When the last employee stepped off the elevator, he clapped his hands together and said, "Okay people,

I need your full attention here! A volcanic eruption on one of the Canary Islands has triggered a huge offshore earthquake. At 11:47 P.M., EDT, a massive landslide on the Isle of Palma occurred. It's been reported that more than half of the volcanic mountain sluffed into the ocean." Mr. Benedict began to pace back and forth. "This is no drill, people! The US Geological Survey says that a cataclysmic tsunami is building and headed our way. They expect it to make landfall sometime around 8:00 A.M.. It's our job to provide factual information, urge the public to remain calm, and encourage people to follow the evacuation plan without delay."

Katrina went to the high-rise window and looked across the span of the city. Lights blinked on in buildings, followed by more lights. *How,* she wondered, *can six million frightened people calmly make their way to high ground?*

Down below, cars squealed through the streets, and people, like ants, scurried about in a frenzy. New York City had been rudely awakened to a portent of doom!

Arizona
Monday, August 12th

At 3:00 A.M., a scream pierced the night—loud enough to rouse Paige and some other residents from their slumber. In an instant, she was at her son's bedside, cradling him in her arms as his body racked with sobs. "Did you have another bad dream?"

"It happened, Mom." Connor rubbed his red rimmed eyes. "I saw it!"

Paige stroked her son's red hair and held him close.

"It was just like the picture on that church," the boy cried. "You know, Saint John the Divine."

"You mean the fresco on the column?"

"Yes, it happened just like that!"

There was a knock on the trailer door, and Paige opened the door to find Priscilla, the young single mother, shivering in her nightgown under the awning.

"Is everything okay?" Priscilla asked.

"Connor has nightmares sometimes, but he'll be fine."

Priscilla stepped closer. "Would it be okay if I talked to him for a moment?"

Paige was surprised by the request. "Sure." She stepped aside, and the young woman went right to her son's bedside.

Priscilla knelt beside the boy who was still gulping sobs. "Hey, Sweetheart. I'm sorry you saw scary things tonight." She smiled gently and that seemed to settle the child. "Can I ask you something?"

Connor nodded as he wiped a tear from his cheek.

She curled her fingers around his. "Did you dream about a wall of water?"

The boy's eyes widened. "How did you know?"

"Because," Priscilla said, "I've been having the same dream."

Paige's cell phone, still on the charger, was blinking and caught her eye. "Excuse me. It's a message from Brody! Hold on a minute," she said and then retrieved the voicemail.

"Listen, Honey, something big is happening here," Brody said. "There's been a massive landslide in the Canary Islands. There is a tsunami headed for the East Coast. I'll try to get out of Manhattan, but as you can imagine, there is already mass panic. I don't want you to worry…" There was a break in his voice. "Give Connor a hug for me. I love you both!"

Immediately, Paige dialed her husband's number, but all circuits were busy!

New York
Tuesday, August 13th

By 6:00 A.M., Anchorwoman Katrina Katz sat at her news desk preparing to address her viewers with another update.

After multiple failed attempts to call loved ones, a fatalistic resolve had settled over the crew. In a few short hours, a wall of water would swallow the city they all called home, and there was nothing they could do to stop it.

Somewhere in the building a woman softly wept, but the rest of Katrina's co-workers carried out their tasks like mute drones.

The lights blinked, signaling the countdown to broadcast. Katrina swallowed a lump in her throat and solemnly faced the cameras. "Friends and neighbors, despite the best efforts of York City's Emergency Response Team, evacuation plans have been suspended. All roads and bridges from the island are blocked by panicked citizens attempting a mass exodus. The airports and railway systems have been closed down due to riots, and the streets have been declared unsafe. You are advised to seek immediate shelter in buildings constructed on New York City's bedrock. Upper floors, roofs, and even stair wells are suggested. Citizens who are fortunate enough to dwell in such properties are being asked to open their doors as good Samaritans. Stay tuned for further updates." Feeling numb, Katrina signed off.

Otto Benedict stepped from his office, pointed at his lead anchorwoman, and motioned for her to join him.

"I've chosen you to cover the events from the air," he said. "The world is watching this drama, and you're the best I've got."

He glanced at the oversized wall clock in his office. "The news chopper is fueled and ready to go. We'll be lifting off in five minutes."

"We?" Katrina queried.

Her new boss seemed annoyed by the question. "If you must know, the pilot will be dropping me off inland at our New Jersey affiliate. I think it's best to headquarter there until this crisis has passed. My safety is vital to operations."

"But, Sir, what about the others?"

"This is the top floor of a stable building. I'm sure they'll be fine," Benedict grumbled as he dashed for the exit.

Thirty minutes later, the news chopper touched down on the roof of the New Jersey UBC affiliate and waited for Otto Benedict to scurry to safety before the helicopter and crew lifted off again.

Filled with trepidation, Katrina Katz, Gar, the field cameraman, and Reed, the pilot, headed back toward Manhattan.

Despite being warned to seek higher shelter in buildings built on the New York City bedrock, many citizens still crowded the streets.

"Are they insane or just stupid?" Gar pointed the camera at people lugging heavy loads as if their belongings were the only thing that mattered. Others stood by like frozen statues.

A flock of pigeons took to the air, and soon the sky was a flutter with birds of all kinds flying up river as the helicopter banked toward Battery Park.

The Hudson River was receding, and water levels were low enough to expose sand bars near upscale riverside high rises. It began to look as though someone could walk to Ellis Island from the Jersey side.

There was a momentary stall, and then Gar yelped out a gen-x expletive and swung the camera to the view beyond the mouth of the harbor toward the Atlantic. A massive ocean swell was building and rolling in fast!

Katrina lifted the microphone to her lips. "New Yorkers, the tsunami has arrived!"

Live video imagery was being broadcast as she spoke. "Please, if you value your lives, abandon everything and find high ground immediately."

Knowing that all the people on the streets below would be unable to hear her broadcast, tears filled her brown eyes. "Oh God—No!" she heard herself saying as she witnessed a towering wall of water. It broke over Brighton Beach and surged with a fury around the Bay Bridge and up the Hudson.

"It must be sixty-feet high!" Katrina cried.

Suddenly, the huge wave crashed against the base of the Statue of Liberty, washing over the pedestal and smashing into the hollow statue with an uncalculatable force. The effigy of American freedom rocked, swayed, and then crashed into the tumult as the world watched on live TV.

Katrina fell mute at the sight. She struggled for words, but there were none.

Next, Gar pointed his camera at the upscale apartments in Battery City, all built on landfill. Knocking buildings off their foundation, the tsunami had hit with the force of a nuclear explosion.

"Whole apartment buildings are being toppled, falling like dominoes," Katrina reported. "Some remain standing, but the streets between them look like raging rivers of destruction choked with debris."

Yellow cabs, buses, delivery trucks, and even capsized yachts rolled among the churning whitecaps. Katrina cried out in sorrow at the sight of people bobbing, reaching, and being tossed about like ragdolls in the powerful surge. "It's horrible," she sobbed.

Gar swung the camera lens her way to capture their anchorwoman's tears. Katrina didn't care. "Pray," she urged her viewers. "They need our prayers."

Overhead, a private jet circled the Manhattan financial district and then banked over the East River.

Katrina recognized the distinctive emblem on the side of the jet—the World Fortress Institute. *We haven't heard the last of Alistair Dormin*, she thought as the chopper headed toward Times Square and Central Park to document the damage.

Chapter 40

New York

Tuesday, August 13ᵗʰ

Katrina's emotions were deadened by the images that played over and over in her mind. When the waters receded, she watched people and clutter being sucked back out to sea. Then, like a bad movie, the whole scene replayed again. Only it was worse when the second tsunami struck.

The anchorwoman's usual professional calm broke and unbridled emotion surfaced as she watched human flotsam clinging and clawing for safety. Some bodies bobbed, unmoving and face down. Many had lost their battle to survive. Others, wide eyed, drifted passively with the surge.

Documenting the trendy window fronts now shattered by the forces of nature, Gar said, "Oh, snap! Bad day to be a merchant."

"Destruction abounds," Katrina reported. As the viewers watched, the stock and trade inventory of retail stores was strewn across the muddy sidewalks. Colorful clothes, once stylish on the rack, but now reduced to soggy rags, were scattered on the streets.

Gar seemed to be enjoying himself a little too much. Zooming in on an empty, toppled wheelchair, he said, "Great human interest shots."

Katrina spotted the lifeless body of a once pampered poodle lying near a child's bicycle. Everywhere, scattered in piles across the city, were the remnants of shattered lives. "I need a break from reporting," she said. With a heavy heart, she began to pray aloud.

"You're wasting your time," Reed interrupted. "Look around! Drugs, alcohol, murder, child abuse, and natural disasters. If God was real, do you think there would be so many problems?"

"It's true that we live in a fallen world, full of suffering, but if people turned their hearts to God, then I believe things would be different," Katrina said.

Reed mumbled a response under his breath and then said, "We're running low on fuel. Better head back and see if there's anything left of the studio." He banked over Central Park, which now resembled a trash-laden swamp.

Katrina closed her eyes and let the sound of the chopper carry her thoughts away.

"Sweet!" Gar gave a thumbs-up. "The old building is still standing."

The pilot hovered over the rooftop platform and settled in for a landing.

"I hope the snack and soda machines are stocked because I don't think we'll be going downtown anytime soon," Gar said with a creepy smile.

No one felt like laughing.

A couple members of the UBC staff were standing at the window when Katrina and the chopper crew arrived.

Setting down his camera, Gar asked, "Where is everybody?"

"Gone," said one of the young production assistants.

"Bad move, Dude!" Not believing anyone would leave the safety of UBC headquarters, the camera man asked, "Like, have you seen it out there?"

"They wanted to try to get back to their families."

Gar dug some change from his pocket and headed for the snack machine.

"Don't bother," the assistant said. "The power is out all over the city." He pointed to the Manhattan skyline and billows of black smoke from fires sparked by shorted electric wires. "Gas mains all over the city are probably breeched. We need to get out of here!" There was panic in his eyes as he turned to Reed. "Will you fly us over to the Jersey affiliate?"

"There's only room for three at a time," Reed said. "Without electricity, I'll need to override the refueling pump and work it by hand."

They heard glass shatter and turned to see Gar standing by the vending machines. "Snacks and sodas are on me!" he said.

———

North Dakota
Tuesday, August 13th

Joel, Coco, and the others gathered around the big screen

at the Bargain Bin waiting for the latest word from the President of the United States. So far, the reports were ominous. A tidal surge had swelled up the Potomac and swamped the Alexandria Historic District. The nation watched in horror as the news footage captured images of the surge lapping at the South Portico of the White House before receding.

Reporters, jammed like sardines in the West Wing Press Room, gathered restlessly for the statement from the President. After a long wait, the Press Secretary arrived and announced that Ira Corbin would be speaking to the country from a secure location. "At this time, all questions for the President will be deferred until the damages are fully assessed."

Above the podium, a large screen came to life with the stoic image of the Commander in Chief. "My fellow Americans, although hardship has again visited our great land, take heart, for we are a people of historic courage!" The president paused for effect. "I have been in direct contact with Chairman Alistair Dormin, and he assures me that international relief efforts are already being organized. With arms linked in the spirit of global unity, coupled with the indomitable strength of our collective humanity, our great nation will rise like a phoenix from the ashes." Corbin's fist rose in defiance. "We shall prevail against this act of nature!"

"Well, I've never heard such pompous nonsense. Excuse my Scandinavian, but this guy is an eel-head, if you ask me," Gertie huffed. "Locust plagues, civil unrest, and tidal waves! Did it ever occur to this doofus that the Man upstairs might be trying to get our attention?"

J. J. O'Shay lifted his finger to his lips and cocked his

ear to listen.

President Ira Corbin laced his fingers together and continued with a quote from the Bible "We will replace the broken bricks of our ruins with finished stone, and replant the felled sycamore-fig trees with cedars."

"That's a quote from Isaiah 9:10, but he's taking it out of context," Nora said. "God was talking about people who say such things in arrogance!"

After scrolling through her Bible app and reading more of Chapter 9, Coco said, "You're right, Nora. This is Isaiah talking about God bringing judgement and the people ignore God, fail to repent, and respond with pride and presumption, saying they will rebuild."

Arizona
Tuesday, August 13th

Above the General Store in their little apartment, David and Elita sat perched on the edge of the couch watching special reports as they came in. Some of the dramatic clips had recycled several times, but they couldn't take their eyes from the screen.

News footage documented the damage that the Mega Tsunami, as it had now been dubbed, had inflicted on the west coast of Africa, the Caribbean Islands, and the entire Eastern Seaboard of the US.

All across the networks, aerial images of the natural disaster replayed again and again to the stunned nation. Swells, estimated to be eighty feet high had swept across the Florida Keys, pulling lives and crumbled real estate out to sea.

David pitched forward on the couch as the cameras shifted to New York City where his brother-in-law lived. The pricey sky-rise apartments at Battery Park had fallen like bowling pins along with many other structures. Images of the Statue of Liberty slammed and toppled by the wall of water left him speechless. The mighty sculpture was swept from her base like a plastic icon. Her torch, once held high, was lost in New York Harbor.

"Paige is probably sick with worry," Elita said with tear-filled eyes.

David glanced at his watch—6:00 A.M. MST. It had been an hour since the Mega Tsunami had struck the East Coast. He reached over and squeezed his wife's hand. "I think we should close up shop today and drive over to Hope Springs."

Without hesitation, Elita woke Joy up and got her dressed. After tossing a hand full of granola bars and a couple of juice boxes into a tote bag, they were on their way.

On the bumpy pickup-truck ride across the desert, Joy drifted back to sleep, while her mother prayed softly for all who were affected by the tragedy.

At Hope Springs, the fire pit was glowing in the center of the pavilion where all the residents were already gathered.

"If my people who are called by my name will humble themselves…," someone prayed from 2 Chronicles.

David scanned the faces for his sister and spotted her near the back of pavilion. "Have you heard from Brody?"

Paige shook her head and fought back tears.

They stood beside her as Raymond Lee began softly

picking an acoustic worship song on his guitar. Beside the former blues artist, young Connor Hays lifted his violin to his chin, and with bow in hand, he coaxed ethereal melodies from the instrument.

"That sounds like angel music," Joy whispered. "I bet my little brother is dancing in Heaven like this." She began twirling like a little bird.

When the songs were over, the group joined hands and began lifting to the Lord heartfelt petitions for those who were suffering.

"Please, God, send angels to help my dad." Connor lifted his eyes skyward, and just then a sudden breeze blew in from the desert.

Chapter 41

New York

Tuesday, August 13th

He awoke to pain thundering in his head, pulsing with an intensity that made him want to meld back into the darkness that surrounded him. There were voices and cries in the distance. Someone screamed.

Slowly, he became aware of a speck of brightness that filtered through the tangled chaos. Something urged him to get moving. The cobbled structure groaned and settled as he slowly labored toward the light.

With lips cracked and tongue dry, he pushed debris from his path. Some obstacles felt as heavy as stone and iron; others were as light as gypsum board. As his progress was measured by inches, he became aware of the constant tick-tock of his wristwatch. *Time?* Intuition told him that it had once ruled him. Now, the concept seemed vague and irrelevant. For the present, the only thing that mattered was the moment and each movement that took him forward.

Nearer the source of light, he paused for a gulp of damp

air that spilled through the opening. His muscles quivered with fatigue as he touched the matted sticky tangle of his hair. *I'm hurt,* he thought as he wedged his frame between two beams.

Sunlight, bright enough to hurt his eyes, spilled into the space. A couple of bent pipes barred his way, but they broke easily. Suddenly, in the confined space, he could smell gas! Instinct urged him to move with caution. Careful not to scrape his belt buckle or the rivets of his jeans on metal, he made his way to freedom.

The street was smeared with wet sediment and soggy debris: paper, rotting food, uprooted plants, and mud. Glass storefronts on either side of the road had been shattered as if they had imploded. Battered cars and cabs were piled against buildings, some entombed the motionless bodies of their drivers. One sedan was leaning precariously against a high rise with its underbelly exposed.

All around, disheveled people stumbled about looking stunned. A few were whimpering or tending to open wounds. There was carnage everywhere he looked.

An elderly woman laid in the middle of the road with a twisted hip. She cried out for help, but when he stooped to offer assistance, she screamed, "Don't touch me!"

On the sidewalk across the road, a man was sitting on a sofa that looked as though it had floated from someone's apartment.

He approached the man who was leaning forward with his head in his hands.

"What happened?"

The stranger looked up, his mouth agape. "Are you serious?"

"I don't remember."

"Well, then you missed a wild ride! When that tsunami hit, I thought I was a goner. It's something I'd just as soon forget." The man's eyebrow rose, and he added, "Say, looks like you took a nasty bump on the head."

"Can you tell me how to get out of here?"

"That's the million-dollar question!" the stranger snorted. "I figure the Holland and Lincoln tunnels are done for, so the way I see it, the George Washington Bridge is probably the only way off this island."

"Island?"

"Manhattan—as in New York City—the Big Apple!" The man's demeanor softened. "Say, maybe you've got amnesia or something."

"Amnesia?"

"You must have a hearing problem, too!" The stranger's lips spread exposing a large gap between his front teeth. "What's your name?"

"I am…" When nothing came to mind, he stuttered, "I…, I…, I don't know."

The stranger rubbed his chin "Sam—that's what I'll call you—as in Sam I Am! My friends call me Yancey." The man hoisted his beefy frame from the water-logged couch and began to lumber away. He stopped, looked over his shoulder, and said, "You coming or not?"

Others joined them on the eerie pilgrimage. Their faces fascinated Sam as he walked beside Yancey. All around him people, some with tears streaming down their cheeks and others with looks of despair, were moaning. Everyone seemed to be experiencing a range of sensations and emotions, but Sam felt oddly indifferent. The only thing he could relate to was his own physical pain. Some of the injured struggled to keep up. Many with grotesque wounds were being carried along on makeshift gurneys.

More drone-like people fell in with the exiles as the hours slipped by. The sky was punctuated with pillars of smoke, and the smell of the air was damp and musky. They faced many obstacles as they traveled on foot: uprooted trees, furniture, buses, electronics, and household goods.

Except for the shuffling of feet, the city had grown strangely quiet. Even the sound of song birds had stopped.

Sam walked around a commercial sink. "Must have been ripped from a diner by the ebb or flow of water—no telling how many people were sucked out to sea."

Yancey shook his head and added, "That first wave was bad enough, but the second one was a real killer."

Sam tried to reconcile want he was seeing, but it was futile. He could recall nothing that happened before his exodus from the ruins of the old building, so he remained silent, like all the survivors who trudged onward as if blind to the death and destruction all around them. Somehow, the whole scene seemed surreal.

At times, the survivors were forced to climb over the rubble of buildings that had been toppled by the force of nature.

"Back in the day before construction codes, they didn't anchor these old buildings to the bedrock," Yancey said as he paused to catch his breath. "Sure could use a drink of water right about now."

Sam pointed to a puddle, but his traveling companion shook his head vigorously. "Look at the film on that water! Could be sewage or gasoline, for all we know!"

"Say, I just noticed you don't have any shoes!" Yancey pointed down at his new friend's bloody socks. "Well, these look like your size, and this poor guy doesn't need them anymore." Without hesitation, Yancey plucked a pair of high-end tennis shoes from a corpse and handed them to Sam.

Reluctantly, he slipped them on his feet and tied the laces thinking, *How do I know how to tie shoes, when I can't even remember my name?* Feeling his soggy socks squishing inside the shoes, he walked on.

Like a specter, a helicopter appeared and hovered overhead. Then, as though Heaven had opened, a pallet loaded with cases of bottled water was lowered.

The thirsty crowd rushed forward, scrambling over each other and clawing their way toward the water. Somehow, in the panic, Yancey managed to grab a couple of bottles. "Quick, slip it under your shirt," he told Sam. "This stuff is more precious than gold right now."

Some gulped their water, others guarded theirs, as they all made their way around some heavy equipment that was trying to clear the debris from the roadway.

Pointing to the George Washington Bridge, someone cried out, "I see it!"

There in the distance was a large double-decked

suspension bridge, built with steel beams and cables.

"What a sight!" Yancey said as they took in the view of the aluminum-colored reversed arches and crisscross bracing that spanned the Hudson River. "Some famous architect named Le Corbusier once said, 'The George Washington Bridge is blessed.' The fact that it's still standing is blessing enough for me!"

Up ahead, thousands of people were also attempting to flee the city. Countless masses inched their way onto footpaths that were built on either side of the bridge. In the center lanes, tow trucks were busy hauling abandoned vehicles out of the way.

Yancey motioned to Sam as others pushed forward. "Listen," he said discreetly, "The way I've got it figured, we'd be better off taking a chance on Martha."

"Who is Martha?" Sam asked.

"That's the nickname for the lower deck of the bridge, as in Martha Washington."

Sam feigned recognition with a nod, and then Yancey continued.

"They'll clear the top deck first, so all we'll have to do is wind around some stranded cars. At least, it shouldn't be so crowded."

Though the majority of travelers chose the footpaths above, Yancey's idea was far from original. The crowd moved like mice through the maze of vehicles, making slow, but steady, progress. Over their heads, the platform creaked and groaned from the added weight of the sojourners. Few spoke, except for some of the children who whimpered in protest as their parents tugged them onward.

On the Jersey side of the bridge, more progress had been made clearing away obstructions. The masses fell into a line that snaked around a fleet of heavy equipment.

Gazing up at the mountain of twisted cars and trucks that had been pushed to the side of the eight-lane roadway, Yancey said, "Will you look at that!"

They crested the bluff of the Hudson River to find that the tsunami had also left a path of destruction there, but to a lesser degree.

"Welcome to New Jersey!" Yancey said and then thrust out a hand. "This is where we part ways Sam I am. Wish I could say it's been a pleasure meeting you!" He flashed another smile, slogged through a deep puddle, turned a corner, and was gone.

⚬⚬⚬

Sam could feel the blisters on his feet with each step. The sun, which earlier had warmed his back, was now in his face and harsh enough to make his eyes water. *I have no idea who I am, where I am, or where I am going,* he thought. Sam paused to catch his breath then trudged on until he encountered streets and buildings that had been untouched by the catastrophic wave.

Sam looked back at the lengthening shadow he cast. Most of his fellow travelers had fallen back. His legs quivered from fatigue, and night was falling, so he decided to hunker down between a dumpster and a brick building. After taking a rationed sip from his water bottle, Sam felt himself sinking into a dreamy state of exhaustion…

He was being chased by a man on a red horse. The sound of hooves closed in on him as he ran. The rider, wearing a green vest, leaned over and raised a machete. Sam heard the blade slice the air as he fled to the safety of a little stone hut. From a window, Sam watched the rider pursue others without mercy. Suddenly, a cornerstone in the little rock building began to glow like molten gold...

Sam was jolted out of his dream by the sound of glass shattering, and he climbed to his swollen feet. From behind the dumpster, he watched a gang of looters kicking out the remaining shards of plate glass from an electronics store. The hoodlums entered with shouts of conquest and returned with arms loaded with big-screen TVs, computers, and other high-end merchandise.

When morning came, Sam proceeded on with caution. Trying to stay out of sight, he moved through alleyways and ducked behind cover when people appeared. By the afternoon of the second day, his feet throbbed with pain so intense that they could no longer be ignored. He found a recessed doorway, sat down on the stoop, and removed his tennis shoes. The fabric of his socks was now plastered to his blistered flesh. He nearly cried as he peeled away the material. Oozing sores covered the entire soles of both feet. *I can't put these shoes back on,* he told himself. *I can't even walk!* He looked at his water bottle, now empty. *Now, what?*

"Did you come from that mess in Manhattan?"

Sam heard the voice and turned to see an old stick figure of a woman looking down at him from the doorway. He nodded.

She motioned him inside. "Hurry, it's not safe on the

streets." Just inside the door, she gasped at the sight of his bloody footprints and ordered him to sit. "I'll be right back with some ointment and gauze."

The elderly lady returned with a first-aid kit and knelt at Sam's feet to gently tend to his wounds.

Sam noticed the pronounced hump on her back and her gnarled fingers. A feeling of gratitude surfaced. "Thank you," he said, and then he offered his hand as she struggled to stand.

"My knees aren't what they used to be." The woman led him to the couch in her tiny studio apartment. "I'm afraid I don't have much to offer, except a sofa to rest on and some bread and peanut butter. You're not allergic to the stuff, are you?"

He shook his head and wondered, *I don't think so…*

"The power's out in Trenton, and I expect all over the Eastern Seaboard. I can't offer you a cold drink, but I've got some soda."

"Thank you. Anything sounds good."

"My name is Greta," the slight old woman said after retrieving a can from her fridge.

"I'm Sam." He popped the tab and gulped down the syrupy liquid.

Greta shook her finger and scolded, "You'd better slow down, or you'll make yourself sick."

Strangely, her maternal words brought feelings of loss, yet he had no memory of a mother. In fact, he had no memories at all.

"I don't know where you're heading, Sam, but I'm going to Michigan. I've got a son, probably about your age, who lives in the Upper Peninsula. He's been pestering me to come live with him for a few years now. I'll be heading out in the morning. I'd be glad to drop you off somewhere along the way."

Sam shook his head.

"Suit yourself, but you shouldn't stick around here. I have a feeling that things are going to get rougher before they get better." Greta disappeared into her tiny kitchen and returned with a peanut butter sandwich.

After Sam finished devouring his food, she opened a hope chest that doubled as her coffee table, retrieved some blankets, and dropped them onto the sofa. "You should get some rest."

It didn't take long for Sam to close his eyes. When he opened them again, morning light was streaming through the window. On the coffee table, he found a note from the old woman.

> Didn't have the heart to wake you. There's a sandwich and another soda on the kitchen table. Help yourself to anything else you might need for your travels. I won't be back. I want you to have my bicycle. With my knees being what they are, I got no use for it anyway.
> God be with you,
> Greta

Wednesday, August 14th

With no particular destination in mind, Sam peddled along the shoulder of US 1 before blundering onto a frontage road that paralleled the New Jersey Turnpike. Though his legs grew weary, he wasn't complaining. Riding a bike minimized the pain of his blistered feet.

Sam stopped along a small brook and ate his sandwich under the shade of a massive maple tree. He would have stayed longer, but a swarm of gnats drove him back to the road.

He counted each turn of the peddle to mark the miles, yet the concept of time still eluded him. The direction and passage of the sun kept him traveling west. As the day wore on, road markers and signs indicated that he was moving around the northern outskirts of Philadelphia. He was thinking about finding a place to stop and rest when a sign with a peculiar name evoked a spark of emotion. "Entering King of Prussia." Feeling perplexed, Sam turned onto Highway 23. He cycled through the city that seemed to be built around shopping malls when, suddenly, one sign stopped him in his tracks!

"Valley Forge National Historic Park," it read. A fleeting memory flashed through his mind so fast that he couldn't catch it, yet something told him that he knew this place. To his own surprise, Sam now had a destination! With single-minded purpose, he pushed on with his eyes keen for markers. On the west side of King of Prussia, the name of the road changed to Valley Forge Road!

Sam peddled faster as he neared a gate that led to the historic park. Unexpectedly, something caught his front tire and sent him catapulting over the handlebars into a patch of thick grass. After brushing himself off, he noticed the front tire was not only flat, but the wheel was bent and useless. He had run over a piece of two by four with a protruding nail. Sam left his bike behind and began to walk. He hobbled along the winding road, amidst a bucolic landscape that looked eerily familiar. Before long, he came to the Washington Memorial Chapel, and he paused to search his soul for any trace of recognition. The gray gothic church with an impressive bell tower invoked no personal feelings, so he continued along the road.

When a two-story stone structure came into view, his heart skipped a beat. This is it! George Washington's Headquarters. Sam limped inside the building and looked around. There were rooms, partitioned by plexiglass dividers, on either side of where he stood. *Yes,* he thought, *I've been here!* The stairs just ahead beckoned, and despite his battered feet, Sam ascended two steps at a time. One room in particular seemed to draw his attention, and he peered inside the place where Washington had spent many a night during the winter of 1777-78.

"You look like a fellow on a mission!"

Sam whirled around to face a little, old man who was wearing an oversized Hawaiian shirt. He turned his gaze back to the window sill in the partitioned room. "I was looking for something," he said.

"Really? It wouldn't happen to be this, would it?" The odd man pulled a plastic army man from the pocket of his baggy shorts. "I must say, though, you look a little old to be playing with toys."

Feeling flushed, Sam asked, "May I see that?"

The old man obliged.

Sam curled his fingers around the figure like it was a hidden treasure. "I'd like to keep this, if you don't mind?"

"Help yourself! Say, you look mighty familiar to me."

The little man's eyebrows kissed, and he twirled the tip of his long, white beard. "Some say I've got a gift for putting faces with names." Suddenly, the ancient man snapped his fingers. "I remember! It was right here in this very room where I first laid eyes on you. Of course, it's been a few years, and you were a sharp-dressed man back then."

Sam looked down at his grass stained and worn jeans, bright tennis shoes, and filthy shirt. His fingers touched the greasy film on his hair. "I don't remember you."

"Well, now, that's been known to happen." The old man smiled. "Let's make this meeting official! My friends call me Zeke."

Epilogue

New Jersey

Saturday, August 17ᵗʰ

"Four days after a catastrophic Mega Tsunami struck the Eastern Seaboard, cleanup efforts are underway. Loss of life in Florida was minimized due to their long-time experience with hurricane evacuation protocol. However, New York City and other outlying areas were not so fortunate. Damages and casualties are still being assessed. Manhattan is under quarantine due to health concerns. The city remains without power, potable water, and gas." Katrina Katz was reporting from her temporary UBC news desk at the New Jersey affiliate, while video images showed New York City crawling with hazmat crews dressed in white-hooded suits. *The scene looks like something from War of the Worlds,* Katrina thought, as more video images played for the viewers—massive bulldozers rolling through the streets, like tanks, pushing debris and twisted cars onto the sidewalks to open avenues for more clean-up crews, and body bags laid out by the thousands. Katrina wrapped up the evening news with, "It is estimated that over a million American's may have perished. Our hearts and prayers go out to those who have lost their loved ones."

From her news desk, a ticker rolled across her teleprompter. "Breaking News," she said as she continued reading the words that rolled across her screen. "Today, during the ribbon cutting for the newly completed Temple in Jerusalem, Alistair Dormin, Chairman of the World Reserve Bank, gave his dedication speech."

The video clip of Dormin came on the screen. "People of the world," he began, "we stand upon holy ground. From this day forward, I consecrate the newly constructed temple in Jerusalem as a universal worship center to be equally shared by all religions of the world."

Katrina was stunned as the camera view shifted to the reaction of Israeli Prime Minister Ezra Yitzhak. "I am outraged by Alistair Dormin's presumptuous diplomatic overreach. This betrayal is nothing less than a breach of the covenant agreement that Israel entered into with the World Reserve Bank. Therefore, we withdraw from the charter, and effective immediately, we reassert Israel's full national rights and sovereignty!"

The studio lights indicated that Katrina was on. With a heavy heart, she read again from the teleprompter, "Chairman Dormin called the Prime Minister's reaction, '…both histrionic and nationalistic.'"

On camera, Dormin went on to say, "Much has been accomplished in the three-and-one-half years since the world has linked arms and resources in the spirit of cooperation. Israel must make concessions, just as we all must, for the greater good." The tall man laced his hands together. His steel-gray eyes looked directly into the lens as if he was gazing into the collective souls of mankind. "We must not stop short of our goal; our planet depends upon our unity. Therefore, I will continue my work to build international solidarity and economic prosperity for all."

The green light blinked. "Katrina Katz, reporting for Universal Broadcasting Corporation." *It has begun!* she thought as the studio lights cut off.

North Dakota
Saturday, August 17th

The whole community of Delmont had gathered at the Bargain Bin to listen to Joel. The place was so crowded that there was standing room only, so he climbed the stairs of the repurposed hotel to address the crowd. "We've called this meeting for two reasons. First, to pray for those who were affected by the devastating tsunami that recently hit the East Coast, and second, to talk about issues that concern the future of all Americans." The young man looked around the room at the seasoned and solemn faces of farmers who had lost everything during the locust plague.

Nora led a prayer for both the Eastern Seaboard and the locust ravaged heartland, and then she waited for her son.

"I am deeply concerned," he began, "that, while the media is fixed upon the East Coast disaster, our government is quietly advancing their agenda to undermine our constitutional rights. Under the cloak of these diversions, American's rights and liberties are being stripped away!"

A murmur rippled about the room.

"The killing of Sergeant Rudd has proven to be a sign of things to come. The ATF has ramped up their efforts to register guns, and any protest or resistance is being squelched by swift and lethal enforcement. There's no way of knowing how many have been killed or jailed."

"That's right!" a leather-faced farmer bellowed. "Last week, I heard that a group of Idaho ranchers had been slaughtered like they were outlaws."

"Ira Corbin is using the Mega Tsunami to divert attention from the fact that he is undermining the US Constitution and denying due process. The authors of the Second Amendment established the right to bear arms in order to protect the citizenry from a tyrannical government." Joel took a deep breath. "Now, our government says they need to protect us from ourselves."

Dabbing her nose with a tissue, Gertie said, "I don't know what's happening to this country. Where's this all going to end?"

"That's a good question," Joel replied. "Maybe we can find an answer in our past." He began to tell a story about the largest mass shooting in US history—the Wounded Knee Massacre.

"After years of government land seizures and broken treaties, there was unrest among the Native Americans on the great plains. The US government felt particularly threatened by the Lakota Sioux who had been practicing a new variant of their religion." Joel paused to make a side point. "This practice concerned the government, which feared this spiritual fervor might spawn uprisings, so officials arrested many of the native chiefs in order to quench the 'Messiah Craze.'

"When they came for Sitting Bull, crowds had gathered in protest. Shots were fired. An officer was killed. More shots were fired, and Sitting Bull lay dead.

"Word soon spread, and many Plains Indians fled from their reservations. In the winter of 1890, Spotted Elk of the Miniconjou Lakota Nation and 350 followers were escorted by a 7th Cavalry detachment to Wounded Knee Creek. There, 500 troops surrounded the encampment with large guns. At daybreak, Colonel James Forsyth ordered the surrender of all Native American weapons. No one knows for sure why the slaughter began, but in less than an hour, fifty Lakota had been wounded and 150 were killed. Only four men and forty-seven women and children survived the massacre. It is important to note that these Americans were killed after being disarmed."

"God help us!" someone cried out.

Joining her son on the stairs, Nora said, "He's the only one who can. Our country has been through drought, war, locusts, and now this tragic, mega tsunami. I believe that God is trying to get our attention. This is not just about guns and economics, but it's also about religious freedom. Our government is already promoting a 'politically-correct' version of the scriptures. If we don't speak out, who knows… Maybe all unadulterated Bibles will be soon confiscated!"

The Third Woe

Arizona

Sunday, August 18th

David and Elita knocked on the door of the Airstream. It was nearly 10:00 A.M., and Paige was still in bed. She answered the door looking like she hadn't slept for days.

"Any word from Brody?" Elita asked.

Paige's eyes were red from crying. "He would have called by now, if…"

Elita threw open her arms and embraced her sister-in-law. "Don't give up hope. We came to worship and pray with you this morning."

David looked around and asked, "Where's Connor?"

"He's already at the pavilion." A wistful smile spread across Paige's face. "Connor thinks his dad will be here soon. Can you believe it?"

"We could all use the faith of a child." Sensing the peace and presence of the Lord himself, David took his sister's hand in his and together they began to pray. When they were finished, a deep peace settled on David's heart, and something told him that everything would, indeed, be okay. "We'll wait for you to get dressed, and then we'll go worship together."

It was a beautiful, hot fall day in the desert as Paige made her way to the place where her friends and neighbors had gathered to give praise. Birds were singing, the cows were lowing in the pasture, yet her heart was weighed down with worry.

416

Unable to worship, she stared across the desert, watching undulating waves of heat rise from the baked soil. Waves that came like grief, and then... "Is that a mirage?" Paige stood and pointed to dust rising from an approaching vehicle.

"It's Zeke!" David called out as the Rambler puttered closer. "And he's got a passenger!"

The community gathered like a welcoming committee as the old man parked alongside the pavilion.

Hoping that he had come with a word of solace, Paige moved through the crowd looking for Zeke.

"Look who I found wandering around the backroads," the old man said when his joyful eyes met hers. "This vagabond didn't even know his own name when I picked him up, but all those photographs you gave me of our road trip jogged his memory!"

Looking weak and weary, a man climbed from the passenger seat, and as he turned, Paige saw the face of her husband and ran into the arms of a living, breathing miracle!